TWELVE
GATES
TO THE
CITY

ALSO BY DANIEL BLACK

They Tell Me of a Home

The Sacred Place

Perfect Peace

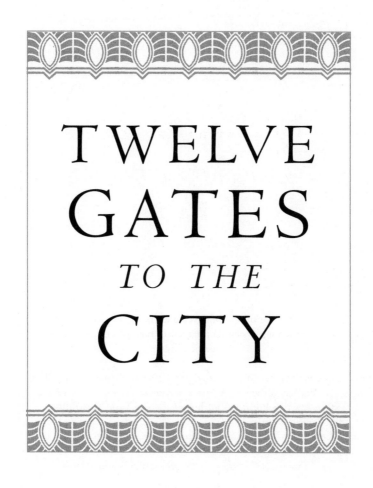

TWELVE GATES

GATES

TO THE

CITY

Daniel Black

ST. MARTIN'S PRESS ▰ NEW YORK

TWELVE GATES TO THE CITY. Copyright © 2011 by Daniel Black. All rights reserved. Printed in the United States of America. For information, address St. Martin's Press, 175 Fifth Avenue, New York, N.Y. 10010.

www.stmartins.com

Library of Congress Cataloging-in-Publication Data

Black, Daniel.
Twelve gates to the city / Daniel Black. — 1st ed.
         p.   cm.
Sequel to: They tell me of a home.
ISBN 978-0-312-58268-5
1. Brothers and sisters—Fiction.   2. African American families—
Fiction.   3. Conflict of generations—Fiction.   4. Supernatural—
Fiction.   5. Arkansas—Fiction.   6. Domestic fiction.   I. Title.
PS3602.L267T84 2011
813'.6—dc22

2011026769

First Edition: December 2011

10   9   8   7   6   5   4   3   2   1

*This novel is dedicated to all the children
of the world who were abandoned
and unloved. This is the story of
your resurrection. . . .*

ACKNOWLEDGMENTS

I celebrate the invaluable criticism of those who read this book in its embryonic form: Anela Ekundayo (Yolanda Smith), Kimathi (Rodney Goode), Tendaji (Reginald Bailey), Chixolisi Sondai (Angelo Pinto), Rashad Burgess, Makata Olakunde (Damali Narcisse), Ibaorimi (Regina Chambers), Adande (Charon Gaskins), Adolphus Herndon, Rose Norment, Nazapa Nzuriwati (Margo Davis), Akinyele Olakunde (Terry Weaver), Molefi Sondai (Asim Williams), and Michelle Weaver.

I also celebrate those who keep me encouraged and convinced that my life is not in vain. THANK YOU!

Might this story assure every soul that you were sent with a mission that promises to save thousands. Find that mission and live it! That is your joy complete!

TWELVE
GATES
TO THE
CITY

HERE WE ARE AGAIN. I'LL HAVE TO TELL THIS PART OF THE STORY. TL can't tell it. Not like I can.

Too many pieces he doesn't have, too much information he doesn't know.

I've waited for this moment an eternity. Or maybe for just a moment, the mere blinking of an eye.

Momma had said TL would return. Her faith was far greater than mine back then. My faith had waned over time. Too much hope, I suppose. Hope can ruin faith, you know? You overanticipate, become impatient, invite doubt, instead of simply believing. But I was a child. Who could blame me? I didn't know much about faith. I was simply a little girl who needed her big brother to come home.

I'll tell you things I took to the grave. They're no good here. They only have meaning to the living. And that's what this story is about—the living. Really, it's about a family, our family, that didn't live, that, in fact, almost died because we couldn't figure out how to love one another. Ain't that crazy? I know. But it happens.

Something else happened, too. My brother finally came home.

His timing was bad, or so I thought at first, but then the pieces came together and everything made sense. Everything. Even the pain.

I'm in the Great City now, the place people go when they leave the earth. At least some people. It's not perfect though, this other realm, but it IS wonderful. Like other human beings, I'd once imagined perfection as the state of the afterlife, only to discover that perfection isn't perfect. That is to say, it isn't joyful. It's stale, uneventful, static, rigid, lacking growth. And that's what's perfect—growth and change. I'm growing now more than ever. We work, citizens of the City, and we enjoy the fruit of our labor.

Before I continue, let me say that you, like TL, will have to put the pieces of this story together for yourself. There are no easy answers. No lives without tragedy. But tragedy begets destiny, you know? All things really do work together in a life to tell one cohesive story. That's where most people lose their way—when things happen that they don't understand. They think something went awry, that maybe some negative energy intruded to destroy their bliss. But it's never that. Never! Tragedy simply comes to remove distractions and keep you on track. You'll see what I mean.

I'm happy now. Happier than I've ever been. I understand what happened to me and why. I'm not saying it was right. I'm saying it was useful in bringing my brother home. And that's what I wanted—for TL to come home—so I offer no complaint. Whether my death was right or not, I never think about. Neither does God. He simply uses human events to get His way. But since His way is always advantageous to a person's purpose, why fight it? Right and wrong are silly concepts anyway, I've learned, conceived by humans trying to understand the ways of God. How ignorant humans are! What God desires most is the manifestation of God in you. That's why I had to come first—so I could tell this story and guide my brother along the way. That was my purpose. TL doesn't know his yet, but he will. He definitely will. And he'll be glad he returned. So will our people.

You must pay attention and follow along carefully so as not to miss any details. I can't tell you any more than what you discover. Yet I assure you the pieces come together, one by one, like the links of a chain, to create a continuity that saved our family. I smile when I think about it now. By the end, you'll smile, too, and you'll know the point of TL's journey, and, with that insight, perhaps you'll discover the point of your own.

CHAPTER I

STANDING AT THE EDGE OF THE ROAD, WHERE THE brown scorched grass confronted the hot, black asphalt, TL looked around in disbelief, just as he'd done a week earlier. He didn't understand the implications of his actions, but he soon would. He'd later explain that something was tugging at his spirit, begging him, as it were, to stay. And he'd be right.

For now, he simply pondered, *What the hell was I thinking?,* as he sighed and watched the bus disappear into a distant heat wave. Across the highway, butterflies hovered peacefully and wildflowers waved, celebrating his return. TL closed his eyes, allowing the sweet fragrance to convince him he'd done the right thing, although he wasn't fully convinced.

"I don't believe this!" he murmured. "How in the world am I supposed to make this work?" A chuckle, deep in the caverns of his chest, rumbled forth as if he finally comprehended what he'd done. Momma's note lay crumbled in his right front pocket. That was the real reason he'd gotten off the bus, wasn't it? He couldn't let it go. Or let *her* go. He'd always wanted her love. Or attention. Or affirmation. At least now they could talk about it. For real. But that would come later. For now, he had to accept that he was home—and he was home to stay.

Sweat broke free across his forehead as if he had a deadly fever. In his imagination, he saw Daddy's stern, cold eyes staring at him, pleading with him to make a decision and stick with it. That's what Daddy always said, that a man—a real, bona fide man—oughta make a decision and stand on it, regardless of what it costs.

TL lifted his bags with tremulous hands. *Who am I kidding? I can't live in Swamp Creek again! Especially not now!* He remembered that he'd lived there before, but that was a different time, he thought, a simpler context. *I was a child then!* He'd convinced himself that the community had tolerated his peculiarities precisely because he wasn't an adult. They'd dismissed all his strange, unsettling ways with the hope that time or education or God would change them, but they hadn't. He was far stranger now than then, and he wasn't convinced homefolks would appreciate what he'd become. Yet, somewhere in his heart, he knew he was supposed to be there.

It was 5:14 P.M., mid-June, 1993, with no shade in sight. The Meetin' Tree was at least two miles away, and the sun sat blazing in the heavens. It promised to bake him three shades darker by the time he arrived at the tree. There were no houses around and, this time of day, people were either lounging before noisy window fans or, like our folks, consumed with outside chores. TL's only option was to bow his head and start walking.

Engulfed in stifling heat, he couldn't tell if he was moving at all. The smoldering air suffocated him like a sauna and scorched his throat. Every tree, rock, blade of dry grass, bird looked exactly alike, as if frozen in time. After twenty minutes or so, he dropped the bags and wiped sweaty palms against his pants. Water drenched his back and gathered in pools of moisture between his thighs. The inner band of his cap was soggy, and the bottom edges of his shirt, serving as a makeshift handkerchief, were saturated with sweat. *I must be a fool,* he thought. Then, with a quick shrug, he dismissed the notion, having decided that this was neither the time nor the place for personal reflection, so he lifted the bags and pressed on.

The blistering sun blinded him. Its unrelenting heat caused the bags to feel heavier now, as if, suddenly, they'd been filled with sand. "I can't believe I did this," he repeated. "How in the world am I going to live in Swamp Creek again?"

A faint strain from Uncle Jesse Lee's harmonica invaded his thoughts. The coarse melody, fumbling across treetops and hay fields, resurrected memories of the old man playing blues at the Meetin' Tree on Saturday evenings. Grandma called it the devil's music. Having crowned himself a virtuoso years ago, he did really bad renditions of B. B. King, Bobby "Blue" Bland, and Johnny T. Walker. Of course he couldn't sing—the community had confirmed that—but he thought he played well—which he didn't—so on Saturday evenings, he sat at the Meetin' Tree, singing loudly and playing his favorite blues tunes. Sometimes folks would stop by and listen for a spell, but most often he sat alone, playing with the same fervor either way. As children, we laughed at him, blowing a few bars, then singing a few, back and forth, until he got tired and went home. His foot kept time against the wooden church pew as his head bobbed with each downbeat. Occasionally, he'd close his eyes and melt into the music while others swayed and swooned, but that didn't happen often. Usually, as people went about their lives, Uncle Jesse Lee sat at the tree, performing for the wind and leaves, mimicking blues masters and composing songs about his own troubled existence. TL was surprised Uncle Jesse Lee was there so early. In bygone years, he hadn't arrived until evening, spending the bulk of his afternoon reading his Sunday school lesson and washing by hand his white formal church shirt. Yet he was supposed to be there. It was all part of the plan.

TL walked on. The damp shirt clung to his back while streams of living water trickled into his underwear. A '79 El Camino sped past, creating a temporary whirlwind of hot, dry air. Consumed therein, TL wondered, again, why the hell he'd gotten off that bus.

Truth was, he didn't know. Or didn't want to know. Momma would definitely ask, and his inability to answer might make him regret having stayed.

Where could he go? He couldn't go home. Not yet. How would he explain his presence, an hour after folks thought he was gone forever? He considered that perhaps everything he'd done in the past ten years was in preparation for this moment. Maybe every hurt, every longing, every heartbreak, every degree was ultimately for this life. TL frowned at the clear, blue sky, hoping for a sign, but saw only a brown chicken hawk gliding above.

Suddenly, amidst that same blank sky, where the heat waves meshed with the heavens, he beheld a city floating midair. Fearing hallucination, he blinked several times, but the image remained. Shielding his brows with his hands, he squinted harder, trying to comprehend whatever it was he was seeing. The streets of this city were paved with gold, and the architecture resembled the buildings of ancient Rome. Twelve huge gates, each guarded by two uniformed elders on either side, marked the city's entrance, and hovering slightly above each elder's head were miniature angels, forty-eight in total, fluttering, like hummingbirds, without moving. A gigantic tower stood in the middle of the city with twin bells in the top, swaying in opposite directions and emitting soprano and alto tones to the melody of "Lily in the Valley." TL had never seen anything so majestic. He would've cried if he hadn't been overwhelmed. The more he blinked, the clearer he saw this city made of gold. There were no people or life of any kind that he could discern. Only buildings and flowers too perfect to be real. Then, slowly, like a whiff of smoke, the image faded and vanished into thin air.

For a moment, TL stared into empty space, breathless. *What the hell was that?* Then, as he looked about in stark confusion, his breathing returned, sharp and labored, as if he'd run a marathon. *Am I losing my mind?* He blinked continually, like one recovering from a trance, searching desperately for clarity he couldn't find. Nothing of the sort had ever happened to him before. He didn't even believe in stuff like that! "Is God trying to tell me something?" he mumbled, glancing once more into the heavens. Already nervous about returning home, he thought the last thing he needed was yet another conundrum.

So, unable to glean meaning from the moment, he dismissed the vision as a psychological reaction to heat and hunger, and approached the Meetin' Tree exhausted and frustrated. Uncle Jesse Lee stopped playing.

"What's the matter wit' you, boy?" He held the harmonica slightly away from his mouth. He had to be at least eighty now, having buried half his children and retired when TL was a small child. "I thought you left here today?"

"I did," TL huffed, frowning from the glare of the sun. "At least I tried to. But I didn't get very far."

Uncle Jesse Lee nodded. "I understand. Sometimes it takes a man a while to figure thangs out. You'll get it."

TL stared across the distant field. "I'm okay. Just . . . confused, I guess."

"Naw, you ain't confused. That ain't the look o' confusion." Tobacco juice splattered onto the dusty earth. "You might be wonderin' 'bout somethin', but you ain't confused. I see it in yo' eyes. That wild look. That's not confusion." Uncle Jesse Lee laughed.

"What's so funny?"

"Life." He blew a blues bar on the harmonica. "Been a long time since I seen a young man stumblin' 'round so. Sorta reminds me o' myself when I was yo' age."

"Really?"

"Yep. Had a wife and five or six kids, and didn't know how I was gon' feed 'em. It was the dead o' winter."

"That's pretty rough."

"Naw, it wasn't pretty rough—it was rough as hell. Cold as the dickens. But we made it."

In TL's silence, Uncle Jesse Lee crooned, off-key,

Walkin' 'round the world

Then blew notes from the harmonica in the bluesy da-da-da-da DA! rhythm.

Tryin' to figure things out
    Da-da-da-da DA!
Walkin' 'round the world
    Da-da-da-da DA!
Tryin' to figure things out
    Da-da-da-da Da!
Walkin' 'round the word, uhm, tryin' to figure things out,
A man's gotta come home sometimes.

TL nodded along awkwardly.

"You ain't got to know everything, son. Just go where yo' spirit leads."

"Is that why I'm back? 'Cause my spirit led me back?"

Uncle Jesse Lee squinted. "You tell me."

"I don't know!"

He played another round of the same, self-composed song. "You gotta decide why you back. Don't nobody know that but you."

"But I don't know!"

"Well, don't worry. You will. When a man starts lookin' for thangs, he starts findin' 'em."

A small blackbird lit on a branch directly above Uncle Jesse Lee's head. He looked up quickly, expectant, then sighed with disappointment. "God'll show you what He need you to know. Just pay attention. Sometimes we miss the signs 'cause we so mad at the way they come, but if you can trust Him, I promise you'll come out better'n you went in." Uncle Jesse Lee chuckled. "He don't lead nowhere He don't go first."

"Hope you're right."

"You ain't got to hope! God sent you back, didn't He?" He spit again, in the exact same spot. "Then look for the signs. He'll tell you what you need to know."

Uncle Jesse Lee switched to a different tune, something a bit more jubilant. TL was thankful for the change. He couldn't discern what Uncle Jesse Lee was implying, but he figured he'd know soon enough.

When the old man finished, TL stood to leave.

"Listen, boy. You can't go nowhere 'less God prepare yo' way. When you try to run from Him, you end up runnin' straight into Him. Don't make no difference what you think. God gon' have His way, any way He gotta have it. You just as well stop fightin' Him. That's what you doin'. I see it on yo' face." He lifted the harmonica to play again, then paused. "You in the right place. Trust me. Everything comes back to where it started out. Everything. That's how life works, son. A man usually ends up exactly where he started out. Ain't that somethin'?"

TL walked away.

Uncle Jesse Lee hollered, "The signs. Look for the signs."

TL KNEW WHERE to go. He didn't bother knocking.

"I knew it!" David shouted and danced when he beheld TL's sweaty face. "You just couldn't leave, huh?"

"It's not funny."

TL dropped his bags and collapsed onto Ms. Swinton's red velvet sofa. His hands still trembled.

"What happened?"

"You already know what happened."

"Yeah, but why?"

"I don't know. That's what I keep asking myself. I must be a fool."

"Naw, you might be a lotta things, but you ain't no fool."

"No?"

"Nope. You're searching for something you ain't found yet. That's what it looks like to me."

TL shrugged. David went to the kitchen and returned with a frosty glass of homemade lemonade.

"Here, man. You sweatin' like a hog."

After three hard gulps, TL sighed and David sat in the chair directly across from him. "What am I searching for?"

"I don't know. You gotta figure that out, I guess."

"But that's the problem. I can't!"

"Well, you knew enough not to leave."

That was true, TL thought.

"My uncle Jesse Lee said God would send me a sign."

David smiled. "Then look for it."

TL leaned forward. "Can I stay here overnight? I'm not ready to go home."

"You're already at home, little brother. This old house is as much yours as it is mine. Probably more."

TL studied the meticulous room, with books that lined the exact edges of the snow-white shelves and red velvet furniture that looked as if no one had ever sat upon it. The oak floors glistened from the glare of the sun and the antique coffee table rested before the sofa like a mouth refusing to smile. Few had ever seen this room. Most would've entered through the back, if they entered at all, meeting Ms. Swinton in the kitchen for the few precious moments she spared. Only now did David and TL lounge there, claiming an inheritance neither of them fully understood, much less deserved.

"You made the right decision, little brother."

"Did I?"

"Sure you did."

David returned the empty glass to the kitchen and hollered from there, "You're gonna make a hell of a teacher for these kids. Just wait and see! It's what Momma wanted."

TL snickered. "Yeah. Just what . . . *she* wanted."

He wasn't ready to call Ms. Swinton *Momma*. He wanted to, deep in his heart, but his head wouldn't give him peace about it. Whenever he considered the matter, he rationalized that, yes, she'd loved him and taught him well, but he wasn't sure she'd actually *mothered* him. Wasn't that a particular kind of love? A personal, intimate, special kind of love? Didn't mothers boast to other mothers about their children, and read them bedtime stories at night, and send them care packages in college? And didn't they believe their child was the most beautiful child in the whole world? Had Ms. Swinton ever said this? Had she believed it? Had anyone?

Perhaps, he thought, this was why he'd come home—and why, now, he couldn't leave. Momma's note implied that she'd at least *wanted* to love him, once upon a time, so now, if they could heal some things, maybe he could know what motherly love felt like. Directly from a mother. TL exhaled.

"How long you gon' hide out?" David asked, taking the chair again.

"Hide out? I didn't know I was hiding out."

"Call it what you like, but sooner or later you gon' have to face your folks."

TL scoffed, "I know, I know."

"What about church in the morning? You're going, aren't you?"

"Yeah. I guess."

"Then you'd better get some rest. You got a lot of explaining to do."

TL REALLY DIDN'T KNOW WHY HE'D GOTTEN OFF THE BUS. HE FELT something in his heart and he followed it, thank God, but he never could've imagined what he was about to encounter.

The heart can be tricky, you know. It'll tell you what to do, and it'll be right, but it won't tell you the pain you're going to experience. Or how to heal from it after it's all said and done.

Like I said before, there are things TL doesn't know, things that would crush him if he knew, but you, reader, need to know. You're like me—we see it all, sitting high and lifted up, but most people can't bear such weight. It's the weight of truth. It burdens them down and destroys their imagination. That's all truth really is, huh? Imagination? So I've been sent to fill the empty spaces, to tell you what you need to know in order to fully understand this story. And to make sure my brother doesn't miss his destiny along the way.

I'll start by saying this: When TL left years ago, I thought I'd die. I stood at the screen, watching him disappear down the road until he vanished into a future I would never know. I was seven, a chubby little kid who couldn't figure out how to get my joy back. Days after he left, I kept looking down the road, hoping he'd forgotten something so he'd return, if only for a moment. My spirit lost its spunk. I couldn't seem to find happiness anywhere I searched. I suppose I was depressed, but I didn't know it then. I simply knew I had no motivation to do anything. I wanted to cry, but the tears wouldn't come. I had that deep down pain, the kind that eases into your pores and settles like a salve. The best I could do was hope. Each morning, I ran to the screen and looked for him, but the sun always set without his return.

I wasn't angry with TL; I knew why he'd left. It was Daddy I didn't understand. Why had he been so hard on the boy? I asked him once and he told me to mind my own business. Said I didn't know nothin' 'bout raisin' a man, so I should keep my mouth shut. I never asked again. I just loved my brother as hard as I could. He loved me, too. That's why he had to leave—'cause a man wasn't supposed to love like that, and TL was almost a man.

I didn't talk for a week. Momma whipped me for being ornery, as she called it, but I didn't care. I needed my brother. He'd been my only friend. I could tell him anything. He even saw my imaginary friends! If I messed up my hair, he'd fix it better than Momma had it at first. I would've traded God for him. I knew TL. He touched me, hugged me, sang to me, and made me feel like I was the most special little girl in the whole world. God wasn't so attentive.

But now I understand that it was all orchestrated. I'm on assignment, you could say. I'll tell you other things as we go along, but I can't tell you what TL will discover. That would be a violation of realms. My job is to make sure he makes it. That's why I came. He loved me then; I love him now. And I can't tell you why things happened the way they did. Even here, you don't understand everything. You just see everything. Except the depth of a person's heart. No one can go there. Not even God goes without an invitation, and few invite Him. So I'm gonna tell you not why things happened, but for what purpose. By the end you'll know that, amidst all the craziness, there were no mistakes.

CHAPTER 2

AVING TOSSED ALL NIGHT, TL ROSE EXHAUSTED. Unable to imagine a new life in an old place, he wrestled with his decision until morning, and even then he was still unsure. But no turning back now.

The thought of skipping church altogether was comforting, but, refusing to live in fear, he decided to go. Standing before the double doors, breathing away anxiety, he tried to brace himself for the imminent confrontation, but when that didn't work, he exhaled one final time and entered, smiling as if he hadn't been there in years. Willie James saw him first and squealed with excitement, then calmed instantly, remembering that they were both men. Grown men. Grown, black men. Yet, unable to contain himself completely, Willie James blinked and covered his mouth like a forlorn lover. Daddy turned and stared, nodding methodically the way he did whenever TL was in trouble. Reverend Lindsay's eyes brightened as he declared, "Well, well! The good Lawd sho' do work in mysterious ways!" Momma swiveled slowly, as if preparing to behold the face of God, and, with narrowed, piercing eyes, studied TL's expectant expression the way one studies a microscropic sample. She clearly wasn't surprised; that was obvious. But she was definitely perplexed. After several excruciating seconds, however, her penetrating gaze softened into curiosity, and TL relaxed as she returned her attention to the pulpit.

He took the space next to Willie James. Mr. Blue whispered, "I thought you left hyeah yesterday on that five o'clock bus?"

"I did, sir. Well, sort of. I didn't get very far. Guess I wasn't ready to leave."

"Well, I wish you'd just stay fo'ever." His mangled arthritic hand patted TL's leg heavily. In Daddy's direction, Mr. Blue asked, "Don't you agree?"

One corner of Daddy's mouth upturned without yielding a full smile. It wasn't clear whether he agreed or not; what was certain was that he wanted Mr. Blue to shut up.

Willie James couldn't sit still. "When'd you get back?"

"I never left. I'll tell you about it later."

Reverend Lindsay asked the choir for an A and B selection. The musician, if we must call him that, banged notes and chords with no logical sequence, and Miss Polly stepped to the mic and screamed, in an annoying, nasal soprano, "It's another day's journey, and I'm glad about it!"

"I'm glad about it!" the other five choir members repeated, each in a different key. TL chewed his bottom lip to keep from laughing.

"I'm so sick o' this song I don't know what to do!" Willie James murmured. "They been singin' it for the last ten years!"

"Longer than that! I used to play it for them myself! And who told Miss Polly—"

"Shhh," Momma hissed without turning. The brothers quieted immediately. Even grown people in Swamp Creek could get slapped in the mouth.

As the choir screeched, a voice intruded from outside. At first, TL thought he was hearing things, but when the deep, coarse alto intensified, he looked around and saw others rolling eyes and shaking heads knowingly. The choir grew louder, almost screaming its love for Christ, while the external voice fought to match its volume. "People, get right while you have a chance!" the voice belted. There was neither rhyme nor reason in the melody or the timing. Clearly someone had made it up. Grandma called these homemade jingles "nigga songs." TL hated them.

"Who is that?" He frowned. Willie James shook his head sadly, but didn't answer.

Everyone knew. They glanced at each other with the look of communal shame and embarrassment.

Daddy rose and stomped toward the entrance. TL followed. Before Daddy opened the double doors, he said, "This heffa oughta get enough o' this crap! Fool 'round and somebody's gon' kill her crazy ass one day. You watch what I tell you!"

When he opened the doors, Cliffesteen stood in the churchyard, in her classic black dress, crooning at the top of her raspy voice: "Time is runnin' out! God ain't gon' wait all day!" She shuffled from one foot to the other, like a nervous drug addict. Her matted wig sat twisted worse than usual, and her extra-long fake eyelashes, which TL felt sure would fall any moment, dangled above yellowing, slanted eyes. Daddy looked at her until his anger exploded: "Git on 'way from here, girl! You interruptin' de Lawd's service!" When she didn't respond, he hollered louder, "Take yo' ass home, Cliff, before I have to get after you!" She stepped backward when Daddy stepped forward, and kept on singing. He hurled rocks and sticks at Cliffesteen, who dodged all but the last stone. It hit her shoulder, and she yelped, "Ow!" and crumbled to the ground. Prepared to beat her, Daddy approached angrily, but she scrambled to her feet and fumbled away. He stopped thirty yards from the church door. She had stopped singing.

"Don't let me have to come back out here, girl! I'm tryin' to be nice, but we ain't gon' have you cuttin' up and clownin' every time we tryin' to have church! This is the Lawd's house! Ain't no room for yo' bullshit here! Now go 'head on and find somethin' to do before we have to find it for you!"

She'd always been crazy, people said, even as a child. Daddy told TL that in school, she would jump up from her desk and dance as if suddenly hearing music in her head. Children laughed and mocked her, but she didn't pay them any mind. Miss Swinton tried to restrain her, but Cliffesteen would always break free and dance the entire room before retiring on her own, sweating as if she'd been working the fields. After the third or fourth outburst, Miss Swinton stopped chasing Cliffesteen and told the children to ignore her. She danced anyway, grateful not to be disturbed. Boys teased each other about liking her, while girls said she had the cooties. When she wasn't dancing, she sat quietly in the back of the room, smiling and mumbling to herself, without ever hearing a word Miss Swinton said. Or so everyone thought. The truth was that Cliffesteen heard everything. She just never repeated it. Not until she got grown. Then, she spent days walking the dirt roads of Swamp Creek, spelling words out loud and reciting times tables.

She'd always been rail thin. Her current 125 pounds was the most she'd ever weighed, and standing five foot ten, she looked like a crack addict before crack came to Swamp Creek. Her hair was short and unkempt and most times covered with the old, matted wig. Even when she was a little girl, her hair wouldn't grow, so her folks covered it with a bandanna and called it a day. Sometimes boys would snatch the rag off her head and run, but they'd pay for it dearly when Cliffesteen caught them. And she *would* catch them. That was her one redeeming quality, her speed, and it resulted, Daddy said, in almost every boy getting his ass whipped at one time or another. No one could outrun Cliff, as the children called her, and, if someone bothered her, she was merciless in her revenge. Daddy said he ran off with her scarf one day, and Cliffesteen caught him before he reached the edge of the schoolyard. "That lil' crazy heffa leapt across the grass like a goddamn gazelle!" he marveled, still unable to believe her agility. "She slapped me so hard I got dizzy and had to lay on the ground a minute before I could move." No one understood her strength. Kids stop trying. They decided it best to leave Cliffesteen alone.

She quit school after the eighth grade. Daddy said her folks didn't object. Hell, they never knew why she went in the first place. At sixteen, she was pregnant. No one knew by whom. In private places, folks asked, "Who in the world fucked that crazy girl?" Besides that, people didn't say much about it, referring to the invisible perpetrator as "a low-life excuse for a man." A few bold ones asked Cliffesteen about the father, and she said, "Ain't nan." At birth, the little girl looked so much like her mother that people stopped asking about a man. When, at age six, she caught polio and died, Cliffesteen went even further out of her mind. Since that day, she never wore anything other than her black funeral dress, black stockings, which were full of runs, scuffed white open-toe shoes, and the ragged black hat her mother had given her.

Frown lines intersected across Daddy's shiny dark forehead as he reentered the church. Cliffesteen's nervous energy subsided. TL watched her shuffle away, then ran after her.

"Hey, Miss Cliffesteen! Miss Cliffesteen! Wait!"

He had to touch her before she'd turn. Even then, she didn't say anything, looking as if she'd taken a vow of silence.

"Are you okay?"

She nodded.

"You didn't seem okay back there. I just wanted to make sure."

"Folk ain't right. Is they, honey?" She glanced at her right shoulder.

TL looked around, puzzled.

"Oh! I'm sorry. This here's my baby girl," Cliffesteen said, smiling suddenly. "She go wit' me wherever I go. Sittin' right here"—Cliffesteen tapped her shoulder—"whisperin' things to help me along the way. My sweet little angel."

TL's eyes bulged.

"She left this world years ago. Too soon, if you ask me. But, hey, ain't nobody asked me." Her smile disintegrated. "She's still wit' me though. I can even see her sometimes."

What?

"She's a special child. Always was. That's why I named her Jezebel."

Cliffesteen noticed TL's shock.

"'Cause can't nobody destroy her."

Probing would've been useless, he decided, so he returned to the original subject. "Why were you so upset a few minutes ago?"

"'Cause they didn't do Aunt Easter right. They didn't have no business doin' her like that!" Her volume increased. "She wunnit no devil! They put her away!"

TL scowled. "What do you mean? What happened?"

Cliffesteen shuffled a bit, realigning her spirit, and told him about Aunt Easter, her father's oldest sister. She lived deep in the woods of Swamp Creek, next to the Jordan River. Her house was hoisted on cinder blocks and stilts, high in the air, so when it rained she didn't get flooded out. TL remembered her vaguely, but he hadn't seen her often. She stayed to herself most of the time. A strange woman, people said. Never married or birthed any children. Not that folks knew of. Her charcoal-black skin was the smoothest, prettiest anyone had ever seen, and those dazzling blue eyes shone in her head like shiny turquoise marbles. TL asked Grandma once how a dark-skinned black person could have blue eyes, and she said they couldn't. That was the devil in her. But the few times he saw Aunt Easter, he didn't see the devil. Granted, she wasn't warm and friendly. She never smiled or said anything. He waved at her once and she lifted her right hand like a courtroom witness being sworn in, then turned casually and walked away. Sometimes menfolk would plow their way through the woods and high grass to check on her, but upon return they never said much. Just shrugged shoulders and shook confused heads.

While TL was away, folks started dyin', Cliffesteen said, whenever they saw her. Not right away, but later the same day. People said whoever looked her in the eyes was sent to hell. Aunt Easter came to town one Saturday—one of the two or three times a year she was seen in public—with a black shawl over her head and a long black dress like pilgrims used to wear. Most people glanced and went about their business, but a few nosy ones lifted the shawl and tried to make Aunt Easter speak.

"So she did, I guess," Cliffesteen said, "and all them folks died befo' the sun went down. Heart attacks, strokes, exilectic fits, everything."

She waited for TL's response, but he didn't give one.

"They didn't have no business botherin' her! She wunnit botherin' nobody! Ain't that right?"

He nodded for the sake of protocol.

"A lotta peoples come together and started talkin' 'bout what had done happened. They said somethin's gotta be done 'bout that woman. I heard 'em. They was in the church. I was standin' right outside. They said they gotta get rid o' her 'cause she the devil."

"The devil?"

"That's what they said!" Cliffesteen shifted again, rubbing her arms like a fiending addict. "The menfolks promised to handle it once and fo' all."

A hawk circled casually above. TL wondered if it could be the same bird he'd seen the day before. He also wondered what it might've been like to live with Aunt Easter down in that house, high and lifted up.

Cliffesteen dramatized how she ran to Aunt Easter's house to tell her what she'd heard, but Aunt Easter told her to hold her peace. She wunnit runnin' from nobody. Plus, she said, you can't run the devil outta nowhere. Devil always around. So Cliffesteen stopped worrying about it.

"A week later, somebody stopped me in front o' the general store, early one mornin', and said Aunt Easter was dead. I knowed they was lyin' 'cause I didn't feel no death 'round her. I woulda felt somethin' if she had'a died fo' real, but I didn't feel nothin', so I knowed somethin' was wrong. I rushed down to her house, but she wunnit there. That's how I knowed them men had done somethin' they didn't have no business. She was always at home, fixin' people's spirits and keepin' demons away from 'round here. She'd just come from town the week befo', so I knowed she shoulda been at home, but she wunnit.

"So I started goin' 'round askin' peoples 'bout her, but they acted like they didn't know nothin'. Some of 'em run in they house like they was scared o' me!" She stomped her scuffed white shoes in the road. "I went to the funeral home and they said they didn't know what I was talkin' 'bout, but I could tell they was lyin'. I felt it. I feels thangs, you know."

"Um . . . Okay," TL mumbled.

"So I waited 'til dark and marched like Joshua 'round that funeral parlor seven times 'til I heard Aunt Easter callin' fo' me."

"What!"

"That's right!" Cliffesteen clapped excitedly. "She was callin' my name, over and over and over. I heard her just as good! I couldn't make out the other stuff she was sayin', so I started talkin' back, askin' her where she was and what had done happened. That's when Mr. Truce come outta his house wit' a shotgun and tried to kill me."

"Tried to kill you?"

"Yeah! He told me to git on 'way from his place with that hoo-doo foolishness or he was gon' shoot me. I told him Aunt Easter was callin' me, and he pointed the gun at my head, so I left. I knowed she was in that funeral parlor. I knowed it! I felt it! I heard her!" She rubbed her arms and frowned. "I just didn't know how to get to her!" Her voice trembled. "She was callin' my name, but I didn't know how to get to her!"

Too afraid to touch Cliffesteen, much less comfort her, TL simply moaned, "Oh no. I'm sorry."

"The next mornin' I went back to the funeral home and saw the menfolks puttin' a casket in the um . . ."

"Hearse."

"Hearst! That's right. I knowed it was Aunt Easter. But she wunnit dead. I knowed she wunnit! Wunnit no death 'round her!"

Chills sprang across TL's arms. Could there be some truth to what Cliffesteen was saying?

"I followed that hearst 'til it come to the church and stopped. Peoples was everywhere, but it wunnit no sadness, you know. Folks just seemed . . ." She squinted and fluttered her fingers, searching for the right word. ". . . restless, I guess. They started tellin' me they was sorry to hear 'bout Aunt Easter's passin', and I told 'em she ain't passed 'cause she was still alive in that casket."

TL wished, for all the money in the world, he'd been there that day.

"Nobody believed me, but when they brung it in the church, womens started mumblin' 'bout how things didn't feel right."

Cliffesteen nodded. TL waited.

"It was 'cause things wasn't right. I felt Aunt Easter's spirit all over me. Then, all o' sudden, I heard her knock, real soft, on the inside o' that casket, and call my name."

"What!"

"That's right. Didn't nobody else hear it but me, but I heard it. I knowed she wunnit dead. I woulda felt it. I told you I feels thangs. People, too."

"She knocked on the inside of the casket? At the funeral?"

"Yep. It was too light for anybody else to hear, but I heard it. I walked toward the casket and she called my name—Honey Bee, Honey Bee—that's what she called me—so I told 'em to open up the casket and let her out, but they wouldn't do it. They said they wasn't gon' open it at all."

"Nobody got to view the body?"

"Nobody. Most folks didn't want to anyway. Guess I scared 'em so bad they wanted to hurry up and get Aunt Easter in the ground. Three or four menfolks held me in my seat like I was some crazy woman. Most folks left early, sayin' she was the devil. I tried to make 'em let her out, but they wouldn't!" Anger began to consume her. "They just rushed through the funeral and buried her. Alive!"

That was all TL could take. "I'ma get on back in the church now, Miss Cliffesteen."

"I'm tellin' you! She knocked on the inside o' that casket! I heard her! Just 'cause other folks didn't don't mean it ain't so. She said, 'Honey Bee! Honey Bee! Honey Bee!' Oh, I cried like it was rainin'. Bet they had her tied up in that thing with somethin' stuffed in her mouth. She probably couldn't move much, but she did knock. It mighta been her feet or hands or whatever, but she definitely knocked and wouldn't nobody let her out! She was callin' my name!"

Cliffesteen's conviction was unnerving. TL couldn't figure out what to believe, but he knew her imagination wasn't *that* enormous. He really wanted to leave.

"They said she was the devil, so they had to get rid o' her, but she wunnit the devil. They was the devil," Cliffesteen yelled, "for buryin' my auntie alive!"

TL tried to ease away without being rude.

"And she wunnit botherin' nobody. They was botherin' her. That's why them people died—'cause they was botherin' her!" she cried and shouted. "I woulda dug her up, but they buried her too deep. That big ol' machine dug a hole so deep you couldn't see the bottom. She died in that hole screamin', 'Honey Bee!' and I couldn't help her!"

As TL turned to leave, she added, "Like the day yo' sister died. I felt it. I knowed it. I went and told Aunt Easter that death was on somebody, and she said she already knowed 'cause she felt it, too. She was sick as a dog, throwin' up all over the ground. The death wasn't na'chel though, she said. The life went too fast. She knowed who it was. I didn't, but she did."

How could he leave now?

"Aunt Easter was so sick she couldn't do nothin' all day. But that night, she got better. That's when she told me 'bout yo' sister's spirit."

Cliffesteen became timid, hesitant.

"What about it?"

"That somebody had done somethin' unna'chel to her. She said the child was dead, but her spirit wasn't restin'."

Their eyes locked.

"Of course her spirit wasn't resting! How could it have been?"

"You right. But it's restin' now. Next to my Jezebel's spirit. In the Valley."

"The valley? What are you talking about?"

Cliffesteen looked heavenward. "You'll understand one day. That's why you back. To understand." Then she continued: "But Aunt Easter ain't in the Valley 'cause she didn't die. They just buried her!" Cliffesteen began to weep and wail, so TL left her in the middle of the road. He questioned why he'd paid her any attention in the first place. She'd been off all her life. Yet something about her sincerity left him troubled. She wasn't *completely* crazy, he knew, so how much of what she'd said was actually true?

He was almost sorry he'd gone after her. This whole thing with Aunt Easter was too real to dismiss. Who could make that up? He'd never seen her house, but Mr. Blue and other men had talked about it sometimes. They talked about Aunt Easter, too. The blue eyes just weren't right, they'd said. It was a sign of some deficiency, something supernatural, some evil omen that had crept among the people, and somebody had to do something about it.

TL didn't know, as a child, that Aunt Easter and Cliffesteen were related. He'd known Mr. Cliff—a tall, skinny dark-skinned man who, like his sister, didn't say much—but he never put the two together. Now that he thought about it, they looked just alike. Aunt Easter was tall and thin, too, and just as dark. Her features were a bit sharper than her brother's—high, pronounced cheekbones and small, narrow eyes. That's probably why folks thought she was the devil. You couldn't really see her eyes unless she looked directly at you. Then she'd bulge them, and their ocean-blue radiance would overwhelm you, and most folks would turn away. But would they have buried the woman alive?

CHAPTER 3

THROUGHOUT THE SERMON, WHICH LATER DADDY called a "travesty of the gospel," Willie James found every excuse to touch TL. Whether with a slight nudge or a sensual rub on the leg, Willie James couldn't contain his joy. He was far more excited than TL was. It was as if he'd finally gotten all he'd ever hoped for. Momma, on the other hand, didn't look at TL again. She sat perfectly still, like one devoid of human emotion, and let Reverend Lindsay scream and foam at the mouth about an Old Testament prophet named Ezekiel who, in a valley somewhere, called dry bones together and they lived again. Momma wasn't moved. Her stoic disposition challenged him to say something of substance, something that might cause her to lift her hands in praise, but Reverend Lindsay seemed oblivious to the call. So, while others shouted, "Amen," simply for the sake of protocol, Momma gazed at Reverend Lindsay until he simply stopped looking in her direction. When he whooped, "Finally, Saints," Momma nodded and retrieved an offering from her good, classic black Sunday pocketbook, holding the dollar bills as ransom for Reverend Lindsay's conclusion.

The deacons rose and collected the money. Before the benediction, Reverend Lindsay chuckled, "Well, bless de Lawd. Looks like ol' TL might stay after all!"

"Hope so!" Willie James shouted.

Momma and Daddy glanced at each other.

After dismissal, people rushed TL with questions of his abrupt return. Daddy exited, slinging over his right shoulder, "See you at the dinner table, boy. Don't be late."

Momma hadn't said anything. She waited for Daddy in the car.

"You have to come with me, David," TL pleaded during the ride home. "Please. I need a buffer."

"Oh no! I can't get in the middle of that. It would be too awkward. Besides, you gotta do this on your own. You the one gotta live here."

"But why can't you help me out? Just this once?"

David wouldn't yield. "'Cause you don't need my help. You just think you do. You'll be fine. They're your folks."

After changing clothes, TL sat in Ms. Swinton's living room, pondering what he'd say. No one would ask much, of course, since that was the Tyson family way, but they'd expect an explanation. Especially Momma. She'd guess that he'd gotten her note, and she'd want to know why it hadn't resolved things between them. *I didn't hate you.* That's what the note said. And that's all he'd ever wanted to know, right? Then why was he back? TL shook his head. He didn't have the slightest idea.

Daddy would ask about his future. He was never too concerned with the past, having told TL years ago that the past was like smoke—it fades before your eyes and reminds you that there's absolutely nothing you or anyone else can do about it. Daddy didn't believe in saying, "I'm sorry"—about anything!—because the truth is, he said, that he was never sorry for his actions. Others ain't, either. They simply feel bad if the outcome isn't good. Daddy didn't embrace feelings of regret, guilt, or shame. He simply acted in the moment and hoped for the best. If the worst resulted, he didn't entertain remorse. "Who controls the outcome of people's choices?" he used to ask TL. But TL didn't know. Daddy said he didn't, either, so obviously it was a power greater than both of them. If there is to be guilt, he concluded, that's who should bear it.

David dropped off TL and wished him luck. Willie James waited outside.

"Man, it's so good to see you again." They embraced and walked into the house.

Smiling sarcastically, Momma stood in the kitchen, draped in her ragged floral duster, with floured hands resting atop narrow hips. "I shoulda guessed," she murmured. TL crumbled the note in his pocket.

"Is y'all gon' talk or is we gon' eat?" Daddy said, waiting impatiently at the head of the table.

Willie James and TL shuffled to their respective seats and sat easily, just as they'd always done.

"I'm fryin' a few last pieces of chicken. They'll be ready in a minute."

Great, TL thought. *Just enough time for Daddy to grill me.*

Willie James wanted to speak further, but, in Daddy's presence, he usually refrained. Instead, he squirmed in his seat and tapped a nervous rhythm onto the tabletop—that is, until Daddy's glance silenced that, too.

"So what happened?" he asked, sucking his teeth.

"I don't know. I tried to leave, even got on the bus, but I got right back off. Well, not *right* back off, but—"

"Why?"

TL sighed. "I don't know. I can't explain it. Just couldn't leave, I guess."

"I see." Daddy's sympathetic nod relaxed TL's anxiety. "I can understand that. A man's got a right to stay home if he wants to. You ain't gotta explain that to nobody."

TL almost mentioned the note, but decided against it. What

good would it do? Anyway, it felt private now, as if, suddenly, in some invisible realm, he and Momma had agreed never to speak about it. When he turned to look at her, she was already looking at him like one struggling to recall where they'd first met. Her vacant stare reignited his apprehension.

Then, as if recovering from a trance, she blinked twice and returned to the skillet of frying chicken. Willie James touched TL's knee beneath the table, retarding his baby brother's impulse to run out the door and hitchhike back to New York.

"Me and this boy here could use some help in the fields."

"Sir? Wow. Um, okay. I was thinking about taking Ms. Swinton's place at the school." He hadn't meant to offer that yet, but, in the moment, he'd say anything to avoid physical labor.

Daddy's brows lifted. "Is that right?"

"Yessir. I mean, I haven't thought it all the way out, but—"

"But what?"

"Um . . . but I guess those kids need somebody."

"Yeah, they do."

"And why not me, huh?"

Momma cackled, shaking her head.

"That's right. Why not you." Daddy nodded slowly.

Willie James took a chance. "You gon' make a great teacher, TL. I just know it!" His giddy demeanor disgusted Daddy. "I can see you now, marchin' up and down between the desks, tellin' kids all 'bout stuff they ain't never heard of, and they tryin' to write it down 'cause they so excited, but they can't write fast as you can talk, and people start comparin' you to Ms. Swinton 'cause you teach just like her."

"That's enough, boy," Daddy murmured.

Momma placed a salad of iceberg lettuce and wedged tomatoes on the table, alongside a pot of black-eyed peas and a platter of pepper-seasoned fried chicken. She laid cutlery before the men and took her usual place, opposite Daddy.

"Lawd, we thank You fo' this food we 'bout to receive," Daddy began without notification, "fo' the nourishment of our bodies and the benefit of our souls."

He didn't say amen, so everyone kept their heads bowed.

"And we thank You, Lawd, fo' . . . um . . ."

Willie James squeezed TL's hand.

". . . family. Amen."

As they served themselves, Momma asked, "Why didn't you bring yo' brother with you? Yo' *other* brother, I mean." She smiled.

"I guess I could've, but I didn't really think about it. Plus, it might've been a little awkward."

"You think so?"

"Let it alone, Marion."

Momma shrugged.

TL couldn't eat fast enough. That was the longest meal he'd ever consumed. With every bite, food seemed to multiply on his plate, holding him captive to a time and place from which he desperately sought escape.

Finally, Daddy rose. "Help yo'self, son. Me & Willie James gon' go check on that ol' pregnant cow."

"Wait!" he shouted a bit too loudly. "I wanted to ask you about Miss Cliffesteen."

Daddy frowned. "What about her? You know that woman ain't well. She ain't neva had no sense. She liable to say anything. Them folks was into that voodoo shit. It drove most of 'em crazy."

Oh no! TL thought. *Don't leave me here with Momma!*

"I didn't know Mr. Cliff was Aunt Easter's brother."

"Didn't? Well, he was. He didn't fool wit' her much though. Told me once that when she was born, she come out babblin' in tongues. I don't know how true it is, but he said she could read and write any language she wanted to. Ain't never been to school a day in her life. Didn't need it."

"What's this about her bein' the devil?"

Daddy's lips protruded. "I don't know much 'bout that. All I know is folks went to dyin' when they looked at her. That much I know."

"Oh come on, Daddy!"

"You believe what you want to, but I know what I seen. I seen her in town one Saturday, walkin' 'round lookin' like a witch. I didn't fool wit' her, but some folks too nosy for they own good. They paid for it, too."

"All of 'em died?"

"Every single one of 'em. Even Mr. Eli's grandson, and I know wunnit nothin' wrong wit' him. Hell, he wunnit but seven years old! She gave him a piece a candy or gum or somethin', and he choked on it."

"Oh my God."

"Yeah. That's how we knowed somethin' was wrong. So we got together at the church, the menfolks, and talked 'bout it, and a few of us volunteered to go see her. When we got there, she wunnit there. Some said she died the night before. Her body was already at Truce's by the time I heard anythin'. I don't know who took it, and I didn't ask. I don't play 'round wit' that shit. Some of it's real."

When the screen door slammed, Momma unleashed a soul-chilling cackle. It was thin and sharp, her laughter, bubbling into a roar that echoed across the table and throughout the house. She laughed until crocodile tears came, then wiped them away. "Whee!"

Damn. I could've been in New York by now.

"It never ends, does it?"

"What?"

"What do you mean 'what'?"

"I don't know what you're talking about, Momma."

"Oh stop it! It's always 'bout you. Always has been. You was here a week ago, in the middle of everybody's attention, and now here you are again. I wish you'd make up yo' mind and stop interruptin' other people's lives."

"Excuse me?"

"You heard what I said. Make a decision and be done wit' it for a change."

His mouth fell open. "I beg your pardon?"

She rose and began clearing the table. "I'm talkin' 'bout yo' life, boy."

"What about it?"

She chuckled again. "Can't you see nothin'? Everything you do is in reaction to somebody else. Grow up. Be a man. Decide where and how you gon' live, and stay there."

TL yelped, "Are you serious?"

"Yeah, I'm serious! You ain't never knowed me to play, have you?

"Stop disturbin' everybody else's life just 'cause you ain't got one."

"I can't believe you're saying this to me! Not after what you did." Momma didn't flinch. "Maybe I should've left."

"Maybe you should've. But that's my point: Decide to go or stay, but decide somethin' and be done wit' it." She put the pot of peas in the refrigerator.

"It's not that simple, Momma."

"Ain't it?"

"No, ma'am, it isn't!"

"Then make it simple."

TL gasped.

"I ain't sayin' you shouldn't've come back. I ain't sayin' you should've. I'm sayin' be man enough to make up yo' mind. Then do it."

Surrendering his hands to the air, TL said, "I really don't believe this. What kind of mother are you?"

Momma closed the refrigerator door easily. "The kind yo' father treats like shit and still expects to cook his food and raise his bastard child. And I did it." She glared at TL. "Can you believe that?"

He paused. "I'm sorry. I was out of line."

"Yes, you were, but what else is new?" She coughed. "It don't matter no way. But now that I've answered yo' question, you answer mine: Is you here to stay or not?" She stood, arms akimbo.

TL wasn't absolutely sure, but he had to decide now. "Yes, ma'am. I'm here to stay."

"Well . . . good for you." She wrapped a breast and two wings in a sheet of foil and sat it atop the stove. "Now, build you a life, like everybody else, and stop walkin' 'round feelin' sorry for yo'self. And, while you at it, pass me the rest of those plates."

TL complied, then asked, "What did you mean by the note?"

"Exactly what it said."

Momma washed the final dishes and wiped her hands on her apron. Unable to articulate his question any clearer, TL left it alone.

Later she added, "You thought I didn't like you. Sometimes I didn't. But I never hated you. That's all you really wanted to know, wasn't it?"

"I guess so."

"Well, now you know."

Instead of feeling free, he felt trapped.

"So what's next?"

"I'm not sure."

"Of course you ain't. When you figure it out, let me know. I'm sure I'll be surprised. I always am. For now, I'ma take me a quick nap."

She touched his arm lovingly as she passed. *Could this all be a dream?* he thought.

"Have a seat and relax," Momma called from the back. "The menfolks'll be back directly."

He had to get out of there. Somehow, Momma had forced him to commit to a future he'd only considered. Now he had to figure out how to live it.

IT WAS 3:38 P.M. in the midst of a sweltering, muggy, Sunday afternoon. Staring at the grave, TL squinted and promised to make Momma pay for what she'd done. Little did he know she'd make him pay, too.

ACTUALLY, IN THE END, THE ENTIRE FAMILY PAID. WE ALL LOST something in our efforts to be loved by people who didn't know how. Truth is, no one goes through life free of charge. People pay precisely because we subtract from others' lives in hopes of increasing our own. It never works. I tried it. I wanted TL's life more than anything I could think of. I wanted to be just like him, to dwell beneath his skin, to bask in his unbridled intelligence. But I couldn't have him. Each day the sun rose, I followed my memory down the crooked lane and into the thicket where he'd vanished. I'll never forget it. It was a quiet, balmy Sunday morning, the day he left, with a chorus of birds chirping sweet, staccato melodies. TL wore blue jeans and a green, short-sleeved polo shirt. Every few steps he turned and waved as I stood on the back steps, crying. He didn't want to leave me, but he had to. I watched him disappear as he struggled with two heavy suitcases. He'd catch the evening bus, he'd said, and be in Atlanta by morning. For several days, I walked the road and into the woods where I'd last seen him. I thought that maybe, if I looked hard enough, I might find some remnant of him, something that he'd left behind. I didn't find anything. Squirrels, birds, and deer glanced curiously, wondering why a little girl was in the middle of the forest alone. And what in the world was she looking for?

Momma told me to let him go. Her advice wasn't malicious. "Disappointment turns into resentment," she said, and she didn't want me to resent him. I didn't know what that meant. "He's coming back," she promised. "How do you know?" I pleaded. With a dry smile, she said, "'Cause you all he got." That comforted me, so I stopped going to the woods and started hoping even more than I'd hoped before. But, as I already said, hope is a dangerous, difficult thing, especially when, after a while, nothing comes of it. But I believed, so I kept hoping until I received TL's letter. I was ten. That's when my hope faded. He was too happy to be away. I felt it in his tone. I'd been obsessed with him while he didn't seem to care about me. That's how I felt. I tried to stop caring, but I couldn't. I'd built my whole life around him, and, with him gone, I was lost. He was my hero, he was gone, and I was lost.

I became silent and withdrawn. All I knew to do was sulk. Days were long and boring. Ms. Swinton prodded me to stay focused, but I'd lost my drive. She had, too. I could tell. Her normal enthusiasm dwindled into mere obligation. We didn't know what to do. I even stopped styling my hair. Momma would press it Saturday nights and I'd sit in the chair like a zombie, then, later, pull it back into a ponytail. I simply didn't care. Nothing mattered except my brother, and I couldn't make him come home. Inspiration was nowhere to be found, and, had I died, I would've been perfectly satisfied. Momma told Daddy, finally, that I was depressed. He said I was too young for that. And anyway, from what he knew, depression was a luxury reserved for rich white women.

Now I know Momma was right. I was indeed depressed, and although TL did come home, he was too late to play with me again. Yet, from God's perspective, he was right on time.

CHAPTER 4

TL TOOK REFUGE BENEATH THE OLD PEAR TREE IN the front yard. His thoughts, like dandelion spores, floated about in his head without congealing into anything sensible. Within minutes, he was drenched and irritable. The slivers of shade the tree provided offered minimal relief from a sun determined to bake him once again. It was even hotter now, he presumed, than the day before—if that could be possible—and he wondered how in the world black people had worked for centuries in that kind of heat. *I would've fainted,* he told himself. *Or perhaps like the rest of my people, I would've put on a hat, closed my mouth, and sweated without public complaint.*

With his back against the tree, the thin limbs, swinging low under the weight of underripe green pears, enshrouded him in a cage. Honeybees buzzed and circled about his head, to his absolute irritation, and humidity left him moist and sticky all over. He was convinced that there was no heat in the world like Arkansas heat. He and Willie James used to say that anybody going to hell could simply come by Arkansas during the summer and they'd know what awaited them. Staring into the distance, he watched the barn shimmy behind a rolling heat wave that stretched the entire width of the field. It was so hot that all the grass had withered, and all of Momma's hostas, lined along the backside of the house, had yellowed and collapsed from sheer heat exhaustion. Cows waded in the pond, up to their bellies, searching frantically for a cool stream, while birds and squirrels sat motionless in the trees, no doubt trying to conserve their precious energy. Only the bees appeared unaffected by the heat. Each time they buzzed near TL's ear, he swung at them and mumbled, "Get away from me, damnit!" until he found himself cursing and fighting creatures a mere fraction of his size.

"No need bein' mad at them," Daddy said, chuckling. "You in they territory. They was here first."

TL hadn't noticed his approach. "I don't see how y'all take this heat. I couldn't do it." He wiped his brow and slung sweat from his fingertips.

Daddy parted the limbs and stood before TL. "Whatchu mean you 'couldn't do it'? You already done it!"

"I guess I have, but I couldn't do it anymore."

"Yeah you could—if you had to."

Daddy's white V-neck T-shirt was soaked, revealing a semi-muscular, hairy chest and rounded beer belly. He was at least 225 pounds now although, while TL was home, Daddy'd never weighed more than 175. Much of his nappy, coarse chest hair had turned white, like his scruffy beard, and TL wondered, for an instant, if his pubic hair had done likewise. Of course he didn't ask. He wouldn't've dared. Besides his being scared to death of the man, Daddy's nakedness always unsettled him. As a teenager, he'd walked in on Daddy stepping out of the bathtub one evening, and all he could do was stammer and look away. Daddy laughed, butt naked and unashamed, and asked, "Ain't you neva seen a grown man naked before?" TL shook his head vigorously and shouted, "No, sir!" "Well, it's 'bout time you do. Hand me that towel." His hands trembled so badly he dropped it twice. "Aw, shit, boy! Throw me the towel and get on out of here." Daddy stood, dripping wet, on the diamond-patterned linoleum floor, mocking TL's insecurity. After closing the door, TL leaned against the adjacent wall and panted. He wasn't supposed to be there, he thought, inside Daddy's vulnerability, and he prayed never to go again. They weren't friends, and he preferred it that way. Something about Daddy's naked confidence made him seem larger and stronger, driving an even deeper wedge between father and son. For days, TL couldn't look at Daddy without visualizing the man's naked, sculpted form, so TL avoided Daddy altogether until, weeks later, the image dismantled and faded. Now, as TL stared at Daddy's chest, the image resurfaced.

After removing his baby-blue fishing hat, Daddy wiped his forehead with it. "Who woulda thought we'd see you again so soon."

TL shrugged. "I know. I certainly couldn't've guessed it."

"I'm sure it's a good thing. Any time a man returns home it's a good thing."

Is it? TL pondered.

"Ms. Swinton must be shoutin' all over heaven, you reckon?"

"Yessir."

"That's probably why you come back. To take over the school."

"Well, maybe that's part of it."

"Oh," Daddy mumbled, feigning surprise. "What's the other part?"

TL cleared his throat. "Sister. And Momma, I guess."

"What about 'em? Sister's dead, and yo' momma . . . well, she's who she is. What is you tryin' to find out?"

"I don't know, but Momma didn't have the right to do Sister like that. She was only a child."

"What is you sayin' yo' momma did?" Daddy fanned with his hat.

TL hadn't wanted to have this conversation, not right there in the midst of honeybees and scorching heat, but having said too much, he had no choice but to continue. "I don't know exactly, but I know she did something bad. Really bad."

"Who told you that?"

"I figured it out. It had to be her."

Daddy nodded. "That boy runs his mouth too much. 'Specially 'bout stuff he don't know."

"You sayin' Momma didn't do anything?"

"I'm sayin' what you think you know ain't necessarily so. That's what *I'm* sayin'."

"I don't need riddles, Daddy. I need truth."

"And be careful where you get it from." He paused. "That boy there?" Willie James walked in from the field. "He ain't strong enough to carry the truth. He can tell you what he *thinks* he know, but it ain't never everything. The least little piece of truth he finds makes him run. He means well. Does the best he can, I guess. Some people just made that way. Ain't you glad you ain't one of 'em?"

"Willie James is fine, Daddy."

"What!" he hollered, laughing. "You gotta be kiddin'. Every screw in that boy's head is loose. Some of 'em done come out altogether."

"There's nothing wrong with Willie James."

"Oh, okay. Sure. If you wanna believe that, go right 'head, but I knows better. You do, too."

Daddy broke free of the cage and moved toward the back door.

TL said, "I'm not saying he's sharp or anything like that. I'm just saying he's not stupid."

"I never said he was stupid," Daddy turned and said, "but you gon' be sorry fo' believin' what he tell you. He don't know how to tell the truth. Not the whole truth."

The slamming of the screen finalized their conversation and left TL wondering what Willie James might've missed. If Daddy were telling the truth. And more than likely he was. He'd never known him to lie. Not ever, to anyone. Let's face it: Any man bold enough to present an illegitimate child to his wife is certainly not a man who fears the truth. Willie James, on the other hand . . . well, TL didn't know him to be a liar, either, but he had to admit that Willie

James was far less trustworthy than Daddy. Daddy didn't fear a living soul.

Willie James waved and joined TL in the sparse shade. "Boy, when I turned 'round in church this mornin' and saw you, I coulda fainted. I asked God to bring you back, but I sho' didn't think He'd do it overnight!"

TL tried to laugh along.

"So tell me what happened. Why didn't you leave?"

"Look, Willie James, I'll tell you about that later. I promise. Right now, I need to ask you something important."

"Okay. What is it?"

A gust of hot air blew across their faces. "Let's walk back to the pond and sit like we used to. Remember?"

"Sure. How could I forget? You, me, and Sister would always . . ."

TL tuned him out until they arrived and sat atop the rise of the bank, shaded by overhanging tree limbs.

"Is you gon' stay this time?"

"Probably. I told Momma I was. I'm not totally sure, but I guess so."

Willie James picked up a small twig. "I hope you do. When you left yesterday, after the funeral, I was real sad 'cause—"

"Listen, man. I don't mean to be rude, but I need to talk to you."

"Okay. Go 'head."

TL sighed. "It's about Sister."

"What 'bout her? I told you everything I know."

"I'm sure you did, but tell me again. About what happened in the barn."

"Why?"

" 'Cause I need to hear it one more time. Please. It's important."

A green-gray lizard scurried between them, and Willie James shooed it away. They were both grateful for the occasional bursts of cool air, lingering among the trees.

Willie James peeled the tender bark from the twig until it rested, smooth and naked, in his left palm. TL couldn't tell if Willie James was trying to remember what he'd said or trying to decide whether to answer him at all.

"I know this sounds crazy," TL said, "but the more I thought about it, the less sense it made. Don't get me wrong—I'm not saying you don't know what you saw. I'm just trying to piece everything together in my mind, you know?"

Willie James glanced up with pierced eyes. "What's the part you don't remember?"

"Well, I'm not sure. I remember you saying that Momma and Sister fought and Momma beat her with the hoe, right?"

"Right," Willie James mumbled.

"And the baby was already dead, lying on the barn floor."

"Yep."

"And Momma wrapped Sister in a sheet and buried her."

"Well, I didn't see her bury her, but I know she did. She wrapped her in the sheet. I saw that much."

"You burned the baby yourself?"

Willie James froze.

"I'm sorry, man. That was insensitive. I shouldn't've brought it up."

He studied the white twig as if having discovered something unknown. "That's right. I burned the baby myself. My own son." He chuckled and withdrew from TL's touch.

"I don't need yo' pity. You don't care what I feel anyway. It's 'bout what you want, right?"

"Willie James, it's not about what—"

In fury, he tossed the naked twig into the pond. "I don't have nothin' else to tell you, TL. I don't know what you lookin' for, and I don't know why you questionin' me."

"I'm sorry, Willie James. Forgive me."

He continued throwing other sticks and rocks into the pond. "Don't worry 'bout it. I know it don't make no sense. How can it?"

"You're right. How can it."

Cows moved about the water easily, barely causing a stir. There were six of them, and one calf that waded closer to the bank. They shared the same shade of brown, like figures cut from construction paper. Standing now, on the top of the bank, Willie James said, "That ol' pregnant cow is back in the woods. She oughta give birth some time today. Or maybe tomorrow. You know how they act right before they deliver."

"Yep, I know."

Willie James stared across the field. "You know what, TL? I'm glad cows don't have to deal wit' the stuff people do."

"That's what separates animals from humans. We think and feel; they don't."

"How you know that? How you know animals don't think and feel?"

"Well, I guess I don't know for sure, but they certainly don't think."

"How you know that?"

TL thought to offer an academic explanation, but instead said, "Because they don't speak."

"Yeah, but that don't mean they don't think. Maybe their language don't require them to speak, you know? Maybe they communicate some other way."

"I guess it's possible, but I doubt it."

"You doubt it because you can't imagine it. That's how people do—if we can't figure somethin' out, we say it don't exist. But I ain't so sho' 'bout that. I mean, I can't *prove* that animals talk, but they might."

TL didn't care if animals had teleconferences; he wanted to know more about what Willie James saw that fateful day.

"Listen, man. I just need to ask you one more thing."

Willie James sighed.

"Did you actually *see* Momma bury Sister?"

"She buried her," he answered quickly. "I know she did. After everything happened, I ran back to the tractor and acted like I hadn't seen nothin', but I did."

TL nodded. "Who put the tombstone on the grave?"

"What?"

"The tombstone. Who put it on the grave?"

"I don't know. When I got home that evenin', I saw the fresh mound, and a couple days later the tombstone appeared. But that day, I fell to the ground and cried until Momma made me come in the house. She said Sister had died, and there was nothin' I or anyone else could do about it. I started questionin' her, but she got mad and started screamin', so I skipped dinner and went to bed. I didn't go to sleep though. I kept tryin' to make all the pieces fit together, but I couldn't, so I laid wide awake until daybreak. At breakfast, I saw that Daddy didn't seem troubled. That's when I knew to keep my mouth shut."

"He and Momma were in on it together?"

"That's what it looked like."

"You didn't say anything more about it?"

"No, I didn't. You try fightin' Momma and Daddy by yo'self."

The thought alone frightened TL. "There's something we don't know, big brother."

Willie James whispered, "And you don't wanna find out."

CHAPTER 5

THE SETTING SUN EASED TL BACK INTO THE LIFE HE once knew. Yet walking from his parents' to Ms. Swinton's, he thought of himself as a stranger in his own homeland. He knew the place, the people, the pace of Swamp Creek. Those things would never change. But his spirit sought something different, something intangible, something man couldn't give.

At Ms. Swinton's, he picked up the phone and dialed.

"Hello?"

"Hey, George. It's me."

"Well, it's about damn time. Where you at?"

"I'm still in Arkansas."

"What! I thought you left there yesterday?"

"I tried to, but I couldn't."

"What do you mean you 'couldn't'?"

"I don't know. I just couldn't."

"Oh shit! Don't tell me you're staying?"

"For a little while at least. I have to."

"What? Why?"

"Because I have unfinished business here."

"Whatchu mean?"

"Hell, I don't know, man! You wouldn't believe all the shit that's happened since I got home."

"Come on, TL. How much can happen in the country in a week?"

"A whole lot! I'm telling you, man, you wouldn't believe it."

George pouted. "Fine. Do whatever you need to, but get back here soon. I'm going out of my mind."

"Well, I can't promise you how soon it'll be. In fact, I know it won't be soon at all. I'ma stay at least a year. I'm taking over the school." TL grimaced, bracing himself.

"What!"

"Yeah. Remember the woman I told you about who was my teacher? The one I was so crazy about?"

"Un-huh. Ms. Swanson . . . or something like that?"

"Swinton."

"Yeah, Swinton. What about her?"

"Well, she died last week and, on her deathbed, she asked me to take over the school. She left me a book collection you wouldn't believe."

"Why would she leave *you* her books? She didn't have any kids?"

"Ha! I am her kid!"

"What?"

Realizing how absurd this sounded, TL said, "I wouldn't've believed it myself if someone hadn't told me."

"Told you what?"

"That she was my mother."

"Huh? You're kidding, right?"

"No, I'm not. It's true. Ms. Swinton was my biological mother."

"Your *mother*? The woman you grew up thinking was your mother isn't?"

"That's right."

"What! Damn. That's some fucked up shit."

"You're telling me!"

"How'd you find out?"

"Long story. I'll tell you one day."

"Wow. Guess Papa was a rolling stone, huh?"

"He definitely was!"

They cackled through TL's discomfort.

"So, one day you find out who your real mother is, and the next day you bury her?"

"That's pretty much it."

"Dang, man. I'm really sorry. That must've been crazy."

"You just don't know how crazy. But it's okay. She was an incredible woman, George. I'd do anything to be like her."

"Looks like you're about to be." George laughed alone this time. "Your mother—or stepmother or whatever—must be a strong woman."

"Why you say that?"

"Because she took her husband's bastard child—no offense— and raised you as her own. How many women you know woulda done that?"

"I guess you're right."

"Damn right, I'm right! I know y'all weren't friends or anything, but she certainly couldn't've been evil."

"I never said she was evil."

"No, but you talked about her like she was."

"Well, you'd have to know the whole story."

"What I know is that any woman who raises her husband's illegitimate child is a woman with a lot of forgiveness in her heart. That's what I know."

"Whatever."

"Aw, come on, TL. I'd whip a man's ass if he brought me his bastard child to raise. Especially if we were married when he conceived it."

"You're right."

"I know I'm right! Shit! He'd see a bitch he ain't never imagined!"

TL yelped.

"So now you know why she couldn't love you. It wasn't your fault, but it wasn't hers, either."

"Okay, George. I can't handle that right now. Look, I need you to send me my stuff."

"What stuff?"

"Clothes. Some of my books. You can have the other stuff if you want it."

"What other stuff? Shit! You ain't got nothin' else! I'll take the futon though."

"That's fine. I'll send you the money to ship it. You have the key."

An awkward silence intruded.

"George? Hey, man. You there?"

"I'm here," he muttered.

"What's the matter?"

"You know what's the matter."

"I'm coming back, man. I promise. I just don't know when."

"That's the matter."

There was nothing more to say. "You know how I feel about you."

"I thought I did."

Click.

"George? Hello? Shit."

TL slammed the receiver on its base. *Just what I need.* Leaning upon the spotless white countertop, he exhaled and picked up the phone again.

"Good afternoon?"

"Hey, Zuri. It's me, TL."

"Oh hey! I've been hoping you'd call. Are you back?"

"Not exactly."

"Not exactly? What does that mean?"

Emotionally drained, he offered simply, "It's a long story, but, suffice it to say, I'm still in Arkansas and I'm staying awhile."

"Suffice it to say? My boyfriend calls and says he isn't coming home, and I'm not supposed to ask any questions?"

TL knew Zuri wouldn't understand. "It's complicated, Zu."

"Complicated? I like complicated. Try me."

He told her about Ms. Swinton and Sister.

"Oh wow. That's a lot. I know how much you loved your sister. Is there anything I can do?"

"I wish there was, but, no, I have to figure this out on my own. That's why I'm staying. At least for a while."

"What did George say?"

"Huh?"

She cackled and repeated louder, "What did George Thornton say?"

"About what?"

"Oh stop, TL. You've already talked to George. I'd bet my life on it."

He couldn't lie. "I only called him first because I needed my things."

"I would've sent you your things," she said pitifully. "Free."

There was no way out. "I didn't want to bother you. I know how busy you are."

"Busy." She paused for an eternity. "Busy. Wow."

"Zuri, don't do this. I don't feel like arguing. I have a lot on my mind. I just wanted to call you and let you know I wasn't coming back to New York. Not for a while."

"Okay. I see," she sang, sarcastically. "And what about us?"

"What *about* us?"

"That's so lame, TL, and you do it all the time. I guess I shouldn't be surprised, but each time I hope it'll be different."

"Do you think we should break up?"

She screeched. "Do *I* think we should break up? You call and tell me you're not coming home, and suddenly the future of our relationship is *my* decision? You're pathetic, man."

"I'll always love you. No matter what. You know that, right?"

"You know what? I'm glad you're staying home. Maybe you can finish growing up."

Click.

With eyes closed, TL listened to the dial tone for several seconds, then, slowly, as if trying not to forget something, he returned the receiver to its base. After weighing the matter further, he tried again.

"Hello, Zuri? Just hear me out."

She waited.

"I'm sorry."

"Yes, you are."

"Don't be mean."

"It's me again, huh? It's always me."

"Nobody's wrong here."

"Yes, *somebody* is."

TL cursed silently. "You know what? Let's just end this."

"End what? The conversation or the relationship?"

He couldn't bear to say.

"Don't worry about it, TL. I can take care of myself. Always have."

"Zuri . . ."

"Just let it go. That's what you want, so let it be."

TL felt like an ass.

"Have a good life. Just do yourself a favor: Decide who you *really* want before you pursue them. Some people'll kill you for playing with their heart. Thank God I'm not one of those people."

"I never meant to hurt you."

She ignored him. "Like I said, have a good life—you and George."

They hung up simultaneously. It was over. No turning back.

She was right of course, he thought. He should've been the one to suggest something, one way or the other, but, in his heart, he didn't want to lose her. Or perhaps he wasn't man enough to face the truth. Either way, he lost her. "Fuck," he muttered, and went to bed.

CHAPTER 6

A LETTER FROM THE CONWAY COUNTY SCHOOL SU-
perintendent arrived the following Monday, expressing his
sympathy for the loss of Ms. Swinton and stating that, in
her absence, a search for a replacement would begin immediately.

"Guess you'd better be going down there," David said. "I'm
afraid this community wouldn't welcome anyone but you."

Come Tuesday morning, dressed in Willie James's best gray pin-
striped suit, TL went to the superintendent's office in downtown
Morrilton. He introduced himself as Dr. Thomas L. Tyson, a pro-
tégé of the legendary Carolyn Swinton. The superintendent shook
his hand warmly and invited him into his office. He was a round,
aged, white fellow with a huge neck and monstrous, soft hands. He
could've been Archie Bunker's twin, TL noted and snickered, praying the man wasn't as bigoted.

In a large, high-backed brown leather chair, TL reclined in front
of the superintendent's shiny cherrywood desk. The man smiled
broadly, relaxing TL's anxiety. He noticed from a glance at the
paneled wall behind the desk that the superintendent held a master's degree in educational administration from the University of

Arkansas at Fayetteville and a BA in English from Hendrix College. A copy of Ellison's *Invisible Man,* on the bookshelf to the left, convinced TL that this wasn't going to be as hard as he'd feared.

"Thank you for your time, sir," TL said. "I know how busy you must be."

"Oh no. It's my pleasure." He appeared genuine.

They exchanged more pleasantries, then the superintendent asked, "What can I do for you, young man?"

TL squirmed slightly. "I want to take Ms. Swinton's position at our school in Swamp Creek."

The man's green eyes brightened as he leaned forward. "Really?"

"Yes sir. It's what she wanted. She asked me herself."

"Oh my. I see."

Bewilderment colored his face pink, so TL explained what happened.

"You could write a hell of a memoir, young man," he said. "Carolyn Swinton was a legend all over this county. This state, really. She worked miracles in the classroom with practically no resources."

"Yessir, I know. I saw her do it. I'm a product of the school."

"And now you have a PhD? Wow. That's mighty impressive."

TL nodded, trying not to be overly confident.

"I have to tell you," the superintendent continued, "that managing the school was harder than it looked. I daresay most people couldn't do for one year what Miss Swinton did for forty."

His wry smile revealed his fear that he had insulted TL. The man folded his hands and placed them gently upon the desktop as his pursed lips quivered, unsure seemingly of what to say next.

"I'm sure you're right, but I think I can handle it. Actually, I know I can." TL looked him in the eye. "It's in my blood."

"Well. This is quite a surprise. Do you have a résumé?"

"No sir, but I can produce one in a few days."

He told the superintendent the specifics of his credentials, including grades and dissertation topic.

"You're quite the scholar, Mr. Tyson."

Dr. Tyson, TL thought, but decided not to say. He needed this ally.

"Your dossier sounds remarkable."

TL flashed a bashful grin. "I've always liked school, sir."

"Apparently!"

They chatted several more minutes, citing books they'd read in common and agreeing, finally, that all students should read *To Kill a Mockingbird.* Then, the superintendent added, "I'm afraid the pay isn't much. It's probably far less than what a man of your caliber is willing to take."

"Exactly what does the position pay?"

The man gritted his teeth, stood, and moved to lean on the front edge of the shiny desktop. "Do you really wanna know?" He folded his arms.

"I doubt it."

"Well, with a PhD you'd certainly make more than she did, but it wouldn't be much more."

"I guess you'd better break it to me gently."

With obvious distress, the superintendent blinked repeatedly and said, "Your starting salary would be somewhere around thirty thousand."

TL leapt from his seat. "No way! You must be kidding me!"

"I'm afraid I'm not," he said, returning to his chair. "I wish I were. I'm embarrassed to admit it."

"How do teachers in Arkansas do it? Who can live off that?"

"I know," the superintendent said, shaking his head. "This country doesn't value education." He stared into TL's eyes. "Especially the education of its minority citizens."

His honesty was both comforting and off-putting. TL almost left.

"But it's worth it," he said. "It produced you."

In a daze, TL stared through a nearby window. "I suppose so."

"And look on the bright side. Ms. Swinton barely cleared twenty-five thousand."

"You're kidding!"

"No sir, I'm not. Teachers in Arkansas have been working miracles for decades, especially the colored ones who, on average, make five or six thousand less than their white colleagues with the same credentials. We'll never know the sacrifice they've made. Never." He sounded like one of the elders at the Meetin' Tree.

"That's so unfair."

"You're right, but it's so systemic you can't figure out how to fix it."

Moments like these made TL wonder what life would've been like had Africans never been enslaved.

"The problem is that this state and this nation doesn't spend as much educating colored children as they do educating white children."

"But this is a *public* system!"

"I know, I know. It's awful, but it's true. I don't want to mislead you. If you do this, you really should know what you're getting into."

They brooded and moaned like cows in a slaughterhouse. TL said, "Racism is going to be America's undoing if she isn't careful."

The superintendent smirked. "You mean if she isn't already undone."

TL liked him now. The man understood things.

They talked another half hour about the nuts and bolts of teaching black kids in a one-room schoolhouse, then the superintendent informed TL that all such schools would close within the next year.

"Why?"

"Federal mandate. They say the schools couldn't possibly be run efficiently, and most reflect a segregated pattern, which the country is trying to dissolve. I don't necessarily agree with it, but, hey, what difference does that make, right?"

TL couldn't hide his disappointment. "Our little school saved my life, sir. I can't imagine having gotten a better education anywhere, regardless of how large and endowed the school was."

"I know, but that's what they've decided." He shrugged helplessly.

Images of Ms. Swinton in the classroom flooded TL's memory. He saw her, in high heels and classy dresses, marching around the classroom, looking over every child's shoulder, prepared to celebrate or reprimand them for their work. "You'll have to forgive me for saying this, sir, but I don't believe teachers in other schools will nurture black childen the way our teachers nurtured us."

The superintendent nodded. "I'm afraid you're right. I'm not naïve, but I'm also not the president of the United States. I believe in equal education for all, regardless of race, but I don't believe it's going to happen."

TL chortled. "I don't think so, either." They offered feigned smiles. "So, once again, black kids lose, huh?"

"Well, I hope not. At least not the ones in Swamp Creek."

TL shuddered as he realized the magnitude of his decision. He assured the superintendent he'd do his best.

"Good. Good. That's the spirit. You'd be surprised at the difference an excellent teacher can make in a child's life." He giggled. "Or maybe *you* wouldn't."

"No sir, I wouldn't."

"Sometimes, that's all it takes—someone who really cares, who's willing to plant the right seeds."

"You're right. Guess it's my turn."

"Guess so. If Carolyn Swinton sent you, you're definitely the one."

I'D WANTED TO BE THE ONE, TOO, BUT I WASN'T. EVERYONE KNEW TL was special. Even the people who didn't like him. That's why they didn't like him—because they wanted his calling. But of course you can't have another person's calling. The mere thought is empty energy. It seemed as if God had forgotten to call me, so I spent my nights writing in a diary. I never slept well anyway. Not after TL left. It wasn't a real diary like the kind you buy from a store. I made it, out of loose-leaf paper. I cut 8 × 11-inch pages in half and stapled them together. From a sheet of purple construction paper, I made a cover on which I drew various types of flowers, which I then colored with Crayola markers. There were petunias, tulips, roses, and others whose names I can't recall. My favorite, the lily, stood in the center. I colored it a deeper purple because that was my favorite color. I'd never seen a purple lily before, but that didn't matter. It was my diary, so I could make it like I wanted it, I presumed.

Usually I wrote letters to TL, which I knew he'd never read, telling him everything that happened to me. Like when I got my cycle. I know this isn't something girls usually tell boys, but TL was different.

He was my closest friend, my only friend really. He was just gone away, out in the world searching for a life he could live. But I still loved him. I could feel him in my heart, laughing and tickling me 'til I cried. So it made sense to tell him. I knew the blood was coming, at some point. Momma had already told me what to do, so there was no surprise. It just made me feel older. That's what I told TL—that I felt older, that the experience made me miss him even more. I don't know why.

I also told him about when I walked in on Momma and Daddy having sex. They never stopped. Momma was groaning mildly, while Daddy's eyes rolled in his head. She must've heard my entry, for she turned and said, "Ain't I done told you 'bout comin' in my room without knockin', child?" I backed away, frightened. There was no pleasure in her expression. Only duty. But not begrudging duty. More like responsible duty. Something that simply needed to be done. She obviously didn't hate the act, but she might've imagined a more perfect life without it. I later thought of them, lying together entangled in sweat and responsibility, like wild vines growing together, crisscrossing on the way upward. You'd think the memory would've left me with a distaste for the erotic, but actually it made me want to try it. I dreamed of the day when I could add pleasure to the act. I began to long for the opportunity.

The other thing I wrote about was my first encounter with Aunt Easter. She was strange, I admit, but not scary. Not like others said. She winked at me as if she knew me. Or was reminding me of something. I must've been eight or nine. There was a picnic at church, and she materialized like a ghost out of the nearby woods. We were playing tag on the left side of the church. As she approached, the others vanished in fear, but I stood and waited. It was her eyes that caught my attention, glistening in her head like blue jewels. She spoke with a dry, soft voice. "Hey, pretty lil' girl," she said. I smiled. "My name's Cynthia," I said, "but everybody calls me Sister." Aunt Easter touched my face, and I jerked away. Her hand was hot as fire. "I'm sorry, baby.

I didn't hurt you, did I?" she said. "No ma'am." Then, after a few seconds, she added, "I know who you are. Been knowin' before you came." I frowned, so she added, "Don't pay me no mind, chile. Just take care o' yo'self. Yo' time ain't long." She floated back into the woods from whence she came. I didn't think much of the encounter. None of it made sense to me, but when I told Momma, she said, "Be careful with that woman, girl. She knows things." I'd assumed as much. Deep in my heart, I wanted to know things, too. Now I do. I just wish someone had told me the price of knowing.

CHAPTER 7

ABOUT UNCLE JESSE LEE . . .

Folks say he's 'bout the most superstitious person the good Lord ever made. He believes in ghosts, or "haints" as he calls them. If you want the worse cussin' imaginable, just sweep across his feet with a sturdy straw broom or toss a dustpan of dirt through his front door at night. He don't play 'bout stuff like that. He says his luck is bad enough already.

A bird flew off with a tuft of his hair one breezy Saturday afternoon thirty years ago—why he was combing his hair outside no one knows—and Uncle Jesse Lee's been looking for the winged demon ever since. He went as far as to climb the tree in which the feathered thief disappeared, hoping to find his silky, black strands entangled in a nest, but there was no nest. There wasn't even a bird, but you couldn't tell Uncle Jesse Lee that. He believed in his heart that the bird had taken his hair away, and would one day return it. Otherwise, he'd have a headache the rest of his life.

He'd descend the tree at sunset, whatever tree he'd chosen that day, rubbing his throbbing forehead, convinced that God would make the bird penitent and he'd be healed. Jesse Lee never did have no sense, folks said. Most waved up at him as they passed, shaking their heads and laughing out loud. Uncle Jesse Lee didn't care. He needed his hair back, and he had the patience to wait for it.

He could've been handsome had he cared about such things. Aunt Clara, his oldest sister, said he had the blackest, smoothest skin she'd ever seen on a baby, and, as he matured, it never blemished. At seventy-something, if not eighty, he lounged beneath Swamp Creek's oaks, cypresses, and maples as the morning sun darkened his already bronze complexion. People's "Ump, ump ump" was more about the waste of his beauty than the shame of him chasing a bird. Graying only at the edges, his soft, curly hair covered his perfectly rounded head like a wig. The two times in life he shaped his unsightly facial hair—his momma's funeral and his wedding—women flirted with the intent to give, although Uncle Jesse Lee never noticed. He shaved only because Aunt Bertha Mae wouldn't have married him otherwise, and he didn't want his momma mad at him from the grave. But even with a scruffy, patchy beard, folks saw a fine Negro underneath, and often told him so. Uncle Jesse Lee shrugged the compliments off as foolishness. The only thing he treasured was his hair, and he'd wait a lifetime, if he had to, he said, for that damn bird to bring it back.

He was blessed with more Indian blood than the other children, Aunt Clara said. Cherokee, no doubt, since that's the only tribe black folk ever heard of. Uncle Jesse Lee's red undertone, which people loved to announce, made him a source of envy in Swamp Creek, since most wanted nothing more desperately than Uncle Jesse Lee's smooth, silky, black hair. Years ago, in celebration of his Native American ancestry, someone gave him a dream catcher they'd bought at a Native American festival. Uncle Jesse Lee didn't know what to do with the thing. He'd never heard of a dream catcher before, but he liked the picture of the bald eagle, standing proudly in the oval center, so he hung it on the wall next to his bed. *His* side of the bed. Aunt Bertha Mae said she believed in Jesus—

Oh praise His name!—not idol worship, so she hung a picture of the crucified Christ on the opposite wall. "We'll see who wins!" she supposedly said.

Daddy warned people not to think of Uncle Jesse Lee as a fool. "He ain't never been dumb. He might be a lil' strange, but strange don't mean stupid." As children, we realized that when folks said Uncle Jesse Lee (or anybody for that matter) didn't have no sense, they didn't mean he didn't have *no* sense, they meant he didn't have *enough* sense. And that was probably true. But he wasn't crazy. Uncle Jesse Lee fed, clothed, and housed thirteen children, practically by himself. Aunt Bertha Mae was *present,* folks loved to say, but she couldn't be counted on for much work. Every now and then, she'd cook a meal or comb the girls' hair, but usually she spent her time visiting and gossiping with women who later gossiped about her. Uncle Jesse Lee was the real cook, and sometimes folks went by at suppertime solely with the hope of being invited to the table. It didn't matter what he cooked; everything tasted scrumptious— squirrel, rabbit, coon, deer, possum, armadillo—and people ate like guests at God's Welcome Table. No one ever knew how Uncle Jesse Lee seasoned possum until it tasted like roast beef, but it did. And he wouldn't tell his secret. The kids ate so well they didn't want to leave home, but Uncle Jesse Lee put all of 'em out at eighteen, whether they had somewhere to go or not. Most of 'em cried 'cause they knew they'd never eat that good again, but oh well. When Jesse Lee said go, he meant it.

He would've put Aunt Bertha Mae out, too, if her performance in the bedroom had ever waned. She loved sex, any way she could get it, and folks said Uncle Jesse Lee loved giving it. She was the top, people teased, riding Uncle Jesse Lee until he simply gave out. Daddy said Uncle Jesse Lee agreed to do everything else around the house if Aunt Bertha Mae never stopped screwing him, and, as far as people knew, she kept her end of the bargain, so he kept his. Af-ter all the children moved away—or got put out—he cooked less, and folks said Bertha Mae did fewer sexual favors, although she never stopped altogether. Then, when the bird flew away with his hair, insomnia set in and left Uncle Jesse Lee sitting up half the night in his old rocker, wondering where in the world that damn bird could be. At first, Aunt Bertha Mae asked, "Ain't you comin' to bed, old man?" but, according to rumor, Uncle Jesse Lee frowned and said, "Bed's for two thangs. We done done one of 'em, and since I ain't sleepy, what's the point?"

He took up reading to pass the time. A King James Bible and a 1955 set of Britannica encyclopedias were the only books he owned. Aunt Bertha Mae had argued years ago that the encyclopedias were a crucial investment in the kids' intellectual development. Uncle Jesse Lee didn't agree, but Aunt Bertha Mae stole the money from him and bought the series anyway. He didn't say a word when the books arrived. He just started hiding his money in a leather pouch and burying it somewhere in the woods. No one ever discovered where. When the family needed things, he'd vanish into the thicket and return with enough money to meet the need. Folks, including his own sons, considered following him to find out where he kept the stash, but Uncle Jesse Lee promised to kill any nigga dead who dared invade his privacy. They knew not to try him.

Reading from the Bible only those passages he liked—most of God's writing was boring, he said—Uncle Jesse Lee spent the majority of his reading time lost in Aunt Bertha Mae's old encyclopedias. He'd thumb pages for hours until encountering a topic that captured his attention. Anything dealing with animals was always a winner. Or foreign countries. He loved learning about life in different places and looking at pictures of people in strange clothes, standing in an environment he could only imagine. Fearing he'd never leave Swamp Creek, he'd close his eyes and travel those foreign lands, eating foods whose names he couldn't pronounce and staring at exotic flowers more grand than anything he'd ever beheld. The day the bird flew off with his hair, he simply took the books with him and sat beneath his favorite tree, passing the time in China, Africa, and Bangladesh.

Back in the thirties, Uncle Jesse Lee learned the harmonica while his siblings chopped cotton. Aunt Clara said he played lame for two years until their father caught him walking from the outhouse one day when Uncle Jesse Lee thought everyone was away. He'd fallen from the old persimmon tree in the front yard and faked his own paralysis. He was seven. No one doubted the authenticity of his injury. Even Doc Henderson was fooled, diagnosing that Uncle Jesse Lee would never walk again. Aunt Clara said he had the act down pat! His legs, like a paraplegic's, hung limp and weak beneath his torso, and his brothers willingly toted him wherever the family went. Miss Liza, the community healer, cooked up all kinds of potions for him to drink, but nothing seemed to help. Of course there was nothing wrong with him. When Great-granddaddy discovered as much, he didn't say anything. Just disappeared into the woods and returned with a hickory limb and commenced to beating Uncle Jesse Lee's ass like an old, nasty rug. Aunt Clara said they found him later that evening, sprawled out facedown in the front yard, covered in his own blood. Granddaddy might've killed him had he had the time. He left him right there on the ground and walked back to the field like nothing had happened. Great-grandmother screamed when she found him. She fell to her knees, Aunt Clara said, and began speaking in unknown tongues. When Uncle Jesse Lee revived, rose, and walked like a natural man, Grandma reached her hands toward heaven and danced in the Holy Ghost. Their father said nothing. He later told Uncle Jesse Lee, "You gon' do all the work you done missed. I'ma see to that."

During the paralysis, Uncle Jesse Lee escaped every day to the honky-tonk, deep in the woods, where he sat with Joe Tex, who taught him the intricacies of the harmonica. Old Man Joe could play any genre of music and make it sound good, but Uncle Jesse Lee loved the blues best. It did something for his soul, he told folks. He saw more God in the blues than in gospel, so he tried to play the blues in church one Sunday, but people had a fit. "We rebuke the devil in the name of Jesus!" they cried, according to Aunt Clara.

Uncle Jesse Lee cried, too. "This *is* Jesus!" he demanded, but they didn't agree, so they formed a circle around him and prayed and laid hands upon him, begging God to destroy his love affair with evil. God didn't do it. Instead, Uncle Jesse Lee played everywhere else he went—the general store, the cornfield, the Jordan River— and opened the doors of the church all by himself when he finished. A few actually accepted Jesus from his ministry. He directed them to the church so they'd have consistent fellowship, but he warned them not to look for Jesus every Sunday. "He don't always do church," he said. "Jesus can't take a lotta bullshit."

What pissed off Uncle Jesse Lee's daddy most was that these clandestine musical lessons occurred while the rest of the family earned the boy's living. And after the crucifixion—or the resurrection, depending on who tells the story—Uncle Jesse Lee's musical interest waned and his days of leisure were replaced by days of excruciatingly hard labor.

Most called Uncle Jesse Lee stubborn in his old age, but he thought of himself as determined. That's why he went to the Meetin' Tree every single Saturday. Sure, he wanted his hair—and he intended to get it—but he also meant for that bird to know his persistence. That was his other crowning glory, his persistence—his hair was the first—and, hell or high water, that bird was going to know whose hair it had taken.

After having waited patiently for a year, Uncle Jesse Lee started shooting every bird he saw. He'd sit still as a decoy, high in the Meetin' Tree, and plant pellets in anything that flew his way. He still didn't find his hair. Folks thought the plague of dead birds signaled the beginning of the end, but when Aunt Clara exposed the truth, they said, "Sheeeeit! Somebody need to take Jesse Lee Chambers's ass off somewhere! That nigga's crazy as hell!" He apologized to God, they said, and stopped killings the birds, but he didn't stop going to the tree.

Never bothering to change his clothes, Uncle Jesse Lee wore the same brown, tan, and white plaid pants for twenty years. He patched holes—*him,* not Aunt Bertha Mae—whenever they grew too big to ignore, and during the winter he simply wore ragged long johns underneath. It didn't take long for the pants to tighten around his extra-high behind, but Uncle Jesse Lee wouldn't let them go. He kept pulling until the waist rested barely beneath his nipples, leaving his droopy balls outlined and pressed against his inner left thigh. He owned three dress shirts of the exact same style, one white, one blue, one gray. The blue was obviously his favorite although it matched least, but Uncle Jesse Lee didn't care. It was that damn bird he was after. And if it took a lifetime, he was determined to sit at the Meetin' Tree and wait. The blues would keep him company.

He told TL something years ago that TL never forgot. He was sixteen. They sat at the Meetin' Tree, just the two of them, lounging away a pretty, warm, fall evening when the weather shifted from calm to chaos. Wind gusts rattled the tree, and miniature tornados, formed from dry Arkansas red dust, skipped across the distant landscape. TL smelled the coming rain. *No need runnin',* he thought. The tree offered the best shelter, tossing its limbs in the wind as though beckoning him to stay, so he obeyed.

Oblivious to the impending storm, Uncle Jesse Lee leaned back onto the worn, splintered church pew and puffed his pipe casually, blowing smoke into the turbulent air. Lone droplets fell at first, precursors of what was to come. Thunder roared, but with no lightning, they felt safe beneath the armored limbs of the tree.

"Looks like we 'bout to get a good rain," TL said.

A halo of tobacoo smoke rose and surrounded Uncle Jesse Lee's head. "Yep, looks like it."

The elder's cool, tranquil demeanor comforted TL. Together, they sat and studied the chaotic heavens as if looking for some new manifestation of God. As always, Uncle Jesse Lee wore his favorite brown, tan, and white plaid slacks and the baby-blue long-sleeved shirt, which badly needed washing. He turned slowly and winked at TL.

"You got to watch God, boy. He always talkin', but we ain't always listenin'."

"Yessir."

"And, anyway, what's a young fella like you doin' sittin' 'round wit' a old man, starin' at a storm?"

"I don't know. Just trying to figure out my future, I guess."

Uncle Jesse Lee's slow, methodical nod reminded TL of those tiny toy dogs, resting on dashboards, with heads that bobbed at the slightest touch. "What is you tryin' to know?"

Thousands of raindrops descended onto leaves above their heads, creating an ensemble of natural rhythms that vibrated into the tumultuous universe.

"I don't know," TL repeated. "I just wonder 'bout things sometimes. Like why I'm here. On the earth."

Again, he nodded slowly and said, "Folks been askin' that question since the beginnin' o' time. Most o' 'em don't never find out."

"Yeah, but I want to."

He puffed the pipe a few times. "What do you wanna do?"

TL had an answer, but he didn't want to say it.

"Listen, son. Don't seek nothin' you ain't strong enough to carry. God don't play wit' chil'ren. A man's destiny is a serious thang."

The wind intensified. "I wanna teach. That's all I've ever wanted to do, but how do I know that's what God wants me to do?"

The right corner of Uncle Jesse Lee's mouth lifted into a half smile. "'Cause he's the one what gave you the desire. You can't want nothin' 'less God plant the yearnin' in you. You's mighty lucky. Most young folks don't even think 'bout such things. Not until they get too old fo' it to make a difference."

Rain fell in horizontal sheets as the wind played hide-and-seek.

"I think about it all the time," TL said.

"Well, good fo' you. You might make somethin' outta yo'self after all. We gon' need a teacha 'round here soon. Swinton can't do it fo'ever."

"Oh, I don't mean here, Uncle Jesse Lee! I mean someplace else."

"Don't care what you mean. When God give a man a gift, He prepares a place fo' him to do it. It ain't yo' decision. He'll direct yo' steps, here o' yonder."

Within seconds, the rain became torrential. Dark clouds gathered and shifted nervously, unsure of where to rest. Uncle Jesse Lee and TL were slightly damp but not wet, and for that TL was grateful. A few savvy droplets meandered through the leaves and fell upon their heads as if to anoint them. With each pellet, TL flinched from the sting of the cold. Uncle Jesse Lee didn't seem to mind. Only when drops ran down his eyelids did he respond, blinking until they moved on. The storm had captured his consciousness and lulled him into a trance, a kind of dreamy hypnotic state, sustained by the rumble of the wind, rain, and thunder. At one point, he closed his eyes and bowed his head, like a man in deep prayer, then, suddenly, he lifted it and looked wide-eyed as if having received a revelation.

"There's always more than one way to do a thang, son. Yo' job is to find the right way fo' you."

TL stared into the purple-gray sky in hopes of seeing what Uncle Jesse Lee had apparently seen, but all he saw was gloom. Then, as if someone had turned the pages of a children's book, the storm subsided, leaving behind a clear blue sky and a light, easy fall breeze.

"See, sometimes, if you wait, yo' change'll come. It *will* come. You young folks get in too big o' hurry to know what you tryin' to know. Just plant yo' seeds and God'll bring the increase. He's good at what He do."

Humid, muggy air returned as the sun resumed its throne.

"See? Change can come just like that!" He snapped. "Don't never underestimate God."

TL told him how frustrated he was at home.

"God's just gettin' you ready, son. He done put all them brains in yo' head, now he gotta teach you what to do wit' 'em. Smarts ain't jus' fo' school. Remember that, you hear?"

"Yessir."

"Sometimes, God makes a man's life hard so he ain't confused 'bout what he wants. If it was too easy, he wouldn't never do nothin'."

TL nodded. It made sense.

"Do yo' learnin' good. If you wanna teach, that's 'xactly what you gon' do. But if God sent you to teach, you ain't gon' be like the rest of 'em. And you ain't gon' get to do it where you want to. You gon' have to do it where He send you. And He might send you right where you at."

TL didn't want to believe that. *God knows my heart,* he thought. *There's no way He'd make me stay here.*

As though reading the boy's mind, Uncle Jesse Lee said, "Son, this place ain't what it used to be. You wouldn't've ever wanted to leave here if you'd seen it in its heyday. I'm tellin' you what I know. Folks can't see it now, but, once upon a time, this was a great city."

"City?"

"Did you hear what I said? Folks came from all 'round to do business here."

"When was this?"

"Long befo' you come along. Befo' yo' daddy, too. But when I was a lil' boy, this was a busy place."

"Come on, Uncle Jesse Lee! There might've been more people, but a city? A city has a—"

"I know what a city got, boy! I ain't crazy! And I know what I'm talkin' 'bout. Hell, I was here! How old you thank I am?"

TL knew not to answer.

"I was a grown man when yo' granddaddy come along!"

How could he challenge him?

"Me and yo' great-grandpa used to run together. We'd come to town on Saturday afternoons, and there'd be people everywhere! From all 'round." He pointed in every direction. "We'd get to play wi' kids we barely knowed and eat Mr. John's homemade ice cream. It was a nickel a scoop, and I mean a big ol' scoop! Some Saturdays, it'd be fifty o' sixty kids in the middle of Swamp Creek playin' while the grown folks talked or handled business." He closed his eyes. "We had all kinda stores—dry good, grocery, hardware, blacksmith, restaurants—"

"Restaurants?"

"Restaurants!" he shouted. "Two o' three o' 'em. And they was owned and runned by colored people. Didn't no white folks own nothin' in Swamp Creek. Not back then. Hell, it wunnit even called Swamp Creek."

"Really? What was it called?"

He smiled as his memory crystallized. "Black Haven. That's what it was called."

"Black Haven? Why?"

"'Cause colored peoples all over Conway County came here to do business. And I mean they came! By the hundreds, from miles around, in every direction. You believe what I tell you!" He dumped the ashes of his pipe onto the roots of the tree. "Black Haven was the train stop, the last one headed west 'til Fort Smith. It was the only town 'round wit' a colored school that went from the first through the twelfth grade. Most children didn't go regular, but some did. They come from Hattieville, Happy Bend, Hickory Hill, Kenwood, Willow Oak . . . all 'round. Black Haven was somethin' else, boy!" He stared into the distance. "There were eleven different towns all together, each with its own road leadin' to Black Haven."

He went on to explain that one could enter from the north by three different paths, or "gates" as he called them, all of which crossed the Jordan River. If it rained, folks were stuck for weeks until the water receded, and even then most couldn't travel since the road was nothing but muck and mire. But during the summer, people came from the north, he said, like the children of Israel bound for the Promised Land. They crossed the Jordan in shallow places, jerking back and forth in homemade wagons that threatened to disassemble with each move. Some crossed on foot, carrying shoes in their hands and delight in their hearts that, once again, they were headed to Black Haven.

"From the west"—he pointed down Highway 64—"folks walked several paths that twisted and turned throughout the Williamses' place. The paths crossed over one 'nother like a spiderweb, but each led to the heart of Black Haven. People from Happy Bend took one road, folk from Hickory Hill took another, and folks from Atkins Bottom took the other. On the east side, traveling was a lot better. Kenwood, Germantown, and Hattieville folks all had they own good roads leadin' to town 'cause white folks lived there and made sure they could get in and out whenever they wanted to. Two o' the roads was even graveled, and that was way back in the thirties!

"From the south"—he nodded toward a field of freshly cut hay—"folks came to Black Haven on what was called the Palmer Trail—a narrow lane that connected the Palmer estate to the rest o' the world. Old Man Palmer lived way, way south of here, almost to the Arkansas River. All the black folk down there worked fo' him, and it was a whole lot of 'em."

"So they just had one way to get to Black Haven?"

"Naw. They had two. The people he liked he let use his road, but the other ones had to walk through the swamp. They'd show up in town wet from the knee down. He was just like that—ol' racist bastard—but wunnit nothin' they could do 'bout it, so they came on and dried off wit' the sun. I 'member laughin' at some o' 'em one day when I seen 'em comin', and Daddy slapped me in the mouth so hard my lip bled all over my shirt. He wouldn't let Momma tend to me. Said if I bled to death that's what I get for mockin' decent folks. 'Course Highway 113 came in from the south but it was too far out o' the way to be useful. Folks didn't start comin' that way 'til I was near 'bout a old man."

TL imagined all the roads leading to Black Haven like eleven winding capillaries pouring into the same river. It was a virtual metropolis, to let Uncle Jesse Lee tell it, a kind of cosmopolitan epicenter where everyone gathered on Saturday afternoons to transact business and fellowship. The more he described it, the more prideful he became until he was standing and shouting.

"You can't imagine it, boy, but I'm tellin' you! It was somethin' else!" The cane trembled under his weight. "Swamp Creek ain't what it used to be. Jus' a shadow of a old town, but once upon a time, it was like goin' to heaven!"

TL cackled.

"I ain't lyin'! There was black doctas and lawyas and school teachas and business peoples. We didn't need white folks fo' nothin'! Hell, they come to us when they needed somethin'!"

Pride had straightened his back a bit.

"You young folks don't know who y'all is. That's the problem!" He shook his head as his cane pounded the damp, bronze earth. "Y'all come from a great people, son. The mistake most young folk make is thinkin' that what we is now is what we always been, but that ain't so. Why you think they called the place Black Haven?"

Didn't you already answer that? TL thought, but remained silent.

" 'Cause o' what we looked like when we stood together! That's why! Peoples came here from miles around to pour into somethin' they believed in." He nodded hard and resumed his seat. "While we was together in town, fellowshippin' and talkin', couldn't nobody bother us. We was one people! Strong!" His arthritic fist trembled before TL's nose. "And couldn't nobody do nothin' 'bout it. I 'member it like it was yesterday."

Sadness replaced his joy.

"The Depression came through here and wiped out everythin'. All the businesses closed, and folks started goin' to Morrilton and Atkins to buy whatnot, but at its height, Black Haven was 'bout as close to heaven as you could get."

Uncle Jesse Lee chatted into the evening. When TL rose to leave, the old man said, "God's gettin' you ready fo' a great work, son. I know 'cause you think like a old man. Whole lotta people's lives gon' be changed 'cause o' you. But remember this: When God lift up a man, He prune him first. You ain't gon' represent God half-steppin'. Not for long."

"Yessir."

"You gon' be all right. Just don't fight Him when you figure out where He's sendin' you. He know what He's doin'."

The old man nodded and chuckled as TL walked away.

CHAPTER 8

I T RAINED MONDAY NIGHT INTO TUESDAY MORNING, settling the dust and leaving small puddles of muddy water scattered across the roads. David offered to drop TL off, but he refused, wanting to walk instead and, again, reaquaint himself with the place. He'd traveled from Ms. Swinton's to his parents' count-less times, of course, even last week, but this was different. There was something he was looking for, something he'd obviously missed a few days ago. Sure, He'd glanced around, but he hadn't studied the place. Not really. Now, he wanted to understand how and why things had changed. He wanted to examine even the small, seem-ingly insignificant shifts in landscape in search of . . . something. Uncle Jesse Lee had told him to look for the signs, and, for whatever reason, he considered that they might be lingering somewhere amidst the countryside he once knew so well.

From Ms. Swinton's, he walked the old access lane, which turned into Fish Lake Road, and veered left at the cluster of plum trees. As a child, he would've taken the shortcut through the Wil-liams place, if it was dry, and stolen peaches from Miss Polly's prize orchard. She would get after him with a broom or a hoe handle, if she caught him, and he would have to pick the rest of the orchard for free. That was worse than a whoppin', since the orchard spread across more than five acres. But he took his chances. Usually she didn't catch him.

It was far too muddy for the shortcut today, so TL took the road, unaware of the hawk perched in a huge pine, watching him. Along the way, he sampled newly ripened blackberries. Vines spiraled up and across the old, rusty, barbed-wire fence he and Willie James had erected years ago. "My God," he declared as the sweet, purple juice drizzled from the corners of his mouth. Blackberry cobbler was the only thing he couldn't live without—besides chitlins—and Grandma made the best around. She'd have him pick a fresh quart, and when he returned, she'd let him roll out the dough with the rolling pin. "Roll it thin, boy! You don't want no thick, gooey crust." After a few disasters, TL mastered the art. Making blackberry cobblers on Saturday evenings became a ritual he looked forward to.

Momma tried to make cobblers, but hers never came out right. Either they were too soupy, too sweet, or the crust wasn't flaky. Not like Grandma's. But she kept trying because she never liked failing. The family appreciated her efforts, but she always knew she'd fallen short. The last time TL brought her a small bucket of blackberries, she sneered, "Take 'em over to yo' grandma. Her cookin' is better'n mine, ain't it?" TL gasped. He recognized the trap. If he'd said yes, she'd have been offended; if he'd said no, she would've called him a liar. So he hung his head and walked away.

He didn't have a bucket now, so he ate the berries he picked. With Grandma gone, so was his hope for a cobbler. He reached for more, and suddenly yelped, "Oh shit!" A black moccasin turned its head to face him. It was coiled around a vine like Christmas tree tinsel. TL used to run at the mere mention of snakes, but this time he didn't. It didn't move, either. They stared at each other, waiting to see who'd give in first. Neither of them intended to lose. For a moment, TL thought the snake might speak. Its mouth trembled like a person preparing to say a difficult thing, then it closed slowly as if the snake had changed its mind. After an eternity, TL eased back and took a deep breath. The snake relaxed. This was the first time he considered that maybe snakes are afraid of humans, too. *Perhaps we're just as poisonous.*

But why hadn't he run? What was different about today? He didn't know, but, as he sauntered home, he sensed that something in the world had shifted.

Knock, knock.

"Whatchu knockin' for, boy?" Momma hollered from somewhere in the house. "What fool knocks on his own door?"

TL entered and met her in the kitchen. "How'd you know it was me?"

"Who else could it be in the middle of the day, like there ain't nothin' else to do?" She blinked repeatedly. TL felt small. "But long as you here, you may as well make yo'self useful and come help me fold these clothes."

Momma led the way into her bedroom. This was strange, too, TL thought. He'd definitely seen it before, of course, but he'd never dwelt in it. None of the children had. And certainly none had been *invited* into it.

TL took the towels, piled upon her bed, and left Momma the undergarments. At least he knew how to fold those the way she preferred. All the corners had to meet, and the tags had to be discreetly tucked away. Momma was known to refold every towel in the closet if someone folded them badly. Or not to her taste, which was the same thing. She was meticulous like that. Always cleaned the kitchen floor on her hands and knees because she said a mop was a poor substitute for human strength. "It barely scratches the surface," she'd say. "It don't scrub to the core the way I like." TL discovered she was right. When he moved in with George and mopped the kitchen floor for the first time, he was disappointed. It just didn't look clean. There was no shine, no sparkle, no smooth slick luster. George said it was fine, but TL knew better. After scrubbing it by hand, he stood, completely exhausted, and saw, finally, what Momma had always seen. There really *was* a difference. And he liked it. He couldn't believe she'd scrubbed the kitchen floor all those years. And he'd walked on it, seconds later, without a care.

"I see you remembered somethin' I taught you," she burbled. "Never would've guessed you got anythin' from me, huh?"

"I learned lots of things from you."

"Well, good. 'Cause I'm still yo' momma. I raised you. Can't no other woman say that." She smirked. "You might not like me, but I did good by you. By all o' y'all. Specially wit' what I had to carry."

"I don't dislike you, Momma."

"You did once. I ain't mad 'bout it." She placed Daddy's underwear in the top drawer of the dresser, then put panties and bras in the second drawer. "I didn't like you, either."

"Why not? I was always a good kid."

"That's true, but you wasn't *mine*. Not at first. And I had to act like you was." She paused. "Put half those towels in the main linen closet, and the other half on Willie James's bed. I'll put 'em away later."

TL obeyed and returned, folding T-shirts and socks.

"It's bad to mistreat a child, I know, but it happens sometimes. You don't never mean for it to, but sometimes it do."

Is this an apology?

She shrugged. "I did the best I could. Can't ask nobody for more than that."

"Guess not."

Humming snippets of church hymns, she proceeded to hang Daddy's work shirts in the closet. After pairing and balling the last set of white tube socks, TL asked, "What really happened to Sister, Momma?"

She never flinched. It seemed as though she hadn't heard him, so he began to repeat himself, but she interrupted. "That ain't for you to know."

He frowned. "Why not? She was my sister. Why can't I know?"

"Because I don't owe you anything. I don't owe anybody anything, and I don't have to do nothin' I don't want to. Not anymore." She smiled. "And I don't want to talk to you 'bout . . . that child."

She took the socks and T-shirts and put them away. TL watched in awe and confusion.

"You think you'll be as good as Ms. Swinton was? Or as good as people *say* she was."

"Momma! You can't do that! You can't just ignore my question."

"I didn't ignore your question. I answered you. There was nothin' else to say." She moved toward the door.

"I wanna know what happened to Sister!"

"First of all, don't you ever holler at me long as you live. Do you understand me?"

TL huffed.

"I said, do you understand me, boy!"

"Yes."

She waited.

TL didn't want to say it, but he had no choice. "Yes . . . ma'am."

She exited with him following.

"This isn't right, Momma. It isn't right."

Turning suddenly, she flung her arms in the air. "Right? You wanna talk 'bout right? Shit! Most things in the world ain't right. I ain't had nothin' right."

"This is different. We're talking about your own daughter! How can you be so . . . so . . . callous?"

Her index finger quivered at the tip of TL's nose. "You don't know nothin' 'bout me, boy!"

He pushed her finger away, and she slapped his hand so hard it burned. TL stared in disbelief.

"Now get out—'til you remember who you talkin' to!"

His eyes watered. She stomped toward the rear bedroom. Several seconds passed before TL regained composure. He wasn't crying because of pain; he was crying because of shame. *Why had she hit me? Don't I have a right to know?*

He exited through the back door and walked around outside, passing the grave and Momma's immaculate vegetable garden. Many things had begun to scorch, but okra, tomatoes, and peas were still making. TL was amazed at how straight the rows were. Well, of course they were straight. Momma wouldn't have had it any other way.

The sting in his hand began to dissipate. She'd slapped him before—when his mouth had gotten the best of him—but he was grown now. This was not supposed to have happened.

Moving from the garden to the nearby pasture, he watched cows graze while field mice played. Willie James bobbed on the tractor in the distance, cutting the first round of summer hay. When he saw TL, he waved enthusiastically. TL lifted his right hand but didn't smile.

That's when he realized he'd missed something in the exchange with Momma. He couldn't put his finger on it, but he felt it. There was something he should've said or done when Momma slapped his hand, but, as usual, he'd acquiesced. It was time for a new response, he determined. Momma needed to know he wasn't the same little boy she'd raised, and how would she know if he didn't tell her?

TL reentered the house. "Momma?"

"Yes?" she called from somewhere in the rear.

"I'm sorry. I shouldn't've yelled."

She emerged in the kitchen, her usual vibrant self. "Very good. It took you long enough."

"I still need to talk to you."

"Well, go ahead." She smiled kindly as if nothing had occurred.

"I'm not trying to accuse you of anything, but—"

"Sure you are! That's why you here. Not here in Swamp Creek, but here in my face. You think I . . . did somethin' bad. Well, what you don't know would make another world, son. And, anyway, I ain't talkin' 'bout it wit' you. I done already told you that."

"I won't go away, Momma. Not this time."

She cackled. "My, my. Well. You finally got some balls, young man."

Her crass language didn't deter TL. "I just wanna know what happened to Sister. I don't see why that's such a difficult question."

She nodded agreeably. "Come wit' me. I wanna show you some-thin'."

He followed her into Sister's old bedroom.

"You big and bad now, right? Then it's time you learned some things."

Momma knelt and reached beneath the bed, dragging out something heavy. "Sit down," she said.

TL sat on the edge of the bed. Momma grunted and pulled forth an ancient-looking wooden trunk. She hesitated a moment, as if second-guessing herself, then proceeded. "I ain't looked in this old thing in years."

"What is it?"

With both hands, she brushed the top as dust rose like dirty clouds.

"You say you lookin' for answers, so I'm 'bout to give you some. Maybe then you'll understand at least a few things."

The cover groaned as she lifted it. At first, TL couldn't tell what all the stuff was, but then he covered his mouth and shrieked, "Oh my God! Are those slave shackles?"

Momma cackled. "Yessir, Mr. Know-It-All. Those are slave shack-les. *My great-granddaddy's* slave shackles."

They were thick and heavy and rusted. A small linked chain connected two braceletlike rings. TL handled them delicately. Momma went on to tell him what she knew: Her great-grandfather had been a belligerent nigga—that's the phrase she used—on a southern Arkansas plantation. She didn't know exactly where. He'd tried to escape several times, but usually never made it past

Tennessee. The fourth time he tried, his master bound him in shackles.

"But not just any shackles," she said. "*Custom-made* shackles. Look on the inside of the rings."

TL looked but didn't see anything.

"Look again, boy!"

When he studied the cuffs closer, he saw the letters EP. "Are those his initials?"

"Hell naw! Those are his master's initials. His first name was Ed or Edward or Eddie and his last name was Prescott, I believe. He put his own initials on the chains so people would know who my granddaddy belonged to. His own name didn't mean nothin', at least not to his master."

TL shook his head.

"Ain't that some shit? You take away a man's freedom, lock him up in chains, and put yo' own initials on his shackles?"

"That's insane."

"He still ran away. Probably made him run harder."

After the sixth or seventh try, Momma said, he made it to Ohio and stayed for years. When emancipation came, he returned, carrying the shackles over his shoulder. His aim was to get back to Arkansas and find his people. He was forty or fifty by then, and he'd never married, promising himself that slavery would never claim any of his seeds. He'd left behind both parents and seven siblings. He was the oldest.

"I'm glad he made it back!"

"Yep. Folks said he walked up one day, sharp as a tack. They didn't know who he was at first, but then his momma recognized him and went to hollerin' and carryin' on and that's when everybody else figured out who he was. They'd heard 'bout him all their lives. He was kinda like a hero to the people, and when he come back, they took it as a sign that good times were to come. His daddy had died a few years before, and the news liked to killed him. That's what

Granddaddy said. His auntie, my great-grandfather's sister, told him the story. She was 'bout thirty when he come back."

"How did you get the chains?"

"Well, before he died, my great-granddaddy gave 'em to my granddaddy. He made him promise to keep 'em in the family and tell the story so we couldn't ever be slaves again. When Grandpa died, he gave 'em to my momma, yo' grandma, and she passed 'em on to me."

"Why haven't you ever told me this before?"

"'Cause you was too busy runnin' in behind some other woman. You didn't care 'bout nothin' I had."

"Oh, Momma."

"But since you back, and done took up studyin' black folks, I thought you might wanna know."

TL felt selfish. And dumb. "What was Great-granddaddy's name?"

"I don't know, but they called him Midnight."

"Midnight? Why? Was he dark?"

"Not at all. 'Bout as light as he could be. Coulda passed for white, they said."

"What!"

"Granddaddy said they called him Midnight so he'd never forget he was black. At least on the inside." Momma closed her eyes and smiled as though seeing him in her mind. She looked at TL again. "They say he could run like lightnin', too. 'Course you can't believe everythin' you hear, but Granddaddy said he was really fast."

"I bet." TL hadn't released the shackles. "Why was he so light? Was he the master's son?"

Momma shook her head. "No. The mistress's."

"Get outta here!"

"Yep. That happened, too, you know."

TL nodded.

"They said she was in love wit' a big black African Master Prescott brung straight from Africa. Didn't speak a word o' English. She went to his cabin at night like white men went to black women. Guess he couldn't do nothin' but what she said. Master Prescott couldn't say much. He went to the slave cabins at night, too. Most times he didn't even know she was gone. Least that's how the story goes.

"Anyway, when she got pregnant, everybody knowed whose it was, but they didn't say nothin'. The day she delivered, she brung the child to the African and asked, 'You want him?' Folks said the man cried and nodded and took the child and raised him. His wife, who was a African, too, accepted the baby and treated him like her own. That story helped me when the same thing happened to me. Well, sorta the same thing."

TL opened his mouth to speak, then pressed his lips together tightly.

"Granddaddy's granddaddy told him all this."

Momma gently pried the shackles from TL's hands.

"First time he run away, he was sixteen. They caught him and brung him back and beat him like a dog. But they didn't break his spirit. He kept runnin' away 'til they put these on him permanently." Her eyes moistened. "When he finally made it and come back, he told folks he kept the chains to prove that nothin' can ever hold you down unless you let it. He scratched his own initial on the outside of both rings." She showed TL the thin outline of the massive, crooked "M"s on each bracelet.

"That's an amazing story."

"It ain't no story, boy. It's the truth." She returned the chains to the trunk and rose. "There's other stuff in there, too, if you wanna go through it. I gotta get these menfolk some lunch ready."

Momma exited and left TL with the open chest. The shackles rested on an old, worn, multicolored quilt, which Momma had obviously inherited from someone. TL lifted it and gasped at what he found beneath.

"Momma! This is someone's emancipation papers! Where'd you get this stuff?"

She hollered from the kitchen, "No one else wanted it! Grand-daddy made me promise to keep it. Said maybe one day somebody in the family might start appreciatin' they history."

TL read the document aloud: '*Let it be known that, on this fifth day of the month of August in the year of our Lord 1857, Katie Prescott is, and forever shall be, free.*'

"This is incredible. I can't believe you have it."

"Yeah. You just never know people, do you?"

"Obviously not," TL murmured.

Minutes later, Momma returned, standing in the doorway.

"Who was Katie?"

"Midnight's momma, the one who raised him."

"I thought she was African?"

"She was. They changed her name. Like they changed everybody else's. I don't know if she accepted it or not. I guess she answered to it though."

"How did she get her freedom?"

Momma's face went blank. "Midnight bought it. He wanted to buy the whole family, but Prescott wouldn't sell 'em. Said Midnight didn't have enough money. Only had enough to buy one, so he bought the woman who raised him. She was so sick she could hardly move, Granddaddy said, but Midnight bought her anyway. He wanted her to feel freedom before she died, and she did."

"When did she die?"

Momma chuckled sadly. "The next day."

"He paid all that money for one day of freedom?"

Momma hollered, "Boy, you ain't got no sense! Don't you know one day o' freedom is worth all the money in the world?"

Having not thought of it that way, TL paused, then offered, "But seems like he woulda bought one of the others since they could've enjoyed it longer."

"Granddaddy said he said they could work hard and buy they own freedom, but his momma needed help, so that's what he did. He carried her out, just past the plantation fence where she'd never been before, and sat her down. Said she cried all day and talked 'bout Africa."

"Do you know what tribe she was from?"

"Nope, but she taught Midnight some African words. He taught my granddaddy a few. She and Midnight's daddy was from the same people. I know that much. Granddaddy said they would talk African when nobody else was 'round."

"I can't believe you haven't told me any of this before."

"Well, like I said, you didn't want anything from me. Not back then. You just wanted to get away from here, and, when you did, I wasn't sure you'd ever come back. But now that you have, and maybe to stay, I thought some o' this old stuff might mean somethin' to you." She nodded. "Momma used to say that sometime what you lookin' for is right under yo' own nose. Now you know how true that is."

TL folded the delicate, yellowed paper and returned it to the trunk.

Down the hallway, Momma shouted, "You still think I killed my own daughter?"

What could TL say?

Her footsteps faded as she mumbled something inaudible. TL didn't know what to think. Only thing he knew for sure was that Momma wasn't the woman he thought she was.

MOMMA SAID GRANDMA ALMOST THREW THE TRUNK AWAY. "WHAT I want wit' all dat junk?" she'd said. Momma was a little girl. Grandma put it out on the porch for the junk man to collect. It rained that day, so he never came, thank God. She then told Granddaddy to take it to the barn, and she never thought about it again. She died before telling Momma what was in it. A few years later, on his deathbed, Granddaddy told Momma to find the trunk and keep it forever. He said she'd understand everything by and by. After his funeral, she found the trunk, covered with cobwebs and dust, bound with large, rusted copper clamps. After opening it, she cried about what the family almost lost.

The day TL left, she opened it again, and told me as much as my little brain could comprehend. I understand now that everything—the chains, the freedom papers, the quilt, the family pictures—was for him. Not me, or Willie James, or anybody else. Sure, it was our history, too, but it was TL's to possess, to use, to interpret. That's how I thought about it. Had he, as a teenager, known the contents, he would've treasured it. But he didn't know. There was so much he didn't know, and Momma wasn't willing to tell him. Things were bad between them then.

Willie James knew about the trunk, too, but he wasn't interested. Or perhaps he didn't understand its significance. Maybe both. He told Momma, "Everybody got free from slavery, so why is one person's papers more important than another's?" She stared at him, then laughed until she cried.

Once TL left, I never saw the trunk again. To think that it rested just beneath me, all those years, waiting for someone to claim it is pretty remarkable now. I suppose that's how Momma knew TL would return. His history was in her hands, lying dormant in that trunk, calling him from the deep, and she knew he couldn't refuse the call. Not forever. He'd searched his whole life to know who he was, and only by coming home would he find out. The trunk would tell him what he needed to know.

CHAPTER 9

L ATER THAT EVENING, TL TOLD DAVID ABOUT THE
discovery. "Something's not right," TL said. "It just doesn't
make sense. A murderer *and* a historian?"

David agreed. "I don't know what to tell you. There's obviously
something you don't know."

"That's for sure. I just wish I knew where to start looking."

"If I was you, I'd go back to the barn."

"The barn? Why?"

"Because that's where everything happened. The scene of a crime
usually holds a clue, most detectives say."

"Yeah, but this happened so long ago. If there had been any
physical evidence, it would've disintegrated by now, right?"

"Maybe. But it's worth a shot."

Shortly after dark, TL took a flashlight and walked through the
woods to the barn. Only the kitchen light shone in the house, but
he knew Momma wasn't asleep. Daddy and Willie James might've
been—they went to bed with the sun—but Momma certainly wasn't.
She lurked around the house at night, talking to herself and tidying
what others had disheveled during the day.

Something felt wrong about what he was doing, but he didn't turn back. Someone had to account for what had happened, he thought, and since no one else was willing, he felt it his duty. Clicking off the flashlight, TL opened the barn door and stood in dark, ominous silence. A cow shifted slightly as streaks of silver moonlight fell across its face. Silhouettes of hay bales and miscellaneous farm equipment made the barn feel both familiar and haunted somehow. Yet he'd come too far to get cold feet now. TL clicked on the flashlight and pointed it toward the floor. A mouse scurried by, scaring him breathless and causing him to stumble upon an empty metal, five-gallon bucket. Noise richoted against the walls and rattled TL's nerves. He covered his ears. There was no way Momma hadn't heard it. He was sure of it. "Shit," he mumbled, struggling to calm himself. The bucket warbled violently, then, slowly, settled onto its side. TL stood it upright again. Silence returned and eased his frazzled nerves. The flashlight flickered as he took a few uneasy steps. *What exactly am I looking for? Why am I here?* Momma was far too meticulous to leave evidence behind, he knew, and, anyway, the scuffle happened years ago, so what could possibly be lying around that might reveal any truth? The more he thought of it, the more ridiculous the moment seemed. But he didn't leave. He shuffled throughout the barn, shifting piles of hay with his right foot and pointing the flashlight behind garden tillers and old, rusty plows. Still, he didn't find anything. Maybe Willie James had made up the whole story. Maybe he hadn't seen anything at all.

Hearing a slight noise, TL turned abruptly, pointing the flashlight as if it were a gun. There was nothing. Just the old milk cow, frustrated that someone had disturbed her peace. Then, out of nowhere, a heavy, raspy voice said, "Leave it alone." TL screeched. Across the barn, near the other exit, a figure stood tall and broad. It scared TL practically to death. His heart pounded against his chest. In the dark, he couldn't see the person's features, only an outline of someone he knew all too well.

TL clicked the flashlight off and joined the figure in the stand-off. They resembled ghosts of cowboys who had died this way and now returned to try their luck again. His knees rattled and buckled like wind chimes beneath his trousers. Yet, he held himself to-gether, refusing to fail this apparent test of manly courage and fortitude.

"You don't know what you doin', boy."

TL's breathing, like a racing greyhound's, became heavy and erratic, but he didn't speak.

"Sometimes the best thing a man can do is leave a thing alone. What he don't know might save him a whole lotta trouble."

The silhouetted figure scratched his head slowly, then returned his arm to his side, shifting slightly like a gunman preparing to draw. TL wanted the figure to feel his bravery, to know that, like him, he was prepared to stand his ground, but fear threatened to consume his confidence.

"I know why you here, and I know what you lookin' for."

Because TL couldn't see his face, the figure's voice sounded distant, strange, hollow, as if he were far away. Neither of them moved.

"But it ain't here. I can tell you that. I know."

TL waited, but, once again, didn't speak.

"You barkin' up the wrong tree." The figure's head rotated slightly. "You don't know what you think you know."

TL's lips parted to tell him that that's why he'd come—to dis-cover what he didn't know—but before any sound emitted, his lips shut like an automatic gate.

"I knowed you was comin'. This ain't no surprise. I always been able to read you. You 'bout the most readable somebody I ever met. But you'd do better leavin' here right now and lettin' things be. You ain't got to understand everything. We think we do, but we don't. That's why God didn't tell man all the secrets of the universe. 'Cause He wanted him to be happy. You can't be happy if you know everything. God ain't happy and He knows everythin'. But He ain't suppose to be happy 'cause He ain't human. He's spirit so He ain't got to worry 'bout human things."

There was so much TL wanted to say.

"We humans? We need at least the chance for happiness. Knowin' everything ruins that chance. God knows this. That's why He don't tell us everything. Not because we couldn't understand it, but because we couldn't have happiness if we did. So just let it go, son." He paused. "And learn to be happy."

A clap of thunder sounded. TL jumped slightly, but the figure didn't move. If he hadn't known better, TL could've convinced himself that the person wasn't real at all. Even after recognizing the voice and the form, he was still open to the possibility that all of this was one long, unbelievable dream, one figment of his insane imagination that now decided to haunt him.

"If you don't, you gon' be sorry. I promise you that. You won't have anyone to blame but yo'self 'cause I tried to warn you."

As TL stared through the dark, the figure's tone softened. "There's so much I wish I didn't know." He nodded. "I'd pay money not to know a whole lot o' stuff. Then, maybe, I'd be happy."

He turned to leave. His shadow looked the same from behind. "Don't make the mistake I made," he said without turning, "tryin' to know everything. People say knowledge is power, but that ain't what the Word says. The Word says: 'Seek ye first the kingdom of God and all His righteous and *then* all other things shall be added unto you.' Don't nobody know what those other things is, and it's best if we don't. We might decide we don't want 'em. Then we'd be mad that we sought the kingdom first. We be done fooled 'round and gave up the whole kingdom o' heaven 'cause o' what we *think* we don't want." He walked to the exit. "I ain't gon' tell you no more. Next time we meet like this, one o' us is gon' be sorry."

The figure slivered through a crack in the barn door and vanished. TL's breathing intensified, as if he'd been holding his breath.

The only thing to do now, he thought, was to get out of there. To think this through. To gather enough strength to figure out what to do next. So, like a phantom, he turned and eased out of the main barn door, tiptoeing as if no one had seen him. He didn't bother flicking on the flashlight. He knew the way.

"FIND ANYTHING?" David asked when TL walked through the back door. David was cleaning the kitchen.

"You wouldn't believe it," he said, half dazed. "They always get me. I don't understand it." Placing the flashlight on the counter he unlaced his sneakers. "Somehow, someway, they always figure me out."

"What are you talking about? What happened?"

TL removed his shoes and sat at the oval table in front of the small bay window. His head fell into his palms.

"I went to the barn, like you suggested, and found more than what I was looking for."

"Would you stop talking in riddles, man, and tell me what happened!" David joined him at the table.

"Daddy caught me! That's what happened!"

"Oh no. Are you serious?"

"Hell yeah, I'm serious. I was looking around with the flashlight when all of a sudden, out of nowhere, he appears and starts talking. Like some shit out of a horror movie! Liked to scared me to death."

"What! How'd he know you were in there?"

"Hell if I know! I stumbled over a bucket, so maybe he heard it, but I doubt it. Momma woulda heard it before Daddy."

"Maybe she sent him out to see what it was."

TL didn't believe that. "Maybe, but Momma ain't that kind of woman. She'd go herself before she'd send a man."

"Did he say anything?"

"Did he!" TL tried to remember his exact words.

David's elbows rested upon the table like a child anticipating the cake bowl batter.

"He told me to drop it, to let it go. He said I'd be sorry if I didn't."

"What'd you say?"

TL chucked. "Nothing. Nothing at all."

"Nothing?"

"Yeah. I know it sounds crazy, but I never opened my mouth. I just stood there and listened."

"You didn't say *anything?*"

"Not a single word."

David relaxed in the chair. "Wow. That's wild."

"You're telling me!"

Their breaths intermingled in silence.

"What's crazier is that I never saw his face."

"What? How is that possible?"

"I heard his voice and knew who it was, so I didn't point the flashlight at him. I don't know why. Guess I thought it would've been rude. And the last thing I wanted was to make him mad."

"That's all he said? Leave it alone?"

TL sighed. "Not exactly. He said that a man can know too much. That sometimes, what you don't know might save you from a lotta trouble. He went on about God knowing everything and being unhappy, but human beings needing happiness, so God doesn't tell us everything or something like that." TL tried to shake the confusion from his head. "I can't remember exactly how he put it, but, in essence, he told me I'd be sorry if I didn't let it go."

David stood and touched TL's shoulder. "I can't help you with this one, little brother."

"I know."

Before exiting the kitchen, David asked, "What are you going to do now?"

"I don't know. But I promise you one thing—I'll find out what happened to my sister. I might be sorry in the end, like Daddy said, and it might cost me everything, but I gotta know. I can't let it go."

I COULDN'T LET HIM GO, EITHER. EVEN YEARS AFTER HIS DEPARTURE, I still had not recovered. I evolved into a shy, quiet child whom no one else seemed to like. I wasn't friendly anymore. I wanted to be, but I couldn't find a reason. My love for reading waned slowly, imperceptibly, like the changing of seasons. There were no other children my age lingering around, and Linda Heart, my closest friend in class, lived too far away for us to spend much time together. So I lost myself in chores. My room stayed spotless, and I learned to cook everything from eggs over medium to turkey and dressing. By twelve, I realized I had become my mother. TL would've gotten a kick out of that.

For several consecutive nights during the fall of my seventh grade year, we watched *Roots*, the four of us, eating popcorn and drinking Pepsi. Daddy grunted about the hell black folks have endured in America, while Momma marveled at Kunta Kinte's sculpted form. "If we was back in Africa," she said, "running 'round like that, chasin' wild animals and stuff, these black kids wouldn't be so damn fat." Willie James and I glanced at each other but didn't dare comment.

I picked up Daddy's watch from the sofa end table as they forced

Kunta Kinte to call himself Toby. I couldn't view the beating. Willie James couldn't, either. He made some excuse to leave the room while I studied the watch intensely. It was golden, but not gold, and round like the face of the grandfather clock in the living room. Momma loved clocks. I loved them, too. I liked to watch the second hand jerk nervously, from number to number, while the hour and minute hands waited for their turn to move. It was a strange concept to me, time, especially considering that it never stopped and was always running out. That's how country folks put it. It was inescapable. Hard as you run, it'll get you one day. It always wins. I suppose I loved clocks because I wanted to see time, to behold this thing that never stopped, that, ultimately, would consume me and the rest of the world. But I never saw it. I'm not sure what I was looking for. All I saw was the second hand, dancing at the edge of the circle, marking the passage of this elusive thing called time. Momma had two or three clocks in every room, chiming throughout the day and night, reminding us that our end was approaching. . . .

CHAPTER 10

WHEN TL ARRIVED AT THE MEETIN' TREE SATUR-
day night, folks were already hollering. Willie James,
sporting his good overalls, squealed with the joy of a
newborn piglet. Someone had just told the story of a woman whose
false teeth fell out as she read the Sunday morning announcements.
TL didn't hear the whole story. He walked up as Mr. Blue stood
and said, "'Our sick and shut-in include Mother Harper, who's
down with the gout, and Brother Taylor who's been diagnosed with
cirrhosis'—and that's when her dentures fell into the palm of her
left hand!" People screamed and doubled over. TL smiled, simply
from watching the master storyteller at work.

Once recovered, folks breathed heavily and welcomed TL to
the gathering. Children played in the distance with stringed june
bugs and lightning bugs, shouting and leaping in the air as if there
was no tomorrow. Such was a child's inheritance in Swamp Creek.
TL had always wondered what his children would be like. Would
they be smart? Tall? Burdened, like he was, with his parents' bondage? In college, he vowed not to have children at all—not until the
world loved the ones God had already sent. How painful it must

be, he used to say, for unwanted children to watch couples con-ceive while they're left crying in the wilderness. He swore he wouldn't do that.

"Years ago, there was a woman 'round here folks called Hallelu-jah," Mr. Somebody began, cackling all the while.

"I remembers her!" a few elders said and nodded.

"People called her Hallelujah 'cause she was so saved and sanc-tified. Everything she did, she did in the name of Jesus."

Mr. Blue shouted, "Hallelujah!" and people screeched, shaking their heads about the level of clowning Mr. Somebody, well into his nineties, was able to sustain.

"If you asked her how she was doing, she'd raise her hands"—Mr. Somebody demonstrated the gesture—"and say"—he assumed the woman's high, scratchy soprano—"'I's blessed and covered in the blood!'"

Some collapsed. Others laughed freely as they waited for Mr. Somebody to continue. He gathered himself and said: "If you called her house, she'd answer the phone 'Praise the Lord, O ye Saints!'"

Miss Polly grabbed her pocketbook and walked away—until she fell in the middle of the road, holding her side to keep from exploding. Mr. Blue's head fell straight back and his shoulders jerked as if he were having a seizure. Tears welled in TL's eyes, but he blinked them away, refusing to lose composure until he'd heard the entirety of the story.

"You ain't nothin' but a fool, Somebody!" Miss Polly repeated, brushing her dress and resuming her seat. "I don't know why folk pay you any mind at all. You ain't nothin' but a stone-cold fool!"

"Well, I ran into Hallelujah one day at the farmer's market. She was prancin' 'round, looking at different things, with her good, black pocketbook danglin' from her elbow and the tail of her dress switchin' like a spawnin' fish. I spoke, and she spoke back right nicely, and I said, 'Hallelujah, you don't want no children or no man?' She looked at me like I had done cussed her out. Before I could apologize, she stared me straight in the eyes and said, 'Jesus is my lover! He rocks me in the midnight hour and comforts me when I'm lonely! I don't need no man! O Hallelujah!'"

TL covered his mouth. This was going to be outrageous.

"I didn't say nothin' else to her. She turned her nose up and went on 'bout her business."

"Yep, she was like that," people confirmed.

"I didn't see her for months, but then I bumped into her one day comin' out of Piggly Wiggly's. She was big 'n' pregnant."

"Pregnant!" TL screamed.

"Did you hear what I said?" He paused. "So I bucked my eyes and told her, 'I guess, Jesus really did rock you all night long, didn't He! Hallelujah!'"

Elders laughed until they couldn't breathe. A few told Mr. Somebody he oughta be ashamed of himself, blaspheming the Holy Ghost, but even they cackled along with others like Daddy and Willie James who screamed without hesitation. TL loved to watch Daddy laugh. He became someone else at the tree, someone lighthearted and easy to get along with. If only he could've lived that way.

TL wondered what Momma would be like at the tree. Daddy had told him years ago not to worry about her. "Everything ain't for everybody," he'd said.

Then Mr. Blue told a story no one had ever heard.

"I used to work for a rich, white lady in Morrilton years ago. I was her driver. This was way back yonder, in the fawties, long before most colored people had cars. Anyway, she hired me 'cause I could drive, and her husband had recently died. She was a foreign woman, wit' a thick accent that made her sound proper. I used to like to hear her talk."

"You talkin' 'bout Miss Mollie?" Miss Polly asked. "That old heffa who used to walk 'round with her nose in the air?"

"She wunnit nearly as uppity as she tried to act. She was actually pretty nice, one on one."

"Sheeeeeeit, that old heffa was nasty as hell!"

"She wasn't nasty! She was just old and lonely."

"Then you shoulda married her! Maybe then the old hag would've spoke to folks who spoke to her."

Mr. Blue waved away Miss Polly's interruption. "Anyway, she was a peculiar woman. She liked everything jus' so. And she loved nothin' more than her cats."

"How many did she have?" TL asked.

"More than I ever knew, but she knew. She could call each of 'em by name. They ate better'n me and you ever dreamed o' eatin'. They didn't eat no table scraps neither. No siree! They got gourmet cat food from the sto'! I seen them damn cats eat fresh grilled tuna. I don't mean no tuna fish out the can; I mean real tuna steaks! Hell, I didn't know tuna even came in steaks 'cause I hadn't never seen it befo', and when I asked Miss Mollie what it was, she laughed and poked fun at me like I was the stupidest man she ever did see."

The crowd tempered its laughter so as not to hurt Mr. Blue's feelings.

"One day I got to her house and she told me to bring the car 'round front 'cause she needed to go to town, and the kids was goin' wit' us. I thought that maybe Alzheimer's was settin' in, so I asked, 'Kids? What kids?' and she said, 'Oh, Horrace!' "—he put his hands on his hips and mimicked a bad French accent—" 'You can be so silly sometimes!' "

His antics were hilarious. That man could transform into anyone in an instant. He definitely had a gift, and he knew how to use it.

"So I went 'round back and got the car and brung it to the front o' the house. I parked and got out to open the passenger door, and here come Ms. Mollie wit' all 'em damn cats followin' in behind her. She opened the back door and seven o' eight of 'em jumped into the backseat. I frowned 'cause I ain't never seen no animals ride in the car wit' people, but since it wasn't my car, and since she was payin' me a pretty penny, I didn't say a word."

Mr. Blue's mouth trembled. He would bubble over any moment.

"Miss Mollie got in the car, and I went 'round and got back in on the driver's side. 'We can go now, Horrace,' she said, like wunnit nothin' wrong, so I started drivin' to town. Well, 'bout halfway, Miss Mollie made the mistake o' her life."

"What she do, Blue?" Mr. Somebody instigated.

"It ain't what she did; it's what she *said*. Outta the blue, she glanced over her shoulder and smiled at the cats, sittin' on the backseat like they was s'pose to be there, then turned back 'round and looked at me and said, 'Don't you like my pussies?'"

People scattered in every direction, screaming, "NO! NO! NO!" and, "I know she didn't!" TL laughed until his throat ached. Mr. Blue stretched out onto the old church pew and howled, too weak to control himself.

"That wunnit the bad part though," he said moments later, panting like a dying man. "The bad part was that I slammed on the brakes 'cause I was jus' so outdone, and one of the cats flew into the front windshield, and she started screamin', 'My pussy, my pussy! You've hurt my pussy!'"

Water poured from Mr. Blue's eyes as he screamed the phrase, over and over. TL almost peed himself. In all his years at the Meetin' Tree, he'd never heard anything so funny.

Half recovered, Mr. Blue said, "No ma'am, Miss Mollie. I ain't hurt yo' pussy! Believe me! It wunnit me! If it hada been me, you wouldn't neva forget it!" and collapsed all over again. Even the few women who found the story a bit distasteful couldn't conceal their joy. Daddy yelped like an excited coon dog while TL held his aching forehead.

Thirty minutes passed before the commotion subsided. Miss Polly leaned toward TL and whispered that she was making a blackberry cobbler so he should come by tomorrow afternoon. Hers didn't approach Grandma's, but TL said he'd be there. She told him to bring his other brother if he wanted to, and he said he'd ask.

"Y'all heard 'bout snagga tooth Tommy finally gettin' married, didn't you?" Mr. Blue asked, wiping his eyes and huffing.

Everyone nodded.

"Who's that?" David asked. "Is that his real name?"

The crowd chuckled.

"He's 'bout the ugliest thang the good Lawd ever made," Mr. Blue said. "Ain't neva had more than one tooth in his head, even as a child. They just didn't come in. He got one big, long tooth, hangin' out the front o' his mouth, lookin' like a jet-black beaver!"

TL tried not to laugh, but he couldn't help it. Mr. Tommy was a nice man who didn't say much to anyone, and whenever he laughed, he covered his mouth and squealed like a hyena. He was usually at the Meetin' Tree, but he wasn't there that night.

"Who he marryin', Blue?" Daddy asked, knowing full well whom he was marrying.

Mr. Blue frowned. "You ain't heard?"

Daddy said no.

"He marrin' Wendell James's baby girl. You knows her. The one you speak to and she look at you like she tryin' to translate yo' words into English."

The crowd bellowed.

"Y'all know somethin's wrong with that girl! I ain't never heard her say a word. Is you? She wave at you real slow like she a beauty queen in a parade, and we know that ain't so! I guess everybody got to have somebody though, and them two is two peas in a pod!" He wailed so hard he could barely speak. "Can you imagine what them children gon' look like? A cross between a toothless go-rilla and a big ol' black walrus!"

Much as TL tried, he couldn't restrain himself.

"Wait 'til you see her," Mr. Blue said, looking at TL. "You ain't never seen nothin' like it. I'm tellin' you what I know."

"Blue, you oughta be 'shame," Daddy said between bouts of laughter.

"No I ain't 'shame! Wendell the one oughta be 'shame! Got that girl lookin' like who-dun-it. She call herself wearin' a natural, but look like to me chickens been playin' in her head!"

"It's a hot mess!" Miss Polly said.

Mr. Somebody added, "I heard her daddy told her not to worry 'bout no weddin' pictures."

Mr. Blue screeched, "I don't see what they havin' a weddin' for period! He oughta just be glad somebody's marryin' that chile."

Had they been present none of this would've been said. It would've been found rude and disrespectful.

"You remember that time we went to Little Rock and ate at that fancy steak house?" Mr. Blue asked Mr. Somebody.

"Stop lyin', man! I ain't been nowhere wit' you! Everybody know this story ain't true."

"The hell it ain't! You wish it wunnit, but it sho' is!"

"Tell it, Blue!" the elders cried.

Mr. Somebody surrendered. "Go 'head and say what you want to. You ain't nothin' but a liar no way."

"Y'all know I wouldn't lie on Somebody, don'chu?"

People murmured, "Oh no!" "Of course not!" "Surely not," just to urge Mr. Blue on. "Well, like I said, we was in Little Rock at this fancy steak house. Somebody had on his good navy-blue Sunday suit, which was 'bout thirty years old then and full of moth holes, but he thought he was sharp!"

"Shut up, fool! Wunnit nothin' wrong wit' dat suit. Hell, I paid fo' hundred dollars fo' that suit."

"Fo' hundred dollars?" Mr. Blue shouted. "Shit, they shoulda gave you three seventy-five back!"

David's laughing rang in TL's ears.

Mr. Blue went on: "So anyway, we walked into the restaurant, and they sat us dead in the middle o' the floor. There were big plants everywhere and lil' lamps on each table. That was fo' the *ambience*."

His overarticulation made TL laugh.

"The place was kinda quiet, although it was full. Mostly rich white folks, but that didn't make us no difference. We jus' wanted one o' those big, juicy steaks we had heard so much 'bout. So anyway the waiter came 'round and spread the pretty white napkins on our laps—"

"They put 'em in your laps fo' you?" Miss Polly asked.

"Hell yeah! Shit! We was eatin' high off de hog!"

"Well I'll say!" people said, clearly impressed.

"A nice-lookin' young man brung us some menus and told us the special o' the day was filet mignon." Mr. Blue exploded with laughter. "Somebody looked at him real strange and asked, 'What kinda fish is that?'"

The tree itself shivered with laughter. People swung their arms like folk doin' the holy dance. Mr. Blue tossed to and fro as David gasped for air.

"Well, hell, I didn't know no better!"

His admission only intensified the screaming.

"That ain't the funny part though," Mr. Blue huffed. "We kept lookin' at the menu 'til, all o' sudden, Somebody jumped up and run out the restaurant."

"Run out the restaurant?" Miss Polly asked.

"That's right! He slammed the menu down like he was offended and run out the restaurant like ninety goin' north!"

"Why?" people asked.

"I didn't know at first. I kept callin' him back, but he shook his head and waved over his shoulder and kept walkin'. White folks turned, lookin' puzzled and confused. I got up and went outside and found Somebody sittin' in the truck wit' his arms folded, like he was mad at the world."

"You really oughta be 'shame, Blue, tellin' lies like that," Mr. Somebody said.

Mr. Blue bellowed. "I asked Somebody what was the matter, but he didn't say nothin'. He jus' didn't want no food outta that place no mo' he said."

No one could've guessed where this was going.

"I kept askin' him why not, 'til he whispered, 'Did you see what kinda gravy they put on they steaks?' I said, 'No, I didn't see it.' He said, 'Go back in there and read it.' I didn't understand, so I went back in and looked at the menu again. When I figured out what he was talkin' 'bout, I fell out on the floor right there in the restaurant!"

"What was it?" Daddy asked.

"I came back out to the truck, with water streamin' from my eyes, and Somebody said, 'Did you see that? Huh? Did you?' I was laughin' so hard I couldn't talk. He said, 'I don't see nothin' funny. Ain't nobody gon' make me pay for no shit take gravy!'"

Folks shouted and fumbled around like zombies in a trance. TL howled. Their voices rose into the branches and leaves of the Meetin' Tree, creating an echo of joy and healing that couldn't be replicated anywhere in the world. Miss Polly lay on the ground, trembling in shock. Others screamed until they were exhausted.

"Stop lyin', Blue!" Mr. Somebody yelled, but no one paid him any mind. "I know what shiitake gravy is!"

"I know you do—after I told you!"

The laughter rumbled on. Nothing Mr. Somebody said could save him now. People were free, and they weren't willing to be anything else.

Jugs of moonshine went around as the night wore on. Even the kids tasted it. They couldn't have much, but they could have enough to spoil their curiosity.

People swatted mosquitoes and complained about the heat until Mr. Blue said, "I wish you young folks coulda seen black people back when we was one people." His peers nodded. "We lived in a community back then. I mean a real community. We took care o' one anotha and raised each other's chil'ren. There was a big bell out at the church that people rang, announcin' births, deaths, weddin's, and different thangs. You could hear it from miles 'round. Different occasions had different rings, and we always hated the death toll most. It was a heavy, deep *BOOM!* that lingered in yo' soul. Folks stopped whatever they was doin', and went to see who had done died. Men would sit with menfolks on the porch and chat into the night as women sat inside doin' whatever women do, makin' sure there was enough food for folks when they come by. I didn't think too much about it then, but now that we done lost them old ways, I thinks 'bout it all the time." His head shook. "I don't know what's gon' happen to black people. We done gave up everything that made us great. We just couldn't see it then." He paused. "We can see it now, but I'm 'fraid it's too late."

Mr. Somebody said it's never too late.

"I don't know 'bout that, Somebody. We let this get *way* outta hand. We was so busy tryin' to get what white folks had that we throwed away what *we* had. It ain't the chil'ren's fault. They didn't know no better. It's the grown people's fault. We sent the chil'ren in the wrong direction. We wanted them to have what we didn't, so we made them love somebody else's way o' life." He looked to see if anyone disagreed. Finding no dissenters, he continued: "And now they can sit anywhere on the bus they want to or go to any school in the country, and they won't even go."

"Cryin' shame!" people murmured.

"Yeah, but the real shame is that *we* did it! That's right. You and me!" He pointed to the elders. "We taught them to love everybody but us. We spent our whole lives givin' our kids what we didn't have, but we never thought to give 'em what we did have. We just couldn't see it then. But we can see it now."

No one spoke.

"You know what I figured out?" Mr. Blue said. "When you tell a child to do better'n you, you really tellin' 'em not to respect you."

Several elders frowned.

"That's right! How in the hell a child gon' do better'n his parents? If the parents go to work every day and teach they children to do right and love the Lord, a child gon' do good simply to do what his folks did! Tellin' chillen to do better than us is like us believin' we didn't do no good job. And that she ain't so! We mighta wanted 'em to have more options, but what we shoulda told 'em was to be just like us! We was their example. If they wasn't s'pose to be like us, who was they s'pose to be like?"

"You talkin' good, Blue," Mr. Somebody said. "I ain't never thought 'bout it like that."

"I know you ain't! Most of us ain't! We taught our kids to be proud of other folks, to long for what white folks had, while we was workin' like a damn dog to give 'em everythin' they needed."

"You right about it!" Miss Polly said.

"I know I am! Hell, I ruined my kids, too. That's why black folks can't keep no young people in our communities no more. We send 'em away. We tell 'em to go find a life when we shoulda been teachin' 'em the beauty o' the life we had!" He paused. "But we didn't know no better. Our folks did it to us, too. Black folks been doin' this since we got here."

TL felt his pockets for a pen, but, finding none, he simply listened more intensely. "Like not too long ago, I heard Helen Faye braggin' 'bout her grandchild goin' to Harvard. Now I ain't neva been to no college, so I don't know much 'bout 'em, but I knowed Harvard musta been a white school from the way she was carryin' on."

"Was she carryin' on, Blue?" an elder asked.

"Oh, her head was way up above the clouds somewhere! You woulda thought that child had died and gone to heaven!"

David nodded knowingly.

"Now I don't know the names of the black schools, but I know black folks don't brag 'bout 'em like that. The shame is that they been doin' just as good a job or better long befo' them white schools decided we was good enough to go there."

"I know that's right!" Mr. Somebody shouted. "That's sho'nuff the truth!"

"We act like any child who go to a black school *had to* 'cause the white schools wouldn't let him in. Like this boy here." He nodded toward TL. "We all knowed he was good in his books. That wunnit no secret. But when some of y'all heard he was goin' to a black school, y'all asked, 'How come?'"

TL looked away. Most denied Mr. Blue's accusation.

"Yes you did! You said it! I heard you. You thought since he was smart enough to study 'longside white kids, he shoulda gone to one of their schools instead o' goin' to a black college. I used to think like that, too. We all did. That's how they made us think. But them black schools did a helluva job educatin' colored chil'ren when nobody else would! I know what I'm talkin' 'bout! We wouldn't be nothin' without 'em. Look at Ms. Swinton. She was the best teacha in the whole state o' Arkansas."

"That's true!" the crowd affirmed.

"And she went to Philander Smith, right there in Little Rock. But see here's the problem: People don't 'sociate black wit' excellence no mo'. But they used to. Once upon a time, a black man could go in a store and buy stuff on credit 'cause folks knew his word was gold."

A few teenagers looked amazed.

"It's true! Gold. Why you think they hired black women to clean their houses? 'Cause when black women cleaned, *they cleaned*! We always had the cleanest houses around. Wunnit much in 'em, but you could eat off the flo'. I'm tellin' you. We was a people of standard, and white folks knew it."

"Amen!"

"The same was true for colored schools. If you went to one, anywhere in the country, you was gon' come outta there knowin' what you was supposed to know. They wunnit gon' have it no other way, 'cause they knowed what you was up against. I didn't go to college, but I betcha them professors could teach up a storm."

TL raised his hands. "I'm a livin' witness!"

"I know it! 'Cause I know what we was like as a people back then. That's what I'm tryin' to say. Didn't make no difference if it was the home or the school or the church or whateva. We knew we had to be good if we was gon' survive in this country, so most times we was twice as good. That made them hate us even mo'. But that didn't really make no difference. We just thought it did. So we traded what we knowed for what we didn't, and you see the good it's done."

TL marveled at Mr. Blue's wisdom. He wished he'd had a tape recorder. The day would come, he feared, when generations of black children would need this insight and it would be nowhere to be found.

Mr. Blue sighed. "But oh well. Guess we gon' have to sleep in the bed we made, ain't we, TL?"

"Yessir. Guess we are."

Mr. Blue's tone lightened. "But the kids 'round here oughta be all right 'long as this boy here teachin' 'em. He went to one of our schools. He know what he doin'."

TL smiled.

Mr. Blue went on about other topics until Mr. Somebody started laughing and said, "Last year, I went out to Hickory Hill wit' Mae Francis fo' their choir musical program. They had every choir in the district on program, so I told her I'd ride out there wit' her. This was 'bout two weeks befo' Christmas. I 'member it because it shoulda been cold but it wunnit."

He laughed again, shaking his head. "Anyway, the church was packed, so I squeezed in on the back pew wit' several other folks. A few choirs sang, then the pastor got up, and said God told him to deliver a word."

Daddy grunted. He'd grown to despise all preachers.

"Folks started grumblin' 'cause this was s'posed to be a musical, and the last thang we wanted to hear was a sermon on a Saturday night."

"I know that's right!" said Mr. Blue.

"We couldn't do much about it though, since he was the pastor, so we rolled our eyes, and prayed he wouldn't be long. They called for Daisy Bell to do a solo befo' the sermon—"

"Why folks always askin' that no-singin' woman to sing?" Daddy asked.

"Hell if I know, 'cause when I say she can't sing, you believe what I'm tellin' you!"

TL had played for Miss Daisy countless times in years past. He hated it, but of course he couldn't say no. And Mr. Blue was right— her singing was horrific. She would wave for TL to come to the piano, and "pick her up," but he never could. No one could. She changed keys every two or three measures, and her vibrato was so heavy that most notes came out flat or sharp. As soon as TL thought he had her, she'd change keys, frustrating him all over again. He usually spent the entirety of a song with his ear to the piano, fingering notes, until, by the chorus, he simply gave up and clapped along. He never knew why people asked her to sing until, as a young adult, he saw how much they enjoyed mocking her. She was too conceited to notice.

"So after Daisy Bell got through messin' up 'Precious Lord,' Reverend Hardy shuffled his fat ass to the podium and said, 'God laid on my heart to talk 'bout Mary.' A man behind me mumbled, 'God shoulda laid on your heart to stop eatin' after sundown!'"

People hollered.

Mr. Somebody reenacted Reverend Hardy's slow pulpit antics. "'Turn in your Bibles with me to Matthew chapter so and so, verse so and so,'" he said, flipping imaginary pages, "'where we find the story of Mary, Joseph, and Jesus.' Now besides the fact that he couldn't half read, he read so slow I thought I was gon' scream. Then, he slammed the Bible shut, leaned over the podium, and said, 'My topic for this evening is this: Mary . . . had a little lamb!'"

Daddy cried, "Sheeeeeeit!" and crumbled. Others walked off, bubbling with laughter. TL and David fell onto each other's shoulders.

After several minutes, Mr. Somebody, panting heavily, said, "I swear fo' God that man said that. I wouldn't lie on him. I couldn't've made that up if I'd tried."

He bellowed again. Daddy tried to stand, but couldn't. He managed to ask, "What did he say, Somebody?"

Mr. Somebody lowered his chin, and, mocking the preacher's deep slow voice, said, " 'Mary had a little lamb, his fleece was white as snow, and everywhere Mary went, the lamb was sho' to go!' "

"That's dumb as hell!" Daddy said, both entertained and angry.

The crowd hollered all over again. Women extracted tissues and handkerchiefs from pocketbooks and wept into them. Men roared and mumbled about Reverend Hardy's immeasurable stupidiy. TL simply laughed, imagining it all.

"Ignorance is a deep thing," Mr. Blue said after everyone calmed. "Especially in a preacher."

"Amen!" TL said. Elders chuckled.

"Most folk in the pulpit ain't got no business there," he added, still cackling and huffing. "What since do it make for God to call somebody to speak for Him who can't even speak? Huh? Do that make any sense at all?"

"No sir!" people cried.

"They make God look like a fool, and they run sinners straight out the church. That's why most churches 'round here can't grow. They ain't got no leadership. These dumb pastors call theyselves shepherding a flock when they don't even know people's names. I ain't sayin' God didn't call 'em; I'm just sayin', if He did, He called 'em to school first. That's the God I serve! He wouldn't put a jackass in front o' people and tell 'em to follow him. He do thangs decent and in order."

Finally, TL thought, someone had said what he'd always wanted to say.

"The best thang these churches 'round here could do is stop payin' these no-count preachers, and come together and form one congregation that everybody could be part of. It don't make no sense! Three members here, nine members there, five members over yonder, and ain't nobody gettin' no sound doctrine nowhere 'cause they can't afford no sound leadership. If they would jus' come together"—he entangled the fingers of his hands—"they could have somethin' worth havin'. As it is, you got fawty people scattered 'round in ten different churches, all wit' clowns as pastors."

No one disagreed.

"Divide and conquer. That's how we gon' destroy ourselves if we ain't mighty careful."

TL wasn't sure he was grown enough to speak, but he risked it anyway. "Why don't the churches combine? Seems like everybody agrees they should."

" 'Cause first of all, everybody don't agree. And, second, we more committed to tradition than to progress. Folks holdin' on to these old churches 'cause they growed up in 'em, but ain't nobody left. Half these congregations ain't got twenty people on the roll. How you gone keep up a church with that kinda population? They don't take up fifty dollars a Sunday! And the pastor gets half of that!" People moaned. "I tried to get these churches to come together years ago, but folk almost cussed me out."

TL frowned. "Are you serious?"

"Ask Polly! She was there. I went to St. Matthew, St. John, Pilgrim Rest, Hickory Hill . . . all of 'em. Sheeeeit! Them niggas looked at me like I had done asked them to take off they clothes and run butt naked down the road!"

"I know they did!" Daddy said.

"Sho' they did! So after that, I ain't said no mo' 'bout it. But it's the only way a black church is gon' survive 'round here. Otherwise, all of 'em gon' die, including ours, 'cause ain't enough people havin' children to keep 'em goin'. But I guess we'll learn—after we done lost everything."

There was nothing more to say, nothing to add, nothing to debate. TL simply wondered why such extraordinary wisdom hadn't transformed Swamp Creek. But like Grandma used to say, people gotta want it first.

Different elders told stories for another hour or so before people began to leave. They were obviously exhausted from laughing. TL's jawbones ached, and he had a slight headache, but he wouldn't've traded the evening for anything. These people, his people, had taught him how to survive. And all the while he'd thought he was the smart one.

THAT WAS THE ONE JOY I NEVER LOST—GOING TO THE MEETIN' TREE. Momma didn't go, so me and Willie James and Daddy would head out Friday evenings at sundown. Linda Heart and I giggled and whispered about how ugly most of the boys were except, of course, Christopher Youngblood. Everyone agreed he was beautiful. Women smiled at him and men told him that looks weren't everything. So while we gawked at his maple brown beauty, grown folks screamed and laughed until their hearts were healed. Sometimes we eased our way into their conversations and laughed along at the unbelievable stories people told. Their performances beat anything I'd ever seen on TV, and the roar of their laughter always made me smile. Even Ms. Swinton cackled along, never losing her classy ways, but obviously refusing to miss her own healing. Everybody was there. When it rained, people sat at home silent, brooding, waiting for the next Friday with great anticipation. And when it came, they unleashed their hearts and the night air took their pain away.

I don't know what would happen to my people if the tree died. But, on second thought, I don't worry about it: Swamp Creek is full of trees.

CHAPTER 11

THE MORNING OF THE FAMILY REUNION, JULY 4TH weekend, TL rose early to help Daddy set up things. He'd complained for weeks about Negroes comin' who hadn't sent in their money, but the truth was that he enjoyed crowds. He wasn't necessarily the center of them, but he liked their energy and he liked watching others make fools of themselves. He'd shake his head slightly or murmur about how ridiculous people looked, trying to impress one another, but any time a crowd gathered, he was in the number.

Momma, on the other hand, possessed a genuine disdain for crowds. When she said she couldn't stand Daddy's people, traipsing across her clean floors and eating like wild boars, she actually meant it and would've told them so had anyone asked. She was cordial for the sake of appearance, but her fury flourished for weeks after the family left—that is, until the house was restored to order. She cooked the sides for the picnic only because Daddy asked her to and because she loved his barbecue ribs. He was never much of a cook, but he knew when to lay ribs atop smoldering white charcoals and let them smoke until they fell off the bones. He made his own barbecue sauce, which everyone envied. No one's ribs rivaled Daddy's, and he knew it. Grilling meat was his crowning glory. Momma's potato salad was her specialty, and although she fussed about it, she smiled proudly when people "oohed" and "awwwed" after tasting it. And it *was* incredible. It was the perfect blend of soft-boiled eggs, dill pickles, onions (diced fine), salt, pepper, a dash of paprika, cubes of perfectly boiled potatoes, a spoonful of mayonnaise, and enough mustard to make it yellow but not soupy. Regardless of the serving size, she knew exactly how much of each ingredient to use to make it come out right. She wouldn't've had it any other way.

TL smelled grilling meat long before he reached the house. Daddy'd probably been cooking since yesterday, he thought. Daddy would never let others say he didn't have enough.

Willie James was mowing the lawn. He lifted his hand quickly when TL passed, but neither spoke. Willie James's cut-off shirt revealed arms and abs far more muscular than TL remembered.

In his work overalls and fishing hat, Daddy stood before the makeshift grill with a white kitchen towel slung over his right shoulder. He basted the ribs, for the umpteenth time, with his magical sauce. When he heard TL's footsteps, he said, "Good afternoon." It was 9:32 A.M.

"Am I late?"

"You is if you intended to help me. I been up since four thirty."

TL rolled his eyes. Daddy prided himself on having never missed a sunrise.

"By the time you get up, boy, I done done a day's work. If I waited on you, it'd be midnight before I finished what I got to do."

His condescension pricked like a bee sting. TL awaited instructions.

"Get a big pan from the kitchen so I can take these ribs off the fire. I guess they done. This the last of 'em."

TL searched the lower cabinets for a container big enough to hold six slabs of ribs. Returning from the bathroom, Momma asked what he was looking for. He glanced up and told her.

"Well, it ain't down there. You know that. Everything is exactly where it's always been. Don't start actin' like you ain't never lived here."

She sat at the table, peeling boiled eggs. TL found a large roasting pan and left before Momma could interrogate him.

The picnic was scheduled for noon. Folks arrived shortly thereafter. Uncle Roscoe struggled out of his candy-apple red Cadillac, with a stomach big enough to carry a full-grown man. Aunt Trucilla exited on the passenger's side.

"Well, I'll be gotdamn!" he yelled at TL. "Where the hell you been all these years, boy? Huh? How come you ain't called nobody?"

"Hey!" TL sang, hugging Aunt Trucilla first, then burying his face between Uncle Roscoe's thick flabby pecs.

"They said you went to school," Uncle Roscoe said. "Then they said they didn't hear from you no mo' so we didn't know what had done happened."

"I got a PhD. It takes a while."

"A PhD? Aww shit!" he said, slapping TL's back so hard he coughed. "We got a doctor in the family!"

"Ooooowe!" Aunt Trucilla sang, twirling her arms. "That's all right! You done made somethin' outta yo'self, boy! We's proud of ya. I hope some of these other kids follow in behind you. Ain't nothin' gon' save us but education. I can promise you that!"

TL shuffled to the tent Daddy had erected in the middle of the field. Others were shocked to see him, too, and each time they asked where he'd been, he simply said away at school. His degrees were enough to satisfy some, but a few said he should be ashamed of himself, disappearing like that and leaving the family worried. He apologized and promised to do better.

With few exceptions, everyone wore baby-blue Tyson family

reunion T-shirts. There was a huge tree sprawled across the chest with children's names printed in tiny letters in the leaves and elders' names scattered among the roots. We were the descendants of Joe-Nathan and Mattie Jo (Williams) Tyson, the shirt said, who'd migrated from South Carolina to central Arkansas after emancipation. "They were looking for work and a place free of the Klan," Uncle Roscoe later chuckled and said. "At least they found the work!"

Most of the cousins were still doing what they'd been doing ten years earlier. Several had married and borne children, and a few male renegades were still living the bachelor's life although they, too, had reproduced. TL asked Marcus, Uncle Roscoe's baby boy, about the reunions TL had missed. Marcus said he hadn't missed much. They'd only had two since TL had been gone, and one of those was in some place nobody wanted to go. He'd missed that one.

"I only come if it's down here." He pointed to the earth. "This is where the family's from. Don't make sense givin' hotels thousands of dollars for rooms and banquet halls when we could save that money and just come on home and enjoy ourselves the way our people grew up doin'." He looked and sounded like Uncle Roscoe. "A family reunion oughta be held wherever the family's from, don't you think so?"

TL agreed, then asked about Jamie.

Marcus wiped his forehead with his sleeve. "Sad story, man." His lips pressed together hard. "He died 'bout two years ago, out in California."

"What!"

"Yeah, man. It was bad. Nobody really talked 'bout it. I called Jocelyn when I heard, and she said he'd lost a bunch o' weight. I asked her what was wrong with him, and she hesitated and said cancer."

"Cancer? What type of cancer?"

Marcus leaned toward TL and whispered, "It wasn't cancer. It was AIDS. I'ma call it what it was 'cause ain't no need in lyin'. We all knew 'bout Jamie, so . . ." He shrugged.

"Oh my God. I can't believe that."

"Yeah, I know, and what's worse is how the family reacted. Nobody wanted to talk 'bout it," he repeated. "Jocelyn said a few people came to the funeral, but only a few. It really hurt her feelins. I could hear it in her voice. I woulda gone, but I had to work. I was mad 'bout how the whole thing went down."

TL restrained his tears.

"This family needs work, man. We need to meet and talk 'bout stuff while we all here together. I hope we will. I might just have to make it happen myself."

He touched TL's shoulder and walked away. If anyone were bold enough to force the family to talk, it was Marcus Tyson. At six foot four, 285 pounds, he had a way of commanding attention that most didn't challenge.

By twelve thirty or so, cars of every make and model lined the dirt road leading to Daddy's house. There had to be fifty or sixty people mulling about the field, laughing and chatting about the good ol' days. Overhearing snippets of conversations, TL wondered why, if the past had been so glorious, all the residents had moved away. Sometimes elders make the past seem dreadful, and other times it seemed heavenly. He guessed it could be whatever they needed it to be—depending on whom they were talking to and the point of the conversation. That's one of the reasons he'd always looked forward to aging. Black elders get to change time, space, and truth without most people ever knowing it. They get to remake themselves and their history so that it becomes precisely what the next generation needs in order to succeed. Truth and historical accuracy don't matter when they speak because most couldn't refute or corroborate their claims anyway. It's as if the older they get, the more like God they become. And in the country, the worst insult ever is to call an elder a liar. That's tantamount to blasphemy, and forgiveness is practically impossible. So children listen to old folks and do what they say. It doesn't matter if the children agree.

TL escaped behind the barn to pee, and when he returned, he heard Momma ask Daddy, "Why don't somebody get that boy some help?" He looked around and saw Thomas, Uncle Jethro's baby boy. He almost didn't recognize him, with his hair permed bone straight and bangs that touched the top of his eyebrows. His lashes fluttered like a bird's tail, and the lipstick was so red it glowed. TL screamed into his palms.

"That's a shame," Momma said, frowning. "His hair look better'n mine."

"Whose fault is that?" Daddy asked,

When Thomas turned, his full-length floral print skirt ballooned. He smiled, waving excitedly at TL as if they were old friends, and began switching across the field toward him.

"That thing look a damn mess!" Momma said, and walked away.

"Tommy! Oh, Tommy!" he sang. Family members looked at TL, puzzled. He wanted to die.

Thomas stumbled about ten yards away and shrieked as if he'd stepped on a snake. His legs wobbled and buckled like the Tin Man's, and that's when TL saw the four-inch black stilettos, with all five of his toes hanging over the edge of the fronts. The family erupted into derisive laughter. TL was glad Thomas didn't fall. The shame would've been irreparable.

"Child, these cheap-ass shoes 'bout to make me cuss!" He tossed fake hair from one side of his head to the other. "And these niggas"—he glared in every direction—"can go to hell!" They only laughed louder.

"How you doin', Thomas?" TL whispered, embarrassed. He hoped Thomas would speak and move on.

"I'm all right, baby," he said, touching TL's chest lightly with humongous hands and beautifully manicured, bloodred nails.

Why is he being so familiar? TL wondered.

"Just takin' care of Daddy." Then he mouthed, "You know how men can be."

TL's eyes bulged. "Excuse me?"

Thomas stepped closer and whispered, "You know what they say 'bout us."

TL scowled. "No, I don't."

"They say me and you was cut from the same cloth." He raised his hand, expecting TL to give him high five, but he didn't. Instead, he said, "I beg your pardon?"

Clearly offended, Thomas sang, "Oh! Okay!" and shuffled uncomfortably from one stiletto to the other. "You don't wanna be 'sociated wit' nobody like me. Is that it?"

"I didn't say that, I'm just saying that . . ."

"Don't worry 'bout it! You can hide the rest of yo' life if you want to, but I ain't. I thought you was different. You was always nice to me when you was younger, but I see you done become just like the rest of these narrow-minded niggas."

"No I'm not."

"Yes you is!" His long fingernail danced before TL's nose. "These folks talk 'bout you like a dog, includin' yo' own family. They say me and you is the"—he made the invisible quotation marks—"funny ones in the family. Just 'cause you don't look like me don't mean folk don't know." He snapped three times.

The cloud of shame hovering over TL felt dark and impenetrable. He didn't know what to say, and he didn't know how he'd ever live down the moment.

Thomas backed away. "Don't worry 'bout it, honey. You'll get yours. Guarantee you that! Life ain't free. You can't live a lie all the time! You can do it for a while, but the spirit ain't gon' take it long. The day gon' come when you won't even care what other folks think! But 'til then"—he was on his toes, tipping carefully—"believe me when I tell you you gon' pay, especially when you throw away people like me who love you, regardless of what other folks say." He swiveled quickly, slinging all his hair to the right side of his head, and added, "I'm a prophetic bitch! I know what I'm talkin' 'bout!" Then he pranced across the field like a runway model.

The family stared at TL.

Suddenly, Momma called, "Let's eat!" and the cloud of shame dispersed.

Everyone moved to the tent. Uncle Roscoe said something funny, easing the tension and restoring order. TL wasn't in the mood for food—who would be after that?—but he went along for the sake of peace.

Momma asked him to help serve, so he scooped potato salad onto paper plates as relatives smiled sympathetically. Then he made himself a plate, which he barely touched, and sat next to Marcus and Jocelyn.

"I wonder what really happened to him," Jocelyn said. "Thomas, I mean. I know what people say about his mother dying and all, but I don't believe that's what made him that way." She glanced into space. Jocelyn had always been a pretty girl. Her eyes were really close together, and she had a bad case of acne, which never seemed to go away, but her butternut complexion and million-dollar smile trumped the blemishes. A pressing comb had burned out the edges of her hair when she was in grade school, but even that didn't ruin her beauty. She was definitely thicker now than TL remembered, but that, too, was an asset, he believed. Marcus told him later that she'd put on weight after Jamie's funeral. Her jeans fit like skin, causing her butt to protrude a foot past her waist. Most of the men wished she weren't related.

"They say his mother was overprotective," she continued. "Wouldn't let him go outside and play or pick out his own clothes. Stuff like that. He was the baby, so maybe she tried to hold on too tight. I don't know." She raised her hands and sighed, releasing the heaviness of her thoughts.

Marcus offered that maybe nothing had happened. Perhaps he was born that way. If people can be born shy or smart or gifted, he said, why can't they be born *like that*? Since God makes people different, who's to say He didn't make some like Thomas? Jocelyn and TL nodded. Nearby cousins acted as if they hadn't heard him. "TL, you different, too. Everybody know it." Horror flushed his face. "Ohh no, man! Not like that. I just mean . . . like . . . special. Daddy always says you the brain in the family. That's why he likes you so much!"

Marcus's chuckling didn't ease TL's embarrassment.

"And even if you was *that way,* you still my favorite cousin. Hell, you gon' be rich one day, and I'll be damned if I ain't gon' get my part."

Jocelyn's forced smile caused TL to change the subject. "I can't believe what happened to Jamie, Jos. Marcus just told me."

Her white plastic fork shuffled between potato salad and baked beans. When she looked up, her misty eyes begged for sympathy. "It wasn't right, TL, the way God took him." Tears multiplied but they didn't fall. "He didn't deserve to die like that. Nobody does."

Clutching her hand and squeezing hard, TL said, "I'm so sorry."

She nodded. "I know." Her mouth quivered as Marcus rubbed her back. "Jamie always loved you. He used to talk about you all the time. Said, one day, you and him were going to change the world. I asked how, but he never did say. Just said it was going to happen." TL wanted to hug her, but decided this wasn't the time or place. "I suppose you'll have to do it alone now. Just don't forget how much Jamie loved you. He never forgot you." TL's throat went dry. Jocelyn dabbed her eyes with a napkin, trying not to smear eyeliner and foundation. "Would you do me a favor?"

"Sure. Anything." TL held both her hands now.

"If you ever make it big, make the world know my brother. Say his name out loud every chance you get." A lone tear sprinted down her right cheek. "Make sure people know he was a human being. Don't let his life be in vain." She covered her mouth quickly.

"I don't know what my future holds, Jocelyn. Looks like I'm back where I started from, so I can't make any promises about changing the world."

"You'll do it," she offered confidently. " 'Cause it's just . . . I don't know . . . in you. Always has been. Jamie said so all the time."

"Yep. Daddy says so, too." Marcus nodded.

"Are you back here to stay?"

"Guess so. I've agreed to take over the school."

"Oh really?" Jocelyn beamed. "That's great. You'll be amazing."

"Hope so."

"Maybe that's how you'll change the world. By changing some kid here."

"Maybe so." TL flashed the polite smile, the one people give when they don't believe what they've just said.

"What kind of cancer was it?"

Marcus shot TL a nasty look.

Jocelyn whispered, "It was AIDS, TL. You knew that. Don't play games with me. I don't need that right now."

TL huffed. "I'm sorry. I was just trying to be polite."

"I'm tired of polite. That's not doing us any good. I've decided to tell the truth from now on, regardless of how much it hurts. That's why the family didn't help me. They couldn't. We're so scared of the truth that we make up whatever we need to believe. I've done it a thousand times. That's why I told everyone Jamie died of cancer. Because I couldn't face the truth. I was ashamed and didn't want people speaking badly of my brother. They knew better, too, but they needed something they could handle, so I gave it to 'em."

"That's such a shame."

"Yeah, it is. Jamie lay in a hospital almost two months and Marcus was the only one who called. But everyone knew."

TL felt guilty.

"It's all right though. I'm not mad at anyone. I just hate that black families can't be honest."

Marcus and TL nodded.

"Before he died, he asked me to tell you something if I ever saw you again."

TL waited.

"He said to tell you thank you for helping him that day Aunt Pearly embarrassed him. At the family reunion years ago. You remember that? He certainly did. No one stood up for him but you. You were his hero, TL, and he needed one badly."

TL couldn't hold the tears any longer. He told Jocelyn how much he loved Jamie. They promised to stay in touch. Momma called for TL to help her take empty pots in the house.

"I won't forget what you asked. I promise. And I'll mention Jamie's name every chance I get—if I ever get the ear of the world."

She waved sweetly as if saying good-bye to a memory.

CHAPTER 12

WHEN THEY ENTERED THE KITCHEN, MOMMA laughed heartily.

"What is it?" TL asked.

"You can't see nothin', child?"

He honestly didn't know what she was talking about.

"Out there. Today. I saved yo' ass and you didn't even notice."

"Saved me? From what?"

"From everybody questionin' you 'bout yo' private life. The food wasn't quite ready yet, but it was a good way to distract folks, don't you think?"

He'd missed it. "Thanks."

She smirked. "The things you miss, boy." Her look was accusatory. "I done saved you a whole lotta times and you never even noticed. I washed yo' dirty draws when you wasn't speakin' to me, and I cooked yo' meals when all you wanted was Ms. Swinton. Did she ever feed you?" TL looked away. "That's what the note meant, fool. I wasn't the momma you wanted. I know that." Her voice softened. "And you wasn't the son I wanted. But we got each other anyway."

The screen door slammed behind her. TL was left standing at the kitchen sink, trying to figure out what other signs he'd missed. It seemed as if Momma was pruning his consciousness, stripping him of everything he thought he knew. He felt naked, exposed, barren. What exactly did the family think of him? And what did they say behind his back? TL chuckled. He knew what they said. There was no woman in his life—at least that they knew of—and that could only mean one thing, right? That's what they assumed. But it wasn't always true. George said most men marry to keep people from talking, but TL felt no need to do that. He was a scholar and an educator, he told himself, who knew his life's purpose. But, from the looks of things, maybe he didn't.

All his life, he'd been too afraid to ask the hard questions. Like what he really believed. He'd grown up in church, but he was never sure how much religious rhetoric to embrace. He didn't believe in hell—he knew that much—and he didn't believe that only Christians were going to heaven. If there was a heaven at all. But he'd always loved Jesus and what He stood for. He was single, too, Jesus, so if His life had meaning, TL thought his could, too. The sexuality question was simply too taboo to touch. Not because TL didn't know his own truth, but because he didn't come from parents or people who would've loved him had he admitted it. He knew that. Everyone knew it. So he carried the shame and silence like a warrior shield. Since college, he'd believed that sexuality is biological, so, to TL, it didn't make sense that God would condemn people for whom they loved. When folks reminded him of what the Bible said, he simply reminded them that God didn't write it.

Outside, Uncle Roscoe called for everyone to create the family circle. Relatives grumbled and moaned about it being too hot for all that, but they obeyed. Uncle Roscoe was even bigger than Marcus and absolutely no one wanted to endure his wrath.

When the circle was complete, Uncle Roscoe stepped into the center with a jug of water and said, "Y'all call the names of people what done passed, and I'ma po' a lil' water on the ground after each name. Y'all know how we do." He winked at TL. "Our folks use to do this back in Africa as a way to say thank you to those who done passed on. They did that 'cause most folks ain't got sense enough to say thank you to folks while they livin'. The water washes away hard feelin's that maybe you never did get a chance to express." He leaned toward TL and whispered, "I reads, too," and nudged him lovingly. Everyone obeyed and summoned the spirits of people the youth had never known. When his turn came, Marcus stepped into the circle and shouted, "Jamie Woodyard!"

No one responded. No ashe, no amen . . . nothing. In his anger, TL stepped forward and said, "Ashe!" Marcus nodded. Jocelyn followed suit. Five or six other cousins their age joined them as they created a smaller circle within the larger one. Then, out of nowhere, Willie James came forth. The crowd mumbled with confusion and surprise, but he stood flat-footed and declared, "Amen," glancing at TL. Most of the elders didn't like it, but Marcus and his peers stood there anyway, representing an ancestor who'd never been celebrated on earth. Uncle Roscoe poured half the gallon of water onto the ground and said, "Ain't no need in y'all bein' mad. These young folks is right. He's a ancestor just like the rest of 'em. And since we didn't treat him right on earth, we gon' treat him right in heaven! Shit. These young folks growed up with that boy. They played together as chil'ren, so they had a personal connection to him. They ain't gon' be satisfied 'til we do right by him. He might've been funny, but he was still family." He looked around. "Yeah, I said it! And I ain't takin' it back!"

The grumbling continued.

Uncle Roscoe said, "Come here, Jocelyn." He placed his hands on her shoulders and massaged soothingly. "On behalf of all of us, we want to apologize for not bein' a family when you needed one. Jamie was a good kid and it's a shame we didn't do better by him and you. But we gon' stop this right here and now. He didn't do no worse than the rest of us. Hell, some of us got kids by two and three different people with no wedlock in sight." The crowd gasped. "Now ashe that!"

The inner circle laughed.

Daddy wasn't amused. He shook his head and said, "You can't make folk call that boy right, Roscoe."

A few said, "Amen."

"I ain't said nothin' 'bout right, Cleatis. Wrong either. 'Cause if we gon' talk right and wrong, you *know* you got to close yo' mouth."

All grumbling ceased.

"I'd have to close mine, too. I got a daughter the same age as my son—and they ain't twins. So if we gon' tell the truth, let's do it. But if we ain't, then we gon' be quiet 'bout everybody. And I mean *everybody*."

Daddy stared at his big brother, but couldn't challenge him.

"So like I said, we gon' do better as a family 'bout bein' a family 'cause we the only folks we got. It's a shame to meet folks on the street who treat you better'n your own family. What's the point in comin' together like this if we don't grow no closer?"

Everyone agreed. Jocelyn wept openly.

"It's all right, baby," Uncle Roscoe consoled, patting her shoulders. "We ain't perfect, but we 'bout to be better. We gon' love all the chil'ren the good Lawd send from now on, don't care what they be like. Hell, we could be throwin' away Jesus Christ."

"That's true," Aunt Trucilla said.

"Yeah it's true! Ain't no tellin' what folks said 'bout Him, either. He was strange, 'cordin' to the Word, so you know people made fun o' Him. That's the way we do. But they didn't kill Him 'cause He was strange. They killed Him 'cause He knowed who He was." Uncle Roscoe paused, believing he'd said something profound. "Think about it. They didn't kill Jesus 'cause He said He was the son of God. Anybody coulda said that. They killed Him 'cause He *knowed* He was the son of God, and He acted like it, too."

Momma laughed.

"I ain't playin'! He knowed who He was. Our job is to love who-ever God sends 'cause, one day, He comin' back, and I'm mighty 'fraid He ain't comin' like we thinkin'. He might come lookin' jus' like Thomas over there."

Thomas raised his hands and twirled. The family hollered.

"Okay. Mark my word. It'd be a shame to treat God like com-mon trash, wouldn't it?"

"Yes it would," people murmured.

"His ways ain't our ways, and His thoughts ain't our thoughts, so be careful of judgin' folks. That's all I'm sayin'."

Jocelyn thanked Uncle Roscoe and they embraced. The inner circle disbanded and rejoined the larger family. After all the names had been called, folks returned to their chairs and resumed general conversation. TL took a seat next to Uncle Roscoe.

"We off to a good start, Professor, but we got a long way to go. You and that crazy-ass son o' mine make sure this family do right after my generation is dead and gone, you hear?"

"Yessir."

"Ain't nothin' harder than livin' wit' your own family. That's 'cause yo' family know yo' history. I mean yo' *real* history. That's why, when people change, they leave home, 'cause yo' family is the first to remind you of what you ain't!"

"I know that's right!" TL said.

Uncle Roscoe's belly shimmied like Jell-O. "But sometimes family's the only ones what'll help you if you get in trouble. I'ma witness to that." He gazed into the sky, searching for his memory. "When I was 'bout sixteen, me and some boys from 'round here was in town lookin' in different shops when one of the boys decided he was gon' steal a watch."

Cousins gathered to hear the story.

"We didn't have no sense, but Joe Nathan Bryers *really* didn't have none. He commenced to goin' in the sto' and actin' like he was browsin'. I stayed outside."

"You knew better, huh?"

"We all knowed better. Parents raised kids back in them days. They didn't just have 'em like y'all doin'."

Young folks snickered.

"Anyway, Joe Nathan piddled around 'til he snuck the watch into his pocket. The two other boys followed him 'round and they all come out the store together. We walked down the street, and went behind the old Grier Clothing store building where he showed me the watch. It was pretty, too. Diamonds all 'round the edge and gold numbers bright as the sun. He let me hold it, and, like a dummy, I put it on. That's when Old Man Grier and another white man come out the back door. Joe Nathan took off runnin' like the devil was after him, and the other boys did the same. I was too scared to move. I didn't wait for the men to ask me nothin'. I handed them the watch and told them what had happened."

"Of course they didn't believe you," TL said.

"Sho' they did! They believed me. They knowed my folks and knowed that Daddy woulda beat the hide off me if I'd ever stole anything. They knowed I didn't take it. Back then, black children rarely got into trouble like that. We wasn't perfect, but we believed in family honor, so we just didn't do stuff like that."

"Did they take you to jail?"

"Hell yeah they took me to jail! Shit. I had the watch in my hands. They knowed I wasn't guilty, but I had to go anyway 'cause I didn't have no business foolin' 'round wit' crazy-ass Joe Nathan in that sto'. I shoulda left when he told me what he was gon' do, but since I didn't, I had to pay the price." He shrugged. "The sheriff went and told Daddy, and he come down to the jailhouse madder'n a fox in a trap. He told the man I didn't do it, and the man said he knowed I didn't, but I had the watch, so he had to take me in. Daddy asked how much it would cost to get me out, and the sheriff said ten dollars, but Daddy didn't have ten dollars. He only had two, and the sheriff wouldn't take it. He told Daddy to go on back home and he'd release me in a few days, but Daddy asked if he could stay. The sheriff said suit yo'self, and Daddy stretched out on the flo' right in front o' the cell. He didn't say a word to me. Just got on his knees and prayed for 'bout fifteen minutes, then stretched out like a tired mule. I never will forget it. The sheriff give Daddy a couple o' old army blankets to cover up wit' and an old, flat feather pillow for his head. In the mornin', I guess he felt sorry for us 'cause he told Daddy to go on home and take me wit' him."

"I bet Granddaddy was mad, huh?" Marcus asked.

"You know he was! He liked to kill me when we got home. Told me years later, befo' he died, why he stayed there that night." Uncle Roscoe choked up. "Said he wanted to make sho' them white men didn't kill his boy. Yeah, they was nice and all, but he didn't trust them completely. I never forgot that. I thought the old man didn't like me, but after that, I realized that, when you least expect it, family stands with you sometimes when nobody else will. You young folks remember that."

They nodded. Uncle Roscoe talked on until slowly, people began to leave. But TL wanted more.

"What kinda man was Granddaddy?" TL asked.

"He was a good man, son. He really was. Times was jus' so hard he had to be hard, too. He didn't have no choice. We thought he was mean, but he wasn't. He jus' meant for us to survive. And we did. Never did have no money, but we ate good every day and always had a warm place to sleep." He laughed. "Well, maybe not warm, but at least it was a place to sleep. In the winter, a bucket of water woulda froze in our bedroom. That's how cold it was."

"How'd y'all stand it?"

"We had so much cover on the bed you couldn't hardly turn over. It was ice cold, boy, but after a while, you got warm enough to go to sleep. If you had to pee in the middle o' the night, you held it 'til mornin', 'cause if you got out o' bed and went to the outhouse, you'd get so cold on the way you never would get back to sleep.

"But it was a good life. We didn't think so then, but I ain't seen nothin' better. Least not yet. I ain't sayin' it was perfect, 'cause it wunnit. People been crazy since the beginnin' o' time, and every family gets a few crazy members. That's the way God do it so won't nobody get the big head. Don't care how great you get, somebody in yo' family is a fool."

He pointed to Marcus and everyone laughed.

"Yo' granddaddy made a lot o' mistakes, boy." Uncle Roscoe paused. "He was the father o' his own grandchild."

"Sir? How is that possible?"

"Oh, it's possible! When yo' aunt Cecelia was fifteen, she come up pregnant. Momma was pregnant wit' Agnes at the same time. Nobody really said nothin', but we knowed what had done happened. Momma knowed, too. Cel hadn't been wit' no boy. She wunnit never allowed to go nowhere. So when she come up pregnant, Momma didn't say a word. She knowed everything. I guess wunnit nothin' she could do 'bout it. Women didn't fight men back in them days. They fussed a little, but most of 'em put up wit' a whole lotta shit while they watched in silence."

Various cousins mumbled their objection.

"That's jus' the way it was. Didn't nobody have enough education to do nothin' else, so we did what was expected of us.

"Anyway, when Cel started showin', they locked her in the back bedroom 'til she delivered."

Jocelyn screeched, "What!"

"That's right. I remember it like it was yesterday. She stayed in that room from March 'til August. 'Course she went to the outhouse, but that was it. And when she did, she covered up like them folks in Iraq! Didn't nobody outside the family see her, and I mean nobody. Even when we was in the house, we didn't go in that room and she didn't come out. Momma took her food and clean clothes, and sometimes days or even weeks went by without any of us kids seein' her at all. Then one day we come in from the field and heard a baby cryin' and we knowed Cel had done delivered. She still didn't come out of that room. Momma delivered a month later and took

Cel's baby and nursed both of 'em. Her and Daddy told everybody that Momma had had twins, and since folks didn't know no better, they believed it."

TL shouted, "Oh my God!"

"Shhhhh. This ain't for everybody. I thought some o' y'all oughta know befo' the good Lawd call me home. I know Cleatis didn't tell you."

"No sir, he didn't."

"Well, he wunnit s'posed to."

"Daddy, you gotta be kiddin'," Marcus said. "You mean to tell me Aunt Cat and Aunt Agnes ain't really twins?"

He cackled. "Did you hear what I said, boy? Shit!"

"They look just alike!"

"I guess so! They got the same daddy!"

Cousins shook their heads in disbelief. TL asked, "And things just went back to normal?"

"Naw, I wouldn't say normal. Momma packed Cel's clothes and put her on a train to Kansas City. She stayed wit' Aunt Luvenia, Momma's oldest sister. I didn't see her no more 'til I got grown and went to Kansas City myself. By then, she was livin' on her own, singin' and dancin' in blues clubs downtown. She was a skinny little thing, but she could sang and sway her hips and have men throwin' their whole wallet at her. She was somethin' to see, I'm tellin' you. But she didn't wanna have nothin' to do with Arkansas, ever again, and you couldn't mention Momma and Daddy without her cussin' you out. I tried to get her to come home wit' me a couple o' times, but that was like askin' God to go to hell. Momma never did see Cel no more. They asked me 'bout her, and I always lied and said she was fine and asked 'bout them. But Cel wasn't fine. She was so hurt she couldn't see straight, and I couldn't do nothin' to help her."

Jocelyn asked, "That's the one everybody talks about who ran away from home and was killed in a train accident?"

"Yep, she's the one, but she didn't run away. They sent her away. Momma was tryin' to protect her, but Cel didn't see it that way. Whenever I mentioned home, she'd start breathin' heavy and fire would burn in her eyes, like she was turnin' into a monster or somethin'. She was so pretty. That was the problem. All the boys in the community talked 'bout marryin' her when she wunnit but twelve or thirteen years old. She was a smooth pretty brown, like a pound cake, and she had big brown eyes the size of marbles. When she smiled, her whole face lit up. I'm tellin' you! Cecelia Ann Tyson was a knockout!" He slammed his right fist into his left palm. "Folks did her so bad she didn't have a chance. And she didn't die in no train wreck." Uncle Roscoe studied their faces. "She was murdered. They found her body behind an old abandoned Folgers factory. Somebody beat her up pretty bad, but it was definitely her. I identified the body."

"What!" TL said. "Then who came up with the train wreck story?"

He pointed to himself. "I didn't want nobody talkin' 'bout my sister as no sleazy tramp. I wanted her to have some dignity." His bottom lip quivered. "I didn't have no money to bury her, so they laid her in a wooden box and put her in an unmarked grave in the city cemetery. I used to go by there sometimes and sit. I stopped goin' years ago. Had to. Needed to move on."

TL touched Uncle Roscoe's massive hands. He wanted to ask a million other questions, but Uncle Roscoe was beginning to tire.

"That's the only time I seen Daddy cry, when I told him 'bout Cel. I drove home wit' the death certificate and gave it to him. He tried to hold it together, but his knees collapsed and he went to the ground. I called for Momma, and when she learned what happened, she walked off down the road like a crazy woman. When she come back, she looked twenty years older. Just like that. Within a year, both of 'em was dead."

"Shouldn't someone tell Aunt Cat and Aunt Agnes they ain't twins?" Jocelyn asked.

Uncle Roscoe hollered. "Girl, git outta here! They *been* knowin'!"

"Stop it! Are you serious?" she said.

"They didn't know at first, when they was lil' girls, but they found out later. I went to 'em when they got grown, ready to tell 'em everything, and they laughed and said they'd been knowin'. They liked the idea of bein' twins though so they decided to live that way."

Jocelyn said, "I can't believe how much they look alike."

"Yeah, well, they oughta."

TL examined the faces of other elders, wondering what they knew that most didn't. Not names or personalities, but truth and family history. *It's funny,* he thought, *how people's faces tell their stories, especially old people.* He'd never noticed this before, but now he could see it. Some of them were a smudgy gray, with a dull, embalmed look. This was particularly true for the men, as if they'd been covered with a permanent ash. Something must've happened back in the forties and fifties, which left them hopeless and discolored. The women didn't share the ashen undertone. Instead, they wore frozen smiles and smirks, masking whatever they couldn't say. The more he studied them, the more he saw the weight of history upon their faces and the price they must've paid to survive. They'd been taught the art of endurance. That was something future generations would long for. The bright innocence of young faces, TL told himself, simply confirmed that they hadn't lived yet.

The last thing Uncle Roscoe said was "Most folks, if they live long enough, end up bein' Jesus *and* the devil. We wanna be Jesus all the time, but we ain't. Every now and then, that old devil has his way. That's what happened to Daddy. He wanted to be a good man. I believe that. But he didn't have enough Jesus on the inside. He did my sister wrong, and I'll never forgive him for that, but he wunnit the devil. Not all the time. I realized that the night he laid in front o' my jail cell. I was mad at him for what he'd done to Cel, but he saved my life that night, far as I know." He paused. "I think he was sorry. He acted like he was. After Cel left, he never did say much.

Me and Cleatis saw him once, out in the middle o' the woods, screamin' and swingin' his arms and cryin' out, 'Forgive me, Lord! I'm sorry!' We turned and ran away. He was a different man after that. I guess that's the best a man can do—beg God for forgiveness and try hard to do better. Daddy did that. I've had to do it, too. Y'all live long enough, you gon' do it, too."

Evening came on easy, purply gray. People's spirits lightened, as if the impending darkness freed them somehow. A few said good night and returned to their hotel rooms in town, while the rest gathered around Uncle Jethro and other elders and listened to family history they'd heard a million times. TL wanted to hear more of the stories they hadn't told, but since he didn't know what to ask, he listened like everybody else until the moon replaced the sun and mosquitoes unleashed their attack. When they became unbearable, the remaining family members said good night and drove away. TL walked Uncle Roscoe and Aunt Trucilla to their shiny red Cadillac, but before saying good night, he asked, "What do you really think happened to Sister, Uncle Roscoe?"

The man squinted hard. "I couldn't tell you, son. Somethin' went wrong between yo' momma and yo' sister. I know that. Yo' daddy called one night right after everything happened, soundin' like he had done lost his mind."

"Really? What did he say?"

Uncle Roscoe shook his head. "I don't remember exactly, but I recall him sayin' he couldn't believe his baby girl was gone away."

"Gone away? You mean passed away?"

"Naw, he said gone away. I asked him where she went, but he didn't say. He just hung up. Next thing I know, somebody called the house sayin' she was dead. It didn't make no sense, so I called him back and asked him 'bout it, but he just said she died suddenly. They didn't know why."

"What about a funeral? Did you ask him about that?"

"Yep, but he said wunnit gon' be none 'cause it was too hard on yo' momma. I didn't ask nothin' else."

TL thanked him and promised to see them at church in the morning. After everyone left, he walked back to Ms. Swinton's in the dark, listening to the cry of crickets and bullfrogs, and wondering what "gone away" could've meant. He never noticed the hawk gliding easily above him.

IT RAINED DURING THE LAST FAMILY REUNION AS IF GOD WERE weeping. Water pounded the roof so hard I thought it might collapse. People had driven from all over the country, but most stayed in their hotel rooms and slept the weekend away. We threw out enough food to feed the world, Momma said. Whole pots of cabbage and green beans gone to waste, and entire containers of potato salad and peach cobbler spoiled. But what could you do? She left the food out all day, thinking that folks might come by, and some did, like Uncle Roscoe's crew, but they didn't eat enough to make a difference. And there wasn't room in the freezer to keep it, so the old dog ate good that day.

I stood at the den window, late in the evening, looking into the downpour, trying to count the droplets, but of course I couldn't. I wondered where they came from, as if perhaps a river in the sky might've overflowed. We'd learned about evaporation and precipitation in school, but I didn't really understand it. The falling water blurred everything outside, smearing images like an excited toddler's hand on a freshly painted canvas. Everything was a dull, slate-blue gray. The scene hypnotized me, temporarily relieving my hopeless misery.

I was sixteen or so, convinced I'd never be happy again. I couldn't think of anything I desired or wanted to do. The whole world seemed irrelevant to me, and Momma and Daddy were no help. The week before, Momma had said I was a spoiled brat who needed to learn how to lose. What? Learn how to lose? How do you say that to a child? Momma seemed to have no trouble. She'd said it more than once. I began to wonder if she were preparing me for some gigantic loss, something greater than I'd already endured, but I soon discovered that her motive wasn't prophetic. It was her way of teaching me the price of womanhood. "A mother gets everything at first," I remember her saying, "then she loses it all in the end. There's nothing you can do about it. It's just the way it works. If you try to avoid the loss, you never have anything to begin with. Kinda sucks, huh?" It was more than I could handle, but Momma extended no sympathy. If I were going to be a woman, and it appeared as if I were, I had to learn how to lose without being broken.

Daddy talked to me a few days later. It was strange, listening to him, since we usually didn't talk. I always spoke—there was no way around that—but we never shared our hearts. Like everyone else, I feared him, so I stayed out of his way. I would never have burdened him with my thoughts. He always seemed to have enough of his own. Yet one morning after breakfast, he told me he'd drop me at school. There was something he wanted to say, something I needed to hear. I waited in the truck, sporting freshly pressed hair, my favorite blue jeans, and a pink and lavender blouse with frills around the neckline. I thought I was in trouble or something, but when we pulled away, he said, "You gon' be a woman soon." I frowned. Had he and Momma been talking? "Which means you gon' need a man. Every woman does." I became defensive. "I think I'm okay by myself." He slammed the brakes. "No, you ain't, girl! You need a man, someone to take care of you. Don't be like these stupid, new-age women, thinkin' they can make it on their own. They just end up lonely and bitter." I wanted to ask how Momma had ended up that way, having had a man all her life, but I didn't. Daddy would've been offended, and, anyway, Momma never wanted independence. She'd never seen the need, she said. Me, on the other hand, I couldn't hide my desire for it, and Daddy thought it his responsibility to save me. By the time I arrived at school, I was crying. The woman's life he'd described was totally un-attractive to me, but I had no choice, he said. It was my lot, and if I wanted to be happy, I had to submit. I exited the truck without saying good-bye, having decided that my life's aim would be to prove him wrong.

I never did. Crazy thing . . . standing at the window, lost in the rain, I realized that the man I couldn't live without happened to be my very own brother.

CHAPTER 13

AVID LEFT SWAMP CREEK EARLY MONDAY MORN-
ing. His church needed him, he said. Parishioners think
more of their pastor than they do each other, he added,
so he had to return before chaos erupted. He laughed although he
didn't think it was funny.

TL had underestimated how much he'd grown to love him.
And need him. David was far more grounded than he was. David's
words gave TL perspective and kept him from doing things he'd
later regret. David tempered TL's drama—something TL didn't
always like, but he definitely needed.

Before leaving, he told TL he could have it all. *Everything.*
"This house, this community, this place is *your life*"—that's how
he'd put it—"so no need haggling. This is your legacy here—not
mine." Envy and sarcasm colored his tone. David had a right to
resentment, TL thought. He believed he did, too. But since both
needed memories of a mother far more grandiose than the mother
they'd actually had, they agreed subconsciously to continue living
the way they'd always lived—without each other—as they imagined how great their mothers must *have been* to someone else.

They'd gone through boxes for days, looking for a will or other significant documents, but found nothing. Just old utility bills and a picture of TL at birth. David held it up and smiled. "You're definitely her child." It was an awkward statement, like one confessing a long-kept secret. He said it as if to say TL was something he wasn't, something he *should've* and *would've* been if things had been different. TL wanted to apologize for his existence, but he didn't want to patronize him. David said there was no reason for TL to fail. He'd had the dream life—a mother who sacrificed everything to be with him and a father who wouldn't leave him. Of course TL didn't see it that way, but his pitiful expressions sounded like a spoiled child's whinings, so he relinquished the fight. He'd never thought of his life as a dream, but he was sure he wouldn't have wanted David's. Not now. What was he returning to? In the weeks they'd known each other, he'd never mentioned anyone important. No girl, no family, no best friend. God seemed to be the center of his life, and maybe that's all he needed. TL hoped it was. It seemed to be all he had.

You're definitely her child. The more TL considered David's words, the more he realized the enormity of what his brother had said. David was suggesting that he'd been the neglected one. And he had, TL thought, but hadn't they both? David obviously didn't think so. From where he stood, TL had spent his whole life in heaven. Ain't it funny how we always want the life we don't get? What he was calling heaven TL had been calling hell. It's only because we don't really see others' lives. We glance at people's exterior and wonder why we aren't blessed to be them when, really, if we examined the interior, we'd understand that our own life is the real blessing. TL began to understand this the day David left.

They hugged as if sure they'd never see each other again. David chuckled, once they released their hold, and TL wiped teary eyes. They didn't say anything more. David simply got in his car, rolled down the window, and waved slowly. In the years to come, TL would wish he'd gotten to know him better, but for now they were long-lost brothers returned—and suddenly estranged again.

TL reentered the house and stood in the center of the living room. How had his life shifted so drastically? And so quickly? He studied the room. David had been wrong, he thought. *This isn't my life. I don't know these walls, these books, these floors, these memories, lounging around windowsills and antique furniture. I'd always admired the house, but from a distance.* Now, in the middle of it, TL had absolutely no idea how to make it his own.

But it *was* his own. It was all he had. Like David, he had to figure out how to make a life from the remnants of what his mother left behind. Make no mistake about it: She'd had as much baggage as Daddy. Maybe more. TL could ask him about his life, but he'd have to piece hers together, with the few precious pieces he had. And he knew that any time you do that, you're bound to get things wrong. Sometimes people get everything wrong, then they pass the error to the next generation and so forth, until, in the end, nobody looks anything like their original selves. That's what happened to black people, Grandma said. Slavery robbed us of so many critical pieces to the puzzle that when we started writing our own history, we told only stories of tragedy, struggle, and loss. The other stories, of triumph, beauty, and achievement, faded into myth and left our young people wanting to be part of someone else's history. TL swore that, if he did nothing else in life, he'd find those missing pieces and tell our children their stories. Their *real* stories. The ones they obviously hadn't heard.

Funny thing—Miss Swinton's house made him think of Momma. It was clean to the point of feeling uninhabitable. That's how Momma kept house, even with kids and a husband. They'd come home on a Saturday evening, and Momma would have the house locked up like a prison. All the doors and windows would be bolted shut as if she were trying to create her own perfect little universe. They'd knock and holler, but Momma would act as if she couldn't hear them, walking around the house touching newly polished ceramic pieces like she was in a museum. Daddy would tolerate it for a while, finding other things outside to occupy his time (and forcing them to do the same) until hunger got the best of him, and he'd call Momma's name slowly, sweetly, seductively—*Marion*—and Momma would open the door as if oblivious to our frustration. Daddy didn't press the matter. He must've understood what she needed. She wanted to enjoy her clean house, she said. At least for a while. It was as close to perfection as she might get.

Momma was kind to TL sometimes. She'd call him first to lick the cake batter bowl. He remembered that. And sometimes she cooked chitlins just for him. She said it wasn't *just* for him, but of course it was—he was the only one who ate them. She hated the odor they left behind, and despised standing at the sink for hours cleaning them, but every now and then, for Thanksgiving or New Year's Day, she'd do it. That was her way of saying she loved him, although TL would've preferred the words. Since he couldn't get them, he settled for the chitlins.

That stopped when Momma had her last child. The day they came home from the hospital, Momma acted like TL was invisible. He was only ten. He stood at the living room window, waiting anxiously for Momma's return, and when she came, she walked past him without saying anything. He went to his room and cried. Nothing he did impressed her anymore, and when he mentioned baking cakes or homemade cookies, she said she didn't have time. Plus, he was too old for cookies. "Boys should be outside playin'," she said. So that's where he went.

Their relationship deteriorated into mere formality. Of course he didn't know then what he knows now. He figured she loved her daughter more because she'd lost a daughter once. Or perhaps she just didn't like him anymore. The best he could do, he thought, was to love whomever she loved. Maybe then he'd be loved again.

That's when he began learning about Momma's life. She was from a little town called Damascus, no more than ten or fifteen miles east of Swamp Creek. He'd only been there once. Momma's parents died before she finished high school, and her only sibling, Uncle Rayford, moved to California when TL was a little boy. He vaguely remembered him. Uncle Rayford was gigantic and muscular like a gladiator. Most kids were scared of him.

Momma said there was nothing in Damascus for her anymore, and since she never liked the place, the family never went. She flew to California once, to show her brother the new baby girl, and when she returned, she said, "I'll never do that again." TL asked what happened, but she told him to stay in a child's place.

One Saturday night, TL came home from a party at the community center in Morrilton and found Momma sitting on the den sofa in the dark. She cleared her throat when he entered, startling him. TL stumbled and froze.

"Be careful, child," she whispered. The voice didn't sound like hers.

"Were you waiting up for me?"

"No. You know I don't do that."

TL took a few steps forward before she said, "Don't never let nobody else have yo' life."

Confused, he stopped and frowned, but she didn't notice. Or maybe she did.

"My daddy took mine. Momma let him."

Did she want to talk? To me? Why?

"He never let me go nowhere. I was *his* little girl, his precious baby, and I liked it at first. He showed me off everywhere we went. I always had nice things although we weren't rich."

TL eased backward and sat in the chair opposite her. She shifted slightly to face him.

"When I got to be a teenager and wanted to go out wit' other kids, he wouldn't let me. Said I was better than them. 'Decent girls don't run the roads at night,' he said. Momma didn't say anything. That's why I was mad at her. She coulda helped me, but she didn't. So I sat 'round on nights like this, listenin' to Daddy read the Bible, when all my friends was out havin' fun. That's why I can't stand the Bible now!

"Then he died. Nobody knew why. Just up and died one day. As much as I had wanted to get away from him, I felt lost without him. That's the way life works, son. You end up lovin' the thing or the person you was determined to hate. It's almost like hate and love is the same thing, you know? Both of 'em have the same result."

She'd never called him *son* before. He'd always been *boy* or *child,* but never *son.*

"So the day we buried Daddy, Momma told me I needed a husband. I wunnit but sixteen. She said I needed to find somebody who would take care o' me and my children. I told her I didn't have no children, but she assured me I would. Guess she was right, huh?"

TL nodded.

"I asked her if we was s'pose to be in love, me and this husband o' mine, and she said that would be good, but it wasn't necessary. 'Love don't make no marriage, girl. Respect is what you better be lookin' for. Any man what respect you will be easy to love.' I disagreed with her, and set out to prove her wrong. When yo' daddy winked at me one day after school, I thought this was my chance. He obviously loved me, I thought, and that made me love him. We started courtin' and carryin' on, and I got pregnant."

She paused for TL's reaction, but he didn't give one.

"We got married a month after we finished school. It was all right at first. We was in love—at least *I* was. After the weddin', yo' daddy disappeared and I didn't see him 'til later that night. I asked him where he went, and he said to celebrate with some of his friends. I told him we was s'pose to be together on our weddin' night, and he said we'd have a lifetime to be together, so what was the rush. I refused to tell Momma she'd been right. I stopped questionin' yo' daddy and let him do whatever he wanted. I learned to do the same. That's how we got along all these years. It ain't been so bad, I guess. We done had some good times. Only bad thing about it is we don't know each other. It's a shame to live wit' somebody thirty or forty years and never know 'em, ain't it?"

"Yes ma'am."

"That's how most folks' marriage works. They just stop expectin' what they once dreamed of. They figure they're better off wit' somebody than wit' nobody, and it usually takes 'em a lifetime to see that, even wit' somebody, they still ain't got nobody. That's why I say don't never give yo' life away, son."

There was that word again.

"You'll never have nobody to blame but yo'self. You can give everything you have, out of the goodness of yo' heart, and, if you ever expect something in return, folks'll turn 'round and tell you they didn't ask you for nothin' you did. They'll tell you you did it 'cause *you* wanted to. Ain't that somethin'? Who in the hell thinks people do anythin' *just because they want to*? I don't care what nobody say—any time we good to others it's 'cause we hopin' they gon' be good to us. I lied to myself for the first ten years of my marriage. I told myself I was cookin' and cleanin' and havin' babies 'cause I wanted to, when the truth was that I was hopin' yo' daddy was gon' love me for it. Well, he didn't. That was my fault 'cause he never said he would. So I had to decide if I could live wit' the life I had created. And I decided I could, although it wasn't *my* life. I guess I ain't gon' never have my own life, but if I could do it all over again, I can't promise you I'd have this one. In fact, I can pretty much promise you I wouldn't."

TL couldn't think of anything to say. He tried to look into her eyes, but, in the dark, all he could see was a silhouette of her face. She reached her right hand toward him and he took it, reluctantly. It felt warm and soft and inviting. Then she extended her left and totally enclosed his right, and TL wondered who this woman was.

"Make sure you have the life you want, you hear me? You ain't gon' have but one, and even then it ain't gon' be perfect, but at least it'll be yours, and you can change it whenever you get ready. Folks been runnin' my life since I was a little girl, and now I ain't got no life. Everybody think bein' a daddy's girl is cute, but I'm here to tell you it kills you in the end 'cause when you wanna start thinkin' for yo'self, you don't know how. So you find another man to finish what yo' daddy started, and at some point you start lookin' for yo'self, I mean yo' *real* self, and you realize you wouldn't recognize it if you saw it. I guess it can happen to men, too, but it usually don't. Men are expected to tell everybody else to go to hell. Women are expected to go to hell *for* everybody else. That's just the way it is. But just in case, I'm tellin' you what to do. You smart. People like you. I'm smart, too, but people don't like me. I don't have the personality. Never did." Her fingers massaged TL's hand sensually. "But you do. So keep yo' life, son. That's all I'm sayin'. You ain't gon' get but one."

She dropped his hand, as if it stung her suddenly, then reclined, sign that she'd said what she'd wanted to say. TL stood and went to his room. He didn't know how much longer she sat there, maybe minutes or until morning, but by sunrise she'd returned to her old self. He'd expected her to be much kinder, after such a vulnerable moment, but she acted as if the conversation never occurred. Maybe, somewhere in the night, she'd regretted having shared her heart, and now she was committed to erasing the memory. So TL forgot it, too. Until now. Standing in the midst of Ms. Swinton's house, he recalled that the mother he'd had hadn't been as awful as he'd once thought.

In the bedroom, where Ms. Swinton once lay, TL reclined across the bed. David had said he couldn't sleep there. The last thing he wanted was to see his mother's spirit. TL didn't believe in spirits, and even if he did, he didn't believe they were bad, so what was there to fear? David agreed, but slept in the guest room.

TL got up and retrieved from his bag the last of Ms. Swinton's journals. Since he wasn't sleepy, he decided to read for a while.

Children never understand. How can they? By the time they grow up, the world's a different place. Circumstances shift, people change, contexts become unexplainable. What once made perfect sense can easily leave one looking like a fool years later. That's how I'll look to TL. Like a fool. How could it be otherwise?

I'm tired of trying to change the past. I did what I thought was right—after I did what I knew was wrong. If someone finds these words, I hope they understand. If that someone is you, TL, if for whatever reason you become the keeper of my secrets, read everything before you judge me. I couldn't possibly have loved you more. That won't be hard to believe. I didn't hide my affection very well. Half the time I didn't even try although I should've. Others noticed, especially the children, and that wasn't fair. But I was far less invested in their opinions than I was in nurturing the gifts in you. You were mine. I owed you something. I owed you everything. I pray I gave it to you. If I didn't, Lord knows I tried.

Who am I fooling? This won't make sense years from now. You can never give children your heart, and that's the only way they'd understanding everything—if they could look into your heart and see why you did what you did. Since that can't happen, all you can do is hope they have a child one day in the midst of their own imperfections. Then they'll know.

TL thought of David. He needed to read this, too.

If God hears my prayers and, TL, if you read this one day, I want you to do me a huge favor. Please.

He paused. Whatever it was, he knew it wouldn't be easy. Somehow he also knew he had no choice.

Tell your mother I'm sorry. I know I should've told her myself, but that wasn't part of the plan. Your father said she didn't want to talk about it. Ever. To anyone. So I honored that. But, still, I should've said something. I was too ashamed, I guess. Or too selfish. But I really meant to do it. Every time I started toward your house, I collapsed with guilt and returned home. I wasn't half the woman people thought I was. Maybe the apology will help. Somehow. I hope she lives long enough to hear you say this for me. She's been waiting a lifetime. We're funny like that, women are. We wait all our lives for people to say what we always knew. You'll understand one day when you get a woman of your own. For now, just tell Marion I'm sorry. And thank her for having done half my job.

Closing the journal, TL turned over and stared at the ceiling. *Yes, you should've apologized.* That would've been the right thing to do. In order to believe that though, he had to relinquish his image of a perfect, polished Ms. Swinton, and he didn't want to do that. She'd always been divine to him, even after he learned the truth. *Everyone messes up once, right?* But now, in her own words, she admitted that she'd been a failure, a coward, a woman he might not've been proud of had he known the truth. And he didn't want *this* Ms. Swinton. He wanted the one he had, the one who read with him after school and told him God smiled when He looked at him. The one whom everybody in the community praised. The one who'd lived as close to Christ as anybody he knew. But *that* Ms. Swinton was dead, and so now was his perfect image of her.

It didn't really matter anymore, he told himself. He was an adult who was supposed to be able to deal with the truth. The real truth, the absolute truth. He just didn't know that the truth could be so ugly. And intrusive. This was the lesson Daddy had been trying to teach him. That everyone's truth is ugly. "No pedestals for nobody," Daddy used to say. Now TL understood why.

But Ms. Swinton's request wasn't about him or his truth. It was about the people who preceded him and the circumstances that had created *their* truths. He was simply being used to mediate the collision. *Just my damn luck! If this was what Ms. Swinton meant by "saving your people," then I don't want the job.*

Turning over again, TL sighed and continued reading:

She knew. Women always know. Cleatis found every excuse to come by here, and I never sent him away. Marion and I were always cordial, even after things got exposed. Occasionally, I'd catch her staring at me or through me and I'd look away, wondering just how much she knew, but she never confronted me. She might've done me a favor, now that I think about it. I would've lost everything had she said anything, so the truth is that Marion was a far greater woman than I was. I never knew her personally, but I know enough to say she isn't crazy. Or selfish. She might be aloof and haughty, but there's another woman deep inside—a woman who had the power to destroy me, but chose not to.

I thought I'd have to leave when I got pregnant, but I didn't. All the superintendent asked was whether I was married, and since I was, he told me I could stay. He couldn't promise people wouldn't talk about me, but that was something I would have to endure.

When I first realized my condition, I left and told my husband the truth. He was disappointed, he said, not that I was pregnant, but that it wasn't his. I told him I wasn't in love with him and he said he knew, but still he had his own private hopes. David, my sweet boy, looked forward to a brother—he prophesied it'd be a boy—with hopes of having someone to play with. I knew they'd never play together, but the gleam in David's eyes kept me from telling him the truth. He'd know soon enough.

Once I returned and began to show, people must've concluded I'd gotten pregnant in Detroit. No one asked anything. No one. They just smiled and glared at my ballooning belly like one stares at a facial abnormality. Of course I didn't volunteer any explanation, so for the last three months of TL's in utero life, I smiled along as Swamp Creek residents ignored the obvious. I wasn't fooled. If there's one thing I know about country folks, it's this: They might not say a word, but they know. Their highest virtue is discretion. They hate nothing more than someone who talks too much about the wrong thing or doesn't know HOW to talk about the right thing. They're indirect, so they could be talking about you to you and you'd never know. If you accused them of doing so, they'd never admit it. But they might say, "A hit dog sho' will holla." I never thought for a second that people didn't know. I just didn't know how much they knew.

Thank God I delivered over the winter break. The midwife came quickly, much to my surprise. I definitely needed her. She didn't ask anything. Just coached me through it, and after the baby came, she cleaned it up, smiled kindly, and left. Cleatis showed up a half hour later. I guessed she told him. Tears came when he looked into the baby's eyes. All he said was "Wow." I remember smiling and thinking we had created something beautiful. Then I thought about Marion and told him we had to tell her. It wasn't right and it wasn't fair. He told me to let him handle her, so I did. That's when he said he should be the one to raise the boy. It was a *boy* after all, he emphasized, one who needed to know how to be a man one day, and what did I know about being a man? Plus, he looked too much like Cleatis for anyone to deny it, so the decision was made. "Keepin' him would ruin you," Cleatis said. "And too many children need you. He'll be right here. Teach him whatever you need to." So that's what I did.

I don't know where he is now. Probably reading a book or arguing with someone about something. That boy was always questioning things! He said that, one day, he was going to call all the citizens of the world together and create one religion. I laughed, but he was serious. He said Jesus, Gandhi, and Muhammad would've been friends had they known each other. "They all taught the same thing!" he declared, sounding like a preacher. So if their followers would just come together, they'd probably discover a new spirituality—or at least throw their old concepts away—and realize that there was only one thing to do to be holy—love. I frowned at this twelve-year-old boy, birthing a theology out of the bowels of his belly. I knew then that he'd never be satisfied until he shifted the course of thinking in the world. I hope he's doing it now. I hope others are listening. . . .

The only thing that could destroy TL is his preoccupation with others' opinions of him. He always cared too much about that. I used to see how his spirit diminished when other children teased him or tried to make him fight. I could've helped him, but I wanted him to learn to stand up for himself. He didn't seek refuge in my authority anyway, not like other children; instead, he recoiled within himself as if bearing self-induced pain. He would have to be tougher to survive. I knew that much. His father's discipline seemed to have done the trick. TL thinks Cleatis is mean and cold, and I guess to a fragile, sensitive son he is, but Cleatis loves that boy. It's a shame he won't tell TL or show him, but I don't interfere. What could I say about doing something the right way?

I remember the day TL changed. Children were playing football in the field beside the school and one of the bigger boys ran into TL intentionally. I thought he'd probably quit the game and sulk, but suddenly he balled his fist and smashed it into the other boy's mouth. The children screamed as the two went at it. Normally, I would've stopped it immediately, but this time I waited to see what TL would do. The other boy's lip was bleeding pretty badly, but that didn't hinder his strength. He punched TL's right shoulder so hard I flinched. TL trembled but he didn't fall. They traded punches for the next few minutes until both of their faces were streaked with blood. That's when I went outside and made them stop. For the rest of the day, children bragged about TL having beaten Henry Joe, acting out the motions as if the two had been in a boxing ring. They were proud and surprised, I think. They didn't expect TL to do anything. Neither did I. But I guess there's a point in every young man's life when he decides whether to live or die, and TL must've been tired of dying.

He and Henry Joe were friends after that, so I stopped worrying about him. He hated fighting, but he could do it if he had to, and that's all I needed to know. His anger with his father was probably the adrenaline he needed to wrestle the world. He surely never knew that Cleatis sparked it intentionally.

"Yeah, right!" TL murmured, refusing to believe that Daddy was smarter than he'd presumed. A month before the incident, Daddy had brought home a set of boxing gloves one evening and tossed them at TL as he walked through the door.

"Put 'em on," he said casually, "and meet me in the barn in five minutes." He turned and exited.

"What?" TL said, but Daddy didn't repeat himself. Momma warned him not to underestimate his father's strength. Her admonition frightened him, but he tried not to show it. Willie James relayed the details later. He said that when TL entered the barn, Daddy was already gloved and dancing like Muhammad Ali. TL looked around, confused.

"You ready?" Daddy said, shuffling toward him.

"For what?"

The punch came so quickly TL didn't see it, but he certainly felt it. He stumbled to the ground.

"Aw shit, boy! Get some balls!" Daddy lumbered back a bit.

TL rose slowly, wondering what had gotten into this crazy man. He didn't want to fight him, but he appeared to have no choice.

"We jus' havin' a lil' fun. Don't take it so seriously. I jus' wanna see what you got. If you got anything at all."

His sarcasm unleashed TL's adrenaline. *I'm not some weak, puny country boy,* he wanted to say, *who doesn't know how to defend himself.* True enough, TL had never fought anyone, except Henry Joe, and that wasn't a real fight, but he wasn't about to let Daddy punk him.

"That's right! Get mad! Come on wit' it, boy!"

As Daddy teased, TL's fuse flamed. With newfound strength and confidence, he joined in the dance. Daddy's gratification increased. TL's aim was to get close enough to deliver one blow. Of course he couldn't beat Daddy—old man strength is real!—but he intended to make Daddy know he wasn't weak. He'd waited a lifetime for the opportunity, and damn if he wasn't going to take it.

TL could imagine his glove slamming into Daddy's wide, flat African nose, releasing a river of blood about which he wouldn't feel badly. After all, Daddy'd brought this on himself. Why did he want to box anyway? What was he trying to prove?

Dancing in closer, TL studied Daddy's eyes as his laughter multiplied. *This is nothing more than a joke to him, a way to humiliate me!* If it was the last thing he did that day, TL intended to make Daddy regret having used him for his own personal pleasure.

Daddy swung a left hook, which would've leveled TL, except that he dodged it quickly. Obviously surprised at the boy's agility, Daddy's laughter calmed to a pensive chuckle. TL watched the old man's movements, his rhythm, his timing. He was far more supple than TL would've guessed for a man his age, but even with that, TL continued plotting how he'd take him down. Or at least wound him.

Wham!

TL's left shoulder trembled from the blow, but he shook it off. Daddy winked. TL smiled patronizingly. Willie James chewed his bottom lip, hoping TL would knock Daddy out. The desire glistened in Willie James's eyes. He knew TL couldn't do it, but he urged TL on until the younger brother bore the weight of every son's subconscious desire to kick his father's ass. Just once. If nothing else, TL had to show the man he wasn't afraid of him anymore.

TL shuffled cautiously to keep from falling. That would've been his luck—to trip and crumble to the floor, inviting a lifetime of ridicule from which he'd never recover. Together, they danced a hypnotic dance, moving from side to side and jabbing the air with gloved fists in preparation for someone's knockout. Daddy moved in closer.

"TL! Watch out!" Willie James cried.

A sudden move to the right saved his left eye. The rush of air following Daddy's failed punch convinced TL that this was no game. The old man had swung to kill.

TL had no choice now. He had to hurt Daddy. Either that, or Daddy was going to hurt him.

Cloaked in a royal-blue, long-sleeved shirt, with sleeves rolled up to the elbows, and worn, bleached blue jeans stained with grease, Daddy actually looked ten years younger than usual. It was amazing, TL noted, how he danced so easily in those heavy, steel-toed brogans. Actually, TL had clearly underestimated the man's finesse, and the more TL looked at him, the more afraid he became. Confidence and pride seeped from Daddy's pores, while TL exhibited nothing but nerves and fragility. Daddy was sure he'd win; he just didn't know how long TL would last. TL didn't know, either. If only he could get close enough to deliver one good punch, he'd quit, he told himself. Yet, from the looks of things, Daddy wasn't going to allow that. If TL hit him, it would result solely from his own cunning and stealth. Something unexpected needed to happen. Something Daddy couldn't foresee.

Willie James coaxed TL along. Whenever he moved, his big brother was behind him, whispering instructions only TL could hear. Daddy glanced at Willie James occasionally and shook his head. *Why hadn't he given Willie James the gloves?* TL asked himself. *He was the oldest! The fight would've made more sense. Willie James was almost Daddy's size, and everyone knew he was strong as an ox. He might not have beaten Daddy, but his chances would've been far greater than TL's.* TL was half Willie James's size, and two inches shorter, so he couldn't understand what achievement it would be for Daddy to level him.

"Hit him on the left, TL. That's his weak side."

TL had forgotten. Years ago, Daddy had broken his arm when the old tractor turned over on him. The wheels had locked and, trying to brace his fall, he splintered his left arm. It healed, but he couldn't lift it quite as high as the other. Most people never noticed.

If he'd had the time, he would've exchanged his tight overalls for something looser and more comfortable. The close fit worked for revealing an amazing physique, but now the snug denim clung to him like the Shroud of Turin, restricting his movements. As he danced, the overalls seemed to tighten until, like the Incredible Hulk, he wanted to scream and break free. But he couldn't worry about that now. He had to concentrate on getting his glove to Daddy's face.

The old man rushed in again, and TL retreated.

"Don't let him intimidate you, man," Willie James murmured. "Make your move this time. It might be the last chance you get."

Hungry for a victory, Daddy gazed at TL and plotted his strategy. He shuffled closer, then closer still, and TL knew something was about to happen. He stopped retreating and stood his ground. If he backed away any farther, he'd look like a coward; if he charged forward, he'd be a fool. So he trembled in place, dancing the dance of terror. Daddy perceived his angst and swung a right jab. Like before, TL barely dodged it, but this time, his glove, like a heavy field plow, burrowed into Daddy's left shoulder. He hadn't meant to hit him there. He'd aimed for Daddy's cheek but his reach fell short. He didn't care. He'd hit him and that had been the point. Daddy closed his eyes momentarily, wincing with pain.

"Knock him out, man! Do it now!"

TL threw a hard right into Daddy's nose, and sent him stumbling backward. Blood trickled down his top lip. Suddenly TL felt ashamed.

"Yes!" Willie James shouted.

Daddy wiped blood on his sleeve, nodded affirmingly, and resumed the dance. TL had hoped they could quit now, but apparently not. Daddy shook his left arm as if it were asleep, then said, "Good. Good." TL didn't know what "good" meant, but he knew it wasn't good for him. Daddy's laughter returned dry and sinister. He eased upon TL and delivered a right hook, which TL thought he had dodged, but when he regained consciousness, he found himself on the barn floor.

"TL! TL!" Willie James shouted, slapping the boy's face.

The room swirled and swayed. TL felt nauseous.

"You okay, man?"

He blinked, but didn't speak. Willie James raised him to a full sit-up position. TL looked around. Daddy was gone.

"What happened?" he mumbled.

Willie James chuckled. "What happened? Daddy knocked you out! That's what happened!"

"And he just walked away?"

"Naw, not at first. He made sure you was breathin'."

With Willie James rubbing his back, TL recovered. Together, they stood. The room swirled again and TL clutched Willie James's arm.

"Take it easy, man."

"I'm all right. I ain't dead." He leaned against a pillar in the center of the barn.

"You want some water?"

"Yeah. That'd be good."

TL's breathing stabilized as Willie James ran into the house. When he returned, TL gulped and said, "At least he didn't punk me."

"Naw, he didn't punk you. You did way better'n I thought you would."

They laughed.

Daddy returned, with a look of sincere concern. He'd changed into ragged boots and a T-shirt, and wore an expression far less aggressive than before. As he approached, Willie James retreated like a young lion conceding his kill to the master.

"I didn't hurt you, did I?"

"No sir. I'm fine."

"All right." Daddy examined TL's face. "You done good, boy. I didn't know you had it in you."

TL wasn't sure, either, but he had to try. Now, he felt proud.

Daddy turned and filled the cows' bucket with feed.

"I didn't mean to hit your bad arm. I was trying to hit—"

"You ain't got to apologize. You did what you had to." Lifting the bucket with his right hand, he added, "That's what a man's 'posed to do."

TL brushed his overalls and walked toward the barn door.

"Sometimes a man'll try you, son, and you gotta be ready. If you ain't, he'll kill you. You don't always get time to prepare. Stay ready and you won't have to get ready."

"You're my father! Why are you trying me?"

" 'Cause it's my job to get you ready. If a man kicks yo' ass, it'll be 'cause you *won't* fight—not 'cause you *can't*."

Daddy hauled the five-gallon bucket of feed through the barn door and into the field. TL never feared another man.

CHAPTER 14

ONVERTING MS. SWINTON'S HOUSE INTO *HIS* HOME
was far more work than TL had imagined. Her spirit per-
meated everything—the floral curtains, cabinets, bed-
spread, glistening white kitchen, immaculate flower bed in the
front. This was simply *her* house, and he was having a hard time
making it his. But he had to do it. He had nowhere else to live, and
he was tired of running. Whenever he attempted to change things
in the house, he felt disrespectful, as if he had no right to be there.
He did have a right, didn't he? Doesn't a son have a right to his
mother's things? Does it matter that they hadn't *lived* as mother
and son? He couldn't even leave a cup in the sink without feeling
bad! He had to do something. He couldn't live like this forever.

TL rose and slid into a pair of old jeans and a brown-and-tan-
striped short-sleeved shirt. He knew what he needed to do, and he
knew that if he didn't do it then, he never would.

An hour or so later, he and Willie James returned from Home
Depot with three gallons of paint, various size brushes and rollers,
and other supplies. Willie James dropped him off, and TL went to

work. He didn't intend to spend another day trapped in someone else's world.

The first thing was to remove those heavy, dusty, red velvet drapes. Standing on a chair, TL unhooked them carefully as streams of sunlight burst into the living room. The brightness energized him. TL wasn't sure if he'd cover the windows again, but if he did, he thought, the material would definitely be thinner and lighter. From the walls, he extracted cherrywood-framed paintings of fruit and landscapes and antique black-and-white portraits of people, probably relatives, he didn't know. Some were beautiful, but none was smiling. They appeared upset about something they couldn't articulate.

His momentum slowed once he began painting. In fact, if someone had told him how exhausting it would be, he probably wouldn't have done it. The initial idea was thrilling, so he rushed forward without thinking it through. The painting itself wasn't so bad; it was the prep work that killed him. First, he taped off the ceiling and moldings. Slowly, tediously, meticulously. It had to be right. He'd inherited two mothers' anal natures, so sloppiness was out of the question. If he messed things up, he'd have to start again, and he definitely didn't intend to do that. Hours later, he covered the furniture and floors with old sheets and plastic so as not to spill any paint on Ms. Swinton's priceless antiques and polished floors.

By sundown, those once-white walls were grass green. All except one. A lady at Home Depot had convinced him to leave an accent wall, as she called it, so he did. It matched the built-in white bookshelves perfectly. TL stepped back and nodded. The red sofa clashed with the green walls, but that was okay for now. New furniture would come in time. He just needed the house to feel like his own, like he was *supposed* to be there.

Willie James helped paint the bedroom the following day. It went from yellow to ocean blue. The floral window dressings got tossed and replaced with three-tone blue curtains. TL kept the fluffy white comforter and matching pillows, more for their feel than their look, but since they complemented the blue color scheme, he wasn't dissatisfied. The nineteenth-century vanity was too pretty to discard, so he let it stay. It definitely disturbed the masculine vibe of the room, but he didn't care. He'd never been very committed to masculinity anyway.

For the rest of the day, he milled about the house, removing shiny ceramic animals from dressers and countertops until he had a paper bag full of them. Most rested on delicate, lace doilies, in the shape of snowflakes. He never understood why southern women collected them. And why so damn many? They definitely had to go!

Once he cleared everything out, including her clothes, which went to the Salvation Army, the house felt empty but free. And it was *his*. He wanted black art everywhere, with the faces of his people overlooking him. He'd always liked paintings of people. He'd told George once that facial portraits give a place a communal feeling and remind you that you're not alone. He needed that reminder now more than ever.

With no rent to pay, TL figured he could live off the thousand dollars or so he had in the bank. It would be tight for a couple of months, but he didn't have anything to buy except food, and, often, people gave him that. He went from house to house each week, visiting families of children he'd be teaching, and folks sent him home with bags of frozen purple hull peas, okra, sweet yellow corn on the cob, tomatoes, cabbage, and turnip greens. And this was the 1990s! Sometimes he got ham shoulders, fresh ground hot sausage, which he loved, and ziplock bags of crappie or catfish (whichever they had at the time), so he never starved.

What surprised him most was how timid the children were. They escaped to back rooms or backyards when he arrived, as if they feared his authority. Children were like that years ago, but hadn't times changed? he wondered. Kids in New York would've laughed at the deference these kids gave teachers. TL chuckled and thanked God he was from the backwoods of Arkansas.

At the McDaniels', he met a nine-year-old boy named Ezekiel. His father, Gary, and TL had gone to school together and traded homework sometimes. Gary wasn't necessarily smart, but he worked harder than anyone in the class. Ms. Swinton liked that about him. He never said much, but he always had his homework. Always. Now, he was married with four children, Ezekiel being the oldest, and everyone agreed the boy was his spitting image.

"Hey in there!" TL hollered, knocking on the old wooden screen door. The main door was open and the screen unlocked, but of course he couldn't enter without invitation. It was an overcast Sunday afternoon.

"Man, come on in here!" Gary said, opening the screen wide. They shook and half hugged. "Angela! TL's here!"

"Oh, don't bother her. She might be in the back, resting." He sat on a brown leather sofa and instantly felt the heat. All the windows were open, but no air was stirring.

"She ain't sleep. Just piddlin' 'round wit' that no-'count sewin' machine."

Angela appeared in a paper-thin, pink-and-white house duster. TL stood. The shadow of her bra and panties shone through, embarrassing him slightly. She was taller than Gary by several inches and much darker, with short, feathered, straight hair. Wide eyes and pearly white teeth made her glamorous.

"Hey, TL," she called sweetly. "How you doin'?" They embraced.

"Good! I didn't mean to bother y'all. Just wanted to come meet the boys."

Angela stood slightly behind Gary as if to assure him he was the head of the house. "Oh, that's fine," she said. "They 'round here somewhere, gettin' into God only knows what."

TL laughed along.

"Sit down, man," Gary said. "I can't believe you 'bout to be the new teacher. Who in the world woulda guessed you'd come back here?"

"I know, right? Man, you couldn't've convinced me in a million years."

"It makes sense though. You was the best student in the class. You gon' be a hell of a teacher, too. I couldn't think of nobody better. Ms. Swinton definitely woulda chose you."

She did choose me!

"I can't believe you're married, Gary. And kids?"

"Yeah, man. Ain't nothin' else to do 'round here."

They talked shop awhile, then Gary rose to get the boys.

"Oh no! I'll go out back and see them myself, if you don't mind."

"Okay, help yo'self. But be careful. They a rowdy bunch!"

"Man, please. I grew up here, too, remember? I know how to handle boys."

TL found his way to the back door and into the yard. The boys stopped playing when they saw him.

"Hey, fellas! What's going on?"

They waved politely and mumbled, "Nothin'."

The three youngest favored their mother. They were skinny, but not frail, probably six, four, and two years old. Each had narrow, piercing eyes that seemed to hide beneath protruding brows, and oval, slender faces with small, sloping foreheads. They'd be handsome one day, TL presumed. Their dark clothes were so worn he could see their flesh in a few places, especially the two-year-old's, and each boy's pants were obviously too short. As TL spoke, they drew together in fear or reverence, and looked at each other before answering any of his questions.

But not Ezekiel. He stood alone beneath a small plum tree, with his round head nodding excitedly as TL talked. More than his brothers, he was warm-spirited and confident. His energy overwhelmed anyone who encountered him. The white of his eyes and teeth contrasted so intensely with his beautiful dark complexion that

TL couldn't stop staring. Clearly the oldest, he was a bit thicker than the others and not quite as athletic in build. His clothes appeared untouched, and his shoes looked brand new. He'd been reading something. As his brothers shied away, he drew nearer.

"What's your name, young man?"

With shoulders back, he shouted, "Ezekiel. But everybody calls me Zeke." His smile revealed a large gap where three front teeth used to be. TL cackled.

"I see. You're mighty friendly, Mr. Ezekiel."

"Yessir!"

"What are you reading?"

He displayed the cover. "I got it for Christmas. I done read it a thousand times, but I like it, so I keep readin' it over and over."

"Do you have a lot of books?"

"No sir, not a lot, but I got a few."

"You mean you *have* a few."

"Yessir, I *have* a few."

The correction didn't dampen his joy. It seemed to invigorate him. TL had never seen a child so eager. Ezekiel danced from one foot to the other as they spoke.

"How old are you, Mr. Ezekiel?"

"Nine years old, sir!"

He shouted like an air force cadet answering a lieutenant.

"I guess you like school, huh?"

"Yessir! I like it a lot!"

They were practically toe-to-toe. The excitement in Ezekiel's eyes radiated, causing TL to shiver with joy.

"I'm in the third grade, sir. Well, I'm goin' to the third, but I just finished the second." He rubbed his hands nervously.

"Oh, I see. I bet you're smart."

His eyes widened. "Yessir, I am!"

Gary called from the back porch, "Don't let him talk you to death, TL. He'll try if you let him."

Ezekiel's enthusiasm never faded.

"Oh no! He's fine. I like this young man."

When TL touched the crown of the boy's head, Ezekiel twitched with glee. His smile exposed the gap again, causing TL to laugh out loud.

"I'm your new teacher, you know?"

"Really?" Ezekiel beamed and clapped lightly.

"Really. I hope we'll get to be good friends."

"Oh, we will, sir! We will!"

They shook on it, then TL said he had to go.

"Okay, but can I ask you somethin' first?"

"Sure. Go ahead."

"What's yo' name?"

"Tommy Lee Tyson. But you can call me Dr. Tyson."

"You a *real* doctor?"

"Yes I am."

"Like the ones in the hospitals?"

"No, not that kind. I'm a PhD doctor. The kind who teaches in colleges and universities."

"Wow. I ain't never met no doctor like that befo'. I'm glad you our new teacher, Dr. Tyson."

"Well, I'm glad, too, Mr. Zeke."

Without announcement or hesitation, Ezekiel threw his arms around TL's waist and squeezed hard. Then he let go. "I'ma be a doctor like you when I grow up!" He raced back to the tree and sat with his back against the trunk. He waved as TL disappeared into the house.

A few other precocious children surfaced throughout the community, like Amanda Cole, Mr. Somebody's great-granddaughter, who shared Ezekiel's intelligence but not his zeal, and Bradley Johnson, the funniest kid the good Lord ever made, although he couldn't spell his own name. Yet Ezekiel McDaniel was in a class by himself.

A week later, TL sat in his newly renovated living room, pondering who else might know about his sister's death, when he heard a light knock on the door.

"Come in."

He saw the small hand push the screen before he saw the face.

"Hello? Dr. Tyson?" Ezekiel called.

"Yes? Yes! Hello there! What a surprise." TL stood. "How good to see you."

"It's good to see you, too, sir!" The child's energy boiled. They nodded in silence until he said, "Daddy said it was okay if I come by to see you. I didn't want nothin' though."

"Well, thank you for thinking of me, Mr. Ezekiel. That's very kind."

His gap made TL smile again. Sporting black slacks and a white short-sleeved shirt with a multicolored bow tie, he stared at his new teacher with unbridled admiration.

"Why are you so dressed up?"

"Oh. Um . . . I don't know. Just thought that since I was comin' to see a doctor I'd better be presentable."

TL nodded. "Yessir. Have a seat. Would you like something to eat or drink?"

"Oh, no sir. We not 'lowed to eat at other folks' houses. Daddy said it makes people think he don't feed us."

"I understand."

Ezekiel sat on the edge of the red velvet sofa, with his feet flat on the hardwood floor and hands on his knees. If TL hadn't known better, he might've thought the boy had come for an interview. Still in pajamas and a white V-neck T-shirt, TL lounged in the opposite chair while Ezekiel surveyed him. There was obviously something he needed.

"So . . . what can I do for you?"

"Oh, nothin'." Ezekiel's wide, bright eyes examined the room. "I like all the different colors, sir. It makes the room feel . . . fun."

"Well, I'm glad you like it."

"I do!" he yelled.

Moments of silence passed. *What does this child want?* "Is there . . . um . . . something you'd like to talk about?"

"No sir." Ezekiel's contentment was all the more troubling.

TL couldn't fake it anymore. "Son, why are you here?"

"'Cause I wanna be a college doctor one day. Just like you. Daddy said I need to see what college doctors do, so I asked him if I could come over here and watch you."

"Ha! That's mighty flattering, Mr. Zeke, but I'm afraid my life isn't very exciting. I'm still settling into my mother's house, as you can see, so that's what I do most of the time. That, and read a few books occasionally."

"What kinda books?" His good Sunday shoes tapped a slow rhythm onto the floor.

"A short story collection called *Some Soul to Keep* and a biography of Paul Laurence Dunbar."

"Who's that?"

For the next hour, Ezekiel drilled TL about everything the boy had ever wondered. He simply never tired. TL became irritated although he tried not to show it. When he moved from the living room to the kitchen, Ezekiel followed like a desperate reporter, oblivious to the possibility that TL might've had other things to do. Ezekiel voluntarily swept the floor as TL washed dishes, all the while asking more questions about life outside of Swamp Creek. He reminded TL of himself at that age.

"You got a wife?"

Here we go. "Excuse me?"

"A wife. You got one?"

"No. Not yet."

"Why not?"

"I don't know. Guess it's not time."

"A grown man's s'pose to have a wife, ain't he?"

"Not necessarily. Who says that?"

"My daddy."

"Well, some men do, some don't."

"Which ones don't?"

TL huffed. "The ones who decide not to, I suppose."

"Oh." Ezekiel muttered. His silence was the first break TL had had since the boy arrived. They sat at Ms. Swinton's oval four-seater dinette set. TL began to tell Ezekiel the story of him and Henry Joe fighting in the schoolyard when, suddenly, Ezekiel's face went blank. He hung his head the way children do when they think they're in trouble. TL waited for an explanation. When he didn't get one, he lifted Ezekiel's chin lovingly and said, "What's wrong, son?"

Zeke looked everywhere except at TL. Tears streaked the child's dark chocolate cheeks as TL touched his hand.

"Daddy hits Momma sometimes."

"What? What are you talking about?"

Ezekiel sniffled. "He beats her, Dr. Tyson, and sometimes it's real bad."

"I don't believe that," TL said, although he knew Zeke wasn't lying.

"It's true. Not all the time, but sometimes." With his free hand he wiped his eyes. "She say it don't hurt, but I know it do. Her face be swole up."

TL's first thought was to accompany Zeke home and confront Gary about the matter, then he considered that maybe Ezekiel was there precisely because he didn't want to be at home. Withholding the impulse to hug the boy, for fear of impropriety, TL grabbed Ezekiel's hands again and squeezed them tighter.

"I'm so sorry, son."

Zeke hung his head. "I thought that maybe if you had a wife and you hit her, you could tell me why men do that." His tone was pitiful.

"I wouldn't hit my wife, son, if I had one. It's wrong. And it's against the law."

"Then why my daddy do it?"

"I don't know, Zeke. I don't know why any man hits his wife, or any woman for that matter. But I know it's wrong. You remember that much, you understand me?"

"Yessir."

After patting the boy's shoulders, TL offered a glass of ice cold, red Kool-Aid. Zeke's spirit revived. "Please don't tell Daddy I told you, Dr. Tyson. Okay? I'll get a killin'."

Against his better judgment, TL promised he wouldn't.

Ezekiel left, but returned almost every day thereafter. TL couldn't get rid of him! Some mornings, the boy sat on Ms. Swinton's porch long before TL rose. He could hear Ezekiel, reading aloud and pacing back and forth like a Shakespearean actor. Gary told TL that Zeke would get up extra early and do his chores so he could go see "the doctor." However, TL's flattery soon dissipated. Some days, he simply didn't want to be bothered, although he endured him anyway. TL left a key under the front mat, which, once discovered, Zeke never hesitated to use, and their daily ritual was discovering some word Zeke didn't know. He'd thumb arbitrary books on the shelves and read until he got stumped. Words like "myopic" and "succinct" became part of his vocabulary long before he needed them, and multiple whippings resulted from his attempt to be what country folks called "uppity."

Whenever Gary was on the rampage, Zeke would come sullen and quiet, as if believing, somehow, that his silence contributed to his mother's healing. He'd explain what she looked like, recoiled and weeping in a corner, or, other times, running out the back door, but Gary would always catch her and reprimand her for some trivial offense. Some days Zeke would cry, others he wouldn't, but he always shared his heart. Involuntarily, TL became his confidant and mentor, but, over time, he feared the boy had grown too emotionally dependent. Yet what other choice did he have?

One blazing hot afternoon in mid-July, they sat on the porch, fanning hot air, when a brand-new, sparkling, olive-green Nissan Maxima turned into the driveway. Ezekiel asked if TL was expecting company. TL said no, he didn't know who it was. The windows were tinted, so neither of them could make out the image. Whoever it was certainly wasn't from Swamp Creek. Folks there didn't believe in buying much of anything brand new.

When the door opened and the gentleman exited, TL rushed Ezekiel away. The boy didn't understand, and TL didn't have time to explain.

"Shit, it's hot down here!" George hollered, dabbing his forehead with a handkerchief.

TL stood trembling at the edge of the porch. *This can't be real. There's no way George Thornton is in Swamp Creek, Arkansas!*

"No, it ain't no ghost, chile!" He slammed the car door shut and looked around. "It's just me in the flesh." His khaki shorts were much too short and his red-and-white, cut-off muscle shirt much too tight. TL's mouth wouldn't close.

"Aw, you knew I was coming. Don't play! You didn't know when, but you should've been expecting me."

TL wasn't. George walked toward the porch, swaying slightly. They embraced a long time as memories, which TL had tried to bury, resurfaced. TL hadn't been hugged like that since he left New York.

"How the hell did you find me!" TL screamed.

George took Ezekiel's chair and shouted even louder, "Very carefully! You live in the goddamn boondocks *for real!*"

Tell me I'm dreaming, oh God!

"Man, I been driving around for thirty minutes trying to find this house. Everybody said 'the white house down the road,' but, hell, all the houses are white down this road!" George crossed his hairy legs. His pants were so tight the crotch bulged.

TL still couldn't believe George was there. "You drove all the way from New York City?"

"Hell naw! I wasn't missing you *that* much! Who drives from New York to rural Arkansas? I flew to Little Rock and rented a car."

"How'd you know how to get here?"

"That's what they make maps for, kiddo. I ain't smart as you, but I can read." He winked. TL's head shook.

Years later, Ezekiel confessed that he didn't go home that day, but rather watched the exchange from the corner of the house. At first he didn't understand George's unorthodox behavior, but then he laughed at him. Had he known the word "queer," he might've used it, and had he known that others would soon think of him similarly, he might've studied George more closely. As it was, Zeke giggled at the New Yorker who left the impressionable country boy with the notion that a man—a real, grown, black man—didn't have to act the way he'd been taught a man was supposed to act.

"What are you doing here?"

George frowned. "What do you mean what am I doing here?"

"I mean, why did you come all the way from New York—"

"Just to see you?" George blinked repeatedly.

"You know what I mean. Who jumps on a plane and flies halfway across America unannounced?"

"Me!" He slapped TL's leg affectionately, then cackled and reclined into the chair. "Relax, man. I'm not stalking you. I just wanted to make sure you were all right. That's what friends do, right?"

"Yep. That's what friends do."

George wiped his brow. "Shit! It's hot as hell down here, man! You ain't got nothin' to drink?"

TL went inside and returned with glasses of cold lemonade.

George swallowed fast and hard, like a dying man in the desert. "I told Miss Zuri I was coming."

"Oh hell! Tell me you didn't!"

"I sure did! Shit, I ain't scared of that chick. That's your role."

If there was any possibility of a future relationship with Zuri, it was gone now.

"I told her she could come with me if she wanted to, but she said no thank you. Stuck-up hussy! I ain't never liked her."

"The feeling's mutual."

"Well, that's fine with me. She can just find herself another man."

What? TL was too afraid to ask what he meant. Something about George's presence left him unsettled. He was certainly glad to see him, and glad that he meant enough to George for him to make such a sacrifice, but TL admitted in his heart that the distance had offered a nice break from questions he hadn't yet answered. *It's funny,* he thought, *how your past has a way of following you, especially the part you don't want.*

They rose to go inside when Daddy's truck pulled behind George's rental.

"Oh no! It's my father. Please be cool, George. I gotta live here."

George smiled, tugging at the frayed edges of his shorts. "This is the man I been waiting to meet!"

CHAPTER 15

DADDY NODDED CASUALLY AS HE STEPPED ONTO THE porch. "Afternoon, fellas! Hot enough for ya?"

"Yessir!" TL said.

George murmured, "I ain't never felt nothin' like this."

"Well, it's hotter'n this someplace else."

Daddy proceeded to tell TL, "Yo' uncle Rayford's low sick. Don't know how much time he got left. Thought you'd wanna know. Call yo' momma when you get a chance."

"I will, I will."

He looked at George. "How you doin', young man? You from 'round here?"

"Oh no, sir. I'm from New York. My name's George Thornton. It's good to meet you." George extended his hand and cringed when Daddy crushed it. "TL talks about you all the time."

"Is that right?" Daddy said, released George's hand. "Well, I hope he said good things. It's good to meet you. What you doin' here?"

"I just came to check up on my buddy. He was due back weeks

ago, but he didn't make it, so I thought I'd make sure nobody kidnapped him!"

Daddy's eyes bulged. "You can't get kidnapped *at home,* son. How much sense that make?"

George gasped.

"He must be where the good Lawd want him, else he'd be in New Yawk wit' you." Daddy descended the steps and slang over his left shoulder, "You fellas have a good afternoon, hear?" From the truck window, he waved and hollered, "And, young man, see if you can't find some britches yo' size. It's too hot down here for all o' that. A man needs to be free, to let his stuff breathe. Talk to you boys later."

When the truck disappeared, TL and George collapsed into the porch chairs.

"Did your father just read me?"

TL's laughter echoed in George's head.

"Oh my God! That man just read the shit out of me!"

They screamed for several minutes. Actually, TL was relieved. Part of his apprehension about George's presence was how others would respond to him. Now TL knew. And he loved it.

They lounged on the porch, talking 'til sundown. George asked about the boy who ran away when he arrived, so TL told him everything. George said they should march over there and kick Gary's black ass. The fact that he didn't know the man was irrelevant, he said. The point was to take a stand against domestic violence and show those boys an example of men fighting for the lives of women. TL didn't disagree; he just wanted to handle the situation differently since he had to live in Swamp Creek. George shrugged and surrendered.

When he asked about Sister, the rhythm of the conversation changed. TL felt overwhelmed all of a sudden, like one finally purging his heart from years of emotional distress. George asked if TL had learned anything new, and he said no, except what Daddy had said—that Willie James didn't know what he thought he knew. George pondered for a moment, then offered what TL already knew—there was more to the story. It just didn't make sense, he said. TL agreed, but didn't know what else to do. George warned him not to play his folks dumb. "That father of yours? That man that just played my card? Don't sleep on him. He's razor sharp! I'm telling you! Hell, he just read me as smooth as anyone I've ever known! You used to say 'country don't mean crazy' and now I know what you mean. Believe me, there's more to this story and this place"—he looked around—"than people are telling you."

They went inside and made spaghetti for supper. When darkness fell, TL and George walked the dirt roads of Swamp Creek, sharing the missing pieces of their lives. TL told George about everyone in Swamp Creek—Cliffesteen, Aunt Easter, Uncle Jesse Lee, Mr. Blue—and showed him where most of them lived. Many stayed on the same land, often in the same houses, as their foreparents. George was amazed at the amount of space individual families owned. Some homes sat on fifty acres and others on more than one hundred. The houses weren't fancy. Most were A-frames with full-length front porches and huge fireplaces that roared in the winter. Residents avoided central heating and cooling, unable to understand why anyone would pay hundreds of dollars a month for heat when all they had to do was build a fire. In the summer, no one needed air-conditioning, since everyone was outdoors all day, and at night people simply opened windows and went to bed, confident that, at some point, God would send a cool breeze. George noted that black people in New York thought they were rich but owned nothing, while black people in Swamp Creek thought they were poor but owned everything.

Overhead, a full moon glistened amid neon stars.

"I like it here, TL. I really do." George gazed upward. "I don't know why. I'm a city boy, but there's something about this slow, easy feel that works for me. Maybe I just like the country."

"I like it, too," TL said. "It's a beautiful place. I realize that more every day."

George took TL's hand and intertwined their fingers. TL felt awkward at first, but then relaxed. It'd been a long time since he'd been touched sensually, in any kind of way, and only now did he realize how much he'd missed it. Plus, in the dark, there was no one to fear.

Before entering the house, they paused again on the front porch. "I ain't never loved nobody the way I love you, TL."

"I love you, too, man. We gon' always be brothers."

George sneered and dropped his hand. "Really? Wow. Okay. If that's the way you want it, that's the way it'll be."

TL hadn't meant to play dumb, but he wasn't ready for that conversation. They went inside to bed. George took the guest room, but he didn't wake up there.

"WE CAN'T live like this," TL said the next morning.

George rubbed sleep from his eyes. "What do you mean?" It was his turn to play dumb. "Live like what? We didn't do anything!"

"I know, but we could've. It's just too much to play with, and now there's too much distance between us. It'd just be easier to be clear." TL wrapped himself with a terry cloth blue robe and shuffled to the bathroom.

"Are you confused?" George shouted sarcastically. "You don't seem confused to me. You made it clear last night that we were brothers, so what else is there to be clear about?"

"You know what I mean!"

George entered the bathroom nude. TL peeked from the shower.

"That's what I mean! You can't do stuff like that!"

"Why not? You've seen me naked a thousand times! Why is it a problem now?"

TL didn't want to say. His feelings vacillated, between a

convoluted heart and a recalcitrant head, leaving him sure he'd soon contradict the clarity he was trying to establish. He felt far more vulnerable in Swamp Creek, for whatever reason, than he'd been in New York. They'd never had sex, but he always knew George was willing. What he didn't know was whether he was. Now, he was too afraid to find out.

"Don't make this harder than it needs to be, George." TL hated he couldn't be honest.

George left the bathroom. "You a trip, man."

By the time TL finished showering, George had already fixed breakfast. Amidst palpable tension, they sat at the little oval table, in front of the bay window, and ate in silence. TL wanted to thank him, again, for having come all the way from New York to make sure he was okay, but he feared George would take it the wrong way. Knowing him, he'd feel insulted and demeaned, TL assumed, because he didn't want to be *thanked*. He wanted to be loved, embraced, coveted, and that was more than TL could do. So, as TL chewed nervously, George glanced from plates to refrigerator to countertops to squirrels in the yard, all the while contemplating why he had come, and reprimanding himself mentally for wanting what he couldn't have.

This is all my fault! Why can't I ever tell George the truth? TL cleared his plate without uttering a word. *Maybe because I can't tell myself!* Pounding the table with his fist, he appeared childish or at least melodramatic in the company of a man who knew precisely what he felt and whom he wanted. George had always been that way. He looked at TL, finally, with an expression of pity. Between the two, TL was the lesser man, he was sure, for remaining bound while holding the keys to his own freedom. George would never have done that.

They finished eating and TL cleared the dishes.

"Don't bother washing them," George said. "I got it."

"Oh no, man. You cooked. This is the least I can do!"

George grabbed TL's wrist firmly but lovingly. "I said don't bother, okay? Just let me do it. I need something to occupy my mind."

There was pleading in George's voice, so TL surrendered. Later, they dressed for church without saying anything. George sported a handsome baby-blue-and-white seersucker suit with white square-toe shoes. The outfit complemented his thick, nicely groomed, jet-black goatee. TL told him he looked handsome. George cackled and said, "Okay. If only it mattered to you." Before exiting the car at the church, he added, "I'm sorry. This is just not what I expected. I thought we had something, but apparently not. I still shouldn't be a baby about it."

"I understand."

"Actually, you don't, but that ain't the point. The point is that I'm too old for this bullshit." He flashed a fake smile. "So let's go in here and praise the Lord."

Neither knew it was Pastor's Anniversary Sunday. Several churches visited from nearby areas, swelling the crowd to capacity. St. Matthew's deacons combined with others and performed devotion like TL hadn't witnessed in years. "Guide me over, Thou great Jehovah! Pilgrim through this barren land!" Deacon Usher cried, in a tenor that penetrated people's souls. The congregation sang back each word. Folks said his was the only voice they'd ever heard that might beat Sam Cooke's. Then, after another deacon knelt before a fold-up chair and prayed himself hoarse, Deacon Usher crooned, "Bread of heaven, bread of heaven! Feed me 'til I want no more!" The walls of the church vibrated as he lined the hymn and people responded. *This was the way black folks use to have church—before we started looking for someone else's God.*

Reverend Lindsay asked the Barnes sisters to come forward and render a selection. They'd been singing together for forty years. Two of them, Miss Ida and Miss Cora Lee, were short, round, full-chested women, and the oldest sister, Miss Johnnie Mae, was tall and lean. She sang lead. People clapped loudly, shouting requests as the sisters shuffled forward.

"First giving honor to God," Miss Johnnie Mae said, "Who is the head of my life, I give thanks and praise just for waking up this morning!"

"Amen!" people roared.

"And for a reasonable portion of health and strength."

"Sho'nuff!"

She talked a while longer, then said, "We gon' sing this little song and get on out of the way."

The crowd hushed and waited. TL prepared to be wrecked like he used to be whenever the Barnes sisters sang.

Miss Johnnie Mae cleared her throat and began in a boisterous soprano, "Have you heeeeeard of a city, the streets are paved with gold!"

TL's hands shot into the air. He hadn't heard them sing that song in years, but he'd always loved it. George chuckled with joy. She continued:

Have you heard of a city, the streets are paved with gold!
Have you heard of a city, the streets are paved with gold!
There are twelve gates to the city, hallelu!

Everyone was standing, swaying, or clapping. Miss Johnnie Mae began to walk the aisles. TL knew he wouldn't make it.

Three gates in the east,

Her sisters backed her up with, "Oh yes!"

  Three gates in the west!
  Three gates in the north!
Oh yes!
  Three gates in the south!
Oh yes!
  There are twelve gates to the city!

> *Twenty-four elders in the city!*
> Oh yes!
> *Forty-eight angels in the city!*
> Oh yes!
> *Great big beautiful city, Hallelu!*

Deacons carried Miss Polly out after Usher Board No. 1 confiscated her glasses. Others shouted, too, but there just weren't enough nurses in the Nurses' Guild to handle everyone. TL's spirit was so invigorated he thought he might sprout wings and fly away.

Miss Johnnie Mae went to the vamp:

Why don't you meet me!

Her sisters responded, "Meet me in the city!"

> *A city built foursquare!*
> *Meet me in the city!*
> *Walls of jasper!*
> *Meet me in the city!*
> *Streets of purest gold!*
> *Meet me in the city!*
> *All the angels there!*
> *Meet me in the city!*
> *No more dying!*
> *Meet me in the city!*
> *Every day like Sunday!*
> *Meet me in the city!*
> *Glory hallelujah!*
> *Meet me in the city!*

She ad-libbed 'til the Holy Ghost came. Even Momma wiped her eyes. She'd always said that, when she died, she wanted the Barnes sisters to sing her in.

There are . . .
      Twelve gates to the city, Hallelu!

Half the congregation cried, the other half shouted. George's eyes streamed with tears. His arms were folded tightly. He was trying not to succumb to the power of the spirit, but he was fighting a losing battle.

Suddenly, Miss Johnnie Mae hollered, "My mother's over there!" and her sisters answered, "Waitin' for me in the city!"

George stood, screaming at the top of his lungs. He fumbled across TL to get to the aisle where he collapsed to his knees, wailing like Mary and Martha at Jesus's tomb.

My father's over there!
      Waitin' for me in the city!
All of God's children!
      Waitin' for me in the city!
My long white robe!
      Waitin' for me in the city!
A crown of gold!
      Waitin' for me in the city!
There are . . .
      Twelve gates to the city, Hallelu!

Miss Johnnie Mae laid hands on George as she sang. He was in another world now. TL had never seen him like that, but TL was happy for him. He knew the feeling. George had told him once that he was agnostic, that he didn't really care whether there was a God or not, but at that moment TL hoped George was having a change of heart. Moments like this made TL appreciate having been forced as a child to go to church.

After the benediction, the Mothers, dressed in first Sunday white, hugged George and told him to keep his hands in God's hands. He nodded and promised he would. Then everyone moved to the church kitchen for dinner, as is the tradition on Pastor's Anniversary Sunday.

TL noticed that George's demeanor had shifted. He wasn't bubbling over, but somewhere in the midst of that city made of gold, he must've decided something or seen something or come to understand something differently. His spirit was jubilant and ecstatic, instead of doubtful and jaded. Perhaps he'd determined that love wasn't worth the trouble, TL told himself, or that he was going to love TL regardless. Or maybe his epiphany had nothing to do with men at all. Perhaps George had witnessed, in another realm, what he'd never thought possible. An aura rested upon him, like it rested upon Moses after descending from the mount of transfiguration. Maybe George had seen the face of God. Who could know? He was still his regular, jovial self, kee-keein' and hee-heein' with everyone around him, but there was definitely something different. He was even more confident than he'd always been. A few frowned at his unrestrained behavior, yet, much to TL's surprise, Momma appeared to like him. Actually she probably loathed him, but she clearly enjoyed making a spectacle of him. When TL introduced them, she became wide-eyed and silly, treating George like a child— and a little girl at that. "Hi, baby!" she said, rubbing his back in a circular motion. George played his part well, careful not to disrespect, while throwing subtle sarcasm into the atmosphere.

"So you TL's lil' friend, huh?"

George blinked and said, "Yes ma'am, I'm George Thornton."

"Well goodie!" She applauded like a toddler.

"I'm just here for a few days, checking to make sure he's all right. Then I'll be headed back to the Big Apple."

"Oh, I see. I'm sure TL's gon' miss you *somethin' terrible.*" Her emphasis caught Daddy's attention. He frowned. TL was too embarrassed to speak. Momma glanced between him and George, saying far more with her eyes than her mouth.

"Sit down, Marion, and let the boys eat," Daddy said.

"Boys?" she screeched. "These ain't no boys!" She sat next to Daddy. "They might be many things, but they sho' ain't no boys!"

George and TL moved to a nearby table. "Was your mother throwing me shade?"

"Don't worry about her. She gets that way sometimes."

George had a mind to go tell her about herself, but, for TL's sake, he held his peace. If George was anything, he was confident. Momma couldn't take that from him. TL, on the other hand, wasn't. Each time she glanced at him and winked, he imagined what she was thinking, and his fury mounted. Why did he care? That's what really frustrated him. All his life he'd sought her approval, and now her belittling of George infuriated him. *I'll hear about this again, but this time, she'll hear from me, too.*

They arrived home a little after four and changed into lounging attire. TL was ready for a nap, but now George wanted to talk.

"I'm leaving tomorrow," he said.

"Tomorrow? I thought you were staying the week?"

"I was, but now I'm not. No need. You're all right. Ha! You're just fine." His brows rose. "You're probably better off than you've ever been."

Two squirrels scampered up a tree outside TL's bedroom window. Lying on the bed, the best friends watched them as if watching their futures unfold. George explained that they were just different people, from different worlds, whose paths had crossed for a moment. He'd wanted more, he admitted, but not at the expense of *this*. Not all of *this*. There was too much at stake, too much to lose. He saw, at church, how Ezekiel clung to TL, like fruit to its seed, and he said, "That boy *needs* you. I just *want* you. He won't make it without you." TL told George he didn't need to leave, but George said he wanted to. No need torturing himself. Like the squirrels, they'd had their playtime. And it was fun. Now they had to figure out what to do with the rest of their lives.

"At least I need to figure out what to do with mine," George said. "You seem pretty clear."

"No I ain't! I mean, I'm home now to teach and all, but that's my career. It's not my life."

"Stop fooling yourself, TL. There's nothing else in the world you'd rather do. I know you didn't dream of doing it here, but that doesn't matter. Destiny—or God—made that decision for you."

"God?"

He laughed and rolled over. "That's what y'all say, ain't it? You know me." One of the squirrels scampered away. The other sat on a limb, looking around quickly. He seemed aware that he was alone.

"I ain't never been no big church person. You know that. But when them ladies sang that song today, I felt like I heard my momma talking to me, and I ain't heard her voice in years. It was the craziest thing. I don't know if that was God or what, but whatever it was, it was real. I done been to a lotta churches in my life, but that ain't never happened to me." He burst into laughter. "Chile, I'm glad the kids didn't see me!"

TL hollered, too. George took his hand. It felt different now.

"I don't know what I'm gon' do without you, but that's for me to figure out. You'd be a fool to leave here. These kids don't know what they 'bout to get, but when they get it, they'll never be the same. You won't be, either."

The lone squirrel dashed into the world, leaving behind the memory of two who once stood together in a brief, fragile place. George and TL turned simultaneously, facing each other, choosing not to speak the vulnerabilities tumbling around in their hearts. They stared for a long time, longer than they ever had before, far beyond their pupils, into that part of the soul that has no voice. They became lovers then, not romantic partners, but keepers of each other's secrets, each other's hearts, each other's private desires. The deafening silence of the soul freed their naked spirits to dance unto an ecstasy far beyond what the body knows. There was nothing to hide, nothing to fear. George loved TL. He understood now why TL had been sent, both to the world and back to Swamp Creek, and George wanted nothing more than for TL to complete his mission. The yearning in Ezekiel's eyes convinced George that TL was where he was supposed to be. That boy had found the man who was sent to set him free. Wasn't that more important than what George desired? His only jealousy was that he didn't know his own calling. As the women sang, he glimpsed the city made of gold, and he saw TL in the midst. But he didn't see himself. *Oh well,* George thought. *Maybe it's not about me this time.*

TL loved George, too, especially for his ability to love beyond TL's capacity to reciprocate. He wished George could stay, not in Swamp Creek, but in the depths of his soul, yet he knew that wasn't possible. No man's soul can ever truly keep another. It's an intensely private place, the human soul, and at some point, without announcement or prewarning, it cleanses and regurgitates all foreign things. Its capacity is for the owner alone, and, selfish as it might seem, it seeks its own healing first. Yet, for the moment, they were there, in the pits of each other's souls, depositing thoughts and collecting memories that would sustain them in the future. They were in the midst of something not made by hands. It wouldn't last forever. It couldn't. But for now it was divine.

They kept staring. The dance became more intense. Farther into the pupils their spirits descended until there was no place else to go. Their energy couldn't be contained. It was wild, frenzied, violent, entangling, and melding into one another in the creation of a third, more perfect soul. It was beautiful, this other being, half one man, half the other, invisible yet tangible, temporal yet everlasting. Now they knew the potential of men.

There was nothing to say. Their season had come and gone, but it had been *their* season, their joy, their creation. Something had bloomed between them, lying on the bed, that would never die. Something full of color and possibility, vast like the ocean, infinite as the baby-blue sky. They were partners now in the truest sense—those who dared to know and love another's truth—and they embraced it as if it were their own, as if it were their death shroud, resting upon them in preparation for eternal life. Then, as they ascended the levels of the soul, they drifted apart, like dandelion spores in a light, summer breeze. They'd be distant friends again in this realm, the kind who call on holidays and birthdays, more out of obligation than sincerity, but they'd be forever indebted to each other for having held hands through the discovery of honesty. TL knew what it meant to love now; he knew what it meant to love *George* now. Perhaps George had always loved him. But love is different when both parties participate, acknowledging the gift of the experience. It becomes a physical, tangible thing, this love, linking people not only here, but in other stratospheres, where shame isn't allowed and love isn't clouded by definitions. TL realized that day, in that moment, that most people never visit this place because their bondage is too secure. Freedom demands too much, insists that people accept others for who they are, and only in freedom can people love so completely. TL knew that now, and he had George to thank for it. No wonder Zuri couldn't stand him.

Instinctively, they gazed through the window again, lifting their heads as if on cue, undoubtedly searching for the same thing—something to say to segue them back to reality. Once again, there was nothing. The squirrels didn't return. TL wondered about their haphazard existence, from one tree to the next, without promise of food or shelter. *They certainly have more faith than me!* When George finally spoke, he mentioned the stillness of the world outside, the way greens, browns, blues, and whites faded without most people ever noticing. "What else have we missed?" he asked. He said that perhaps clouds were God's thoughts, lingering in the sky, sometimes thick, sometimes thin, and sometimes vanishing in an instant. They hovered above us, unreachable, elusive, as a sign that there is always something greater, something beyond what we think we know. How marvelous it would be, TL said, to know the thoughts of God. George shook his head and said, "Or how dreadful."

They didn't say much more that night. Just sat back and let their lives drift apart. They watched Jay Leno and fell asleep. TL let George have the bed. He took the rocker. He would've sent him to the other room, but something about it felt disrespectful.

By morning, George was packed and ready to go. TL's back hurt from the chair, but he didn't complain. It was a bright, hot July day with heat rays flooding the kitchen through every crack they could find. TL lifted the window above the sink, and the sounds of country living poured in. It would be their last breakfast. At least until TL made it back to New York. Someday.

George wore faded denim, formfitting shorts just as before and a white tank. He had the body for it, and he knew it. They fixed breakfast together, joking and laughing the while, then sat at the little oval table and said grace. With their mouths full, truth joined in and forced them to accept life as they'd come to know it.

George blinked as he chewed. He tried to look away, but sadness covered his face like a thin, gray veil. TL refused to cry. It would only have made things worse, and he didn't intend to be an emotional wreck once George left. So they ate in silence, glancing occasionally at each other with weepy eyes, daring not to say what their hearts were begging them to say.

George left the table and retrieved his things. TL laid dishes in the sink and waited. When George returned, they stepped onto the front porch and stopped.

Gazing across the road at a field of golden, round hay bales, George said, "On the plane ride here, I dreamed our future. We were happy, man, together. It was really nice." He smiled. "But dreams don't always come true, huh?"

No they don't, TL thought but didn't say.

George sniffled. They avoided each other's eyes. "Hope you find out what happened to Sister. I mean, for real."

"I intend to."

He turned and looked at TL. "And I hope you find someone to love."

"I intend to do that, too!" TL laughed, but George didn't. They embraced for the last time, then, slowly, sorrowfully, relinquished their hold. "I can't fight your destiny, TL. This is where you're supposed to be. I know that now. You'd be wrong to go anywhere else. But me? I don't have any business here. Not anymore."

TL wanted to protest, but there was no point. He thanked George for having come to see about him. George nodded and descended the stairs. In the car, he lowered the window and said, "I think I believe now, TL. In God, I mean."

"Really? Why?"

"Because of you. Your life. This." He frowned from the glare of the sun. "It would take a God to make a man's life fit a people's needs so perfectly. I think I'm jealous."

TL smiled to keep from crying.

"These people need you, TL. Especially that boy."

"Ezekiel."

"Yeah, Ezekiel. But not just him. Even people who don't know they need you yet. This place has been waiting for you since you left it. The way these people love you is crazy! Even your mother. She's too hurt to show you, but she's glad you're back."

TL smacked his lips.

"Trust me. I've seen something in the last few days I've never seen in my life. The only people who hate you, TL, are the ones who need your love but can't get it." He backed into the road. "Pray for me, man. I don't know what I'm going to do now, but I gotta do something."

TL said he'd pray.

"And whatsoever you do, never leave here. You were made for this place."

With that, George drove away. An emptiness surged within

TL, like billowing black smoke, and all he could do was close his teary eyes and remember how good George had been to him. He'd saved his life in New York! TL owed him everything, but he had nothing to give.

Sitting on the edge of the porch, TL thought about what George had said—how TL's life had made him believe—and TL wondered what exactly God was up to.

POOR GEORGE. HAVE YOU EVER LOVED SOMEONE YOU COULDN'T have? It's a pain you can't describe. I knew that pain, knew it all too well. It can be deadly, you know. Make you decide life has no purpose, no meaning. Or it can make you desperate, like a wilted rose, longing for a mere drop of someone else's living water. I know. I've been there.

That's how I found myself in Willie James's arms. I was seventeen, and so lonely I could taste it. Willie James and I had become friends. I had no other choice. We were never as close as TL and I, but he was there, and when you're starving emotionally, "there" is everything. So I made use of him. The bad part is that the more I discovered his limitations, his frailties, his personal insecurities, the more I longed for TL. Willie James's company was a poor substitute for the fun TL and I used to have. Willie James tried so hard, but he just didn't have TL's internal drive, his spark for life. When Willie James spoke, I drifted farther into loneliness until, often, his lips moved without me hearing him. A few times I looked down the road and swore I saw TL coming, dressed in a nice stately suit with an accompanying leather briefcase, smiling all the while, having missed me as much as I'd missed him. Each time, the mirage disintegrated into nothing, leaving me angry and physically ill. Some days I cried so hard I vomited. My stomach twisted into knots, and I stopped eating regularly. Nothing anyone said or did assuaged my need for just one day, one hour, with the only person in the world I ever truly loved. My weight dwindled from a healthy 150 to barely 120. Momma worried that I had become anorexic, but that wasn't it. I needed nourishment no food could provide.

So I went to Willie James. That's right—I went to him. He didn't come to me. He was willing to love me, hold me, make me believe I was special—if only for a moment—and that's what I needed. Had he not been there, I'm convinced I would've died. I would've gone to the Valley before my time and I would've had to wait 'til God was ready for me before I could enter the Great City. You don't just walk in. It's gotta be your time. There's order here like you wouldn't believe! I've heard of people who've waited thirty and forty years before they could enter. Others were right on time. Most are, from what I hear. I was.

My point is that Willie James helped me. You may not agree, and that's okay. Humans don't see heart issues very well anyway. But I know what I needed, and I'm grateful he didn't reject me. Some of you are thinking how wrong this is, and I understand why. Remember, though, that we don't deal with right and wrong here. Our question is always one of honor, and I know for a fact that we were honorable. To each other, I mean. We never meant to go that far, much less conceive a child, but our needs were beyond our control, so it happened. God took the baby back. He knows what's best. I'm with my son now, and everything's fine. He's beautiful. His name is Judah.

I need to tell you something else. Can you try not to judge me? I made a mistake in the midst of it all, an error that alienated Willie James and me for a long time. I muttered TL's name while lost in Willie James's arms. It's not what you think, though. Yet Willie James stopped. He stared as if I'd violated a sacred pact between us. I wanted to tell him I'd called TL's name in hopes that someone somewhere was loving him, too, but before I could speak, Willie James rolled over and left. His feelings were hurt, of course, and I couldn't retract what I'd said. And since this isn't a topic you discuss casually, we never spoke about it again. We acted as if the moment never occurred.

And if this isn't bad enough, I had a boyfriend at the time, well, sorta. We didn't date or see each other outside of school, but we liked each other exclusively. His name was Christopher Youngblood. We were the same age almost to the day. He was the fourteenth and I was the twelfth of February. He was the cutest, sweetest boy in the whole class. Even Ms. Swinton said so. Almost a foot taller than me, he was easily six three or four and wore a size-fourteen shoe. The ironic thing is that his size clashed with his soft demeanor. He wasn't weak or puny, but he was definitely shy and reserved, to the point of being quiet most of the time. I suppose that's what I liked about him—that I could talk and he never tired of listening. Sometimes he walked me home and never said a word. He knew when to laugh along and when to grunt just enough to let me know he was listening. I wasn't in love with him though. At least I don't think so. I'm not sure I knew what that meant. But I liked him. I might've even had sex with him, but he seemed uninterested. Every time I took his hand, he withdrew, as if we were doing something wrong, so I didn't press the matter. I just wanted someone to hold and hear me. Since he couldn't hold me, I settled for him hearing me.

Every now and then he'd talk about different things, like rock-skipping or fishing, but for the most part he lived a silent life. When the thing happened between Willie James and me, I felt guilty, as if I'd broken a promise to Chris, so I told him about it. His response was surprising. "What about us? I thought we had something special." "We do!" I affirmed. "But it just happened." We were in the middle of Fish Lake Road. "Things like that don't just happen, Sister." That's all he said before turning and walking away. The next day, he told me he couldn't see me anymore. I understood, but it hurt like hell. An aching grew in my heart that never quite went away.

CHAPTER 16

A KNOCK AT THE DOOR STARTLED TL. IT WAS early—6:13 A.M.—and he couldn't imagine who in the world it could be. He lay still a moment, thinking he'd been dreaming, then the banging intensified, so he scrambled out of bed, clutching his robe. When he opened the door, Momma's fist was raised to knock again.

"Oh. I'm sorry. Were you asleep?" She glanced at her thin, silver Timex.

TL almost apologized for what he was thinking. "Yes ma'am, I was."

"At this hour?"

The only way to remain honorable, he determined, was to remain silent. She stared and waited. He rubbed his crusty eyes.

"Well, ain't you gon' invite me in?"

TL stepped aside, and Momma entered.

"Is something wrong?" he asked, clearing phlegm from his throat.

"So . . . this is what this house looks like on the inside." She sauntered around casually. "It needs dustin'. You could at least dust, boy."

"Momma . . . day on need something?"

"And look at those drapes layin' there! If you'd put 'em in the cleaners, they'd look brand new. Well, almost brand new. No one really has velvet drapes anymore, but—"

"Momma! I know you didn't come all the way over here at this hour to critique Ms. Swinton's house!"

"*Ms. Swinton's* house? You mean *yo'* house, don't you? I wouldn't ever have come in if I thought it was still *her* house."

TL huffed. "Momma, please."

"Okay, okay. I just came to tell you yo' uncle Rayford passed yesterday." She said it casually, like one might announce the coming of spring. "Just in case you wanted to know." She turned to leave.

"Oh no. I'm sorry. I didn't know he was *that* sick."

"Yes you did. Your daddy come by and told you." She smiled and patted his shoulder.

What could he say?

Only then did TL realize what was really going on. Momma was dressed in a soft purple-and-pink-striped dress with a wide-brimmed lavender hat. Her good black shoes sparkled and matched her black leather pocketbook. She was on her way out of town.

"Heart attack. Least that's what they say."

"Who called you?"

"Sharon, wit' her dramatic self. That child can't handle nothin'!"

"It's her father, Momma! She oughta be upset!"

"Okay. Whatever. Personally, I don't think it takes all of that, but that's just me."

She stepped onto the porch. TL followed.

"You flyin'?"

"How else I'm gettin' to California from here? Hell, it'd take me a week on the bus. By the time I got there, he'd be a skeleton!" She laughed.

"Momma."

"Look, I ain't like y'all young folks. Y'all can't take nothin'! Death don't disturb me. Everybody gotta go. We jus' sittin' 'round waitin' on God to call our number. When He do, you goin'. That's all there is to it."

"I know, but you could be a little sympathetic."

"I *am* sympathetic. He was my brother. My *only* brother."

Her mouth quivered. TL would've hugged her had they been the hugging types.

"It's all right. He's better off now."

She blinked, like one recovering from an unconscious state.

"What about Daddy? Is he going with you?"

Her cackle rang with sarcasm. "Believe it or not, he is. I told him he didn't have to, but he said he wanted to."

"I'm glad. It's always good to have support in times like this."

"Guess so."

She eased down the steps and into the yard. "Check on Willie James for me while we gone. We'll be back Saturday."

Her heels sunk slightly in the yard as she made her way to the car. There was a walkway, but she ignored it. Or she simply refused to use it.

"Get those drapes cleaned!" she hollered, backing out of the driveway. "If you gon' keep 'em at all."

TL nodded but didn't wave. Something about Momma's visit left him uneasy, but he couldn't put his finger on it. She hadn't come all the way to Ms. Swinton's—well, *his house,* he thought— just to relay the news about Uncle Rayford. It wasn't like her. At best, she would've called. She was looking for something. Maybe she'd always wanted to know what the inside of the house looked like, and this was the perfect way to find out. But even that wasn't like her. Momma wasn't shy. She wouldn't've entered the house while Ms. Swinton lived in it, but the moment it became TL's she would've. No, there was something else, something about him she was after. What was it? Should he have offered to go to the funeral? he wondered. She knew he didn't have the money, but the gesture would've been nice. Too late for that now. Maybe she was really worried about Willie James. His welfare had always been her obsession, not because he couldn't handle himself but because she knew he wouldn't, so she'd found meaning and purpose in taking care of a fully grown, capable man. He liked it, too. He acted as if he didn't, but of course he did. Three home-cooked meals a day, clothes washed and ironed every week, fresh linens twice a month—what man wouldn't like it? That he couldn't leave was a small price to pay, he probably thought, for a life he saw as perfect. Or as close to perfect as a life can get.

TL returned to bed, but not to sleep. Strange dreams teased his subconscious until he sat up, frustrated. He would've had a pity party had there been someone to invite, but there wasn't, so he huffed, tired of feeling sorry for himself, and read until dreams came again.

VEILED IN pale, sandy dust, Willie James stopped by Friday evening. TL had heard the loud, ragged tractor miles away. Willie James hopped off, obviously tired, but not exhausted. He reclined onto the porch, flat on his back, with his knees bent upward.

"You remember Uncle Rayford? I mean, do you remember him well?" Willie James asked.

"Not really." TL sat in a metal folding chair. "I only saw him twice."

"Yeah? Well, I remember him." Willie James slapped a rhythm against his thighs. "He used to come by all the time when I was little. Before he moved to California."

"Oh."

"Yeah. He was nice. At least to me. He was kinda weird though."

"Weird how?"

Willie James's thick, bushy brows met in the middle of his forehead. He licked his lips and said, "He . . ."

TL scowled. "He what?"

"He . . . showed hisself to me. Once."

Willie James said it so quickly it didn't register at first. Then TL squealed, "What!"

"Yeah. It was crazy how it happened." Willie James tried to shrug the memory away. "I don't know. He didn't mean no harm. He put it away real fast and said he was sorry. I believed him. He looked like he was real sorry."

"Stop it, man! I don't care how sorry he says he was, he was wrong!"

"I know. But he wasn't a bad man. He was jus' sad, I think."

"Willie James! Do you hear yourself? You can't be defending this man."

"I'm not defendin' him. I'm tryin' to share somethin' wit' you."

"Why? After all this time?"

"'Cause I felt sorry for him. He never did get over it. He kept apologizin' every time he saw me. I told him I didn't think about it, but he couldn't let it go. He started doin' drugs, and nobody understood why, but I knew. I thought he might get in trouble if I said somethin', so I never did. It don't matter no more. He's dead now."

TL relaxed a bit. Willie James sat up and clutched his legs to his chest like an insecure child.

"Yes, he's gone," TL said.

"He used to send me birthday cards every year wit' money inside. I never read 'em. I just took the money and throwed the cards away. I didn't really think 'bout him much. I mean, he didn't make me touch it or nothin'. He just made me look, and I guess the expression on my face told him he was wrong, so, like I said, he put it away real fast and apologized."

"How old were you?"

"I don't know . . . six or seven."

"That's sexual abuse, Willie James. You should've told someone, and they should've had his ass locked up."

"He wasn't a bad man, TL. I know what he did, and I know it wasn't right, but he wasn't a bad man. He didn't abuse me."

"Yes, he did!"

"No, he didn't. I was there. I know what happened. It didn't happen like you thinkin'. He wasn't tryin' to hurt me. You didn't see the look in his eyes when he realized what he had done. He really was sorry. He jus' couldn't forgive hisself."

TL couldn't figure out how to make Willie James understand. "It's not about him forgiving himself, man. It's about you knowing how wrong he was!"

"I said he was wrong!"

"Yeah, but you're still defending him, and that's a problem!"

"See! You don't never listen. I ain't defendin' him. I'm just sayin' he wasn't a bad man. That's all. Jus' 'cause you do somethin' bad once don't make you bad forever."

"Depends on what it is, Willie James."

"Who decides that?"

TL sighed.

"God, right?"

"I suppose."

"And how we know which bad things God won't forgive?"

"We don't."

"Right, but I know Uncle Rayford wasn't bad—not most of the time."

TL shook his head.

"He's dead now anyway, so it don't matter. I don't even know why I told you."

TL leaned forward in the chair. "Did you ever tell Momma?"

"Nope." Willie James bit his fingernails.

"You should've. Back when it happened. You don't know what he did to somebody else's child somewhere."

Willie James leapt and shouted, "He didn't do nothin', TL! That's what I keep tellin' you! He didn't hurt me or anybody else!"

"How would you know?"

"'Cause he promised he wouldn't!"

"What? Come on, man!"

Like a child caught in a lie, Willie James's arms dropped to his sides. He looked at TL finally. "I made him promise not to do it to nobody else. I told him I wouldn't tell if he swore never to do it again, and he did."

TL gawked. "Are you crazy, man? Anybody would've said that to stay out of trouble!"

Willie James huffed angrily. "Everybody ain't like you, TL! Some people make promises and actually keep 'em!"

He stormed off the porch and onto the tractor. TL frowned. *Did I miss something? Why is he angry with me? Is this his way of grieving Uncle Rayford's death?* Perhaps, TL considered, Willie James had come to clear his consciousness—not to be lectured and reprimanded. But wasn't it right to say something? You can't hear that kind of thing and say nothing at all, can you?

And what the hell did he mean by some people *actually* keep their promises? TL almost called after him, but Willie James was gone. *I haven't broken any promises to him! Maybe to others, but not to him.*

By dusk, as much as TL tried, he couldn't get Willie James's outburst out of his head. If he hadn't known better, he might've believed Willie James was bipolar. Or schizophrenic. TL had never seen him act that way, and he didn't believe it was because of him. Nothing he'd said was enough to ignite anyone's rage. It just didn't make sense.

TL stepped into his sneakers, grabbed a flashlight, and went to find his brother. It was almost dark when he arrived at the house—it would be pitch black when he returned—but he wasn't afraid of the dark. Not anymore. Daddy had taught him not to be. He'd pulled over one night when TL was ten or so, where the service road meets the highway, and told him to get out and find his way home. It was more than a mile away. Daddy said the moonlight would guide him if he'd just follow it. He was too nervous to cry. When he made it home, his chest was puffed with pride. He wasn't afraid of much of anything after that.

The house was dark and still, as if no one lived there. TL

couldn't imagine where Willie James could be. He knocked on the door, but no one answered. There wasn't even a stir. Then TL turned and saw a flickering light. He followed it and found Willie James behind the barn.

The beam blinded TL as he approached.

"You can't never leave nothin' alone, can you?" He'd obviously been crying.

"What are you talking about?"

Willie James's head dropped. "It happened right here. Right in this spot." He paused. "It scared me, lil' brother. I hadn't never seen nothin' like it. And I lied to you before. He did ask me to touch it."

"Oh, Willie James, no! Why didn't you tell somebody?"

"'Cause I was too 'shame. I didn't do it, though. I swear I didn't. That's when he said he was sorry. I guess he saw how scared I was."

Willie James sniffled. TL touched his shoulder. "This is a big deal, man. Don't you see how it's affected you? You might need somebody to talk to."

"I'm talkin' to you."

TL grabbed his hand and Willie James crumbled, sobbing as if he'd committed the crime. TL didn't know how to help him. The more Willie James wept, the tighter he squeezed TL's hand until, several minutes later, Willie James loosened his grip and stood upright again, sighing heavily.

"I guess I never let it go either, huh?" He wiped his eyes with his sleeves.

"Willie James, I can't believe you didn't tell somebody. That man should've been in jail."

"Maybe. But he was so nice to me after that. I knew he was sorry. I could tell. And since he hadn't hurt me—"

"But he had! You're still crying about it!"

"I'm not sad about that."

"Then what's the problem?"

He stared into the forest. "I hate I never got up enough strength to tell him how he made me feel. That's what I'm sad about. Now I can't."

They stood in silence awhile. Willie James eventually smiled and said, "I'm okay though. I guess I just had to let it go. You know how I am."

"You sure you're okay?"

"Yeah, I'm sure. It's just that . . . well . . . I got so close to tellin' him."

"When?"

"A few years ago. I called, but when he answered, his voice scared me so I hung up."

"Damn, man. I wish you had told him."

"I know. I just kept thinkin' 'bout what might happen if people found out."

"What could've happened?"

His shoulders hunched. "I don't know. Anything. He might've gone to jail or people might've thought I made up the whole thing."

"No way, man. People know you. They know you wouldn't make up something like that."

"Maybe. Maybe not. What about Momma? Who was she supposed to believe? Her brother or her son?"

Willie James had obviously wrestled with this a while. "Her son! She raised you. She knows the kind of man you are!"

"She knew the kind of man he was, too! They grew up together. She said he practically raised her, so why would she believe me over him?"

TL had no explanation.

"That's another reason I hung up the phone. I didn't wanna put her in that kinda position."

"This isn't about Momma, Willie James! It's about you and what that filthy scum did to you. She needed to know so she could've protected you!"

"If she had found out, she would've hated him, then who would she have had left?"

"What?"

"She didn't have nobody as it was, TL, and I wasn't gonna make her hate her only brother."

"You can't be serious, Willie James!"

"You bet I'm serious. You don't understand 'cause you always had somebody. The truth would've killed Momma."

"Momma? Look at what it's done to you!"

He paused. "Well, this is better'n what it woulda done to her. I might be a little messed up, but she woulda been devastated. I wunnit gon' do that to her."

Nothing TL said moved Willie James, so TL stopped trying.

"Just leave it alone, okay? I made a decision and I gotta live with it."

Willie James turned off the flashlight and walked toward the house. TL followed. "I think you should still tell Momma."

"Why? What good would that do now?" He continued walking.

"It would free you."

"No it wouldn't. It wouldn't free me at all. It'd be the worst thing I could do, 'cause then Momma would feel guilty, and what could she do about it? She'd have to carry the pain the rest of her life. Like me. She'd never have no peace, and it'd be because of me. I know that don't mean nothin' to you, but she the only momma I got, and she's done took care of me my whole life. I ain't takin' nothin' from her, especially the memory of her brother. "

Willie James entered the house, allowing the screen to slam behind him. TL stood on the back steps, looking at the old landscape of cows, the barn, farm equipment, and the old tractor in the field. Maybe Willie James was right, he thought. Maybe he was just too selfish to understand Willie James's position. *There's no way Momma would've ruled me like that!* She would've known the truth, TL told himself, if it were up to him, and she would've been responsible for her own heart. Like everybody else. Certainly Willie James meant well, but his stance seemed to pamper her, to shield her from the truth, and TL had grown to believe that adults should know the truth—however painful it might be.

In the dark, Sister's grave resembled an oversized ant mound. TL couldn't make out the words on the tombstone, but of course he knew what it said. He exhaled. Willie James thought he needed to protect Momma, of all people? How funny was that! How had she manipulated him so? She probably already knew about Uncle Rayford, he thought. He wouldn't be surprised. The man might've moved to California precisely because she threatened to go to the authorities if he didn't. That way, she protected her son without him ever knowing. No need traumatizing the boy, she might've reasoned. Let him move on and just forget about it. That was Momma's way. She arranged people's lives without telling them. *She'd done it to me!* He knew she'd meant well. In her heart, she probably thought she was doing people a favor.

But she wasn't. That's partially why TL left. He couldn't think. She was smothering him, just as she'd smothered everyone else. Like the time she applied to those colleges *for him*! He never even knew! She got the acceptance letters and danced around as if she'd won the lottery. We didn't know what was going on. At supper she announced proudly, "You're going to Yale, boy."

"Ma'am?" TL inquired.

"Or Brown." She smiled.

He'd never heard of Brown.

"For college. They're Ivy Leagues schools. They're the best. They only take a few black kids each year." She handed him the acceptance letters.

"I didn't apply to these schools."

Her sigh caught him off guard. "Don't you know a blessin' when you see one, fool? Just go and be glad you got in. Most students don't, black or white."

Her pride radiated. That's how we knew what she'd done.

"I wanna go to a black school, Momma. You know . . . like Ms. Swinton did."

Plates rattled when her fists hit the table. "You ain't got no sense, boy? Young folk die for the chance to go to Ivy League schools, and you throw away the opportunity like it ain't nothin'?"

"I'm sure they're good schools, Momma, but—"

"But nothin'! Colored schools ain't got shit! Don't you know white folks got all the power? A degree from one of their schools opens all kinds of doors for you. Don't waste yo' time foolin' wit' niggas!"

Daddy intervened. "You can't say that, woman. You ain't never been to no college, black or white."

"Maybe I ain't, but I see who got the money. Folks come out of those black schools and barely make more than the rest of us! Hell, Carolyn Swinton broke as I am!"

"Yep," Daddy said, "but she done educated a whole community all by herself, and she did a hell of a job doin' it. I don't see nobody from Yale tryin' to teach 'round here."

TL shut up and waited. Momma's heavy breathing made him nervous. Finally she said, "Fine. Do what you want to, but you'll regret it later. Smart as you is? I might be dead and gone, but you'll definitely regret it."

Smart? Momma thinks I'm smart? She'd been careful not to admit that before. Daddy closed the matter: "He'll make up his own mind 'bout where he wanna go. Either he'll get a good education or he won't, but it won't be the school's fault if he don't."

Willie James looked at TL with pity. He'd never dreamed of college. Or going anywhere for that matter. Courage was an attribute he couldn't seem to find, and even if he mustered the nerve to leave, he couldn't think of why he would. Whatever Momma said, he believed. He didn't need the truth, it seemed. He just needed to believe someone cared about him, and Momma kept him assured of that. TL was different. She and Daddy told him, his whole life, that he tried to know too much, that he needed to learn how to be content. Well, he never learned it.

SUDDENLY TL ran to the barn and returned with a shovel and started digging at the mound. *A man can always know the truth if he's willing to pay the price,* Daddy used to say. TL wasn't sure what the price would be, but he was sure he wanted to know what happened to his sister, so he kept digging.

Willie James heard the commotion and came to the screen. "What the hell are you doin'?"

"You know what I'm doing! I should've done this the first time I laid eyes on this grave!" Clumps of dry, Arkansas red clay flew into the night.

Willie James rushed through the door and tried to take the shovel from him, but TL's adrenaline wouldn't allow it. "Stop it!" Willie James yelled as they tussled. "You don't know what you doin'!"

"The hell I don't!"

Willie James tripped and stumbled to the ground. TL resumed digging. Within seconds they were fighting again.

"Don't do this, TL! Just leave it alone!" With hands clutched around the shovel handle, the brothers pulled in opposite directions.

"You can let me do it now, or I'll do it later!"

When Willie James loosened his grip, TL snatched the shovel and continued digging. Sitting on the ground, Indian style, shaking his head slowly, Willie James surrendered the fight. TL didn't pay him much attention after that. He was determined to find out what he wasn't supposed to know.

After fifteen minutes or so, he had dug a sizeable depression in the earth. Willie James began humming, in a strange key, something sad and deep and slow. He was obviously mourning. TL heard it in his voice. The melody sounded familiar and painful, like the exhausted purring of a mother cat that simply can't find her kittens. Willie James's head hung low, almost to his knees. An outside observer might've thought he was lost in heavy meditation. TL didn't really care what he was doing. He was bracing himself for whatever he was about to discover.

An hour passed. The hole grew deeper and wider. Streaks of sweat marked TL's face and chest. The song of the crickets and hoot owls intensified as if they were singing background for Willie James. Out of nowhere, his soft, off-key humming evolved into words:

Hush, hush . . . Somebody's calling my name,
Hush, hush . . . Somebody's calling my name,
Hush, hush . . . Somebody's calling my name!
Oh my Lord, oh my Lord, what shall I do?

A strange feeling swept over TL, as if he were doing something wrong. He was three feet deep into the grave. His resolve weakened, but he pressed on. He had to know.

Sounds like Jesus . . . Somebody's calling my name!

Willie James's arms enclosed his torso as he swayed. He resembled Grandma, with eyes closed, rocking as she sang. TL kept digging.

Oh my Lord, oh my Lord, what shall I do?

Banjo, the dog, appeared out of nowhere and sniffed around the fresh pile of dirt. He'd stopped barking years ago when Daddy beat him for barking too much. Willie James had found him in the woods somewhere, covered in blood and motor oil, and brought him home to nurse his wounds. He named him Banjo because he'd always liked the instrument, although he'd never played it, and because he saw a dog on TV just like him with the same name. He wasn't worth a shit, Daddy said. Instead of chasing wild animals, they chased him, and he only barked at small children. He tried to bite a child once, Willie James told TL later, and Daddy beat him so badly he ran into the woods and stayed for three days. He returned, but never barked again.

Banjo walked around Willie James slowly. He stared at his master, leaning his head from one side to the other and perking up his ears, as if trying to ascertain exactly what Willie James was doing. Unable to do so, Banjo curled at Willie James's feet and watched TL sling dirt over his shoulder as he burrowed the hole deeper.

Hush, hush . . . Somebody's callin' my name!

There was a hollow *cling*! Willie James must've heard it, too. He stopped singing. TL jabbed the shovel in the same place harder and the sound rang louder.

"Please don't do this, TL. Please," Willie James droned.

TL retired the shovel and retrieved the flashlight. He saw the edge of something shiny, so he bent and brushed away loose dirt. It was a large stone. He didn't know what it meant or why it was there, but he had a feeling he was near the truth. He scooped out more dirt until he found shreds of a sheet. Willie James began singing again. TL shivered.

Run, sinner, run . . . find you a hidin' place!

Dropping the shovel, TL scrambled nervously out of the hole. He wasn't ready. The thought of seeing a skeleton in the dark overwhelmed him and made him wish he hadn't done this. He sat on the ground next to the hole, huffing and shuddering. Willie James's singing died to a soft rumble. Only Banjo appeared unmoved.

After several minutes, TL's breathing slowed. He would've dropped the whole matter except that he'd done so much work.

He'd never get this opportunity again. He knew that. And, come what may, he wanted to know the truth. So he sighed one last time and looked at the moon and stars glistening brightly above. They encouraged him not to be afraid. To be bold, like them, regardless of what others thought. He stood and grabbed the shovel again.

"Stop, TL! I'm beggin' you! Please. This ain't right."

"I gotta know what happened to Sister, man. I just gotta know. I can't live like this!"

Willie James wanted to know, too, TL assumed, or he would've fought harder to stop him. He would've at least gone inside, although TL was glad he didn't. He would've been scared to death in the dark without him.

TL reentered the open grave and uncovered what must've been the bundle Willie James saw Momma bury. After taking a deep breath, he opened it slowly, pointing the flashlight with his trembling right hand.

"Oh my God," he cried. "I don't believe this." It was all his personal things: framed school pictures, report cards, writing journals, awards, the rocks he'd painted in fifth grade. That's probably what he'd hit with the shovel, he assumed. Willie James crawled over and looked into the hole. TL unfolded and searched the dirty sheet completely.

Then he screeched, "Willie James! Where's the body? Oh my God! Ain't no body! Sister's not here!"

FROM THIS POINT FORWARD, READER, BE VERY CAREFUL. THINGS ARE never as they seem. Sometimes we think we know a person, only to discover we don't know them at all. There are pieces of their story we could never have imagined, and when we find out, even then we don't believe. I've discovered that belief is not an issue of what's true; it's an issue of what you can imagine to be true. So you must drop all preconceived notions of reality. If I've learned nothing else in this realm, I've learned that humans have no reliable conception of reality. They only believe what they've seen. Or what they can prove. But truth lies far outside of human perception. And in order for TL to know the truth, he, too, must step outside of what he thinks he knows, what he perceives as possible. You'll never guess what really happened to me. No one could've. But it was real. And it was wonderful. Yet it was totally unimaginable, at least to the human psyche. However, to the spiritual mind, it made sense. I give thanks, now, to those who dared to be different, who refused to relinquish spiritual insight and power for mere human acceptance. They made my travel easy. And guess what? They govern in the next realm, and those who mocked them bow low in humble reverence.

So . . . walk easy, reader. Step beyond what you think you know. Follow wherever the story goes, far out into the deep, and learn how earth and sky merge sometimes in preparation for the coming of a promise.

CHAPTER 17

TOO NUMB TO SPEAK OR MOVE, TL STOOD FROZEN with disbelief. *Where is my sister's body? What has someone done?* Banjo sniffed around the open grave, then returned to the darkness of the forest. Upon their return, Momma and Daddy would definitely know that TL had disturbed the grave, but that was the least of his concerns now. He was determined to find out what happened if it cost him everything.

Willie James wiped snot from his upper lip and resumed a seat on the earth. He couldn't stop shaking his head. "I can't believe this. It don't make no sense."

They sat together awhile, unable to comprehend the magnitude of their discovery. Each wanted to speak, but their convoluted thoughts wouldn't congeal into sensible words.

Eventually, TL rose and, after extracting his personal things, began refilling the grave. Putting dirt back in the hole was far easier, he discovered, than taking it out. He tried to restore the mound to its original shape, but of course Momma and Daddy would see the difference. *But, hell, so what? What had they done with Sister? Wouldn't somebody have to know?*

When the task was complete, they went inside and sat in the den. TL clicked on the small lamp on the end table, casting just enough light to make shadows of everything. Neither of them spoke at first, then Willie James sighed like a man taking his last breath.

"I don't understand it, TL. I know what I saw! I ain't crazy. Momma killed her wit' that hoe!"

TL nodded. "I believe you, man. I just can't figure out what she did after that."

"She buried her! Right there in that grave. I saw her pulling the body, wrapped up in that sheet."

"Did you actually *see* the body in it?"

He didn't answer at first. "No, but what else could it be?"

"All my old stuff, looks like."

"But she's dead, TL. I know that. There was too much blood. Looked like somebody had done slaughtered a hog. It was all over the barn floor."

"I know, Willie James, but what did they do with her body?"

"I don't know," he whined. "I just don't know. It's all so crazy."

Reliving the details of things, he closed his eyes and traveled back in time, describing precisely what he'd seen. TL had heard it all before, but hearing it again reignited his emotions. What had been going through Momma's head to make her do something like that? Willie James smiled slightly when he spoke of how valiantly Sister fought, and he noted that Momma had overcome her only because she'd caught her off guard. The first blow leveled her, he said, and she never quite recovered. Willie James's right eye twitched as he talked. He was sure Momma hadn't meant to kill her, but once the struggle ensued, she lost control. Even her face changed, he said, from its usual calm to something dark and monstrous. TL tried to connect the dots, to have a clearer, more reliable understanding of exactly what had happened, but there were holes in the story he hadn't noticed before.

"So you *saw* Momma drag Sister's body out of the barn?"

Willie James hesitated. "No, I didn't actually *see* it. I saw her draggin' *somethin'*, and when I saw all the blood, I assumed it had to be Sister's body." He shrugged. "But I guess it wasn't."

"Guess it wasn't."

"Whatchu think she did wit' it?"

"I don't know."

Willie James rubbed his thighs. "She *is* dead, ain't she, TL? I mean, ain't no way . . ."

"She's dead, Willie James. She's definitely dead. It just didn't happen the way we think."

"I saw the blood! It was everywhere!"

"I know, man, but there's something we *don't* know."

Willie James closed his eyes and exhaled. "There's apparently *a lot* we don't know."

It was after one in the morning when TL returned home. He didn't remember the journey. Surely he'd walked his usual route, across the Williams place to the access road, through the woods, and into Ms. Swinton's backyard, but it seemed as if he'd simply been transported. Nothing was real. The noises of the forest hadn't frightened him as usual. He didn't remember hearing anything at all. All he remembered was walking out the back door of the house, glancing at the newly shaped mound, then stumbling like a helpless drunkard until he reached home. He then went inside and stripped away dirty clothes and collapsed across the bed, confused and semiconscious.

In the midst of exhaustion, the vision came again. Streets of gold, stained-glass windows in steepled architecture, fields of flowers of every kind, and "Lily in the Valley" echoing from the church bells. The whole shebang all over again. TL just didn't get it. *What in the world is this?* He saw it clearer now than before, so he wasn't startled. He simply couldn't figure out what it meant. And what about that hawk? *Why is he always following me?*

A gray and black sparrow awakened him the next morning. It

tapped lightly on the window, as if trying to get his attention, then, when TL looked up, it flew away.

The doorbell rang. He knew who it was. When he flung the door open and saw Momma, distraught and disheveled, his defenses weakened. Her eyes were cranberry red as if she'd been awake all night, and, without makeup, she looked broken and fragile. He'd never seen her so unkempt. Intersecting streaks of tears covered her mahogany-brown cheeks, and, for the first time in TL's life, he felt sorry for her. He thought to touch her face, but remembered that Momma hated public expressions of emotion, especially pity, so, instead, he looked away. Her condition embarrassed him. Something was horribly wrong. Something more than what he would've guessed.

She sniffled and blew into a white, floral-trimmed handkerchief. "Did you have to do it? You couldn't let me have *nothin'* for myself?" She folded the handkerchief neatly and returned it to her pocketbook. "I mean, I just never thought you'd do nothin' like that."

"I had to, Momma. How else was I supposed to learn the truth? You wouldn't tell me."

Slap!

The strike was quick and invisible, like a fleeting thought—he never saw her raise her hand!—but the sting lingered, leaving his left cheek burning. *Was it my tone?* TL massaged his face lightly.

"You didn't have no right! She was *my* child!" Momma poked her chest. "*Mine!* MINE!"

"She was my sister, too!"

"And you left her!"

"I didn't leave *her.* I left *here.*"

"Same thing."

"No, it isn't. I would've taken her if I could've."

Momma looked surprised. "Then what would I have had?"

"The same things you've always had. Daddy, Willie James, the house. Everything."

She blinked. "You got all that education and still don't know a goddamn thing."

The tail of her dress brushed his pant leg as she walked into the house like a social worker in search of an endangered child. TL followed, sure now that all his mental preparation was about to prove futile.

Momma sat on the edge of the red velvet sofa, her forehead buried in her right palm. TL took the ancient high-back rocker, with the glass-topped coffee table resting between them, and waited. Seconds later, she looked up.

"You must think I ain't got no feelin's at all."

"Momma, this ain't about your—"

"I know what it's about. And, like I said, you must think"—her voice trembled—"I ain't got no feelin's at all. But I do."

"I know that, Momma."

"No you don't!" She stomped the hardwood floor. "You think I killed my own daughter and threw her in the ground! What kinda mother would do somethin' like that?"

TL chewed his thumbnail.

"You always thought you knowed more than you really knowed."

"Willie James told me what happened. He saw you."

"Willie James ain't seen me! He ain't seen shit! You know better'n believin' anything that boy say. He ain't never been smart enough to fully understand nothin'. Come on, TL! Stop actin' like you dumb!"

"I ain't dumb."

"I didn't say you was dumb. I said stop *actin'* like you dumb. Try listenin' to me sometimes instead of playin' deef when I talk."

Momma rested her pocketbook on the coffee table.

"I always knowed you didn't think much of me, but for you to think I could murder my own child means you think I'm some kind of crazy woman or somethin'."

"Momma."

"Aw hell, boy, be honest for once in yo' life! It ain't gon' kill you. Irregardless of what you say, I'ma still be yo' momma—at least the only one you ever really had."

Fine! "Yeah, I think you killed her. Who else coulda done it? Willie James said Daddy was out plowing the field."

She nodded. "Good. Finally. 'Bout time."

"And the way you treated me? I wouldn't put anything past you."

Her thunderous applause echoed throughout the living room. "Yeah! Now he tells the truth. The real, naked truth. For once in his life."

"Don't patronize me, Momma."

"Don't judge me, either!" she shouted. Their eyes locked. "I might not of been the sweetest or kindest woman you knew, but I gave you what I had." Her voice cracked again. "And I ain't never killed nobody—even the ones I shoulda."

"So what happened?"

She paused, unsure of whether TL could handle what she was about to say. "We was in the barn, arguin'. 'Bout you." Momma blew her nose again as the intensity between them subsided.

"She said she was leavin' Swamp Creek once and for all. Said she was goin' to find you, since you was the only person who ever really cared 'bout her. I was so hurt." She fought not to cry. "I tried to convince her that if you cared so much you woulda come back for her, but she couldn't see it. I told her to go 'head on then. That's when she told me she was pregnant, but I already knowed it. I knowed whose it was, too. I ain't never been no fool. Never. I see things. So I told her she couldn't go 'til she had the baby. She was four or five months, I guess. I'd take care of the baby, I said, me and Willie James, 'til she found you and come back. Or didn't find you and come back. Whichever way, the baby was gon' be fine. But she didn't wanna do that. She said she was takin' the baby wit' her, and if I didn't never see neither one of 'em again, that was too bad. I told her she didn't have no right to take that baby 'cause it wasn't just hers, but she said she could do whatever she wanted to." Momma chuckled. "Well, you know me. I slapped her and told her to watch her mouth. I asked her who she thought she was talkin' to, and she said, 'I'm talkin' to you!' and that's when we started fightin'. It wunnit nothin' at first, but then it got out of hand. She fell on the hoe blade and damn near cut herself in half. I hollered, but wunnit nobody 'round to help me. Blood gushed 'cross piles of hay like burgundy syrup over a snow cone. She was cryin' and I was cryin', but wunnit nothin' I could do. I knew if I went to get help, she'd be dead by the time I got back. She was bleedin' just that bad. So I got some old rags and tried to stop the bleedin', but it didn't work. She grabbed her stomach and started screamin', 'My baby! My baby!' She was in labor."

Tears poured faster than Momma could wipe them away, so she stopped trying. Snot ran from her nose.

"I managed to walk her in the house and lay her across the bed. I ain't never seen that much blood in my life. She kept screamin' 'bout the baby 'til it come. It was so tiny. The whole body fit right in the palm o' my hands. I knowed it was dead, but for a minute I loved it. It was a boy. A beautiful, little precious boy. He'd just come too soon."

TL offered Momma a tissue from his pocket, and she blew a mound of mucus into it.

"I knew she'd die. Can't nobody lose that much blood and live."

Pity colored her face red and wrinkled it where it had once been smooth. It was as if Momma was transforming before TL's eyes into a worn, beaten-down, old woman.

"What did you do?"

"What *could* I do?" She shrugged helplessly. "I found a shoe box and wrapped the baby in a towel and laid him in it. Then I prayed like I ain't never prayed before." She lifted her right hand. "I'm tellin' you, I begged God to make it right. To give me my daughter back and give her her son back. I begged God to forgive me for fightin' her in the first place. I begged Him to forgive me for re-sentin' you. I begged Him to take my life instead of my child's!"

Her sobbing rushed TL like an unexpected breeze. It was a

long, dry cry, full of sorrow and regret. He'd never seen her so disheveled, and now he wanted her to stop. Our family didn't do vulnerability, and certainly not with each other.

"But He wouldn't do it, so I had to live with what I'd done."

TL went to the bathroom for more tissue, and Momma received it gracefully.

"How did you manage to carry her body outside and bury it?"

"*I* didn't." She paused. "Willie James did."

"What!" TL leapt up. "Willie James?"

"You heard what I said."

"But he told me—"

She pursed her lips.

"Oh, Momma, no." TL crumbled into the chair.

"He lied. We agreed not to tell anybody. Ever. Even you."

"Why!"

"Because you wouldn't understand. Nobody does."

"Then why tell me now?"

She smirked. "'Cause, from the looks of things, you gotta live here, too. At least now. You gotta carry the weight of bein' in this family just like the rest of us—since it's the only family you got. Plus, you givin' this community somethin' it needs, so it's only right to give you somethin' you need."

They paused.

". . . and we didn't bury her."

TL gasped. "What do you mean you didn't bury her?"

Momma touched her hair in a meager attempt to recompose herself. She sighed and melted into the cushions of the sofa. "We had to do somethin', TL. Something drastic. Somethin' outside the norm. Nobody was gon' believe the truth. Hell, I wouldn't've believed it myself if I hadn't been there. So we had to do somethin' believable, somethin' that would make sense to people in this world."

"Momma, what are you talking about?"

"Can you listen for once? Huh? Can you just try to hear me out?"

TL huffed and waited.

"I called Willie James into the back room where Sister was layin,' and he started hollin' and cryin' like he didn't have no sense."

"What else did you expect, Momma?"

"I expected him to calm down and listen like he eventually did. He understood. He knew I wouldn't never hurt my own child. When I explained things, he understood."

"Understood what?"

Momma shouted, "That I've been the best mother I knew how to be! To him, you, Sister, and every damn body else! He didn't assume I was no murderer like you did!" Her spittle sprayed TL's arm like a mist. "That's the only reason the lie worked—'cause of what you and everybody else 'round here think about me." Tears returned. "Just think about it, boy! Who in the world would believe that a mother killed her own child, then buried her in the backyard? Huh?"

TL didn't answer.

"Nobody!"

She was right, but he refused to admit it.

"Unless folks *already* thought the woman was crazy. Then they'd believe anything they heard about her. That shit hurts, TL."

Her mouth trembled as she licked her upper lip.

"The fact that my own son believed it is even worse! But I knew you would. I *knew* you would." She hung her head sadly.

"What did y'all do, Momma?"

She smiled peevishly. "We created a truth people could believe. That's what people like—things that make sense to them. They hate bein' forced to consider things they ain't never considered. That's why you can't never get rid of ignorance, son, because people like it. They know it. It feels natural to them. Even when they know it's not right or don't make no sense, it still *feels* right. You know what I mean?"

"Momma."

"Listen to what I'm tellin' you, boy! This is why we couldn't tell you the truth—'cause you wasn't lookin' for the truth. You was lookin' for confirmation of what you already believed. The truth was starin' you in the face and you didn't want it. How the hell could I get away wit' killin' somebody and authorities never come? Huh? I know we in the country, but we ain't on Mars! That don't make no sense! But you couldn't swallow the truth that I had done changed, so you held on to the ignorance you always believed—that I was a mean, nasty, evil woman. That's what's wrong wit' the world. We don't let people change." She paused, frowning. "Sometimes, when people change, we change 'em right back into what they was 'cause the change don't fit how we know 'em. So people get tired of fightin' to make other folks see 'em differently. Most stop tryin'."

TL knew the feeling.

"I thought education was s'posed to make people open to things. I see that ain't necessarily so."

He refused to defend himself.

"Anyway, I stripped the sheets from the bed and burned them behind the barn. I had to burn the mattress, too. Yo' daddy musta seen the clouds of black smoke 'cause he come runnin' home on the tractor, frownin' wit' confusion. I told him what happened, and he run to the barn to find Willie James, but Willie James wunnit there. Sister's body wunnit, either."

"This is really hard to believe, Momma."

"What other choice you got? If it's one thing you know 'bout me, it's that I don't lie. No time, to nobody. I don't need to. Anybody I ever needed to lie to been dead a long time."

TL tried to recall when Momma had lied, but his memory was as vacant as a cloudless sky.

She closed her eyes: "He had done took the body off somewhere. Yo' daddy went lookin' for him, all 'round the woods, but couldn't find him. We knowed he had done done somethin', so we startin' diggin' the grave. That made sense. When people disappear, we think of death. She was dead already anyway. I knew that. We just had to make the story make sense to everybody else."

"What doesn't make sense is why you put the grave in the back-yard."

"That's where the crazy woman part comes in." She laughed at herself. "See, I'm really not like that anymore. That was the old me. But it worked 'cause people like you wanted the old me more than the new me. So I used it—the crazy black woman act—one last time."

Anger flooded TL's thoughts, but he kept them to himself.

"People come by and frowned, and a few asked what happened and I told them Sister died with a contagious disease, so we had to bury her right away. They wanted to ask more—I saw it on their faces!—but they didn't. Some looked at the grave and scowled, others acted like they didn't see it at all."

"Oh come on, Momma!"

"I'm tellin' you. They walked right past it. They didn't wanna know, TL. The thought of what might've happened was probably more than they could bear, so they left it alone and come on in the house and laughed and talked like we always do."

TL stood and paced before the coffee table. "Are you kidding?"

"Live long enough, and you gon' learn to ignore some stuff, too. Some things you better off not knowin'."

"But something like this? What's wrong with people?"

She rose and hung her purse from the bend of her elbow. "Nothin'. They just got enough to carry without carryin' other folks' stuff. That's all." She wiped her eyes, sighed, then moved toward the door.

"What did Willie James do, Momma? With the body, I mean."

She shook her head slowly, trying to see into her own imagina-tion. "I don't know. I really don't know. He come home later that day, walking like a drunk man. Me and Cleatis stared at him 'til he told us he took care of everything. I asked him what he meant, but he wouldn't say. Said it was best if we didn't know, that way we wouldn't have to lie if somebody asked us 'bout it. 'What if somebody ask you?'

I said. He looked at me strange and said, 'Ain't nobody never asked me nothin'. I don't 'xpect they gon' start now."

TL's head swam. He felt faint.

"And you know what's funny? Until you come back, ain't nobody asked him a single, solitary thing. Ain't that somethin'?"

Unable to discern, in his heart, between sympathy and fury, TL remained quiet. Maybe he was feeling both.

"So"—she clapped once loudly—"there you have it!" and reached for the doorknob.

"Did you ever ask him *yourself*?"

Momma turned. "I didn't have to. A mother always knows, deep in her heart, 'bout her children." She blinked. "It had somethin' to do wit' Aunt Easter. I know that much. They had a strange connection since the day he was born. Guess you didn't know that."

"No ma'am, I didn't."

"Well, it's true. When he come out, he wasn't breathin'. Aunt Easter happened to be outside 'cause she said she knowed he was comin', and knowed he was gon' have a hard time gettin' here. I screamed when the midwife slapped his ass and he didn't cry, and that's when Aunt Easter come runnin' and shoutin', 'He ain't dead! He ain't dead!' She picked him up real gentle and put her mouth on his mouth and went to breathin' real slow. I didn't know what she was doin', but I knowed she was tryin' to help. At first, nothin' happened, but then, after a while, the baby shivered and started breathin'. He looked at Aunt Easter like he knowed her. Like a grown man looks at a woman. Never did cry. I wanted him to cry but Aunt Easter said he wouldn't. Said he didn't have nothin' to cry 'bout. He was happy. I asked her what she did, and she said, 'I blew into him the breath of life.'"

"You have to be kidding!"

"No, I ain't. That's exactly what she said. She gave me the baby and said, 'He lives and walked away. I ain't never seen nothin' like it. Ain't seen her 'round here since, either. But I used to see the way her and Willie James looked at one another. They had some kinda bond. That's all I know."

Momma eased toward the door. With her hand on the knob, she said, "Whatever else you need to know you gon' have to find out from someone else. I done told you everything I know, and I done gave you everything I got."

She left without saying good-bye.

CAN YOU SEE THE PIECES COMING TOGETHER? MOMMA ISN'T THE woman TL believes she is. He isn't the man she thinks he is. They never really understood each other although, funny enough, they're so much alike. Determined. Bullheaded. Sensitive. Oh so sensitive! Both of them! I heard Momma praying for TL one night, begging God to take care of him, out there in the harsh, cruel world. She was crying and talking all at the same time. I peeked through her bedroom door and saw her on her knees. She'd never expressed that kind of love to him directly, so it caught me by surprise. But over the years it made sense. She'd raised him, so of course she wanted the best for him. He never would've guessed she cared one way or the other, but she did. She was just poor at showing it. Daddy was, too.

But Momma had been sweet to me. We baked cookies sometimes and gave them out to folks in the community. Neither of us was very big on sweets, but we enjoyed cooking together. Usually she did the talking, telling me about her life, its disappointments and revelations. How, if she could do it all over again, she would definitely have married a different man. Or not married at all. If she could die and come back again, she said, she'd be a butterfly. They're all so beautiful. No one seeks to hurt them. People stand in awe when they flutter past, as if they're royalty among insects. "I'd like to feel royal for once," she said.

I told her my only dream was to find TL. She stiffened and told me not to worry about him. He was out in the world, making a life for himself, so I should do the same. I didn't believe her. I mean, I knew he was at school studying hard to become something, but I also believed he never stopped thinking about me. And I was right.

Not until I came to the Great City did I realize Momma's main problem: She thought she was insignificant. That's a hard life to live, giving constantly and believing no one cares. But that was her plight, and no one could convince her otherwise. Things just didn't turn out the way she had dreamed. Yet, with TL's return, she was in for the surprise of her life.

CHAPTER 18

TL REALIZED HE DIDN'T KNOW WILLIE JAMES AT all. He'd thought of him as weak-minded, but apparently he'd been wrong. Everyone was wrong. Willie James was the only one who knew everything! And all this time he'd been lying to protect Momma. *I should've known! If I'd stopped grieving long enough to think about it, I mean really think about it, I could've figured it out. That's why he let me dig up the grave—because he knew she wasn't there! Yeah, he'd fought, but not really. Willie James could've stopped me if he'd wanted to. Damn! I can't believe I missed it!*

TL poured another cup of coffee, and sat at the little oval dinette table. It was 5:00 A.M.

Yet what had all the singing and moaning been for? It had sounded genuine. Willie James wasn't dramatic enough to pull off that kind of performance. TL blew across the steaming black coffee and sipped slowly. Then, suddenly, he got it! Willie James wasn't grieving for Sister; he was grieving because his plan, their plan, was falling apart. *If he'd fought me too hard,* TL reasoned, *I would've known something was wrong from the start. So letting me discover that Sister's body wasn't in the grave was the only thing he could do.* TL shook his head slowly. Willie James knew TL wouldn't quit until he knew the truth. Willie James had counted on Momma keeping the contract never to tell. As long as she did, he could deter TL forever. But Momma told. She knew he'd come home one day, but she absolutely never dreamed he'd stay. Now that he was back . . . "Oh my God!" TL mumbled, sitting the cup on the table. "She *wants* me to stay. She gave me the truth so I'd have no reason, ever again, to leave. Or to think she didn't love me. She'd breached the contract with Willie James precisely so I'd know how much she was willing to sacrifice for me. For *me*! At whatever cost. Oh my God!"

He dressed quickly and walked home. Willie James was slopping the hogs. Their eyes met for an instant, daring either of them to tell what they knew, but both nodded simultaneously like distant neighbors and went their way. Daddy's truck was gone, so Momma was obviously home alone. TL entered unannounced.

"Hey," he called.

Momma was sweeping an already clean floor.

"Thanks for telling me the truth yesterday. You didn't have to. You really didn't."

"No, I didn't, but I wanted to. You needed to know."

TL got the dustpan and held it as she swept microscopic particles onto it. "I won't tell Willie James you told me. I promise."

Momma nodded. "Well, I'll be damn!" She appeared shocked. "Finally!"

"What?"

"You startin' to act like you got some sense. Like you belong in this family. Like you actually one of us."

They didn't speak for a while, then Momma said, "Let the boy have *somethin'*, TL. It'd do him good to think he know somethin' you don't. He done spent his whole life tryin' to measure up to you, tryin' to beat you at somethin'. What difference does it make if he don't never know the truth?"

TL hadn't thought about it.

"He was just protectin' the people he love. Same way you woulda done Carolyn Swinton."

Her innuendo was painful, but true. She moved to the sink of dirty dishes. "Been a long time since I trusted somebody like that. Kinda felt good." She giggled slightly. "Whatever else you find out, just remember I didn't do it."

From somewhere deep within, TL gathered strength to say, "Ms. Swinton said she's sorry."

Momma stiffened without turning. "What did you say?"

"It's in her journals. She asked me to tell you."

Every conceivable emotion—rage, sadness, nonchalance, regret, pity—shaded Momma's face. She resumed the dishes and looked straight ahead, through the small kitchen window, and out into nothing.

"She wanted to tell you herself, she really did, but—"

"Then she should've!" Momma snapped. "She didn't have no right, sendin' you to do her dirty work." She wiped her hands and face with a blue dishcloth.

"She would've told you, she said, but Daddy asked her not to. He made her promise to let him handle you."

"Handle me?" she screeched. "Handle me. Damn. That's what that man's been tryin' to do? *Handle me?*"

"She really wanted to talk to you, Momma. It's all in her journals. She knew she was wrong. She wanted to apologize."

Momma mumbled something TL didn't hear. She shook her head slightly, like one recovering from a spell. "I shoulda knowed it was all yo' daddy's doin'. If I woulda followed my first mind, I woulda went to her myself. But, no, I was too busy tryin' to be a good wife, so I kept my mouth closed."

"She meant well, Momma. She just didn't do well."

"I meant well, too."

Momma looked at TL as if he had the power to forgive. They exchanged forced smiles, and TL moved toward the door.

"I ain't mad at her no more. We was both grown women who made serious mistakes. One of them was mutual."

TL knew what she meant.

"Well," Momma said, "tell her it's over. I'm through wit' it. All of it. And"—she peered past TL's eyes, into some internal place—"tell her we lost. Both of us."

TL left. Willie James waved this time, wondering what in the world TL and Momma might've talked about, especially at six o'clock in the morning.

A quarter mile down the road, TL bumped into Cliffesteen. Her black dress was cleaned and ironed like new. The wig and hat were still a hot mess though, and her once-white shoes were scuffed so badly she should've thrown them away. She marched like a soldier in a regiment.

Her name was a combination of her father's, Cliff, and her mother's, Ernestine. Mr. Cliff Ross had been well liked in the community, although he was crazy, too. On Saturday nights, he'd get drunk and beat up Miss Ernestine, then stumble around the county talking trash until people got sick of him and told him to leave. You could hear him a mile away, singing and shouting about the goodness of the Lord. Somehow, after making his dreaded rounds, he'd find his way to the church steps and collapse until morning. Whoever arrived first would wake him and make him go in the back and freshen up. Then he'd reappear new, like a transfigured Christ, and lead devotion until there wasn't a dry eye in the house. That man could sing! He'd lean back and belt hymns like somebody hollering across the field. He died long before TL left home, and any time people hummed church songs, it was Mr. Cliff's voice they heard in their heads.

Cliffesteen went to his funeral, but stood outside. Folks begged her to sit with her mother, who, whenever anyone asked, said that Cliff Ross was the sweetest man the good Lord ever made, but Cliffesteen refused. "I ain't right wit' God. Ain't got no business in His house." So she paced the front steps, weeping occasionally not for her father but for her mother, who would now be alone. She worried about what Miss Ernestine would do with a farm and no man to work it. Her worries didn't last long. Miss Ernestine died of cancer in the head a few months later, having left Cliffesteen a note, which simply said, "Gone."

After that, folks said Cliffesteen never went back to the house again. Some said her daddy was her baby's daddy, but no one knew for sure. And no one knew where Cliffesteen stayed. She'd appear out of nowhere, talking loud like her father, then walk away and vanish into the same invisible realm from which she'd come. The old farm fell apart, and the county took it over since no one paid the taxes. Daddy said a wealthy white family bought it and pissed off everybody in Swamp Creek. "I coulda beat Cliffesteen's ass for that. She coulda at least tried to keep up the farm and pay the taxes, even if she ain't got no sense. Hell, how much sense it take to sweep and mop and raise a few tomatoes? Now we gotta live next to white folks—again!"

TL waved first, but Cliffesteen waited until she stood before him to speak.

"Saw yo' sister yesterday," she said, biting her bottom lip and smiling at Jezebel.

"What? What do you mean you *saw* my sister yesterday?"

She fidgeted. "I mean . . . I saw her. Like I'm lookin' at you now."

TL smirked.

"You ain't gotta believe it. Aunt Easter used to say most people can't believe what they can't see. Ain't that a shame?"

"I don't know."

Cliffesteen danced from one foot to the other. "Well, *I* know."

TL's head said walk away, but his heart said stay.

"She misses you," Cliffesteen said sweetly.

"How do you know that?"

"She said so."

TL rolled his eyes and glanced at the trees and barbed-wire fence behind her. "What else did she say?"

"Oh, that's all. She didn't have much time."

Didn't have much time? What else did she have but time?

"Spirits be busy. They have work to do."

None of this made sense. He understood now why people dismissed her.

"Come on," she said. "Let me show you somethin'."

TL wasn't sure why he followed her—and Jezebel—but he did. They walked across the Williamses' land, then crossed the Jordan in a shallow place. He'd been that far, but when she proceeded into another expanse of thick, dense forest, TL almost turned around. She stopped and beckoned him on, so he huffed and continued.

In the woods, the morning sun disappeared. Darkness lingered like fog on the tops of trees. *How does Cliffesteen see?* All he could do was follow her, and even then he could hardly keep up. Occasionally, she'd wait, then press on, and soon he'd be lagging behind again.

He learned to follow her voice. She made up songs along the way about God, humans, spirits, and animals. Hers was a rough contralto with heavy vibrato, but it was strangely soothing. She sang loudly, too, like a person walking the planet alone, and doing so in complete contentment. The sound echoed through the woods, then hid among the leaves, but he could always tell its origin. Some notes were louder than others, blazing a melodic trail that assured he wouldn't get lost. The journey became easier. His eyes adjusted to the dark. Somewhere along the way, he grew to trust Cliffesteen.

One of the songs stayed with him. It spoke of a rabbit that had died, and all the animals of the forest that attended its funeral. Some wept aloud, others more softly, but everyone grieved. It was a bizarre tale set to music, but perhaps that's why it was memorable. The refrain stuck out most:

And ye shall rest where the spirits dwell
In the Valley . . .
Until you become like God again

Until you become like God again
Until you become like God again

At the close of each line, she held the final "n" with perfect vo-
cal control as the note reverberated through time. TL wondered if
anyone else had ever heard her sing. Not like in front of the church,
but for real. It probably wouldn't have mattered. They would've
called her crazy anyway.

When the songs ended, he saw the log cabin house, high and
lifted up. It sat among the trees of the forest, as if it were shy, as if it
were hiding from someone. There was no yard, no space between the
house and the woods. Tall pines shielded it on every side like soldiers
guarding a fort. One might've thought the house had sprung natu-
rally from the earth, sitting on eight-foot stilts like a wooden throne.
It resembled a military fort, with a tin roof and one window on each
of its four sides. A porch, extending from the front, was accessible
only by a long, steep staircase that looked too fragile to climb. Cliffesteen climbed it, though, and called, "Come on!" so TL took a
chance and mounted the stairs, too. She stood on the porch proudly.

"This is Aunt Easter's house. She built it years ago. All by herself. I been keepin' it up since the Put Away. Come on in."

When he stepped through the doorway, he saw the vision again,
that city made of gold. It was just as before, with the hawk sitting
atop one of the steeples, glancing around as if he were guarding the
place. When the bird took flight, his enormous wings flapped slowly,
propelling him through the air and allowing him to circle the city
without detection. Then, as quickly as the vision came, it vanished.

Cliffesteen nodded with excitement as she rocked. She didn't
know what he'd seen, but she knew he'd seen something. The revelation must've rested on his face.

"I see stuff all the time! Don't let it scare you."

Except for twin rockers, the huge living room was totally bare.
It felt eerie. No paintings or pictures on the walls, no rug on the
floor, no tables. Nothing.

"Have a seat."

He did, but he didn't rock. Instead, he looked around for something memorable, something normal, but didn't find anything. Not right away.

"Aunt Easter liked it like this so her company would have plenty o' room. Plus, she always hated clutter."

Cliffesteen looked toward the windowsill. TL turned and yelped "Aww!", prepared to run away.

"Oh, he don't bother nobody. That's just Ol' Jack, lay 'round waitin' fo' mice o' frogs o' somethin' else to eat."

Clutching the arms of the chair with all his strength, TL wondered what he'd gotten himself into. "I think I'd better go," he said, and stood.

"Don't leave," Cliffesteen pleaded. "Please. Not yet. You s'pose to be here."

TL's soul rumbled. How could he make sense of a woman who lived with a gigantic black snake? Yet the yearning in Cliffesteen's eyes compelled him to stay. *What does this woman want? Why am I supposed to be here?* He resumed his seat.

"Ole Jack was Aunt Easter's friend. Well, one o' them. Wherever she went, he wasn't far behind. She said she found him one evenin', sliverin' up a tree after a bird's eggs. She told him he oughta be 'shame o' hisself. Plenty o' mice runnin' 'round here without him havin' to take somebody else's babies." Cliffesteen cackled. "So he come down out o' the tree and followed her home. He been here every since. She said he stayed 'cause she was the only person ever respected him enough to speak."

What the hell? TL changed the subject. "Was Easter her real name?"

"Yep. She said it was. Said her momma named her Easter 'cause she was born Easter Sunday mornin'. That's the way colored peoples used to do. They'd name chil'ren accordin' to when they was born. Or what day they was born on."

"What about her father? Who was he?"

Cliffesteen shrunk a bit, rocking easily. "Said she didn't have none. Said her momma had her all by herself."

TL's brows furrowed. "Come on. That ain't true. It's not possible."

Cliffesteen shrugged. "Jesus didn't have no daddy. Not no earthly one."

"God was His daddy."

"Then God was her daddy, too."

There was no way to win this, so TL dropped it.

"Aunt Easter was special. She knowed thangs other people didn't know. She could see what people couldn't see. Animals minded her like lil' chil'ren. I seen 'em."

"Okay."

"No, for real." She moved to the edge of the chair. "She wunnit na'chel. She was . . . outta this world."

"That's what everybody said, that she was different."

"But not just different. Special. She could go between levels, talkin' to the livin' and the not livin'."

Their eyes met.

"That's how come she knowed 'bout yo' sister. She felt it. She knowed it was comin', she just didn't know when or how. A sharp pain started in her side that day and went all the way down her hip. She couldn't hardly move. Said she seen yo' sister in her mind, cryin' and hollin', and she knowed somebody had done hurt her. She woulda went over there if she coulda got 'round. Next day, when the pain let her go, she seen the grave."

Cliffesteen touched TL's hand. He shivered. It was ice cold.

"She talked to the spirits, and they told her what happened. She didn't tell me what they said. It wunnit my business."

TL's chair began to rock, involuntarily.

"But, like I told you, I seen her spirit. More than once. Seen it a few times. She's so pretty."

Cliffesteen closed her eyes and smiled. She knew TL wouldn't leave now.

"I always see her in the same place, down by the Jordan River."

"The river?"

"Yeah. There's a little cave I go to sometimes. It ain't for most folks, but I like to sit there and let the spirits talk to me."

"I ain't never heard of no cave by the river."

"Nobody has. Weeds and vines keep it covered up. Aunt Easter showed it to me when I was a little girl. It was her favorite place. Jezebel likes it, too."

"Well, take me there."

"I can't. Not yet."

"Why not?"

She hesitated. " 'Cause you don't believe."

"In what?"

"The spirits."

"What difference does that make?"

"You gotta believe, Aunt Easter said, to go to the cave. She made me promise not to take nobody what don't believe. Said the spirits get real offended. If it ever happen, they might not come again."

"This is crazy!" TL said getting up and walking toward the door.

"That's where I saw yo' sister. In the cave. In the Valley."

His feet got heavy. He didn't turn around.

"Don't you wanna believe?"

TL couldn't have cared less about believing, but he wanted to see his sister, so he stayed.

Cliffesteen stood. "Let me show you how to believe." She extended her hands.

TL blinked cautiously. He felt as if he were getting into something he'd never get out of.

She moved toward him and took his hands and led him back to the rockers. Once they sat, she started clapping and humming.

"Trust me. I wouldn't hurt you. I'm just gettin' you ready. I wouldn't take you nowhere I can't bring you back from."

TL didn't know what she meant or what to do.

"Breathe and relax. Stop thinkin' and start feelin'."

What?

"You get on outta here, Jack! TL's scared o' you. Come back later on." The snake raised his head and slivered away.

She kept humming something in a low, minor key. TL knew the melody but couldn't think of the words.

After several minutes, her humming increased. TL studied her, but she didn't look at him. Then her clapping intensified. She was lost in this makeshift ritual. Her feet began to stomp the floor to the same rhythm with which she clapped, and the house began to vibrate. TL knew there was no turning back.

She rose and danced like Indians at a powwow. Again, TL knew the song she hummed, but the words just wouldn't come. He would've left had he not thought it rude.

Cliffesteen moved counterclockwise around TL. It was the song that drew him in. The rhythm and melody were so intense he couldn't help but close his eyes and sway his head. He didn't know if he was beginning to believe, but he was definitely beginning to feel.

Most frightening was that the rockers kept rocking. Not fast, but easy. TL didn't try to figure that out. He just accepted it for what it was. Whatever it was.

Cliffesteen circled faster now. The rhythm hypnotized him. If only he could figure it out!

Suddenly, it came and he started singing. He hadn't meant to—in fact, he'd intended to maintain safe distance from this *thing* Cliffesteen was doing—but the sound came forth on its own. She nodded vigorously. There they were, stomping and singing and dancing in the middle of Aunt Easter's house, high and lifted up, trying to free TL from disbelief.

This lasted ten or fifteen minutes, TL guessed. He couldn't tell. It might've been hours, since time was probably different, he thought, in the spirit realm. It had gotten hot. Sweat appeared across his forehead and inched its way downward. He blinked often to keep the salty droplets out of his eyes. The more he wiped them, the more they multiplied, until streams of water covered his face. Cliffesteen was feeling something. She mumbled, "Um-hm," and looked at him. Her eyes glowed red like smoldering coals. It scared TL at first, but everything scared him in Aunt Easter's house. All he could do was continue singing, hoping that, soon, he would become a believer.

Cliffesteen was sweating, too. The edges of her black, straight, stubby wig were soggy and clinging to her temples. She'd unbuttoned the top of her dress, revealing moist cleavage and a ragged, white bra. Her scuffed, off-white shoes rested slightly outside the circle.

After another rotation, TL sang loudly and Cliffesteen went berserk.

> *Talk about a child*
> *That do love Jesus . . .*
>   *Here's one!*

She flung her arms wide and hollered, "Yeeeeeeees!" Perhaps she already knew the words or maybe simply hearing them excited her. It didn't matter. She'd heard the song before, somewhere, and the melody had moved her and she'd recorded it in her soul and apparently she had kept it all these years. TL had learned the spiritual in college, singing with the Clark College Philharmonic Society, and he remembered it because the organ prelude always wrecked him long before any words were uttered. When the lyrics ushered forth, they always made him cry:

> *Talk about a child that do love Jesus,*
> *Talk about a child that's been converted,*
> *Talk about a child that do love Jesus . . .*
>   *Here's one!*

Their voices meshed into a loud, brash harmony. Cliffesteen wailed like a mother before a dying child. TL cried softly. There was an energy in the room he couldn't explain. Or control.

TL repeated "Here's one" until his hands floated into the air. He didn't know why. In church, he'd had context for this kind of thing, but deep in the woods, in a cabin high and lifted up, he wasn't sure what it was. They were in the spirit, he presumed, he and Cliffesteen, right in the middle of Aunt Easter's living room. TL wasn't afraid anymore. Watching Cliffesteen's wild antics confirmed that she wasn't of this world; she was Aunt Easter's kin. She knew things others didn't.

While TL sang, he imagined himself talking to God. The glory around the throne overwhelmed him. He told God all about his troubles, and God told him to hold out a little while longer. The house trembled. He was the child now that's been converted, and he was too joyous to stop. Had Daddy seen him he would've laughed at how ridiculous TL looked, dancing in this house with Cliffesteen, lost in a dimension between heaven and earth, or perhaps he would've grabbed him and dragged him away from this crazy place in the middle of the forest. But no one knew they were there. No one in the human realm.

Suddenly TL heard a heavy *thud*! He turned and covered his mouth, muting a desperate scream. Cliffesteen turned, too. Sitting on the window ledge, as if he'd been conjured, was the huge, brown hawk with the snow-white head. "No way!" TL said. "I don't believe this!"

Cliffesteen gawked as if a kidnapped child had been returned. She moved toward the window slowly, with deliberate ease and grace, and stroked the back of the bird sensually. TL couldn't close his mouth.

"Been a long time since the Messenger come 'round. This is a good sign. Seem like after the Put Away, he just disappeared. I didn't think I'd see him no mo', but here he is."

After swallowing hard, TL said, "I've seen that bird before! It's been following me!"

Cliffesteen nodded.

"No, really!"

She wasn't surprised. He explained that he'd seen the bird everywhere, walking down the road and sitting atop the building in the golden city, but again Cliffesteen wasn't moved.

"The Messenger gets around," she said. "He's the go-between for this world and the next."

TL was still in shock. "I just don't believe this," he murmured. "I've seen that bird almost every day!"

"Yeah, well, then he's got a message fo' you. That's the only reason he'd be followin' you. Guess you can't help but believe now."

Nothing felt real. What he'd once thought was simply a figment of his imagination was now standing before him in the flesh. How was this possible? It couldn't be mere coincidence. He stared at the bird, which stared back, as if any moment he might open his beak and speak. Ol' Jack returned and coiled himself in the corner, burying his head beneath his body.

"Aunt Easter used to call the Messenger whenever the wind blowed. She'd stand on the porch and make some kinda strange sound and the wind would carry it into the sky. I guess he heard it, 'cause wouldn't be long befo' he showed up. He'd swoop from the clouds like a bullet and land smack in the middle of the porch, right next to where Aunt Easter was standin'. She'd talk to him awhile, 'bout invisible thangs, I guess, then he'd fly off and tell everybody else what she said." Cliffesteen laughed as she remembered. "Him and Aunt Easter was real close!"

This is insane! he thought. But he couldn't leave.

"I guess that's why they call him the Messenger, 'cause he spreads the message 'round the world."

TL wanted to touch the bird, but he was too afraid. "What's the message?"

Cliffesteen hesitated, then, in a voice that didn't sound like hers, she said, "If I tell you, you ain't never gon' be the same again."

TL held his breath. Did he really want to know?

She took his silence as compliance. "There's a special place, between earth and sky, where life dwells together after this life. That's how Aunt Easter put it. It's a beautiful city."

"Oh no . . ." TL began to back away, toward the door.

"She used to say it was made o' pure gold. All spirits live there—humans, animals, trees . . . everything."

TL trembled. How could she know about the city? He bumped into the door. Cliffesteen and the Messenger looked at him simultaneously.

"Aunt Easter described it as a great big majestic city, not made by man's hands."

Turning abruptly, TL ran through the door and down the long staircase. Cliffesteen and the Messenger peered at him from the cabin window.

"Don't you wanna go there?" she hollered. "It's the most beautiful place you've ever seen! No need to be afraid!"

TL slowed his steps, but only slightly.

"Everything righteous goes there! Everything! You don't never lose life! That's the secret message, Mr. Professor! Life can't be destroyed. It jus' changes forms!" The Messenger spread his gigantic wings and leapt into the air. "Ain't no death!" she hollered. "Ain't nothin' but life! These are jus' bodies we livin' in fo' now! Our spirits live fo'ever in that city made o' purest gooooooooold!"

Dashing through the woods, TL reprimanded himself for having followed Cliffesteen. He couldn't listen to anything more. It was too much. Too true, too real. At home, he collapsed onto his own porch and cried tears of belief.

"YOU CAN'T STAY IN THIS REALM."

That's what Cliffesteen had said. It was a week after my sixteenth birthday. I had no idea what she meant. Momma rebuked her. She told Cliffesteen to keep her mouth off her child. Cliffesteen apologized sweetly. That's what startled me—her sincerity, her authentic kindness. She looked into my confused eyes and loved me. I can't really explain it, but I felt it. And I smelled her. It was a sweet aroma that soothed and relaxed me. Like the scent of rain. Or perhaps the scent before a rain, that mixture of fresh earth and heavenly moisture. It intoxicated me. Momma called for me to get in the car—we were leaving church—but my feet wouldn't move. After several seconds, Cliffesteen blinked and sighed and the spell broke. My breathing became erratic, labored. I got in the car and Momma drove away. But I knew Cliffesteen was trying to tell me something. Something important. Something I desperately needed to know.

I saw her months later, in front of the general store. The smile captured me again. I wasn't afraid. I didn't see why I should be. Others said she was a demon, like that crazy aunt of hers, but I didn't sense any of that. She just seemed . . . I don't know . . . different. Like she wasn't from this world. She was too tall to be an average woman, and she always wore that dusty black dress, as if she were going to a funeral. Perhaps sympathy is what I felt for her. She fidgeted like she was nervous about something. I wanted to know what it was. "Yo' time ain't long," she whispered, and winked, as if letting me in on a secret. "What do you mean, ma'am?" I asked and she repeated herself. I couldn't've imagined what I know now, partially because her expression contained no sorrow. The smile plus the gleam in her eyes gave her the look of sheer excitement, like one in great anticipation. I chuckled, thinking she was talking nonsense, but I still liked her. She shuffled down the road, singing something in a voice so deep it sounded like a man. Her body fumbled from side to side, like a sapling in the wind, but I knew she wasn't drunk. She was zoned, as I thought of it, lost somewhere in the sky. I hoped she'd get home someday.

CHAPTER 19

WHEN HE ARRIVED AT AUNT EASTER'S THE NEXT day, Cliffesteen was sitting on the front steps, tapping a rhythm with her bare feet.

"What took you so long? I been waitin' over a hour!" She laughed.

TL wasn't humored. He stood, slightly irritated, at the bottom of the stairway.

"You wanna know why I wear this dress all the time? I got other clothes. Got Aunt Easter's clothes, too."

TL didn't care, but he nodded anyway and met her on the porch.

"'Cause I cain't wait to go to the City. And since this body gotta die first, I stay dressed fo' death. I ain't scared. I hope it come anytime!" Her eyes brightened. "Aunt Easter talked about the city so much it made me wanna go there, you know what I mean?"

Again, TL nodded.

"You done seen it, ain't you? You done seen the city."

Sigh. "Yes. I've seen it. In a vision."

"I knowed it!" She clapped once, hard. "I could tell the way you left here. I guess the Messenger scared you."

That was an understatement. "Everything scared me, but it

seemed so real." TL shrugged. "I saw it in my head before I ever came over here. Been seein' it off and on since I got back."

Cliffesteeen shrugged, too. "Well, now you know."

She entered the house. TL remained on the porch, glancing around at gigantic trees and bushes. They were beautiful. All the leaves had their own shade of green. Some were a light, yellowish tint, others a richer, kelly green, and the needles of the pines were dark, forest green. *What an incredible backdrop,* TL thought, for a log cabin, high and lifted up, in the middle of the woods.

Cliffesteen exited the house and descended the stairs. There was one more thing to do. "Follow me," she said without pausing.

"Follow you? Are you serious?" TL shouted.

She never turned. He huffed and, against his heart's advice, shuffled behind her. They came to the river.

"Aunt Easter said people used to call this the Jordan. I don't know why. She said it was holy. Said a man used to come every year, during the rains, and cry his heart clean. I don't know if it's true o' not, but that's what she said."

TL wasn't interested in stories. He wanted to know where they were going. Crossing in a shallow place farther downstream, he and Cliffesteen entered the water without hesitation. She didn't bother lifting her dress, so he didn't roll up his pant legs, either. As hot as it was, they'd dry within seconds. TL carried his socks and sneakers in his right hand. On the north bank, they walked at least half a mile before Cliffesteen turned into a field of high grass. He knew he'd be covered with chiggers and ticks by dark, but oh well. He'd come too far to turn back now.

She led him into another patch of forest and stopped. He'd never been there, but he knew they weren't far from the river. He could still hear its rumbling.

"Ain't nobody never been where I'm 'bout to take you but me and Aunt Easter. Not that I know of." She smiled and touched his shoulder. "But now that you believe, I guess it'll be okay for you to see it."

He returned the smile. She proceeded into a thick, overgrown mass of bushes and vines. He struggled hard behind her. There was no opening. He simply pried his way forward, like all the other beasts of the forest. Cliffesteen slithered through like Ol' Jack might've. Within seconds, she'd disappeared. TL fought his way, pulling thorny vines apart and stepping over things he couldn't identify. His short-sleeved shirt left his forearms scratched and bleeding slightly, but his curiosity propelled him on. In a voice that sounded far away, Cliffesteen said, "Don't give up the fight. Jus' come on." TL obeyed.

Suddenly he stumbled into an open space. It was totally dark, except for the lighted candle Cliffesteen bore. "This is it," she whispered. "Don't talk too loud. They don't like a buncha noise."

TL couldn't've escaped if he'd wanted to. The green mass behind him closed up like a black hole in space, and everything in front of him looked like an ancient cave. He was totally at Cliffesteen's mercy.

She sat on the ground, so he did likewise. Where the candle and matches came from he didn't know. Perhaps they were always there, or maybe she had them tucked somewhere beneath her dress. He didn't ask. This wasn't the time for questions.

She began humming a tune he didn't know. After a few bars, she blew out the candlelight. They were engulfed in darkness. She must've sensed his fear because she touched his leg as she continued humming. TL couldn't see a thing. Whether his eyes were closed or opened didn't matter at all.

She stopped humming and took his hand. "Sing the song you sung yesterday. I like that song. Never did know the words. They'll like 'em, too. Trust me."

Trust you? That's all I've been doing!

When he completed the first line, the vision came again, stronger than ever. The streets shimmied under the brilliance of the sun. Perched atop the church steeple was the Messenger, glancing east to west, standing guard over the Great City. Unlike before, forms of people were now discernible, although faces were not, and animals of all species lounged easily or grazed in verdant fields. Everything seemed to exist in perfect balance. A light breeze bent the grass and made dress tails sway. No one spoke. *Maybe they're telepathic,* TL considered.

He kept singing. Then, suddenly, a warm feeling engulfed him. He shivered. It was Sister's spirit. He knew it. And he saw her form, sauntering through a flower garden, picking purple lilies and laying them in a basket. He didn't see her face, but he knew who it was. He wanted to cry.

"Do you see her?" Cliffesteen asked in the dark.

TL nodded, but couldn't speak.

Talk about a child that do love Jesus, here's one!

With the basket full, Sister took a lily, kissed it, and tossed it to the wind. TL gasped and stopped singing.

Cliffesteen relit the candle. "What did you see?"

TL sat transfixed. He'd never believed in such things, but now he was in the midst of them. "The City. I saw the City."

"Ain't it beautiful?"

Words proved insufficient. "I've never seen anything like it, Cliffesteen. I've just never seen anything that majestic."

Cliffesteen giggled with excitement. "I know! I cain't wait to get there."

"And I saw my sister, standing in a flower garden. We both loved flowers as kids. In the spring, we'd comb the forest for all different types and bring home bouquets and put them in vases throughout the house. They smelled so good Momma didn't mind. Sister's favorite was the lily."

"Told you you'd see her!"

"Well, I didn't exactly *see* her. Not her face. But I knew it was her. I felt her more than I saw her."

"Feelin' *is* seein'! Aunt Easter used to say the heart can see way more than the eyes. The eyes lie too much."

TL sighed and wished the feeling would return.

"I like flowers, too," Cliffesteen volunteered. "They so easy to get along wit'. Don't never argue or fight nobody . . . know what I mean? And they be so pretty! All the different colors and shapes bloomin' right next to one another, and don't nobody be mad 'bout the other takin' their glory. And they love when you talk to 'em! They bloom so much bigger when folks stop and say hey. Aunt Easter use to talk to 'em all the time! She had 'em all over the house, too, smellin' like heaven."

TL wasn't saying what Cliffesteen was saying, but he didn't object. She added, "It makes sense now. I saw yo' sister in the garden last time I was there."

"Did you talk to her?"

"Yep."

"How? Spirits don't talk, do they?"

"Not to livin' people, but they talk to one another."

"You livin'!"

"Yeah, but Aunt Easter showed me how to move in between."

"In between what?"

Unable to explain herself, Cliffesteen settled for, "Let's just say I went there. To the City. For a minute. Aunt Easter came and got me in my sleep, but, since I hadn't died yet, I couldn't stay. Yo' sister asked 'bout you. We recognized each other. I looked way better over there!" She cackled.

TL asked, "Why do I keep getting this vision? Am I about to die?"

Her smile reassured him. "Chile, please! You cain't never tell 'bout Ol' Death. Just remember the message: Death ain't the end. People think it is, but really it's the beginning." Then she whooped like an old country Baptist preacher, "Death ain't got no *power*! It's just the way we get outta here. That's all."

TL chewed the inside of his jaw.

"Come on. I'ma show you somethin' else."

Cliffesteen struggled to her feet and moved toward the back of the cave. TL followed. They seemed to be entering the depths of the black hole. The small candlelight flickered nervously, as if intimidated by the darkness. "Where are we going?" he asked, but she didn't say. Soon, the rounded walls of a tunnel confined them. It was barely five feet high and three feet wide. Cliffesteen blew out the flame. *What the hell you do that for?* TL thought. She answered, "They don't like a buncha light, either. Just stay behind me." He was totally blinded. She could've murdered him right there if she'd wanted to, but he knew better. She didn't even believe in death, so what would've been the point?

They walked on, bodies bent practically in half. If he'd've stretched his arms wide, he could've touched both sides of the tunnel at once, but, afraid of losing his guide, he held on to Cliffesteen's waist while she plowed forward. It twisted and turned, the tunnel, until TL was sure they'd made a complete circle. They must've walked a quarter mile or so. Then Cliffesteen stopped. TL relinquished her waist. She relit the candle, and they sat on the hard, rocky base of the tunnel.

"Look," she said, lifting the light above her head.

When TL looked up, his breathing stopped. "Jesus Christ!" he screeched. There were names etched everywhere, in childlike penmanship. Some of the letters were small and barely distinguishable, others were large and bold. A rock or some hard instrument had obviously been used as the writing utensil. His head wouldn't stop shaking.

"These the people what run through here fo' freedom, Aunt Easter said. They left their names so we'd know their story one day."

TL blinked, trying hard to focus. Chills raced across his arms. He began to read aloud, though still at a whisper: "Nancy, Willie Joe, Bertha Mae, Tom, Columbus, Gladys, Annie Lou, Conklin, Bimma, Joe T, Dot, Earl, Stella, Harry, JoNathan, Hezekiah, Margaret Ann, Oliver C, Ray Charles." He touched each name as if the letters gave life. He'd studied this history, but he'd never seen it. Not like this.

TL took the candle from Cliffesteen and illumined, on all sides of the passageway, hundreds of names of people who'd once dwelt there, trembling undoubtedly with fear and excitement, believing that a day would come when they'd be freed. As he read the names, he felt their pain and anguish. He couldn't explain it, but something within him came alive. It was as if he knew these people personally, as if he were calling roll at the Great Camp Meeting black folks always sang about. He believed they knew him, too, or had dreamed of him, as they sat in this tunnel, a century ago, calling his name.

"Aunt Easter memorized all the names. Every single one of 'em. She'd come in here and stay fo' hours, talkin' to folks like they was sittin' right in front o' her. I came wit' her sometimes."

Shadows moved around them. TL inched forward, discovering still more names. He read each of them with pride, standing as living proof that his ancestor's struggle had not been in vain.

Returning to Cliffesteen, TL knelt in reverence. He had come back to the womb of his people. His soul knew this place. His spirit was born here. And all of this just happened to be in Swamp Creek. Or, rather, Black Haven. Were these the voices beckoning him when he got off that bus?

Cliffesteen hummed softly. "You doin' good. But this ain't all. Come on."

The candlelight led their way. They walked another mile or so, encountering more names of people on their way to Freedomland. "You don't see as many names down here as you did back there," Cliffesteen explained, "'cause folks was runnin' through this part. They didn't have time for writin' when they got this far. Back there was the restin' place."

"Oh."

They continued until reaching a fork in the tunnel. The candle burned low. Cliffesteen took the path to the right. Of course TL wondered where the other led to, but he wasn't about to find out on his own.

Soon, streaks of light danced in the distance. Cliffesteen put the candle away and said, "We're almost there now." TL felt the earth rise beneath them.

As before, they fought through a fortress of overgrown bushes and intertwining vines. TL couldn't figure out where they were. Then he looked around and saw Old Man Birch's house.

"You've gotta be kidding! I don't believe this!"

"What?"

"Folks always said the Birch place was part of the Underground Railroad. It must've been true."

Cliffesteen frowned. "Part o' what?"

"The Underground Railroad. The system slaves used to escape to freedom. That's what they called it. They probably ran from the river through the tunnel just like we did. Then Old Man Birch hid 'em away somewhere."

"Probably in that dungeon under his flo'."

"What!" TL screamed.

Cliffesteen frowned. "You didn't know 'bout that?"

"Yes! Well, I mean no. I'd heard about it, but I didn't think it was real."

"Oh yeah it's real all right! Aunt Easter told me 'bout it. Said Old Man Birch's granddaddy was one o' them people what fought against slavery. He built the house hisself just fo' that reason."

The dilapidated shack looked sad. TL imagined desperate days when slaves dashed from the woods, another fifty yards, into Birch's holding cell. He'd taken the risk of a lifetime, and, from the names inscribed on the walls of the tunnel, he'd taken it more often than anyone ever knew. TL stared at the house. Uncle Jesse Lee was right—Black Haven was something else!

After his surprise subsided, TL inquired about the other route, the one they didn't take. Cliffesteen's demeanor shifted. "You sho you wanna know?"

TL said yes, so she led him, reluctantly, back into the underground passageway. At the fork, she stopped, rubbing her arms fretfully.

"Is you really sho'?"

TL said, "I think so."

She lit the candle for the last time. "Ain't nobody been that way but me and Aunt Easter. Never. Not nobody livin'."

"What about the slaves?" he whispered, unsure of why he was whispering. "Wouldn't they have gone that way sometimes?"

"Naw. It didn't exist back then. Aunt Easter dug it out."

"What? *She* made it?"

"Yeah."

He almost asked why, but decided it didn't matter. He just wanted to know where it led.

Still, Cliffesteen didn't move.

"Is something wrong?"

Her head shook, and she flashed a fake smile. He waited. She finally gave in. "It's what yo' spirit wants, so come on." So TL went.

It was narrower than the first tunnel. A cold, eerie feeling accompanied them, like a draft you can feel but never find. TL knew Cliffesteen was withholding something, but he couldn't decipher what it was. They were stooped so low they were practically crawling. The candle had burned down to a small wick. TL prayed the tunnel wouldn't collapse while they were in it. There'd be no chance of survival.

At least Aunt Easter had had the good sense to support the passageway with plywood and other uneven boards. TL couldn't imagine how she did it by herself, hauling dirt away and carrying in materials too heavy for the average woman, but of course she wasn't the average woman. Not by a long shot.

The tunnel twisted and turned until TL couldn't tell north from south. His breathing became labored, as if, at some point, the altitude had shifted, but he was too anxious to complain. They moved slowly now, like cautious, discreet thieves. That's how he knew Cliffesteen was concealing something. They'd blazed through the other tunnel, running the way their ancestors must've, only to find themselves in Old Man Birch's backyard. This was no discovery for her. She knew the genesis and revelation of it all. Her joy was watching TL learn what only she and Aunt Easter once knew, but somehow, in this other direction, she was timid, hesitant, seemingly calculative of the price she'd pay for what she was doing. TL didn't understand.

She stopped and lit the small wick. Enshrouded by her left palm, the nervous, flickering flame cast shadows against the walls of the narrow passageway. Cliffesteen turned to the right and removed her hand, and TL released a scream that echoed throughout the tunnel. *Am I seeing things? Or is that what it looks like?* She never flinched. She already knew.

Clutching her right arm in mortal fear, TL trembled. The fragile flame illumined, off to the right, a collection of skulls and bones.

"This is it," she said. "You finally made it. This is the Valley. The Valley of the Dry Bones."

TL felt light-headed.

"And these are they, Aunt Easter used to say, who've been washed in the blood of the lamb."

TL swallowed hard, then blinked, convinced he was dreaming.

"Don't be scared. They love you. They love everyone."

What the hell!

She knelt before the bones like one kneeling before an altar. "It's the Valley of the Dry Bones," she repeated, "the final restin' place of the righteous."

"What are you talking about, Cliffesteen?"

Seconds passed while she prayed. When she lifted her head, TL said, "This is crazy! It ain't right!"

" 'Course it's right. What else could it be but right?"

"It's insane!"

TL would've run if he could've, but his limbs were shaking too badly. Then it all came together. "Oh no! No! No!"

"Shhhhhhh," she warned. "She and the others don't like a lotta confusion. They like peace."

He squeezed his head.

"It's what she wanted. It's the only way she was gonna be happy. She had to be here, right here, next to my Jezebel and the others until she went to the Great City. This way, she didn't travel alone."

TL couldn't look at the bones, he couldn't look at Cliffesteen, and he couldn't breathe. He felt semiconscious.

"Everybody don't get to come here, though. None but the righteous. Aunt Easter brought 'em. Couldn't nobody bring 'em but her. She was the *only* one." Cliffesteen wiggled her index finger. "Not even me. I couldn't bring 'em. But Aunt Easter could talk to 'em. She had them kinda powers."

Composing himself a bit, TL shook his head. "But how did Aunt Easter get—"

"I don't know. I never did see her bring nobody, but she told me 'bout yo' sister. She felt the whole thing. Said yo' sister had to be here. That's the only way the child could have peace."

TL looked at the bones again. The skeletons were indistinguishable, so in his mind, none of them had ever been his sister, although, in his heart, he believed otherwise.

A dim halo of light hovered above the bones.

"Aunt Easter never would tell me everythin'. Said it was better if I didn't know, so I stopped askin'."

"How did she get Sister's body?"

"I don't know that either. She was sick as a dog the day yo' sister died. I told you 'bout that. But I guess it mighta happened later that evenin' or the next day."

The eye sockets of the skulls winked each time the candlelight flickered. TL refused to let go of Cliffesteen's arm.

"But, like I said, didn't nobody come here unless Aunt Easter brung 'em. Yo' sister was number twenty-three. Then they put Aunt Easter away."

For a brief second, in TL's mind, the bones came together—reconnected, as it were—and told their stories. They spoke of tragic and triumphant black people who never got their due and a way of life so hard it seemed unimaginable. Each was cloaked in royal white robes with puff sleeves. TL was proud to be among them, proud to be their son. "We need you," he heard them say. "The battle is far from over." TL nodded. "For this reason, we give you our strength. Go forth—and win!" TL promised to give his all. Only in that moment did he believe he'd be enough, that he'd actually been called for the task at hand. Then, moments later, when reality returned, he saw himself running like hell out of the tunnel, past Swamp Creek, and out of the state of Arkansas forever. But since that wasn't an option, he shivered where he was, wondering how he had let Cliffesteen usher him into this place of no return.

She said other things, but he wasn't listening. He was ready to go. Cliffesteen pried his hands from her arms. "'Course this ain't her. Not no mo'. She *been* gone. You saw her yo'self. This here"—she pointed to the bones—"is just proof that she *was* here—once upon a time."

Cliffesteen touched the bones lovingly. TL thought he heard them moan. "They all right. They don't bother nobody."

"Can we just go?"

She stood and rubbed her hands together. "You can't tell nobody 'bout this. Nobody. Ever." They began walking through the tunnel again. After a few steps, she paused and added, "'Cause if you do, you can't go to the Great City."

"Why not?"

Cliffesteen didn't say. She simply pressed on. Soon the air became breathable and TL knew they were approaching the end.

"Don't forget what I said. You wanna be wit' yo' sister, don't you?"

TL nodded.

"Good. Then never speak what you saw today."

They fought through overgrown brush and thick, intersecting

vines. When TL noticed where they were, he froze, mouth agape, and muttered in total awe and wonder, "Oh . . . my . . . God! I don't believe this! It can't be!" Before him stood the old run-down general store, a mere relic of a time and town long forgotten. TL fell to his knees and, with lifted hands gave thanks and praise. The Messenger glided alone. He'd just discovered the twelfth gate to the city of Black Haven.

HE'S READY NOW. HE'S BEEN TO THE VALLEY. BUT THIS IS ONLY THE first part of the journey. Now comes the second part . . .

A person's life assignment always includes others. We're sent to the world because of what others lack. It's not always glorious, this calling, but it *is* always fruitful. Our payment is often someone else's growth. That's what TL must figure out now—who else this newfound knowledge is for and how that person is supposed to use it. See, the joy is not his own. It's not some personal ecstasy sent to excite him alone. It's a communal inheritance, which has no real power until he passes it on. Just as Cliffesteen did. How can he do that, you ask, when he can't talk about it? That's for him to discover. And until he does, the journey is not complete. . . .

CHAPTER 20

TL LEFT CLIFFESTEEN WHERE SHE STOOD. HE HAD to get away. There was no one to talk to, no one who would understand, no one who would even believe all that he'd seen. On top of that, he *couldn't* tell it—ever!—if he wanted to go to the City. Perhaps Cliffesteen was lying, he thought. Maybe she'd said those things simply to keep him from talking. But he doubted it.

Uncle Jesse Lee's unpolished baritone relaxed his anxiety. Thoughts churned in his head like tumbleweeds in the desert. TL looked drunk, stumbling along the side of the road, trying to make sense of what only three sets of human eyes had ever beheld. *Were those really Sister's bones? Really?* He wanted so badly not to believe it, to dismiss everything as a joke, a fantasy, a mere foolish dream about a crazy woman and a desperate man who had followed her, but his heart wouldn't allow it. It reminded him that, like those who'd once trembled in the cave, he couldn't deny the truth. He was part of it now, co-conspirator, in fact, with those unseen gate-keepers who traverse the boundary between the visible and the invisible. Self-deception was no longer an option.

And, anyway, he'd felt it all. That's why he couldn't lie about it. He'd actually felt his sister's spirit, as sure as people feel the wind. He knew it as well as he knew his own. She had always calmed him, he said, like the soothing sensation of a cool, ocean breeze. It was just her way. TL, on the other hand, was the high-strung, melodramatic one who cared too much what others said about him. Sister was the earth, revolving without notice, while TL was fire, explosive in all his passions. She was his other half, his soul mate, so he definitely knew what her spirit felt like. And they were together in that city made of gold! He'd never be the same again. His heart's desire was to stay with Sister, although, unlike Cliffesteen, he wasn't prepared to die.

Sweat streaked TL's face like African warrior marks. It's a wonder he'd walked in the right direction, baffled as he was. As he approached the tree, his sensibilities returned. He began to breathe normally. Cliffesteen and Aunt Easter didn't have to worry about him talking. He was too afraid of what he knew to tell anyone.

"Fooled around and got me a life," Uncle Jesse Lee sang, head leaning back and swaying in a figure-eight pattern. The coarse harmonica filled in the empty spaces. Some of the notes didn't sound right, or at least didn't sound clean, and, on a different day, TL probably would've laughed, but at the moment he needed clarity more than entertainment. He didn't care where it came from. Uncle Jesse Lee repeated the line twice before belting the final quatrain: "Now I ain't got no choice but to live it!"

He sat on a rusted, tan folding chair, tapping worn, battered, brown brogans against the dusty earth. TL rested at the end of the old church pew. He wasn't sure the elder had noticed him. Rocking and crooning before an invisible audience of millions, Uncle Jesse Lee reiterated the homemade ballad as if the crowd had begged for an encore. He was a study in contentment. It didn't matter what others said—and they said a lot!—about him wasting time at the tree when he should've been home tending his overgrown garden or making love to his overgrown wife. Their comments went in one ear and out the other. Uncle Jesse Lee felt music in his marrow, and the devil in hell couldn't've kept him from playing it. He'd raised his kids and loved Aunt Bertha Mae the first forty-five years of his life. The second forty-five, he said, were his.

After a slight pause, he relaxed into the chair and said, "Trouble don't last always, son." He didn't look at TL; TL didn't look at him, either. His mind was still somewhere in the tunnel.

"Worry sits like that on a man sometimes." Uncle Jesse Lee nodded. "Trust me, I know. I done wore it."

Staring into the leaves of the Meetin' Tree, TL asked, "How do you get rid of it?"

"Every man's gotta find his own way o' handlin' thangs. Me, I sings it off. Or plays this ol' thing. " He blew into the harmonica, creating a bizarre run of disjointed, chaotic notes. "But you gotta find yo' own thang, son. Ain't nothin' else gon' help you. Can't nobody live without somethin' to restore they mind when it gets outta whack." He repeated the chaotic chord progression.

Something about the world seemed different to TL. Or perhaps he was simply more aware of things, now that he'd glimpsed the city made of gold. Like the worm he noticed struggling through the earth at the base of the tree. He'd seen worms before, but he'd never paid them much attention. It rose, like a miniature cobra, wiggling from side to side until it freed itself. Then it stretched forth and rested. *Could it be exhausted from its own journey? Do worms get tired?* TL was a stranger in its world. How many other worlds had he overlooked?

An eighteen-wheeler hummed by, leaving a matrix of hot, humid, suffocating air. Uncle Jesse Lee fanned with his ragged fishing hat. "Gotta be somethin' that feeds yo' spirit. Man can't live by bread alone."

The only thing TL could think of was writing. He did it a lot as a kid, reading short stories and poems to whoever was willing to listen. It was usually Grandma. She loved to watch him act like different people as he created worlds no one else could've imagined. By the time he left for college, he had notebooks full of stuff he'd written (and abandoned). Most of his writings were about the experiences of black children in the country and the private hurts and abuses they endured. Some were funny, but he was never much good at humor. He wrote what he knew, and most of it simply wasn't funny. That's probably the real reason he stopped writing. It conjured too much pain. After eighteen, he found himself depressed or wanting a drink whenever he wrote. And he didn't even drink! Yet, somehow, regardless of his attempt to avoid it, he couldn't stop writing. Not altogether. Most everything he conceived featured his heart as the protagonist, and he wasn't prepared to offer the public that much of his truth. The few times it wasn't true, the stories were contrived and artificial, but even so, he loved himself when he was writing. Lost in the imagination, he became his own god, shaping people and circumstances precisely as he needed them. But, unlike God, his creations weren't everlasting.

"I used to write," TL said. "But I stopped. Well . . . sorta."

"Why? Why would you stop writin'? In the beginnin' was the Word."

TL chuckled. Uncle Jesse Lee had a way of putting things.

"You don't know yo' Bible, boy." His frown reprimanded. "In the beginnin' was the Word!" Uncle Jesse Lee shouted louder as if TL hadn't heard him. Or as if he'd missed the point. "And the Word was *wit'* God, and the Word *was* God. The same was in the beginnin' *wit'* God."

TL didn't understand his emphasis, much less the overall meaning.

Uncle Jesse Lee ran his tongue across his false teeth, then offered, "Anybody what know how to write oughta do it every chance he get. The word is powerful, son. God created the world wit' words. He just said 'Let there be' and stuff showed up. I 'magine that's what writers do—put words on a piece o' paper and stuff show up in people's minds."

Wow. TL had taken Uncle Jesse Lee too lightly. He'd told him to look for the signs, but TL had missed most of them. As it was, his comprehension still had holes and gaps where understanding should've been. Now he had to search harder for what Uncle Jesse Lee was trying to tell them.

"If I could write, I would. But I can't. I wasn't good in school. But you? You oughta be able to do somethin' wit' a pencil and a sheet o' paper, smart as you is."

TL listened more closely than before.

"It ain't but a few people who can do what you do. Whole lotta folks tell stories, but they can't write 'em. The ones what can write 'em gets the credit. They gets somethin' else, too." His expression bore confidence and self-assurance. "They get the ear o' the whole world. The *whole world*!" He smiled. "Now that's power, boy, 'cause they gets to say 'xactly what they want to say, and people ain't got no choice but to listen. And they get to say it however they want to say it. Can't get no closer to God than that, can you?"

"No sir."

"Naw, you can't." His head shook vigorously. "I do's music, but you do the word. And the Word came first."

Another vehicle sped past, giving TL time to think. He'd resolved to teach for the rest of his life, but now Uncle Jesse Lee had disturbed his plans.

"So if you can write, don't neva stop. Most of our stories ain't neva been told. Not to the world. So people ain't neva really seen colored people. Not for what we really are. But maybe that's yo' job—to show the world who we really are so we can hold our heads up again."

Without transition, Uncle Jesse Lee returned to the harmonica, playing a really bad rendition of B. B. King's "The Thrill Is Gone." TL had heard it on the radio several times, and knew which parts the old man didn't have quite right, but that didn't bother Uncle Jesse Lee. His point was simply to play because he liked music. It didn't matter how excellent he was. He wasn't trying to be excellent; he was trying to keep his mind right. That had been TL's problem—he dreamed of Pulitzers and the applause of other writers, although he hadn't published anything. Maybe if he just wrote, he'd have peace and wouldn't care what others thought. Wasn't that Uncle Jesse Lee's lesson? And if he never won anything, simply by publishing he'd change the world? *Wow. Knowledge is good, but wisdom is irreplaceable.*

He left Uncle Jesse Lee like he'd left Cliffesteen—abruptly—without looking back. Racing home with renewed motivation, TL had decided to write again. The topic didn't matter. That would come. If Uncle Jesse Lee could sing without shame—and folks said he should be ashamed—TL could definitely write. He had a zillion stories in his head, but he'd left them there because they were too personal and painful. "Ugh!" he grunted. *There you go again! Worrying before you even start!* Of course he wanted to write about the cave, but he couldn't. Even if he could, who would believe it?

He began to imagine what Willie James might've done with Sister's body. That would be a story! Had he brought it to Aunt Easter, who then took it to the Valley? How would Willie James have known to take it to Aunt Easter in the first place? What was the nature of their relationship? Yes, this would intrigue a reader for sure! Even how he'd led TL on a wild-goose chase, when, all the while, he knew everything. Willie James was Br'er Rabbit, outsmarting the fox every time. Just when the fox thought he had the rabbit trapped and bound, the rabbit introduced some new element in the story, designed specifically to set him free. That's how country folks do! They act like they don't know things, just to see how far you'll go to find out. TL was country, too, but education had dulled his rural sensibilities. If he was going to live in Swamp Creek, and it looked as if he was, he would have to be far shrewder, far stealthier, far subtler than he preferred. He'd have to become the sly rabbit again. Or else the fox would get him every time.

AFTER DRAFTING the story, which didn't transfer to paper so well, he took a walk and ended up at the family home. As usual,

Willie James was fixing the old tractor. TL didn't think he saw him until Willie James said, "What are you lookin' for now?"

Dust and grease covered his face and hands while muscular biceps bulged from his short sleeves. Small, rounded balls of kinky, coarse, black hair stood on his chest, pushed forward by full, hard pecs. A few gray strands stood among them.

"Nothin'." TL lingered like a bored child.

"It's always *somethin'* wit' you."

If TL said anything, he feared he'd say too much, so he looked heavenward and begged God to help him hold his peace. Leaning on the big, rear tractor wheel, he waited as Willie James circled the machine, greasing each joint.

Tension mounted. TL wasn't sure why he was there. Maybe he hoped Willie James would volunteer enough information to confirm what Cliffesteen had said, but so far he didn't say anything. Willie James seemed his regular, naïve self. Now TL knew better.

"Why didn't you tell me Sister wasn't in the grave?"

Willie James's rustling on the other side of the tractor stopped. "'Cause it didn't make no difference. She was gone. That was the important thing."

"But you knew I'd wanna know. That's the only reason I came back."

Willie James grunted, "Ump."

"I'm sorry. You know what I mean."

"Hey, man, look," he said, peering over the front end of the tractor. "Everybody know why you come back. That ain't no secret. Most know why you stayin', too." He lowered his head and returned to work. "It's them kids. What else could it be? You never liked Arkansas so—"

"Never liked Arkansas? Are you crazy? I love it here. Always have."

Willie James frowned.

"I just couldn't stand the way people treated me. Especially my own folks."

Willie James couldn't defend the guilty.

"It was hell, man. Don't you remember? The way people talked about me behind my back?"

"Yep, I know."

"It was Momma half the time!"

"I know that, too."

"Then why you act so surprised I didn't come home more often?"

He stood before TL. "'Cause I thought you was stronger than what people said."

"I was a kid, man! Ain't no kid stronger than what people say!"

He shrugged. "Guess you right."

TL felt insulted. "Man, I love this place! Our folks worked this land for generations! This is my home!"

"You mean *our* home."

"Of course it's our home. I thought about it every day I was gone. I just couldn't relive the pain. I couldn't."

Willie James looked down.

"I wasn't Momma's favorite. I never knew why back then. I'm not sure I know now, but at least I know why she struggled. It hurt so bad, man, watching her adore the rest of you. I couldn't figure out what was wrong with me! And Daddy didn't help. He acted like he didn't even know what was going on. He let me live my whole life believing something that wasn't true. Shit! He didn't love me enough to make sure I knew my own mother!"

Willie James drew circles in the dirt with the toe of his right brogan. "I understand what you sayin'."

TL wasn't sure he did.

"I just didn't know you liked the old place. Not like *that*."

A honeybee circled TL's head until he swung at it with all his might. "Like it? Man, I love it! Don't you remember how I used to walk these roads by myself, singing at the top of my lungs?"

Willie James smiled. "Hell yeah! We could hear you all through the woods."

"That's because I loved it, man. I'd walk and see a hawk chase another bird down and peck it apart or I'd see a snake choke a mouse to death right in the middle of the road and I'd say, 'God's Glory,' just like Grandma used to say. Or I'd go fishing back on the creek and come home with a mess of crappie and when we ate them, I'd be so proud. I fished more than anybody else in the family!"

"That's true."

"If the fish didn't bite, I'd walk the banks, skipping rocks and picking up turtles or talkin' to myself about how I wanted to teach like Ms. Swinton one day."

Willie James said, "Guess you can't never tell what's in a man's heart, huh?"

"No, you can't."

A young fawn caught their attention, darting across the field and into the forest. Willie James aimed at it with his finger and said, "Pow!" TL had never cared for hunting. Watching beasts writhe and squeal in pain was more than his fragile spirit could stand. Daddy took him coon hunting once, but each shot left him trembling. He promised to leave him at home next time. That was fine with TL. He probably should've been ashamed, but he wasn't. Not about that. He'd be soft for the rest of his life, he decided, if it meant he didn't have to kill things.

Yet, make no mistake about it: His objection didn't result from any moral principle. Everything Daddy killed TL ate. Anxiously. He'd sit at the table and devour pork, beef, coon, squirrel, rabbit, fish—he could kill fish—like a starving grizzly. That boy could eat! He didn't appear troubled at all that someone had killed it. He just couldn't do it himself.

Time waited patiently to see which brother would break and tell it all, but neither did. Both had signed verbal contracts that simply couldn't be broken. Willie James needed Momma, and TL needed to believe that nothing—real or imagined—would ever keep him from going to the Great City.

Several awkward moments passed. Willie James breathed deeply and returned to the other side of the tractor. It was early evening, but the sun still blazed relentlessly. Arkansas heat is like that. In mid-July or August, it's ninety degrees at night. TL wiped his brow and moved to the tractor seat, staring across the field of cut hay, longing for the comfort of the window-unit air-conditioner in his bedroom. Daddy had air-conditioning, too, but he never used it, didn't care how hot it got. As children, we'd lay in bed, wet with sweat, and Daddy still wouldn't turn it on. When we complained, he'd say, "Go outdoors. Plenty o' air movin' 'round out there."

Hours passed as Willie James worked. He simply didn't intend to talk. When night fell, he clicked on a flashlight and said, "Guess I'ma turn in soon."

TL descended the tractor and said good night. Down the road, he heard rustling behind him. He knew who it was.

"I can't tell you what I did," Willie James said, approaching slowly. "I made a promise."

The glare from his flashlight blinded TL. "I understand."

Willie James clicked it off. They didn't need it. A full moon shone above.

"If I told you, you'd be responsible for doin' somethin' 'bout it. That's why I did what I did—so no one else would be responsible but me."

"Just tell me one thing. Was Aunt Easter involved?"

He shook his head. "I can't tell you anything. Ever. This way, can't nobody be charged with nothin'. Even if the police come, ain't no evidence or witnesses."

"Do you think this is right?"

"I don't know, but I think it's best. It's worked so far. It'll be okay."

TL didn't press the matter.

"I loved her as much as you did, man."

TL felt Willie James's sorrow. He thought again of the Valley of the Dry Bones. He still wasn't sure those were Sister's remains, but now, without his brother's corroboration, he'd have to trust Cliff-esteen's word.

"You not gon' know this one, lil' brother. Not 'til we get on the other side."

TL parted his lips to tell Willie James about the vision—*that's not off limits, is it?*—but fearing it was too connected to everything else, he closed his mouth and grunted, "All right."

"It just seemed like the family was fallin' apart. You was gone, then the whole thing happened with Sister. It looked like we didn't have no future. I knowed what folks woulda done if they found out the truth, and I woulda lost what little I had left. Can you imagine me livin' the rest of my life by myself?"

"No, brother. I can't."

"Well, I couldn't, either. That's why I decided to do somethin'. To save us. What was left of us. I had to. It was all I had." With extended palms, he shrugged like a helpless child. "I promised God I'd take the truth to my grave, and that's what I'm gon' do. I'm doin' you a favor, man. Believe me."

Unable to share what he knew, TL realized he was now a legitimate citizen of Swamp Creek, a keeper of someone else's secret.

Before stepping back into darkness, Willie James said, "I'll tell you one thing." He hesitated. "Someone helped me."

"Who?"

"Someone. That's all I can say."

Willie James vanished without using the flashlight. He knew the forest better than its inhabitants. Years ago, he'd laughed at TL for using a flashlight at night. Neither of them needed it, Willie James had said. TL just *wanted* it. Yes, he could've walked the woods in the dark, TL admitted, but the flashlight kept him from walking up on things. "Things like what?" Willie James teased, but TL wouldn't say. It was those spirits that people spoke of incessantly that he feared. He couldn't explain why. In his mind, they lived in the forest, lurking behind trees and bushes. The cloak of darkness allowed them to roam, and, without the flashlight, he'd convinced himself he'd shit his pants if he saw one. Willie James would've screamed had he heard this. He would've told Daddy and, together, they would've mocked TL into eternity. So he took the flashlight and kept his fears to himself.

After the day's experience with Cliffesteen, his fear of spirits diminished. Not totally, but greatly. *If they'd wanted to hurt me,* he rationalized, *they certainly could've.* Of course he didn't *see* anything, not really, but he knew what he felt. And, in many ways, that was even more real. The names, etched in stone across the ceiling of the cave, were as eerie to TL as the bones. In a strange way, they *were* bones, he thought, introducing him to people, lives, and stories he'd never known. They were alive, those names, trembling with energy and hope that someone might see them, touch them, and believe and be transformed. He chuckled now at his childish theory of spirits living in the woods. They *lived* wherever they liked, he concluded. And some of them apparently liked that cave.

TL walked home and sat at the small oval kitchen table and began writing another story about a young man with a terminal illness. He had no name. TL wasn't even sure it mattered. The protagonist hadn't told anyone about his illness because he felt he'd never meant much. Most with such limited time surround themselves with family, but this character went to the sea. He sat, feeble and frail, and watched the waves lick the sandy shore. Memories of hurt and loneliness consumed him. He cried out his mother's name—Laura, Laura—but she never heard him. At sunrise, a group of children found him, cold and stiff, balled in a fetal position, wet from the rising tide.

There was a sad yet sanguine beauty to the story. How the sea tried to love him, to touch him, to reinvigorate him with life. How, throughout the night, as the water rose, it rocked him like a mother trying to calm an anxious infant. He'd never known his dad. Well, he knew him, but he never knew his love. That had never been part of the bargain, the love thing, so the son spent thirty-three years wondering if his father ever really wanted him.

It was 2:43 A.M. TL couldn't think anymore, so he went to bed, but before he went to sleep, he asked himself, one last time, *Were those really Sister's bones?*

CHAPTER 21

ON THE FIRST DAY OF SCHOOL, TL ARRIVED IN THE dark. It was just after six. He'd been too excited to sleep. He was about to either make a royal fool of himself, he thought, or, if things went well, birth a legacy similar to Ms. Swinton's. It could go either way. He'd prepared lessons weeks in advance, and imagined himself walking the aisles between desks, quenching the thirst of children whose parents had only dreamed of an education. He'd once been one of them. Maybe that's why he was so nervous. He knew the price of a failed teacher, and he knew the children couldn't afford it. For some of them, the quaint, A-framed schoolhouse was their last hope, and TL prayed he could deliver.

He unlocked the door and, looking across the dim, empty room, froze with nostalgia. This was where it all began. He saw himself, sitting at the desk in the front row, directly in front of Ms. Swinton, absorbing every word she uttered. He never took his eyes off her. Whenever she used a word he didn't know, he'd thumb the dictionary frantically until he found it. Only TL possessed a personal dictionary, which lay concealed in his lap the entire school year. He wanted to be smart, to make her proud, to mean something to somebody, and she loved every minute of it. No surprise that he quickly became her favorite. She tried to hide it, but all the children knew. Some days, he'd get to school early and wait on the front steps, reviewing his homework for the umpteenth time. It had to be perfect! He lived for her approval. TL felt embarrassed now about how far he'd gone to get it. Many evenings, he rewrote essays far into the night—with what Daddy called a girl's penmanship— because he'd made some trivial error. Students were allowed to draw a single line through mistakes, Ms. Swinton had said, but TL never did. He simply rewrote the whole page again whenever he erred. Willie James said he was crazy, but TL dismissed Willie James, sure that he didn't understand what was at stake.

TL would get one year, the superintendent had said, to do what Ms. Swinton had done for forty. Then, through forced consolidation, all schools in the county would integrate. Court orders. Wow. One year to plant the seeds of transformation in the lives of poor, black children no one else cared about. TL wasn't naïve enough to think he could actually transform them in a year, but he was certainly arrogant enough to try.

When he switched on the lights, he chuckled. There, in perfect rows, were the same wooden, antique, lift-top desks he'd used ten years earlier! And they were in mint condition! Ms. Swinton had made sure of that. She'd fine a child's family if she found writing or other marks on "the furniture," as she called it, and one's ass would be sore for a good week. There were no questions asked. If she said it, it was so.

One day at recess, Matt Henson gave TL a piece of Wrigley's Spearmint chewing gum. That was one of Ms. Swinton's cardinal rules—no gum in the schoolhouse—but he thought he could chew it subtly. Matt warned TL not to, especially since he sat in the front row, but TL proceeded anyway, convinced she'd never know. Matt bet him fifty cents she'd call him out. By the end of the day, she hadn't said a word. TL boasted to Matt on the way home about his shrewd, smooth demeanor, and Matt reluctantly gave him his last two quarters. When TL arrived home and entered through the back door, Daddy commenced to beating him with a long hickory limb. "What did I do?" he hollered. Daddy said, "Take yo' ass right back up to that schoolhouse!" so of course TL obeyed. Ms. Swinton stood behind her desk, waiting. TL tiptoed through the doorway.

"I'm sure this might catch you by surprise, young man, but we don't chew gum in my classroom."

How had she found out? Why hadn't she mentioned it earlier?

"You know better! Therefore, you will clean this room, inch by inch, until it sparkles like the resplendent sun!"

The *what* sun?

She exited through the rear. TL never discovered how she knew, and, at the time, it didn't matter. What he knew for sure was that the entire room was his to clean—until it sparkled. He wanted to cry. It would take him all night to clean the room thoroughly, but the consequences of not doing it were far more frightening, so he retrieved dust rags, Lemon Pledge, a broom, and a mop from the supply closet and went to work. The room wasn't nasty, but Ms. Swinton would definitely know if he hadn't completed the task. He finished in the wee hours of the morning and collapsed onto the floor behind her desk. An hour later, it seemed, she aroused him with her foot.

"Get up, boy!"

TL leapt quickly, wiping drool from the corners of his mouth, and stood at attention. He was too ashamed to speak.

She inspected the room, running fingers across the tops of desks and studying the floor with her microscopic gaze. He would've sucked his teeth, but he wanted to keep them.

"Very well. I suppose it's resplendent." She returned to her desk. Before sitting, she asked, "And what does 'resplendent' mean?"

TL didn't want to answer, but she knew he'd looked it up.

"It means bright, shiny, or brilliant," he murmured, thankful she didn't slap him for his insolence.

"And what is its part of speech?"

TL huffed. "Adjective."

She sat. "You're free to go now."

Before he exited, she added, "And the next time you use that tone with me, you will be sorry."

TL closed the door softly. He knew she meant business. Ms. Swinton was sweet and all, but she definitely didn't play.

At home, he barely had time to wash up, get breakfast, and feed the cows before he had to return to school. Sleep teased him all day, but he refused to submit. Ms. Swinton would've beaten him to death! He was totally miserable, nodding off and on, and, on top of that, he had to give Matt Henson his fifty cents back.

Standing there now, TL cackled. Those had been his best days, he thought, in that little one-room schoolhouse. It wasn't much physically, but it had been his haven. He remembered when Mr. Archer replaced the hardwood floors. Come Monday morning, Ms. Swinton stopped everyone at the entrance and said, "Children, I want to show you the work of a master craftsman." She made everyone close their eyes until she'd positioned them around the edges of the floor. "You may open your eyes now," she said, and students gawked at the most beautiful, red oak floor they'd ever seen. It glistened like polished brass. "This is yours," she said. "It's amazing—just like you." The children beamed with pride. "No one can take excellence from you once you have it. You don't get quality work without great sacrifice and years of apprenticeship. Now your job is to take care of it."

And they did. Each week, two students had cleaning detail, which included dusting the floor. It took hours, but they didn't complain. It was their school and Ms. Swinton had taught them to treasure it.

Each of the four walls contained a blackboard on which daily assignments were posted. Behind the teacher's desk, the main board instructed preprimers, grades one through three. The one on the right, grades four through six, the left, seven through nine, and the rear board told "the big kids" what to do. Upper grades assisted lower ones, and, on report card day, everyone received a grade for "Commitment to the Community." Ms. Swinton had constructed the category, surely, but students took it seriously since any bad grade resulted in an automatic whipping. No grounding or lecturing children in Swamp Creek! Locals believed in beatings that left children wounded and covered with welts. They believed in education, too, but they believed far more in respecting grown folks. Bad grades were a sign that someone had violated this sacred pact. Rest assured the violation never lasted long.

Lost in memory, TL shuffled to the front of the room and sat at Ms. Swinton's desk. *His* desk now. Dr. Thomas Lee Tyson. He marveled at it all. How had this happened? Who would've guessed? *Life has a funny way of making sure you find your destiny,* he thought. And it doesn't care if you like it or not. Uncle Jesse Lee had been right. "The destiny's not really for you anyway," Ms. Swinton used to say. "It's for the world. You'll benefit, but it might transform others before it touches you. No worry though. If you live it out," she said, "you'll thrive. That's God's solemn promise."

TL sniffled and sighed. Here he was, in the center of something he'd never longed for. Or always longed for. Perhaps, deep within, he'd wanted this very life, this exact mission, this one chance to see if he had what his mother had. Of course he didn't know then that their connection was biological, but life works out that way sometimes. Grandma used to call God "the Great Orchestrator" because, when you look back over your life, she said, you realize that things happened just so other things would happen and God would get His way. It might look crazy at first, but, in the end, it all makes sense. TL was beginning to understand that now.

"No turning back," he said. Streaks of morning sun burst through the windows, ushering in a new day. He wrote assignments on each board, then returned to his desk—*his* desk!—and began unpacking supplies. An unexpected commotion at the door caught his attention. He looked up.

"Good mornin', Dr. Tyson!" Ezekiel yelled. His wide, nervous grin made TL laugh. The collar of the boy's white shirt was starched stiff, and his new Levi's, three sizes too big, were gathered at the waist by a tattered brown belt. The thick bulky cuffs would be rolled down each year until he grew into the pants or wore them out, whichever came first. The belt was probably his father's.

"Well, good morning, son. You're mighty early, aren't you?"

"Yessir!" he shouted and nodded. TL laughed louder. The boy didn't move.

"Come on in."

Ezekiel ran forward, like a mighty, rushing wind, and sat at the desk before TL. His excitement was electrifying.

"What's your hurry, son?"

He shrugged. "I don't know, sir. Just didn't wanna miss nothin', I guess."

TL resumed working. Ezekiel studied him like a mother bird studies a nearby predator. Occasionally their eyes met, and Zeke smiled, causing his teacher to cackle every time.

"I like yo' suit, Dr. Tyson. I ain't never seen one like that."

"Thank you, sir."

"Why you call me 'sir,' sir? You the teacher."

"Yes I am, but everyone deserves respect."

"Even kids?"

"Yes, even kids. Plus, you'll be a man one day, so I'm practicing a little early." TL winked. Ezekiel glowed.

"When I get big I might wanna teach, too."

"Oh really?"

"Maybe. Daddy say ain't no money in it, but that's all right wit' me. I don't need much money."

TL almost said, *That's good, 'cause if you teach, you sho' ain't gon' have none,* but he held his tongue.

"Have you heard from yo' friend?"

TL frowned. "Excuse me?"

"Mr. George. The man that came to visit you this summer. You know, the one—"

"Yes, yes, I know. And, no, I haven't heard from him in a while." The inquiry seemed bizarre. "Is there a reason you ask?"

"Oh no, sir! I was just wonderin'. I liked him. He was funny."

Ezekiel snickered into his palms. *My, how times have changed,* TL thought. *I would never have asked Ms. Swinton such a personal thing.*

Seconds later, the boy continued: "Is Mr. George yo' best friend?"

What is he getting at? "I don't know," TL said without looking up. "I guess you could say that."

"Then why don't you talk to him?"

Ezekiel's chin rested on folded hands. He meant no harm, TL was sure, but something about his innocuous questions made TL horribly uneasy, although he tried not to show it.

"Friends don't talk all the time, son. Sometimes they go weeks or even months without speaking at all."

"Yessir!" The matter appeared closed, but then Zeke added, "But not best friends, right?"

"Look, Zeke! I don't know what best friends do, and I'm not very concerned about that right now."

"Okay," he moaned.

The gawking resumed. Everywhere TL walked, Zeke's eyes followed. Whenever he glanced at the boy, he'd smile and wave, happy as a newborn chick. TL wondered if every morning would be like this.

"I watched you and Mr. George a few times."

Turning from the rear board, TL said, "I beg your pardon?"

"Them days you sent me home. I didn't exactly go home. Not at first. I hid on the side o' yo' house and listened to y'all talk. Mr. George is funny!"

TL breathed deeply. *Temper yourself. He's just a child.*

"Y'all looked like y'all was havin' so much fun! I ain't never seen menfolks have fun like that. I seen 'em carry on and laugh and all, but not like y'all was doin'."

"And how were we doin' it?"

His mouth twisted. "I can't really explain it, sir, but it was different. Y'all just seemed . . . I don't know . . . like y'all was best friends. I didn't think grown men had best friends."

"Why not?"

"'Cause the men 'round here don't talk much or tell they feelin's and stuff."

Now TL understood. "Well, son, anybody can have a best friend, including men. And you're right—most men here aren't very open with their hearts, but that doesn't mean they don't have best friends. That also doesn't mean you have to be that way."

"I know! I wanna be like you!"

Other children trickled in. Most were far less gregarious than Ezekiel although all of them seemed excited. The girls floated to the front while the boys lingered in the rear, as if the final row were the Throne of Men. *Poor Zeke,* TL thought.

A few children sported designer apparel—Nike sneakers, Calvin Klein or Jordache jeans, Izod shirts—but most simply wore plain jeans and tops from Walmart or Fred's. The day had not come when it mattered much, yet from the admiration of the less fortunate, TL knew that day was on its way.

"Good morning!" he said, calling the class to order.

"Good morning, Dr. Tyson!" they returned loudly, and sprang to their feet.

He was taken aback. They'd certainly stood for Ms. Swinton, but he was sure those days were gone.

"You may have your seats."

The children obeyed and waited in perfect silence. TL walked each aisle, peering into hungry eyes, trying desperately to connect with them on some metaphysical level. Most looked down or away. He returned to the front. Something in him began to shift.

"I don't know what you think about yourselves, young people, but I'm here for only one reason: to convince you that you are black *and* brilliant."

No one responded. Ezekiel blinked and smiled.

"You come from a long tradition of people who died so you could sit here today. They would've done anything—anything!—for this opportunity, but it didn't come to them. It came to you." He walked among them again. "You." He looked into their faces. "And you. And you, ma'am. You, sir. And you." This wasn't the lesson he'd planned. "You cannot begin to learn unless you understand the precious, priceless cost your people paid for freedom. They stole books and sneaked down by the river at night to read. Our ancestors risked their lives simply to learn their ABCs. Not too long ago, reading was illegal for black people, children! Illegal! Do you know what that means?"

They nodded together.

"They would've been killed had they been caught! Many learned anyway. They knew that knowledge was power! They knew that the only way to be truly free was to transform the mind. The mind, young people! The mind!" He touched their heads. "Whoever controls your mind controls your thoughts, and whoever controls your thoughts becomes your god!"

Ezekiel began to raise his hand, but put it down quickly.

"So we're here to do what your ancestors only dreamed of. We're here to figure out how to thrive in the land of our bondage. We're here to understand how to love ourselves again and to lead the world in alleviating oppression. We're here to figure out how to be human beings. Real human beings. Not just humans, but humans *being.*"

He feared it went over their heads.

"Our people picked cotton in these fields for a dollar a week sometimes."

The children swiveled in their desks to look at him as he walked by.

"All the while dreaming of sitting in a classroom like this. Even your parents, who probably went to this school, didn't get to go consistently. They had to work in order that the family could eat and buy other necessary supplies. My generation was the first to go to school every day, and look at how things have changed. We now have a country full of black doctors and teachers and lawyers and entrepreneurs who live like kings and queens. It's your turn to contribute to the strength of your people. Yes, we've come a long way, but we're nowhere near the goal, and we won't get there without you."

He was back at the front.

"So your job is to learn. Every word, every concept, every mathematical equation, every historical figure, every geographical place, every poem . . . LEARN IT! Show the world who you are!"

As if reading his mind, the children extracted paper and pencil from their bags and waited for further instruction. He almost told them to copy their lessons from the board, but another idea materialized.

"I know some of you are young and just beginning to write, but there's something I need all of you to know. Right now. Once you learn it, it'll stay with you forever. It'll never let you forget who you are."

The children waited with pencils in hand. TL hadn't planned this either, but it felt right.

"I shall dictate the words slowly as you write them down. Write them precisely as I give them, line by line, so you can understand the beauty, structure, and rhyme scheme of the poem. I'll explain later. You young ones do the best you can. Here we go."

Ezekiel could hardly sit still. TL thought he'd have to tie the child to his desk.

"Lift every voice and sing," he began, walking the aisles once more. " 'Til earth and heaven ring."

Children wrote feverishly. Those too young to keep up wrote what they could. Even the first graders tried.

"Ring with the harmonies of liberty!"

TL touched each child's shoulder as he passed.

"Let our rejoicing rise, high as the listening skies! Let it resound loud as the rolling sea!"

He was practically shouting. Why did his voice tremble? Had he never really studied the lyrics himself? It was as if the ancestors had taken control of him and were reminding all of them of a time past and a time to come, which they'd not seen. The ancestors were telling students and teacher alike to press on, to believe even when there were no signs, to sing our songs regardless of what others said about them or about us. They were *our* songs, written for *our* tongues, sent to set *our* spirits free. And, like the rolling sea, the children would keep coming, and, if they stayed consistent, they would win. That was the promise! The children and TL both were guaranteed to win.

"Sing a song, full of the faith that the dark past has taught us! Sing a song, full of the hope that the present has brought us!"

Zeke sniffled up front. It was more than TL could bear. He didn't want to be dramatic, but he definitely wanted the children to feel—not just hear—the power of their anthem. Watching them write the words moved him because, in that moment, he knew they were the hope of the slaves. Those old souls had surely dreamed of the day when their offspring would study them and fight to understand the enormity of the legacy they'd left behind. TL envisioned the ancestors clapping and weeping and nudging each other as they beheld the manifestation of their prayers. That image left him *full*, as Swamp Creek folks called it, but he couldn't stop now.

"Facing the rising sun, of our new day begun, let us march on 'til victory is won! March on, children. March on!"

Several smeared tears across their cheeks. All TL could do was shake his head. He didn't understand why the words were moving him so. Maybe it was because these were his children now, those who came from the same soil and lived the same struggles he'd known. Children whose lives were just as fragile as his had been, and now he had the responsibility and the privilege to help save them. In his soul, he loved them. Every single one of them. He knew their beauty and their possibilities, and he knew that most of them had no idea why God had sent him to them. And them to him. But he didn't need them to know that. He needed them simply to trust him. If they could trust him, TL believed, he could take them to the Promised Land.

"Stoney the road we trod . . . ," he continued until they'd written the entire song. Then he sang it, trying hard not to crumble. They stood and sang it, too. Their voices weren't polished or even harmonious, but standing beside their desks in battered, holey attire, they'd begun to believe. He could feel it! That's when he knew why he'd come home.

They asked various questions, like who wrote the song and why black people had an anthem different from whites. TL explained DuBois's notion of double consciousness—what it means to be simultaneously part of a thing and outside of it—and the children understood. They would sing the song every morning, he told them, until they sang it in their sleep. Jophelia Bobo surfaced as the classroom vocalist. She had a thin, high soprano with not much volume but incredible control and tone. Whenever asked to sing, she was more than willing, and her voice always left the classroom spellbound. She'd fold her hands like a child delivering an Easter speech and barely crack her lips as the melody floated into the atmosphere. Before the children realized it, their eyes would close and they'd sway slightly until she slowed the rhythm and sang sweetly, "True to our God," where she'd pause and lift her hands, then finish with some unexpected run, "True to our native land." Someone always eased the tension with "Girl, you know you can sang!" or "If I had a voice like that, you couldn't tell me nothin'!"

TL separated the children by grade level, then, as they copied their lessons for the day, he moved between them, assisting whenever necessary. It was far more exhausting than he'd imagined. Some asked questions he'd already answered, and others wanted him to affirm anything they put on paper. He wasn't sure he had the patience to endure this a lifetime.

A skinny, light-skinned boy named Elijah Hooker was determined to be the class clown. Everyone called him EJ. He was fourteen or fifteen and easily TL's height. He heard him giggle, and when he turned, EJ acted as if he were lost in his lesson. Others cackled. This happened a third time, and TL snapped.

"That's enough, young man!"

EJ flinched.

"I won't have you clowning in my classroom!"

Ezekiel frowned. Others looked from the corners of their eyes.

"Did you hear me, son?"

EJ mumbled something rude and sucked his teeth. TL rushed to the boy's desk, grabbed his skeletal arm, and said, "You WILL obey me! And you WILL answer with 'yessir' when I ask you a question! Am I clear?"

Anger flushed the boy's narrow face. Rage trembled on his lips, but TL wasn't frightened. He knew that if he didn't establish authority that day, he'd never have it.

EJ tried to snatch his arm from TL's grip, but the professor wouldn't let it go.

"Don't make me take you out of here and show you what's really happening! You might be big, but I promise you you're not stronger than me!"

He sighed and backed down with an insincere "Yessir."

TL released his arm, but continued to stare. He'd whip the child if he had to, he told himself, and he wouldn't be sorry about it.

Things calmed. TL spent the majority of the day learning each child's name and capabilities and convincing a few that they were smarter than they believed. Whenever he moved, Ezekiel's eyes followed. If TL knelt next to a desk, Zeke strained his neck like a crane to see and hear what he was saying. "Do your own work, son," TL said countless times, and Zeke relaxed in his seat, disappointed.

Yet within minutes his enthusiam returned. TL couldn't reprimand him hard because, when he checked, the boy's work was flaw-
less. He searched for errors and simply couldn't find them. Zeke's
penmanship was absolutely beautiful. It looked typewritten. Either
TL would have to do something else with him, he determined, or
Zeke would drain his teacher's annual supply of energy long before
the school year ended.

The bell rang at three. One would've thought a bomb exploded,
the way the children came to life. All except you-know-who.

He never moved. He simply sat at his desk and read. TL didn't
want to feed his insatiable thirst for attention, but he also didn't
want to discourage his love for learning. So for a while, TL ignored
him and tidied the room. Zeke wasn't disturbed in the least. After
a half hour or so, TL relented.

"What are you reading?"

He shivered with joy. "Just an old magazine Momma had laying around the house."

"Anything interesting?"

"Naw, not really." He paused. "Well, one article was okay. But
most of it's kinda boring. I got some other books at the house, too,
but I done read 'em so many times I don't wanna read 'em no more.
Daddy say I oughta read the Bible 'cause it's got some of the best
stories in the world, but I don't really like the Bible. I mean, I like it,
but it's not very inter-restin'. Do you like the Bible, Dr. Tyson?"

God deliver me! "The Bible is fine, son."

"But do you like it?"

"It's . . . all right."

"Do you think the stories are inter-restin'?"

"Some of them."

"Which ones?"

TL exhaled. "The story of Job is a good one."

Ezekiel smiled. "I'll read that one tonight and we'll talk about
it tomorrow, okay?"

"Okay." TL gathered his things. Zeke did likewise.

"I'll see you tomorrow, sir. Bright and early!"

"I'll be here."

Ezekiel approached the teacher's desk and hesitated.

"Is there something else I can help you with?"

He darted around the teacher's desk and hugged TL with all his might. TL had no choice but to hug him back.

"You're the best teacher in the whole wide world, Dr. Tyson! See ya tomorrow!" He ran out the door.

"See ya, boy." TL chuckled and sighed.

THERE'S A PRICE TO PAY FOR THAT KIND OF ADMIRATION, AND TL'S ABOUT to pay it. But it's worth it. A good teacher can be a child's salvation. Thousands of precious, fragile lives would've been lost, ruined, thrown away if some caring, nurturing teacher hadn't come along. Parents aren't necessarily the people who love you most. They're the people who secure your arrival, and that is certainly important—you couldn't make it to earth without them—but the human error is to believe that, since you come through them, they MUST love you. Or even like you. This simply isn't true. They're used by God for your conception and delivery, and that's where the contract ends. It's certainly a blessing if they adore you, but if they don't, someone else will. That's the divine promise. And that someone else is often found in the classroom. But, again, teachers pay a price to meet such needs. They're crucified daily as they spend money, time, and energy to save those who'd otherwise not make it. Ms. Swinton saved thousands, including my brother. He couldn't get enough of her, and now I know why. It wasn't because she was his mother; it was because she facilitated his destiny. Daddy thought it should've been him, but it wasn't.

That's how life works. God makes everyone relevant to someone, and it's not always who we prefer. But if we follow His lead, we always get what we need. God does not abandon people. Ain't it funny that, often, we spend an entire lifetime trying to make someone love us who was never obligated to do so? This includes family. But be clear about it: The issue is not willingness; the issue is capacity. CAN they love ME? is the question we should ask, and if the answer is no, instead of pondering personal failings, we should simply look for those who can. They're waiting for us. They're our angels. God has them in place. Take the love wherever it comes from. Remember that love itself is the only promise—not who brings it.

CHAPTER 22

THE NEXT DAY, EZEKIEL WAS LATE. THEY'D ALREADY sung the anthem when he arrived, and most students were busy copying their lessons for the day. TL knew something was wrong.

Zeke's head hung so low TL couldn't see his eyes. Children whispered when he entered, the way people whisper when they feel sorry for someone. TL met him mid-aisle. Zeke didn't say a word.

"What's the problem, son?"

His head shook slightly. TL lifted his chin.

"Oh my Lord!" Jophelia Bobo screeched when she saw his eye. TL knelt and asked, "What in the world happened to you?"

Still, he wouldn't talk.

"Don't you hear me, son?"

Zeke's mouth quivered. The look in his eyes begged TL not to embarrass him in front of the others.

"Come with me."

They exited through the rear and walked some distance down the shady lane leading to the Rose of Sharon Cemetery.

Turning abruptly, TL asked, "Now what happened?"

Zeke licked tears from his upper lip. "I was readin' Job last night," his voice shimmied, "and I asked Daddy why God would do somethin' like that to somebody who had been so obedient, and Daddy told me I didn't have no business questionin' God. I told him I wasn't questionin' God, I just didn't understand why God would let the devil ruin Job's life," he sniffled, "and he started screamin' at me 'bout thinkin' I know so much 'cause I read all the time"—*sniffle*—"and I told him I wasn't smart, but it didn't make sense to me that God would waste His time talkin' to the devil"—*sniffle*—"and that's when he started beatin' me!"

TL rubbed the boy's head as he sobbed.

"He beat me all the time, Dr. Tyson," he added once he calmed. "He beat Momma, too." Snot ran from his nose.

"What about the others?"

Zeke shook his head. "Only me and Momma. He say we talk back too much. My brothers don't neva say nothin'."

TL offered a handkerchief. "It'll be all right, son. We'll handle everything." He felt himself getting too involved.

"I wunnit doin' nothin', Dr. Tyson, but askin' a question! I wanted to read the story so you and me could talk 'bout it like we said!"

"I know, son, I know, and we'll talk about it. I'm not going anywhere." *God, what am I saying?*

Gently, TL clutched Zeke's shoulders. "Now listen, son. We have a lot of work to do today, so let's get that done first. Then we'll go and have a talk with your father." TL had no idea what he was getting into.

"Okay. But . . ."

"But what?"

"He told me to stay away from you."

TL's eyes narrowed. "Why?"

Ezekiel shrugged. "I don't know."

They walked back to the schoolhouse with TL's right arm around Ezekiel's small shoulders. TL began to plan his strategy. He knew why Gary wanted Zeke to stay away from him—at least he thought he knew—but he didn't intend to surrender without a fight. Eze-kiel meant far too much to lose him.

At the end of the day, they marched to the boy's house with hopes of resolving things quickly and easily. At least that was TL's hope. Yet, as they walked, his confidence disintegrated. He wasn't sure he even had a right to intrude, but Zeke needed a mediator, so TL pressed on. He certainly couldn't act as if a black eye on a nine-year-old was no big deal, especially when a grown man had put it there. He'd be wrong, he thought, not to say *something*. Even if Gary cursed him and insisted he leave, he could know in his heart he'd tried, and Zeke would always remember how far his teacher had gone to protect him. This could save his life, right? Such was the conversation he was having with himself as they walked. There'd be a price to pay, certainly, for such an act since men hate nothing more than another man questioning their authority, but oh well. TL couldn't have lived with himself if he hadn't tried.

As they approached, Zeke got cold feet. "Daddy might not be home yet," he said, walking slower. "Sometimes he don't get home 'til dark."

TL tried to remain strong. "Well, we'll just have to wait for him in that case, won't we."

Disappointment colored the boy's cheeks a burgundy rouge. "Yessir."

"It'll be all right, son. Don't worry. Just let me do the talking." *What the hell am I going to say?*

Angela greeted them at the door. Her attempt at politeness was disingenuous though not unpleasant. She knew why he'd come, and she knew her husband wouldn't like it. TL saw sympathy in her eyes, but she couldn't say much. That was the southern wom-an's way, especially when she feared her husband.

They drank lemonade, TL and Angela, and made small talk about every topic conceivable. Then, with nothing more to say, she excused herself and left him sitting alone in the small living room, with only a noisy fan to keep him company. Occasionally, she'd holler from the back room, assuring him that Gary would be along directly, and he'd holler, "No problem!" and continue waiting. Ezekiel had disappeared when his mother and teacher began to talk. With each passing hour, TL's anxiety mounted until, a little after six, he stood, having decided this was a bad idea from the start. Then Gary entered.

"Good evening," TL said cheerfully, hoping to disguise his intentions.

Gary saw straight through the façade. They shook hands, for the sake of protocol, and Gary took the high-backed chair opposite the sofa. TL sat again, unsure of how to begin.

"Um . . . this isn't a very comfortable conversation, Gary, but um . . ."—TL massaged his thighs—"I have to ask you about Ezekiel's eye."

With absolutely no trepidation, Gary asked, "What 'bout it?"

TL licked his lips. "He said you hit him." He hadn't meant to be curt, but Gary's indifference angered him.

"I did."

"Why?"

"That ain't yo' business."

"I'm sorry, but yes it is. When a student comes to school visibly scarred, especially by a parent, I have no choice but to investigate. I'm not trying to be in your business, Gary, but Ezekiel is the best—"

"Look, TL. Don't come over here tellin' me how to raise my kids. I'll discipline that boy any way I see fit."

"I understand that, but you can't blacken his eye! He's just a kid!"

Gary stood slowly. "I can do whatever I want to. He's *my* kid."

Looking up and into Gary's eyes, TL felt awkward and belittled, but he endured. "That doesn't give you the right to knock his eye out, does it?"

"I didn't knock his eye out. I wunnit even tryin' to hit him. Not *that* hard."

"Oh, come on, Gary!" Frustration lifted TL from the sofa. "I don't believe that. I'm sorry, but I don't."

Angela peeked around the corner of the kitchen. The menfolks were eye to eye now. Ezekiel lurked somewhere nearby, TL was certain, listening with fear.

"Yo' job is to teach—not to tell me how to raise my kids. That's my job."

TL swallowed, trying hard to remain calm. "Don't do him like that, Gary. I know he's gotta lotta mouth, but he's just curious."

"He ain't jus' curious," Gary said. "Somethin's wrong wit' that boy."

"What do you mean?"

The couple glanced at each other, then Angela vanished. Gary continued: "Did he tell you what he did?"

"Yes. He said he was reading Job and he asked you whether you thought—"

"No, not that. It didn't have nothin' to do wit' that."

TL relaxed his guard. "I don't understand."

"You think I'd whip my son just for askin' questions?"

TL didn't answer.

"Zeke!" he yelled. "Get in here!"

Ezekiel came running. He didn't look at TL.

"Why didn't you tell yo' teacher what you did? Huh?"

Zeke stared at the floor. Gary slapped the back of his head. "Answer me when I talk to you, boy!"

TL wanted to intervene, but instead folded his arms and waited. Zeke still didn't speak.

"You see? This right here is why he got his ass beat. I ain't gon' have no child in my house what can't answer me when I talk to him."

Praying Gary wouldn't slap the child again, TL squatted in front of him and asked, "What did you do, son?"

He sniffled but said nothing.

"Tell me. Before your father gets after you again."

"Mess wit' me, I'll beat his ass for real," Gary said. "He bet not ever do that again. Not in my house! He ain't seen no black eye yet!"

"Gary!" his wife called, but he ignored her.

"Listen, son," TL whispered. "It can't be that bad. Just tell me and get it over with so you don't get in any more trouble."

Zeke wanted to speak, even opened his mouth, but nothing came out. TL stood and faced Gary again.

"Would you mind if I spoke with him privately?"

Gary stared at the boy.

"Please? I don't wanna embarrass him."

"I don't care nothin' 'bout embarrassin' him. He oughta be embarrassed!"

"Yessir. I understand. But just give us a minute if you would. Please."

Gary walked into the kitchen. TL grabbed Zeke's right arm and stared him in the face. "You tell me the truth, boy, and you tell me right now! What in the world did you do?"

Zeke muttered, "I can't tell you, Dr. Tyson."

"Yes you can, and you will! You should've told me earlier today when I asked you about it. Now take a deep breath and start talking!"

He sighed and sniffled again. "You not gon' like me no more if I tell you."

"I'll always like you, son. Don't worry about that. Just say it!"

After wiping his nose, he mumbled, "Daddy caught me lookin' at a dirty magazine."

TL scowled. That couldn't be all, could it? No, there had to be more to the story, so he huffed with impatience.

"I was behind the smokehouse," Zeke whispered. "Touchin' myself." He squeezed his eyes shut.

TL's frustration broke free. "Aw, Zeke! Every boy does that. There's nothing wrong with you." He touched the child's head. "You don't have to be ashamed. It's just as natural as breathing."

"No it's not."

"Yes it is! I looked at naked magazines when I was your age."

Actually he hadn't, but the comfort was more important than the truth.

"I bet you didn't touch yo'self while you was doin' it."

TL yelped. "Boy, if you only knew!"

Ezekiel's eyes yearned for compassion.

"Trust me. You're perfectly normal."

"No I'm not. Daddy said it's an abomilation, and God hates it."

TL shook his head. "Abomination, son, and I don't think God cares one way or the other." He knew he was on thin ice, but he refused to let Zeke hate himself. "I'm not telling you to look at the pictures. I'm just saying be more careful. Learn to be discreet."

"What does that mean?"

His swollen eye justified TL saying, "Be more careful what you do and where you do it."

"Learn how to hide better?"

"I guess that's what I'm saying. This is between you and me though. Don't ever repeat what I've said."

He nodded. "I understand. I won't."

Peering deep into Zeke's eye, TL added, "And I still like you."

The boy's broad smile returned. TL told him to go play while he finished speaking with his father. The men met on the porch.

"Did he tell you?"

"Yes, he told me."

"Did he tell you everything?"

"I think so. About the picture?"

"Yep. And 'bout the fact that he wasn't lookin' at the woman?"

"Oh, Gary, come on! How would you know?"

"Because the picture was folded in half!"

TL tried to think of another explanation, but he couldn't.

"That's why I whipped him."

"Gary, you didn't whip him. You beat him. That's the problem. Plus, what he did is perfectly normal, man."

"Normal? That shit ain't normal." The disgust on Gary's face put a bad taste in TL's mouth. "I ain't gon' have no son o' mine doin' nothin' like that 'round here. He ain't gon' be that way. I'ma see to it."

"Are you serious?"

"Hell yeah I'm serious!" He stepped back, offended. "A man s'pose to look at a woman! That's Bible!"

TL rolled his eyes. "Gary . . . really. This isn't that big of a deal. He's still young. He doesn't know who he is yet."

"Well, I know who he is! And I say I ain't gon' have that shit in my house!"

Backing down a bit, TL raised his hands and said, "I'm not here to challenge your authority, Gary, but all of us have sinned and fallen short of the glory of God."

"It ain't the same!" Anger wrinkled Gary's otherwise soft, smooth features. "Maybe it's natural for people *like you,* but not for most folks. And definitely not for no boy in *my* house!"

This is fruitless, TL thought, so he said, "Okay, okay. Just don't beat him, Gary. He doesn't deserve that, regardless of what he's done. He's a really good kid. Probably the smartest in the class."

"I don't give a damn how smart he is! He gon' be what I say he gon' be or I'll put his lil' ass out!"

TL surrendered. "I've said my peace, sir. Tell Angela good evening."

When he stepped off the porch, Gary said, "I 'preciate you comin' back to Swamp Creek and teachin' and all, I really do, but . . ." TL looked directly at him. "I don't want Zeke to be like you."

"Excuse me? What?"

"I don't mean no harm, TL, and don't take it personally, but my son is gon' be regular, like all the other boys 'round here."

"What are you saying?" TL's feelings were obviously hurt.

"Just what I said. Every since you got back, that boy can't get enough o' you. He sniffin' 'round yo' place and talkin' 'bout you like you some kinda god or somethin'."

"What's wrong with that? He just wants to learn!"

"Learnin' ain't the issue. He wants to *be* you, and I ain't havin' it."

"What's wrong with me?"

Gary looked away. "I don't know. I know you smart and all. You always been that, but you strange, TL. You always been that, too."

Slowly, TL inched back onto the porch. They were practically eye to eye again. "What are you trying to say, Gary?"

"I ain't tryin' to say nothin'. Not in particular. I'm just sayin' you was always . . . different, and I guess you couldn't help it, but I don't want my boy like that. It's too hard a life. I remember how we talked 'bout you. We growed up together, remember?"

"Yes I do, and I'm not going to act as if I had a smooth, easy life, but there's nothing wrong with me. Not now, not ever."

"That's yo' opinion."

TL wanted to say other things, but he thought of Zeke's future. Gary pressed the issue. "Like . . . where's yo' wife?"

"Pardon me?"

"Yo' wife. Why ain't you got one?"

TL was flustered. "Because I don't!" he cried. "I don't need one. Every man's not supposed to be married."

"Well, if that works for you, fine, but that ain't what I want for my boy."

TL's voice jumped an octave. "You can't determine the direction of Ezekiel's life, Gary! You're his father, but you're not God!"

"I didn't say I was God, but I *am* sayin' that my boy is gon' be a boy in my house! If you gon' feed him and clothe him, he can be whatever you say, but since you ain't, he gon' mind me or pay the cost!" The men stared each other down. *"Dr. Tyson this, Dr. Tyson that"*—he mocked Zeke's voice—"that's all I hear. I ain't mad at him likin' you, but I do *not* intend for him to be like you. Ain't no boy s'pose to talk 'bout no man like that!"

"Oh, Gary, stop it! I'm his teacher!"

"You right! And I'm his daddy, and I say it's gon' stop!"

"You can't direct the boy's heart."

"The hell I can't! And I will!"

TL descended the steps again and stomped home, fussing to the wind. *How dare he! He doesn't know anything about my personal life! And I might have a wife—one day. Who knows? But if I don't, I'm still a good man. And a damn good one at that! I've sacrificed everything to teach these children!* Your *children! And you don't want your boy to be like me? Kiss my ass! You can't intimidate me! I'm gon' be exactly what I always been, exactly what I'm supposed to be, and these children will make it because I came home to teach. If some of 'em end up like me, good! I'd be proud! You'd be proud, too—if you had any damn sense!*

Before he knew it, he was standing on his own porch, preaching the gospel of TL. He hadn't been that pissed off in a long time. *Who the hell does he think he is, assessing the quality of my life? I'm not some insecure upstart, brought in from some distant place, to teach children I don't know or care about. I'm at home, goddamnit! Home! These are my children, too, and my job is to teach them. And, in the name of my mother, Carolyn Swinton, I intend to do just that! All the demons in hell can't keep me from it!*

He was in bed before realizing he'd said "in the name of my mother." Smiling in the dark, he nodded, amazed at how everything in his life was coming together.

ZEKE ARRIVED with the other children the next day. He was cordial, but guarded. His enthusiasm was clearly tempered. He sat at the same desk, and occasionally squirmed with excitement, but TL could tell his father had gotten to him. At the end of the day, TL retained him for a moment.

"I need to speak with you, sir," he called as the boy dashed toward the door.

Zeke froze, then turned slowly like a porcelain figurine in a music box.

"Sit down." TL pointed to Zeke's desk. He obeyed.

"Listen to me: There's nothing wrong with you. And there's nothing wrong with me. Your job is to be yourself. Not your mother, not your father, not me, or anybody else. Being you might feel strange at first, but you have to do it. It's the only way you can love yourself."

Zeke blinked as his eyes moistened. TL vowed not to cry.

When he finished, he told Zeke he could go, but he didn't. He sat still, like a department store mannequin, staring straight through TL. TL didn't know if he should hug him or say something more, so he remained still and let Zeke control the moment.

Eventually, the boy said, "Dr. Tyson?"

"Yes?"

"Can I ask you somethin'?"

"Sure. Go ahead."

"How you make people like you?" His eyes pleaded for understanding.

"What do you mean, son?"

"Daddy said people don't like me, but I want people to like me."

TL gazed into his pupils. "People already like you, boy. Don't ever forget that."

"I know *you* like me, Dr. Tyson, but I want other people to like me, too. I wanna be special."

"Why?"

"'Cause special people are the ones everybody else like."

TL cackled. "That's not always true!"

Zeke shrugged. "Seem like to me it is. Even in the Bible, God always called people He thought was special."

TL couldn't argue that.

"Don't you know how to be somebody special, Dr. Tyson?"

"I'm not so sure, son."

"*You* somebody special."

TL smirked.

"Daddy told me not to be like you."

"I know."

"But I don't know nobody else 'round here to be like. You the most special man I know, and I like you."

Everything TL thought to say was too dangerous. "Just be yourself, Zeke. That'll do the trick."

"Daddy ain't gon' like it."

"I know, son. I know."

"Will you help me, Dr. Tyson? Will you help me be myself?"

TL coughed over the lump in his throat.

"I'll do what I can, son, but I don't want to make matters worse for you at home."

"I know you don't, Dr. Tyson, but I wanna be somebody special. Even if Daddy thinks I ain't."

TL knew what to say. It was time. He directed Zeke to sit down again.

"Can you keep a secret?"

"Yeah," Zeke said. "Sure. I like secrets!"

"Okay. I'm going to tell you something about this place we call home, this town we know as Swamp Creek."

"Okay."

"Something that might not mean much now, but in the future it'll mean everything."

"Okay." His eyes brightened.

"We're not really from Swamp Creek, Zeke."

"We not?"

"No, we're not. We're from another place far more magical."

"Huh?"

TL smiled. "We're from Black Haven, son. That's what this town used to be called, long before you or I ever came along. Uncle Jesse Lee told me all about it. He said it was an incredible place back then, and he was right."

"Really!" Zek squirmed. "Black Heaven?"

"Not heaven, son. *Haven. Black Haven.* People came from all around to go to school, shop, everything. There were eleven different ways to get here—Uncle Jesse Lee called each entrance a 'gate'—some roads, some paths through the woods, but they all led to the center of town."

"Eleven different ways, huh?"

TL sighed and took a chance. "No, son, there were actually twelve gates to the city of Black Haven. Your job, one day, will be to find them all. Then you'll understand everything, especially yourself. I've just given you your first clue."

"Wow. That's pretty neat!"

"Yeah. We're more than we think we are, son. When you start defining yourself, remember where you came from. That's the first step. But be sure you know where you *really* came from. Sometimes there's a difference."

TL told him about the vision and the city made of gold. Zeke listened as if his life depended upon it.

"Can we go there, Dr. Tyson? Please? I'd love to see a place like that."

"I know, son. So would I. And we *will* go there. One day. I promise."

Zeke's excitement bubbled over, but it was time to go. TL told him to run along and mind his manners.

"Thanks, Dr. Tyson," he said, skipping to the exit. "I'll never forget what you said. I'll never forget you, either." Running down the road, he screamed, "And I'll find those gates one day! I swear! All twelve of 'em!"

Behind his back, TL whispered, "I'm sure you will, boy. I'm sure you will."

CHAPTER 23

TL COULDN'T FORGET WHAT GARY HAD SAID. HE thought of paying him another visit, but decided nothing good could come of it. He didn't want to antagonize Gary to the point where he'd make Zeke stop coming to school. The man valued education, of course, but he valued an obedient, "regular" son far more. The best TL could do, he told himself, was to keep his distance and close his mouth.

Daddy stopped by the house just as TL arrived home. "Broke the handle of my shovel," he said, "so I'm headed to Walmart to make Sam Walton richer." TL met him at the driver's door of his old pickup.

"So what you think 'bout teachin 'round here so far?"

"It's fine. I like it. Just a lotta work."

"Are the kids obedient?"

"For the most part. E. J. Hooker is a trip though. He's determined to try me every doggone day."

Daddy nodded. "God know who to put in front of them kids 'cause if it was me, I'd beat his ass 'til he couldn't walk outta that schoolhouse."

TL hollered. "People don't do that anymore, Daddy."

"I know they don't! And you see what you got, don't you?"

He had a point.

"Read yo' Bible! It tells you to beat a child's ass! Spare the rod and spoil the child—same thing. If you don't, both o' y'all gon' be sorry and you ain't gon' be able to fix it later. You gon' have to half kill him to teach him anything."

TL hated the idea of beating a child, but since he had no equally fruitful alternative, he couldn't challenge Daddy's position. TL changed the subject slightly and told him about Gary and Ezekiel.

"You ain't got to fight that man, boy. Relax. If it's in the child's spirit to follow you, he gon' follow you. Ain't nothin' gon' keep him from it. I learned that the hard way."

"What do you mean?"

Daddy cackled. "You can influence a child, but you ain't gon' keep him from goin' where his spirit sends him. I can promise you that. I tried!"

Now TL knew what he meant.

"I wanted you to be a farmer. Thought you'd make a good one. And, yeah, I could make you go to the field, but I couldn't make you like it. Don't care how much I talked 'bout fresh peas and greens and corn, you just didn't want that life. All you wanted was a pencil and a sheet o' paper. I couldn't understand it. I never liked school that much and neither did yo' momma, so I don't know where you got yo' desire from. You musta been born wit' it, I decided one day, so I couldn't take it from you. I stopped tryin'."

"I probably got it from Ms. Swinton."

"Maybe you did. All I know is that God sends chil'en wit' somethin' already in they spirit, and they gon' itch and squirm 'til they find out what it is. Then they gon' itch and squirm some more 'til they do it."

TL nodded.

"That boy you talkin' 'bout? What's his name?"

"Ezekiel."

"Yeah, 'Zekiel. I see him 'round, grinnin' like a chess cat. He gon' be all right. You ain't gotta do nothin' special. Just stand in front o' him and teach. If he wanna follow you, he will. A black eye ain't gon' stop him. It might slow him down a lil', but it ain't gon' stop him. "

Leaning on the driver's door, TL asked, "What did God put in you?"

Daddy shifted the truck into gear, prepared to pull away. "I ain't never found out. That's how come I ain't happy. But I ain't gave up lookin'." He flashed a fake grin. "I'll holla at you later."

"See ya," TL called, and waved slowly.

LATER THAT day, Cliffesteen appeared. TL literally ran into her. Jogging along the old two-lane highway, he was in the middle of a nice stride when she dashed from behind a pecan tree growing next to the road. Her black dress was wrinkled and dirty, as if she'd been doing construction work, and the once-white shoes were more scuffed and battered than before. The wig sat straight this time, but the heavy, thick, sky-blue eye shadow and inch-long lashes startled him. She blinked repeatedly. He tried to jog in place, so as not to lose his rhythm, but her erratic energy overwhelmed him. She offered a tissue from her black patent-leather pocketbook, and TL took it and wiped his brow. They stood beneath the pecan tree.

"Do I look pretty?" she asked, batting her eyes.

TL couldn't lie, but he couldn't tell the truth, either. "You look okay, Cliffesteen. Where'd you get the makeup?"

"I been had it! Jus' don't wear it much."

"Why are you wearing it now?"

She smiled. " 'Cause I got a date tonight!"

"A date?"

"Yep. I think somebody loves me."

"You think so?"

"Un-huh. He's s'pose to meet me in the woods by Aunt Easter's house."

All the money in the world couldn't have made TL ask who that somebody was. He was afraid to know.

"Yo' sister got a message fo' you."

TL wiped sweat from his eyes. "Cliffesteen . . ."

"I told her you didn't wanna come back, not the way you run off, but she said she got somethin' to tell you—befo' you make a big mistake."

"What mistake?"

"I don't know. That's all she said."

"Why can't she just tell me then?"

"You know why. You gotta go where she is. She can't come to you. It ain't allowed."

"Ain't allowed by who?" TL was getting angry.

Cliffesteen didn't answer. She started that nervous dance thing that lets people know she's on the edge.

"I gotta finish my run."

"All righty." She nodded. "You know where I am."

TL took off. *Sister wants to talk to me. How crazy is that? Cliffesteen ain't got no sense!* But even after returning home, TL couldn't dismiss what she'd said. He had to know. She knew he was coming.

He arrived at Aunt Easter's at sundown. Cliffesteen sat atop the steps, painting her fingernails.

"Yo' date ain't showed up yet?" TL teased.

"He jus' did!" she hollered, blowing her fingernails dry.

TL felt like a fool. Cliffesteen had planned the whole thing. She wasn't nearly as crazy as folks made her out to be. *Clearly she's smarter than me,* he thought.

"Spirits don't lie, you see. They told me you was comin'. Come on in." She stood and beckoned him forward.

TL refused. "No thank you. I just wanna know what Sister said. That's all."

Cliffesteen looked offended, but TL didn't care. She shrugged and said, "That's fine. Jus' give me a second and I'll be ready."

She vanished into the house as silence settled upon everything. TL wasn't about to go in there again! He'd seen enough the last time. He didn't want to see the snake again, he didn't want to see the Messenger, and he wasn't in the mood for another ritual. But he had to find out if what Cliffesteen said was true.

She emerged with the ragged, black hat sitting lopsided atop her wig. It was wide-brimmed with one fake white flower in the front. TL started to ask why she needed it, but then remembered he didn't care.

"I'm ready!" she called like an anxious teenager.

TL didn't respond. He simply waited for her at the bottom of the steps. He knew where they were going, and he knew he couldn't go without her. *My date. Unbelievable!*

She led the way, once again, humming something he didn't know. His attitude was far less than pleasant. He felt manipulated, but he couldn't justify it. He was the one who had to know, right? That wasn't Cliffesteen's fault. She simply knew he had to know, and she'd capitalized upon it. He couldn't blame her for that. Actually, he was using her, wasn't he? She knew he didn't care about her one way or the other, and she also knew he couldn't get to his sister without her. She'd *made* herself significant in the midst of his need. Who could be angry with her for that?

They crossed the chilly Jordan at dusk. The water grabbed TL's ankles as if angry that he'd interrupted its flow. He couldn't figure out why it was so cold, hot as it was in Arkansas that summer, and though they'd had almost no rain, why hadn't it dwindled to a mere, easy-flowing stream? Maybe it did have magical powers, like folks said. Townsfolks told children about the man who used to come to the Jordan to weep with the spring rains. Some said you could hear him for miles around, wailing in the midst of thunder and lightning, and soon as the rains ended, he'd return home and plant his crops like everyone else. But something would be different, folks said. Some energy in the air or some spirit that made people love one another unintentionally. You could feel it, they said, like morning dew falling silently over everything. TL thought it was just an old legend until Uncle Jesse Lee told him that the Wailin' Man, as he called him, was the Peace boys' daddy. TL knew Mr. Authorly Peace, Reverend Woody Peace, and Mr. Bartimaeus Peace. They called him Blind Bartimaeus because he was born blind. Uncle Jesse Lee said that was his real name—*Blind* Bartimaeus—but TL didn't believe it. What mother in her right mind would name a child "Blind"? Uncle Jesse Lee laughed out loud and said, "I wish you coulda met his momma. That Emma Jean Peace? Boy, she was more than a notion! You wouldn't have no mo' questions if you'd ever met her!" The way he hollered TL knew she must've been a piece of work. "It was fo' mo' boys, too! The oldest one died first. He was kinda slow. Then there was one what could sing like a angel. He was smart, too. Left and never did come back. I think he got the same degree you got. Went to college and never did go to high school."

"Stop it, Uncle Jesse Lee!"

"Did you hear what I said? That boy had a gift! Authorly said he could hear a thang once and he'd have it the rest o' his life. He was what you call a genius. His name was King Solomon."

"Get outta here!"

"I'm tellin' you what I know!"

They laughed together, although for different reasons.

"What about the other two boys? What happened to them?"

Uncle Jesse Lee's demeanor shifted. "I don't know exactly. Folks said one o' 'em left here in behind some man. I don't 'member his name. And the last one . . ." Uncle Jesse Lee paused and bowed his head.

"What? Was something wrong with him?"

"Well, I guess it depends on how you look at it."

TL frowned.

"The last one was a girl—at first."

"Huh? I thought you said it was a family full of boys."

"It was. I said he was a girl *at first.*" Uncle Jesse Lee flung his arms in the air. "Hell, I don't know 'bout them people. Folks said his momma raised him as a girl fo' the first half o' his life, then told him he was a boy when he got to be a teenager."

"Uncle Jesse Lee!"

"Looka here! I'm just tellin' you what I heard. He left, too, and ain't nobody heard from him since."

"Why not just ask Mr. Authorly 'bout it?"

"'Cause he won't say nothin'. He'll laugh and talk all day long, but the minute you ask him 'bout his brothers, 'specially his baby brother, he get deef all o' sudden, so peoples stopped askin'. The other two won't say nothin' neither. Guess they wanna forget about it."

Stepping out of the Jordan behind Cliffesteen, TL tried to imagine the life of the Wailin' Man and his family. A boy who they raised as a girl, a blind son, a genius, a preacher, a gay one . . . wow. That family must've been something!

They made their way to the Valley of the Dry Bones. TL got the same eerie feeling he had the first time. It was pitch black, but energy vibrated everywhere. He rubbed his arms because it felt like things were crawling all over him. When Cliffesteen struck the match, he could've sworn he saw shadows dash into the darkness. The tingling sensation across his arms subsided.

"She didn't tell me what she wanted," Cliffesteen said. "Jus' asked me to bring you."

"Okay. Well I'm here." His sarcasm was almost rude.

Cliffesteen shone the dim light in the direction of the bones. TL trembled once again. Something was different from before.

"They move 'round sometimes," she whispered. "One day I'll come and he'll be over there"—she pointed to the right—"then the next day he'll be someplace else."

"How can you tell them apart?"

"Oh, I just know. Seem like they all look alike, but they don't. You gotta be 'round 'em more often. You could tell 'em apart, too."

No ma'am!

"There's twenty-three in all, like I told you. There probably woulda been more, but they put Aunt Easter away. She was the only one what could bring 'em."

Good!

Cliffesteen sat and started one of her songs in a minor key:

Time ain't long
I'm watchin' and waitin'
Ready to come any day now
Please don't pass me by!

The pleading in her voice soothed TL's irritation. His attitude shifted against his will. She sounded like Nina Simone, crying in the dark, growling through her troubled soul. TL's spirit followed Cliffesteen's. The song never grew loud, but it became so intense he found himself squeezing his torso. "Please don't pass me by!" Each time she sang the refrain, his emotional resolve weakened until, lost in a trance, he knelt beside the bones and reached forth his hand as if one of them might touch him. He wasn't afraid anymore. He believed. And he wasn't going anywhere until he heard what Sister had to say.

Out of nowhere, the vision returned. Streets of sparkling gold and buildings studded with gems and jasper. Flowers blanketed the fields, and spirits moved to and fro with perfect ease. The church bells swayed, but TL heard no tones. Perched atop the tallest structure was the Messenger, high and lifted up, standing guard over the Great City. Everything looked and felt so real!

In the rear of TL's consciousness, Cliffesteen's voice reverberated like an echo. She repeated the refrain—"Please don't pass me by!"—as if begging God not to forget about her. TL heard her, but his mind was elsewhere. He was looking for Sister in that Great City not made by hands.

The Messenger took flight. Cliffesteen's voice calmed to a painful moan. TL couldn't see her, but he knew where she sat. Before him, in his mind's eye, was a council of ancestors sitting in a semi-circle, resting easily in the Valley of the Dry Bones. They seemed to be waiting for him to say something, but he didn't know what. In the interim, Cliffesteen changed songs.

> *There's a lily in the valley,*
> *And it's bright as the morning star!*

Goose bumps broke across TL's arms. He knew that song. Deacon Ausler used to sing it until folks couldn't control themselves.

> *There's a lily in the valley,*
> *And it's bright as the morning star,*
> *Amen, amen, amen!*

Cliffesteen stopped singing. "TL?"

"Yes."

"I jus' heard her."

"I didn't hear anything."

"Well, I did. Sometimes you gotta listen wit' yo' heart, not yo' ears."

TL sighed. "What did she say?"

Cliffesteen took his hand. "She said . . . 'forgive.'"

"What? Forgive?"

"That's what she said."

TL's shoulders slumped. "What does she mean?"

"You s'pose to know that."

"Well, I don't."

"Yes, you do. You might not wanna know, but you do. It's in yo' spirit."

Relinquishing the fight, he said, "I suppose I have to forgive everyone. For everything."

"That's right. Aunt Easter used to say none but the righteous shall see God. And ain't no righteousness in grudges." Feeling the weight of TL's heart, Cliffesteen rubbed his hands. "We gotta leave all that stuff behind, don't make no difference what it is."

"How do you do that?"

She cleared her throat and looked at the bones. "It ain't easy. Aunt Easter told me to stop lookin' back. She said every time you look back, you stop lookin' forward."

TL nodded.

"These folks here?" She lifted several bones. "They want us to make it to the City, so they send us messages and angels whenever we 'bout to lose our way. Most folks don't get the messages 'cause they don't believe. Or they don't see the signs. Either way, they don't ever know what they need to know. But the few that believe get to be born again. That's how Aunt Easter put it. They get a second chance to get it right so they can live forever."

It was making sense now. "That's why the City's not full," TL said.

"That's why. Most people ain't goin' there. Their heart ain't clean." Cliffesteen's eyes glowed in the dark.

"Is your heart clean?"

Her head dropped. "No, not yet. Almost. I just got one more thing to let go of."

"Aunt Easter's Put Away."

"Yeah. I know she's all right though. The Messenger done told me a thousand times. But the way people did it was so wrong I ain't been able to let it go. They took the only real momma I ever had."

Cliffesteen's vulnerability made TL love her. He'd never imagined she cried about anything. Before they left, TL knelt and embraced her, believer to believer, and together they decided, without saying a word, to drop the weight of memories and pain in preparation for the journey to the magical, golden city in the sky.

GOD TOLD ME THAT THE PROBLEM WITH FORGIVENESS IS THAT PEOPLE think they know everything. They don't. If they did, forgiveness would be easy. People are often angry with others because they think they know the seed of another's behavior and they're arrogant enough to believe that they even comprehend the fullness of another's motives, when, in truth, most of their assumptions are grossly incorrect. Even when something appears obvious to the human eye, it is often *not* what it seems. The eye is governed by the limitations of the mind. Don't trust it!

Unforgiveness can't come to the City because it breeds death. There is no death here. Only life. And perfect love. Yet if we actually knew the details of most people's lives, we could love them easily. Most have fought demons and men to overcome what should've killed them, but since we didn't behold the battles, we have no appreciation for the scars. It's the scars that tell you who people are and that help you understand their motives. Understanding scars breeds compassion, and compassion breeds sight, and sight leads to forgiveness. How blind humans are while they think they see so clearly. . . .

CHAPTER 24

THE NEXT DAY WAS OVERCAST AND BREEZY. IT smelled of rain, so TL took an umbrella. He'd tried to rehearse what he'd say, but now he couldn't remember the words. *It should come from the heart*, he thought, so he walked on and asked God to be his help.

Momma was on her knees, scrubbing the off-white, tan-striped kitchen linoleum. A red bandanna circled her poofy, half-pressed hair, and only in this position did her cleavage bulge through the top of her button-down shirt. TL thought she hadn't heard him enter.

"Can't wait to hear this one," she said without looking up. "You musta found out somethin' else."

He couldn't let her distract him. There was too much at stake. He'd wrestled overnight between forgiving Momma sincerely and forgiving her simply for the sake of the City. But that would never work. God would know the difference. So would the ancestors. Any fake display would only make matters worse. And, anyway, he didn't want to be fake. He wanted to be honest and free—for the rest of his life.

TL sat on the sofa in the den and waited for Momma to finish the floor. *The Young and the Restless* played softly in the background. Jill and Mrs. Chandler were at it again, as usual, while Victor battled desperately to save his marriage to Nikki. He'd cheated or something, and now, with Jack Abbott as his foe, he seemed to be fighting a losing battle. Yet, even against the odds, Victor Newman never, ever lost. TL had watched the soap long enough to know that. Things always worked out in his favor because of money, power, or influence, so the real question was *how*—not *whether*—he was going to win.

Momma rose to her knees when she reached the edge of the floor. "I don't know why I keep doin' this. It ain't gon' make no difference. Menfolk don't care nothin' 'bout a clean floor."

"It looks nice."

She stood and huffed. "Well, I guess it does. Maybe that's why I do it—'cause I like to look at it—for the few minutes it's gon' last."

TL tossed the bucket of dirty water outside. When he returned, Momma was dusting the floor-model console TV. He grabbed the broom and began sweeping. He needed something to lean on.

At first, they didn't say anything. Every phrase TL conceived sounded too formal or too insincere in his head. Momma moved about as if he weren't there. Who could blame her? Whatever TL had to say, she still had work to do.

Finally, overcoming his nerves, TL said, "I don't understand it all, Momma, but I love you." It just came out. Just like that.

She jerked around to face him. "What? What did you say?"

He didn't think he could say it again, but he did. "I love you. That's what I said. I know I don't act like it, but I do."

She didn't respond. Instead, she studied him, squinted eyes and all, like a specimen under a microscope. Then she nodded twice and returned to dusting.

"I'm sorry for how I've acted." Words came slowly. "Everything just caught me off guard, I guess."

"I can understand that." She moved from the TV to walled picture frames.

"I never thought I'd live here again. Never in a million years." TL retrieved the dustpan.

"Well," she cackled, "most people end up doin' exactly what they thought they'd never do. I'm proof of that!" She couldn't disguise the regret in her voice.

"What did you wanna do?"

Momma sprayed the glass in the picture frames with Windex and wiped them with newspaper. "Nothin' in particular. I just wanted to be happy."

"You never wanted to travel or go to school or anything like that?"

She shook her head. "Nope. I like home. I ain't never wanted to go 'round the world. I can't imagine nothin' they got that we ain't. When I see foreign folks on TV, seem like to me they ain't got much as we got!"

It was useless, TL knew, to try to convince Momma that the media's portrayal of foreigners was biased, to say the least, so he listened as she continued.

"And I never could think of nothin' I wanted to do worse than be a mother."

"Really? That's all?" TL's tone was unflattering.

"Yes, *really*," she said, sneering. "What could be more important?"

TL thought it best not to answer.

"Even as a little girl, I dreamed of havin' a house full of chillen and a husband who sat at the head of the table and blessed the food like he knowed he was the head. I'd be sittin' at the other end, watchin' everyone eat, and I'd be smilin' 'cause my family was healthy and happy."

"Then I guess you pretty much got what you wanted."

Momma laughed as if someone were tickling her. "What? Boy,

is you crazy? I tell you the truth. You must be blind. Do you *ever* remember us sittin' 'round the table like that? Huh? Ever?"

"Well, not exactly, but we sat at the table and ate almost every day."

"Yeah, but where was the joy?"

TL sighed. "I don't know. You and Daddy were the parents."

"Yep, we were." She moved from one picture to the next. "I thought he was s'pose to set the tone of the family, but he never did. I asked him 'bout it one day, and you know what he said?"

"No ma'am." TL, leaned upon the broom handle.

"He said, 'Oh! Why didn't you tell me you wanted that? I coulda done that a long time ago.'"

Momma looked at TL, who smiled sympathetically.

"Ain't that some shit? Here I was waitin' on a man to set the tone of my family and he didn't even know he was s'pose to do it? I doubt he knew how!"

They chuckled together.

"He told me he didn't see nothin' wrong with the family. Everybody ate and had clean clothes and a roof over they heads. Anything else was theirs to get on their own. It took me years to see he was talkin' to me, too. He had done gave me everything he intended to give."

"So why didn't you set whatever tone you wanted?"

She nodded. "'Cause I didn't know how to do it, either. He was the man! That was s'pose to mean somethin'! Hell, I married him 'cause he was s'pose to know how to *make* a family, not just have one."

"Well, when you saw he didn't, why'd you stay?"

"'Cause I kept hopin' he was gon' learn. I couldn't figure out how a man could have peace in his heart when his family was so disconnected, but I guess he never wanted that kind of family. He just wanted offspring, and when he got 'em, he was pretty much done. What they became was up to them."

Momma stepped down from the chair and took it back to the kitchen table. "I can't blame him totally though. A lot of it is my own fault." She stood at the threshold between the den and kitchen. "I kept hopin' when wunnit no sign. That's called a fool. Don't never do that! Not unless it's God you hopin' on!"

She chuckled again but TL didn't.

"Now I got a husband, if you wanna call him that, and a son too scared to do anything. How far you think I am from what I wanted?"

She opened the refrigerator and retrieved a whole chicken, which she sat in the sink. Had TL said what he'd come to say?

"You got another son, too, Momma."

She turned abruptly. "Do I?"

"Yes you do."

"Well, I'll be damned. I thought he had done found his *real* momma."

TL shuffled to the kitchen and sat at the table. He didn't know why he'd thought this would be smooth and easy.

"I just wanted whoever loved me, Momma. That's all."

She began cutting the chicken into parts. "Love comes in a whole lotta ways, son. I gave you the only love I had, which was my home. I took you in. I couldn't think of a better way to love you."

"You're right. I just couldn't see it then. Or even now, I guess."

"Guess so."

She asked him to peel a bag of potatoes. He sat in Daddy's chair.

"It just seemed like Ms. Swinton liked me."

"I'm sure she did. She should've."

"And it seemed like you didn't."

"I'm sure 'bout that, too." She appeared unmoved. "You didn't need nobody else to like you. Plenty o' people liked you. You needed somebody to take care of you."

"Yes ma'am."

"And since I didn't see nobody willin' to do that, I decided to do it. Maybe this gon' be my dream child, I told myself. But I was the last person you wanted."

"That's not true! I couldn't figure out why *you* didn't want *me*!"

"You probably right. I didn't want you at first, but I grew to want you. At least I thought I did."

"I never felt that. You certainly never told me."

"No, I never told you. You right 'bout that."

TL's nerves settled. He wasn't fighting Momma anymore.

"Thanks for taking me in. You didn't have to. That was a lot to ask of somebody."

"Lord knows you right 'bout that!" She cackled. "But I'd do it again."

"I feel like we would've done so much better if I'd simply known the truth."

"Maybe. You can't never tell. We mighta done worse. At least back then you *wanted* me to like you. Now, I ain't sure it matters one way or the other."

"It matters." TL nodded. "It matters a lot."

She glanced at him as if she were shocked. "Well, I'll say! Look like you 'bout to grow up, boy!"

From one of the lower cabinets, she extracted a black cast-iron skillet and sat it on the right eye of the gas stove. Then she filled it, three quarters of the way, with Crisco oil.

"Guess ain't nothin' to do but go from here, huh?" TL said.

"Guess so."

She joined him at the table with a peeling knife.

"I don't hold anything against you anymore, Momma. I don't guess I ever had a right to."

"Everybody got a right to feel however they feel, son. It might not *be* right, but they got a right to feel it."

Her culinary skills were far superior to his. TL was amazed at how she manipulated the knife around the potato without ever breaking the peel.

"You can have that old trunk under the bed if you want it. I

318 ❦ DANIEL BLACK

can't do nothin' with it. You the only one with sense enough to understand what's in it."

TL gasped and dropped the knife. "Momma! Are you serious? Those things are priceless!"

"I know it! Shit. Why you think I kept them all these years?" She winked. "Don't nobody else want that stuff."

"I want it! It's our history."

She nodded. "Then take it. Just make sure you use it. Show it to them children or somethin'. Don't let it go to waste."

"Yes ma'am, I will. I promise."

"I was s'pose to pass it on to someone in the family, and now looks like you clear you in the family." They cackled at the irony of things.

"I'm sorry, Momma. For everything. I really am. You deserve so much better."

"Yeah. I'm sorry, too." She didn't look up. "And yo' daddy is the sorriest of all!"

Their laughter echoed throughout the house. TL was no longer thinking about the City made of gold.

Daddy entered shortly thereafter. He said good evening and asked what the hell they were cackling about. They spoke and then finished the potatoes. He washed up, which meant washing his face, hands, and arms, then returned to the kitchen.

"What's good, Professa?" he said. "What you doin' here?"

Momma intervened playfully. "He ain't got to 'xplain that to you or nobody else. He got as much right to be here as you do."

Daddy frowned. He sensed something had changed.

"I was just chattin' with Momma. That's all."

Now he *knew* something had changed.

"Well, good for y'all," he mumbled. "Good for y'all." Moving toward the door, he told TL, "Come out to the barn when you get through. I wanna show you somethin'."

Half hour later, TL went. Not wanting to appear anxious, he strolled casually like a tourist. Daddy was sitting on a bale of hay.

"I been thinkin' 'bout what we talked 'bout at yo' house the other day."

TL couldn't recall the conversation. "What?"

"The piece o' God in me."

"Oh yeah. That. What about it?"

"Well"—Daddy rose slowly—"I told you I ain't never knowed what it was, and I ain't. Not 'til now."

His subtle excitement was refreshing.

"I been thinkin' 'bout this a long time, and I tried it once, but I didn't think I could make no money doin' it, so I stopped. Now I don't care 'bout the money. I just wanna do it."

TL couldn't guess what it was. "What made you try again?"

"You," he said. "The way you talked 'bout them kids. That's the way a teacher is s'pose to be. Ms. Swinton was like that. Never will forget it. I knowed there was somethin' in me, too. It's somethin' in everybody if they can find it. But like I told you that day, once you find it, you gotta do it. So I come home thinkin' 'bout you and that boy and how much you was willin' to give to make sho' he survive, and I said, 'Shit, I'm gon' give it another try.'"

Daddy moved to the wall next to the exit.

"Tell me what you think."

He yanked an old sheet hanging from a nail, and TL stumbled with disbelief.

"Pretty good, huh?"

"Oh my God . . . Daddy! You did that?"

The portrait was breathtaking. It looked real! Ms. Swinton stood in the middle, with her hands at her sides, staring as if, any minute, she might blink and come to life.

"I think it's pretty good. Kinda surprised myself!"

"Daddy!" TL approached the painting like a viewer in a gallery. "How did you . . . When did you know . . . What!"

Pride glowed on Daddy's face. "I ain't never really knowed. I just kinda had a feelin'. I used to draw stuff in school when I didn't understand the lesson, and, one time, Ms. Swinton took the picture away from me. She was gon' whoop me for not payin' attention, but when she opened up the paper, she stared at it so hard I knowed somethin'. She looked at me, then looked back at the paper like she couldn't believe it. I still got the whoopin', but she kept the picture. It stayed in her top drawer the whole time she was the teacher. Sometimes she'd pull it out and look at it, then look at me. Other kids didn't know what it was, but I knowed."

"She didn't ever talk to you about it?"

"Uh-huh, she didn't. I don't know why. Maybe she knowed I couldn't do nothin' wit' it."

"I doubt that. But I guess we'll never know." TL couldn't stop gawking. "It's so amazing, Daddy."

"Pretty good, I guess. Just never thought much about bein' no artist. I sho' didn't know no black men who painted pictures for a livin', so I never did try it seriously. Not 'til the other day."

"You did this in a few days?"

"Yep." He stepped forward. "I'd eat my supper, then come on out here and get to work. Yo' momma kept worryin' me 'bout what I was doin', but I didn't want her to know. I was up past midnight last night."

"Midnight? You?"

"That's right. It was in me and I had to get it out."

TL reached toward the portrait. Daddy grabbed his arm. "No, no! It ain't quite dry yet. Give it another minute."

"Okay, forgive me!" *Who is this man?*

Daddy released his wrist. "Tell me whatcha think fo' real, son. Don't bullshit me."

"What I think? Are you serious? It's unbelievable, Daddy. I mean . . . it's incredible. She looks alive!"

Daddy nodded without smiling.

"Your attention to detail is remarkable! It really looks exactly like her. Even the little mole on her neck. Everything!"

"Well, ain't no need in doin' a thing if you ain't gon' do it right."

"Yessir. You're right. *You* taught *me* that." TL slapped his back.

"Then you come home and taught me. Ain't that somethin'? I guess that's how it's s'pose to work."

"If you say so."

Had anyone seen the portrait in a museum, they wouldn't have been more impressed. It really was incredible. Her face looked alive. It was almost frightening. The closer TL examined it, the more amazed he became. Daddy hadn't simply painted her complexion a smooth, fake brown, but rather milk chocolate with dark splotches across the forehead. She'd been a pretty woman, far prettier in her youth, Daddy once said, but even beneath makeup she couldn't completely hide her blemishes. Now, in Daddy's hands, the imperfections looked right, as if they'd been ordained, or as if, in their absence, she'd have been less perfect. Her thick, wavy hair—which, of course, folks attributed to a mere drop of Indian blood—was pulled back in a bun, as it always was, with not one disobedient strand gone astray. TL had never seen the long red dress before, but she wore it elegantly. Nor had he seen the chandelier-shaped diamond earrings, but they gave her the look of royalty. He glanced at Daddy, who finally smiled. He knew this woman well. Far better than TL. Far, far better than TL.

"Once I got started, I couldn't quit. I saw it in my mind first."

"Really." TL's head rotated. "It's unbelievable."

"Glad you like it."

"Like it? Daddy! I love it. I can't believe you did this!"

"I can't believe it, either. But I'm startin' to now." He nodded. "I got you to thank for that."

"Oh no, sir! I didn't have anything to do with this."

"We all got somethin' to do with one another, son. Whether we know it or not."

Before TL could take it back, he said, "You loved her, didn't you?"

Daddy stared past the picture, past the barn wall, into a corner of his own private heart. He closed his eyes. "I was wrong, boy. We was both wrong."

"Can the heart be wrong?"

Turning slightly, he said, "I don't know, but I know one thing for sure: Followin' it can kill you. I know that!"

TL knew that, too. He thought of George.

"Ain't nothin' wrong wit' havin' feelin's for a person. That's normal. The problem is thinkin' you gotta do somethin' wit' them. That's when we get in trouble."

"Yessir."

Daddy returned his attention to the portrait. "You ever loved somebody?"

"Yessir. I have." TL hoped Daddy didn't ask for details.

"Well . . . then you know."

TL sighed, relieved.

"Life is funny, boy. Man can go all the way to the moon, but we still cain't control the heart."

"No we can't."

"No, we can't," he repeated. "The best we can do is try to make the heart line up wit' the head. And that ain't easy." He chuckled. "I ain't done good at all."

TL laughed, too. "I ain't either! Believe me!"

It was strange, these two laughing together about love, although neither of them was willing to reveal details. TL was grateful for both the sharing and the limitations.

Daddy lifted the painting from the barn wall. "I guess it's dry now. I want you to have it. I can't keep it. Not in this lifetime."

TL's mouth opened. "Sir? Are you serious?"

"Yeah, I'm serious. I sho' can't hang it nowhere 'round here!"

"No, you can't."

Daddy handed TL the canvas. "It'll remind you that you come from a great woman."

TL felt sorry for him. He had the same look in his eyes George had the day he left.

"You can come by, Daddy, and see it any time you like. I'll hang it in the living room."

Dazed for a moment, Daddy suddenly blinked back to reality. "No, don't put it there. Everybody'll see it and wonder where you got it from, and you'll have to either tell the truth or lie, and either way we'd be in trouble." The right side of his mouth twitched. "That's kinda funny, ain't it? That a lie and the truth can both leave you in the same place?"

TL had never thought about it. "Yeah, that's kinda funny I guess."

Daddy walked toward the exit.

"Thanks, old man. It's an incredible portrait. I can't believe you've had this gift all these years."

"Well," Daddy said, turning, "most folks don't know what they got inside of 'em 'cause they too scared to look. I looked, so now I know."

He exited.

"I looked and I know, too," TL whispered.

CHAPTER 25

WITH THE PORTRAIT BENEATH HIS ARM, TL AP-
proached the Meetin' Tree as Uncle Jesse Lee's harsh
blues filled the air. He sang something that made
absolutely no sense. You'd think a musician might get better over
time simply because he plays continuously, but obviously not. He
sounded exactly like he did twenty years before, and, for the most
part, he sang the same songs. Unlike professional musicians, he
didn't seek mastery or even proficiency. He was playing for himself, he'd told TL one day, so what difference did it make?

Leaning the picture against the trunk of the tree, TL huffed
and relaxed. He took the space at the opposite end of the worn
church pew. Uncle Jesse Lee stopped playing.

"What you got there?"

TL didn't see any harm in telling him. Uncle Jesse Lee was the
last person in Swamp Creek whose mouth he feared. "A painting."

"Of what?" He blew a chorus of strange, illogical notes.

"Ms. Swinton."

The disjointed melody evolved into a song about a man who

searched the world over for a woman he loved, only to find her in bed with his brother.

"Lemme see it."

TL held it up.

"Good-lookin' picture. Looks jus' like her."

"Yessir."

"You do it?"

"No sir. Somebody else did."

"Well, *somebody* know what they doin' wit' a paintbrush."

"Yessir."

Uncle Jesse Lee sang louder:

Lookin' for my baby, my sweet honey chile!
Searched all over for my sweet honey chile!
Spent all my money lookin' for my sweet honey chile!
Then went to my brother's house and found her, safe and sound!

A few people came by, but didn't stop. If they noticed the painting, they didn't acknowledge it. After fifteen or twenty minutes, Uncle Jesse Lee and TL were alone again. The elder seemed happier than usual. Even smiled at folks when they walked by. TL envied his contentment.

"I got this back," he said, opening his palm. And there it was: a tuft of silky black hair.

"What! Are you serious? How?" TL wasn't sure he believed it was really his, but who else's could it be?

"From him." Uncle Jesse Lee looked heavenward.

Circling the top of the tree was the Messenger, high and lifted up. Maybe he'd been there the whole time, or maybe he'd accompanied TL from home. TL didn't know. He hadn't looked up in a while.

"This afternoon. Jus' a few hours ago. I was sittin' here like I always do, playin' my music, when all o' sudden I felt somethin'

brush 'cross my head. When I reached to wipe it away, I found it."
He smiled. "Jus' cain't never tell, son. The Bible say wait on the Lord
and be o' good courage. Well, I did that, and look what happened!"

The Messenger never flapped his wings. He hovered midair,
gliding in a circle as if creating an invisible shield of protection. TL
knew it was the same bird. There was no doubt in his mind. He just
didn't understand how the bird could be here and there at the same
time.

"Everything ain't to be understood, son. Some thangs is just to
be appreciated."

"Why can't we understand?"

"'Cause, sometimes, tryin' to understand make you miss the
point. We can be so busy tryin' to make a thang make sense that
we overlook the thing itself. Take folks what argue 'bout God, for
instance. It's a whole lot more fun jus' to walk wit' Him. Least I
think so." He rolled the ball of hair in his hand. "Plus, it's some
stuff you ain't gon' never know, don't care how hard you try. That's
just the way it is. The quicker a man accepts that, the better off
he'll be." Uncle Jesse Lee shoved the hair into his shirt pocket and
licked his lips. "I been waitin' all these years, and finally today I
got what I been waitin' for." He nodded. "I'm mighty grateful, but
I guess I had done got used to askin' wit'out expectin' an answer.
Now, I ain't sho' I got nothin' else to live for."

TL looked up again. The Messenger was gone.

"Just be careful what you think you need to know. You might
be better off not knowin'."

TL retrieved the picture and walked home. Uncle Jesse Lee's
coarse melody followed him most of the way, reinforcing what he'd
come to know: You can believe without understanding, but you'll
never understand if you don't believe.

THE PICTURE hung in TL's bedroom. Whenever he entered, she
looked at him, waiting for details of the day and secrets of his heart.

His evening ritual became talking to her, building the intimate, mother-son relationship they'd never had. He told her about George and how, sometimes, he wished he'd return. He was convinced that another soul would never love him that way again, and he feared his return to Swamp Creek might mean he'd be alone the rest of his life. She didn't say anything. Just held the smile as if she knew something he didn't. He confessed that he'd been too ashamed to call Zuri again, so he filed the memory away in his heart and hoped she didn't hate him. He also told her about Cliffesteen and the Valley. Again, she didn't flinch. She looked like she knew.

Sometimes they'd talk for hours. It was like having a personal, private therapist who simply never said anything. But she wasn't uninterested. Quite the contrary, her eyes suggested she wanted to know everything, so he told her. Even in the dark, they chatted about things he never would've told a living soul. When he awoke, she was there, smiling, welcoming him into a new day. If he hadn't known better, he would've believed Daddy had painted the picture specifically for him, apologizing, perhaps, and attempting to replace what he'd stolen. But when he thought about it, he admitted that, no, Daddy had done the portrait for himself, and that made sense. TL's benefit was simply an incredible, unexpected by-product.

Stepping onto the porch weeks later, he literally stumbled over Ezekiel, who was reading a small, thin children's book. It was a bright, hot Saturday morning.

"Excuse me, son! I didn't see you. What are you doing here so early?"

"Oh, I don't know." He shrugged spryly. "Finished up my chores and thought I'd come by."

"Your daddy knows you're here?"

"Yessir," he lied. "He know."

"All right. Good to see you. What are you reading?"

He lifted the book. "I done read it a hundred times. I know it's for little kids, but I didn't have nothin' else to read."

TL invited him in for breakfast, and, against his rearing, he accepted. They both hoped it didn't result in another black eye come Monday morning.

Zeke sat at the little oval table as TL fried bacon, eggs, and homemade hash browns.

"I dream 'bout dead people sometimes, Dr. Tyson," he blurted out. "They be walkin' 'round like they livin', but they ain't." His feet swung freely beneath the table. "It just be skeletons, but the bones be connected." He looked at TL. "What you think it means?"

"I don't know, son."

"I don't, either. But . . ."

"But what?"

He began to squirm. "I been thinkin' 'bout killin' Daddy."

TL swiveled abruptly, sure he hadn't heard him right.

"Excuse me?"

Zeke looked out the window. "I done thought about it a lot."

"Son, don't say that. Don't you ever say that again. You don't mean that."

"Yes I do!" His anger flared. "He ain't gon' keep beatin' my momma, Dr. Tyson. He can beat me, but he cain't beat my momma."

There was resolution in his tone. That's what scared TL. Zeke was almost joyful, like a puny, frightened child who decides, once and for all, to confront the bully. *One of us is going down. Him or me.* And Ezekiel had decided it wasn't him. Not this time.

This was too much for TL. He'd hoped for a quiet, easy Saturday morning in the country, and this was what he got? He tried not to say anything, but silence felt totally irresponsible. "Beating people isn't right, Ezekiel. I'll give you that. But killing them is worse."

"Okay. Then what can I do?"

TL returned to the stove. "I don't know. What about calling the police?" He knew better before he said it.

"Will they come up here? I ain't never seen no polices in Swamp Creek."

"I haven't either."

TL tried to think of something else, something to sway the boy's thinking in another direction, but nothing came. Ezekiel rose and went to the living room, perusing bookshelves as the smell of slab bacon and fried potatoes and onions filled the house.

Twenty minutes later, TL called, "Let's eat, son."

He'd followed a honeybee from one title to the next until it walked the spine of *Go Tell It on the Mountain*. He snatched it from the shelf and reentered the kitchen. "What's this 'bout?"

TL chuckled. "Ms. Swinton gave me that book years ago, when I was just a little older than you."

"Really? What's it 'bout?"

He gave the safe answer: "A young, black boy in New York City who struggles with a stepfather who doesn't seem to love him. The man's a preacher, so they go to church all the time. The boy's name is John, and he loves school more than church, and his stepfather hates it. So the book is about how John wrestles with his stepfather and the church as he tries to figure out how he fits into either one."

"Does he figure it out?"

"You'll have to read the book one day."

They sat, and Ezekiel offered the blessing. Once he finished, he continued his line of questioning: "How many books you done read?"

"Ezekiel! Come on! You can speak better English than that!"

He already had a mouth full of food, although TL was still spreading jelly on his toast. Zeke chewed a few seconds, nodding slightly, then, with the help of a gulp of orange juice, said, "Yessir. I mean, how many books have you read already?"

"I don't know. Hundreds I guess."

"Wow. I'ma read like that one day. When I leave here."

"Where are you going? Nothing's wrong with Swamp Creek, son."

"Yeah, I know," he mumbled through his food, "but ain't no libraries or nothin'."

"That's true, but be careful. Lots of places with libraries have horrible standards of living. You can't even go outside without locking your door."

Zeke's brows furrowed.

"That's right. I'm telling you what I know."

The child continued chewing, then asked, "Why did you leave?"

TL sighed. "For the same reason you're talking about. I just know better now."

"So you wish you woulda stayed?"

Shut up, boy! "No, I don't. I needed to go."

"See! That's what I mean. I need to go, too. I'll prob'ly come back though. One day. Just like you did."

They stopped talking. Ezekiel's plan was impenetrable, so TL had nothing else to say. *Funny how God shows you yourself.*

Zeke washed dishes as TL wiped counters and swept the floor. The resolve in Zeke's eyes was unsettling, so TL tried not to look at him. What more could he say without being a hypocrite? The boy was simply following his teacher's path, right?

After cleaning up, they returned to the porch.

"Can I read that book? I'll give it back. I promise."

TL had hoped to suggest others first, but what the hell. He saw where this was going, and he couldn't do a damn thing about it. "Sure. It might take you a minute to finish, so don't get in a hurry."

"Oh, I won't" Zeke sang. "I'll take my time."

With that, he jumped off the porch and into the countryside. TL had meant to remind him not to mention the breakfast or the book, but he didn't worry. Zeke knew the routine by now. In TL's heart, he felt as if he had taught the boy to lie and deceive, and, in truth, he had. But that was the only way the boy would survive. And TL needed him to survive. The world did, too.

CHAPTER 26

T HE FOLLOWING FRIDAY EVENING, TL WAS MEN-
tally exhausted and ready for the therapy of the Meetin'
Tree.

He arrived around nine. Folks were already laughing and falling over. TL chuckled simply from watching them.

"Polly, I ain't stuttin' you!" Mr. Blue screeched. "You know
good and damn well you lyin'!"

She could hardly breathe. Her chest rose and fell like the ocean's
tide. "No I ain't! I'm tellin' you, she used to let her cat sleep right on
top o' her titties every night. Whenever the cat got hungry"—she
slumped over, almost to the ground—"I guess she just got some
milk!"

People screamed. TL had missed the first part of the joke, but the
last part was funny by itself. When everyone calmed, he spoke and
they nodded kindly. These were the elders, so a nod was more than
sufficient for him to feel welcome. Many of the kids waved, and TL
waved back, but they kept their distance. They weren't grown.

TL shook hands with Daddy and Willie James like men meeting
for the first time. Daddy despised public—and private—displays of

affection, so, like the other elders, he dropped TL's hand quickly and invited him to "sit down and join us." Willie James made room, and TL took a seat.

Dusk faded to darkness. That's when Swamp Creek folk got free—in the dark. Everything they did fun was at night. The light of day was for work.

Laughter intensified and people shared jugs of deep purple grape wine. TL hated the stuff, but he drank it anyway. It would've been rude not to. Then, suddenly, squinting at something in the distance. Mr. Blue hushed the crowd. Everyone turned.

"Well, I'll be damned!" he said. "It's 'bout time!"

Miss Polly waved her hands. "Oh! This is so wonderful!"

Out of the void of darkness, Momma emerged. She smiled that nervous smile, like one unsure of how they're going to be received. She'd never been to a Meetin', as we called it, except the one time people laughed her away, and TL could feel her awkwardness as she approached.

Mr. Blue offered his folding chair. "Sit down, Marion. Good to see you! Where you been all these years?"

Her smile broadened as she sat. "Cleatis had me locked up!" she teased. "This boy hyeah"—she nodded at TL—"come by and let me out!"

People's laughter eased the tension. No one had expected Momma to fit in so easily, much less contribute a joke. TL and Willie James couldn't believe she was there at all. No one else could, either. But they made room for her, just like that.

"I went to see Lula Bell the other day," Mr. Blue began.

"Lula Bell?" folks murmured.

Mr. Somebody said, "I thought she was in the hospital?"

"She was, she was, but they let her out yestiddy." Mr. Blue's shoulders jerked already. TL's head shook. He knew this was going to be crazy.

"How she doin'?" Daddy asked.

"You tell me how she doin' after I tell you this!"

Miss Polly's hyena cackle echoed into the evening breeze. TL loved her laughter. It was full of life and rhythm.

"I went by there last evenin'," Mr. Blue panted, "and she was sittin' up on the couch, lookin' crazy. I asked her how she was gettin' 'long, and she said she was all right. I told her she looked good—"

"Looked good?" Mr. Somebody said. "Sheeeeit, Lula Bell ain't never looked good! Hell, in her heyday she scared me!"

Momma covered her mouth, muting a scream. Everyone else hollered openly.

"Y'all know that woman used to be a man!" Mr. Somebody teased. "Shit, her features harder'n mine!"

TL pictured her in his mind and couldn't restrain from chuckling. She'd always had a beard, not a few whiskers like many women, but a full, bona fide beard she couldn't pluck away, and her brows were thicker than any man's around. On top of that, her voice sounded like James Earl Jones. Children avoided her and grown people acknowledged her from a distance. She'd had a son, but he died years ago. Folks said she must've had him with another woman 'cause she wasn't ever pregnant. TL didn't know any details, and he certainly wasn't bold enough to ask her.

Mr. Blue resumed: "She said the Lawd had done healed her— *to one extent*."

"To one extent?" Momma whispered. "That don't make no sense."

"I know it don't, but that's what she said. I said praise the Lawd, but she told me not to praise Him too soon. She wasn't out o' the woods yet."

Folks hollered.

"I asked her what she meant, and she said that God had done healed her from one disease, but she still had one mo'."

Mr. Blue practically collapsed. TL tried to anticipate what the old man was about to say, but no normal mind could've conceived it. Mr. Somebody's hands waved back and forth as he prepared for what none of them could've imagined.

"'You got *two* diseases?' I asked and she shook her head and said, 'Naw, Blue, I got one. I *had two* berculosis but now I just got one!'"

In all his days at the Meetin' Tree, TL had never seen people scream like that. The jug of wine spilled onto the earth without anyone noticing. Mr. Blue squealed like someone being bullwhipped. Everyone hollered at the insanity of it all, while understanding the context from which it came, which of course made it even funnier. Momma kept her hand over her mouth, but she couldn't stifle her screeching. With a bright moon overhead, tears glistened in her eyes, and TL gave thanks for whatever had compelled her to come. Miss Polly walked in a circle, shouting, "Shut up, Blue! Shut up! You oughta be 'shame!" as her laughter overwhelmed her every few steps. Daddy's head was hung so low his forehead practically rested on his knees. His whole body trembled, like an epileptic's. TL wasn't sure folks would ever recover from something so hilarious.

Barely able to look up, Daddy panted and said, "What did she say, Blue?"

Mr. Blue couldn't answer. He frowned from the pain in his right side. Mr. Somebody had walked off, hobbling on his cane, so full of mirth people feared he might fall. He was twenty or thirty yards down the highway, shrieking like someone being tickled. TL couldn't stop laughing, either. Who, in God's name, had thought of something that brilliantly funny?

Fifteen minutes later, folks began to reconvene. They looked exhausted, as if they'd just finished a hard day's labor. Many had.

"Can you believe that?" Mr. Blue huffed. "That's exactly what she said! 'I *had* two berculosis'"—he held up two fingers—"'but now'"—he lowered one of them—"'I just got one!'"

The crowd crumbled again. TL laughed at them laughing. Never in his life had he heard anything so comical, and never had he seen Momma so . . . free. She hollered and trembled, back and forth, like one lost in a sea of revelry. TL was happy for her. She deserved all the joy she could get.

Suddenly, out of the same darkness from which Momma had emerged, Cliffesteen came—timid and unsure, dragging her feet like a disappointed child. Everyone knew something was wrong. She wasn't a regular, so people wondered what she was doing there. All laughter ceased as she eased forward, closer, capturing the attention of adults and children alike. Staring from a distance, Ezekiel gawked in curiosity while TL rose and met her in the road.

"You all right, Miss Cliffesteen?"

Her eyes glowed red. "No, I ain't." Inching closer still, she did the nervous dance until she stood before the people.

"Well . . . what's wrong?"

Their silence reprimanded her for the interruption. She looked at each face, and then began to cry.

"What is it?" TL repeated, caressing her right hand with his left. "Did something happen?"

"No, no. I jus' come . . . to get my heart clean."

Mr. Blue shouted, "What is you talkin' 'bout, chile? Go 'head on somewhere! We ain't got time for yo' hoodoo foolishness."

Cliffesteen twitched and fidgeted. Where had her confidence gone?

"Is there something you need?" TL asked sweetly.

She nodded and dropped his hand. He stepped aside and let Cliffesteen scuffle forward. "I jus' wanted to say . . . um . . . I'm sorry . . . fo' the way I . . . um . . . been actin' since . . . you know . . . the Put Away. Y'all remember, right? What happened to Aunt Easter?"

The crowd grumbled its impatience. People knew what she was talking about, but they didn't understand why she was apologizing—not in the midnight hour. They'd read her behavior over the years simply as confirmation of her insanity, so now there was no room in their heads for a human, sensitive, vulnerable Cliffesteen like the one standing before them.

"Go on home now, Cliff," Mr. Blue said. "It's gettin' late."

She rubbed her arms and continued: "I know she wasn't dead.

Y'all couldn't hear it, but I heard her knockin' inside that casket. And you buried her anyway." Cliffesteen tried not to cry. "But she's okay now. She's gone to the Great City!"

Mocking erupted. A few repeated her words and antics right before her eyes. Others laughed along, dismantling any possibility that Cliffesteen might be taken seriously.

"She is! She's in the Great City! I'm tellin' you! I seen her! I been there myself! I know she is!" Cliffesteen became flustered. TL tried to comfort her, but she rejected his touch.

"Chile, please!" someone bellowed. "You 'bout crazy as a Betsy bug!"

The roaring intensified until Cliffesteen covered her ears. TL wanted to ask people to listen, to pause long enough to hear her out, but no one was interested. No one except Momma. She looked on with heartfelt sympathy, like a mother witnessing her child's demise. Cliffesteen began to withdraw. TL accompanied her.

"Don't worry about them," he said. "They don't mean any harm."

Again, he tried to touch her, but she resisted.

"It's just that they come here to laugh and have a good time, not to hear anything serious. You know what I mean?"

Cliffesteen trembled in shame. Her palms still covered her ears as she stumbled backward. She'd come to make things right, she thought, and all she'd gotten was contempt.

"They don't believe," she muttered over TL's words. "I see it now." Her head shook. She never uncovered her ears. "They don't believe. They don't know what we know."

"No ma'am, they don't."

A gust of wind blew. With a look of panic, Momma rushed to Cliffesteen's side and embraced her. They melted into one being, one reconnected self, as if they'd once been separated. People frowned. Did those two know each other *like that*? If anyone had dared or cared join them, they would've heard Momma whisper, simply and sincerely, "Forgive yourself." Cliffesteen nodded. "And thank you. For everything. Tell Aunt Easter the same." They held one another tightly, clutching far more than flesh and blood. TL didn't know what to make of things, this sudden intimacy between assumed strangers. Or perhaps they were linked in some other way, some other place, some realm where men couldn't go.

When they relaxed their hold, Momma looked into Cliffesteen's fiery eyes. "I believe." Cliffesteen smiled and said, "Blessed are those who believe but haven't seen." Then she dashed into the darkness.

Momma rejoined the baffled crowd. Folks grumbled and mumbled about what they apparently didn't know, and someone offered that, sometimes, angels dwell among us unaware. No one knew the whole story, how or when the two women's lives had intersected, but Daddy knew enough to clutch Momma's hand and stare at her lovingly. TL smiled and nodded. Now he understood that every life is sent simply to save another.

He wanted to ask Momma what she'd meant—what, exactly, did she believe?—but he didn't think it his place. She couldn't've known what he knew, but apparently she knew something he didn't.

The crowd returned to its revelry until, a little after midnight, people dispersed and went home. TL walked alone, both exhausted and revived. Before stepping onto his porch, he felt a presence above him. He knew what it was this time, and he knew what it meant: Someone was getting ready; someone was on the way.

NO ONE EVER SAW CLIFFESTEEN AGAIN. NOT IN THE FLESH. AFTER THE encounter at the tree, she vanished from human sight as if someone had erased her very existence. Conjecture swirled concerning her whereabouts, not out of communal concern but out of the desire to mock one who actually believed in a life, a place, a people after this life. A few went to the wooden house, high and lifted up, but didn't go in. They reported having looked around and found nothing. When TL arrived, the Messenger lingered on the rooftop, like a figure prepared to lead the way. He spread his wings and took flight, up, up, up in the air until he disappeared among the clouds. Inside, lying neatly across the back of one of the twin rockers, was Cliffesteen's dusty black dress. The other held her white scuffed shoes and battered church hat. At first, TL didn't understand, but, then, piece by precious piece, it all came together. He clapped and whispered, "She's free now. She's gone to the Valley."

How right he was! And there she sat, holding her Jezebel to her bosom, waiting for the time of her appointed hour. When it came, Aunt Easter came, too, to accompany her Honey Bee into a permanent stay in the City made of gold. That's all she'd ever wanted—to say "I'm sorry" to Aunt Easter for being unable to save her and to dwell forever in a land flowing with milk and honey. Cliffesteen confessed to Aunt Easter that she'd been right. A savior had indeed been born in Black Haven who'd returned to complete what his people had begun. Now, he would prepare another, the last king to sit upon the throne, before the Great Waters would come and swallow the Valley whole and it would be no more. But until then, TL visited the place alone, talking to those he loved and those who had opened the way.

Ezekiel was that last king, sent to make Swamp Creek's dry bones live again, and once he touched a thousand and forgave his father for being . . . well . . . a man, it rained until the Jordan consumed everything—first the house, high and lifted up, then the Valley—closing the twelfth gate forever. Those souls sent to save the lost, those twenty-four elders in the City, stand guard now and forever along the streets of purest gold, in the great, big, beautiful City not made by man's hands.